BRIGHAM PLAZA

BRIGHAM PLAZA

DANIEL VERASTIQUI

CHANNEL 8 PRESS
Austin, Texas

Second Edition, April 2025

ISBN: 978-1-967847-10-5

danielverastiqui.com

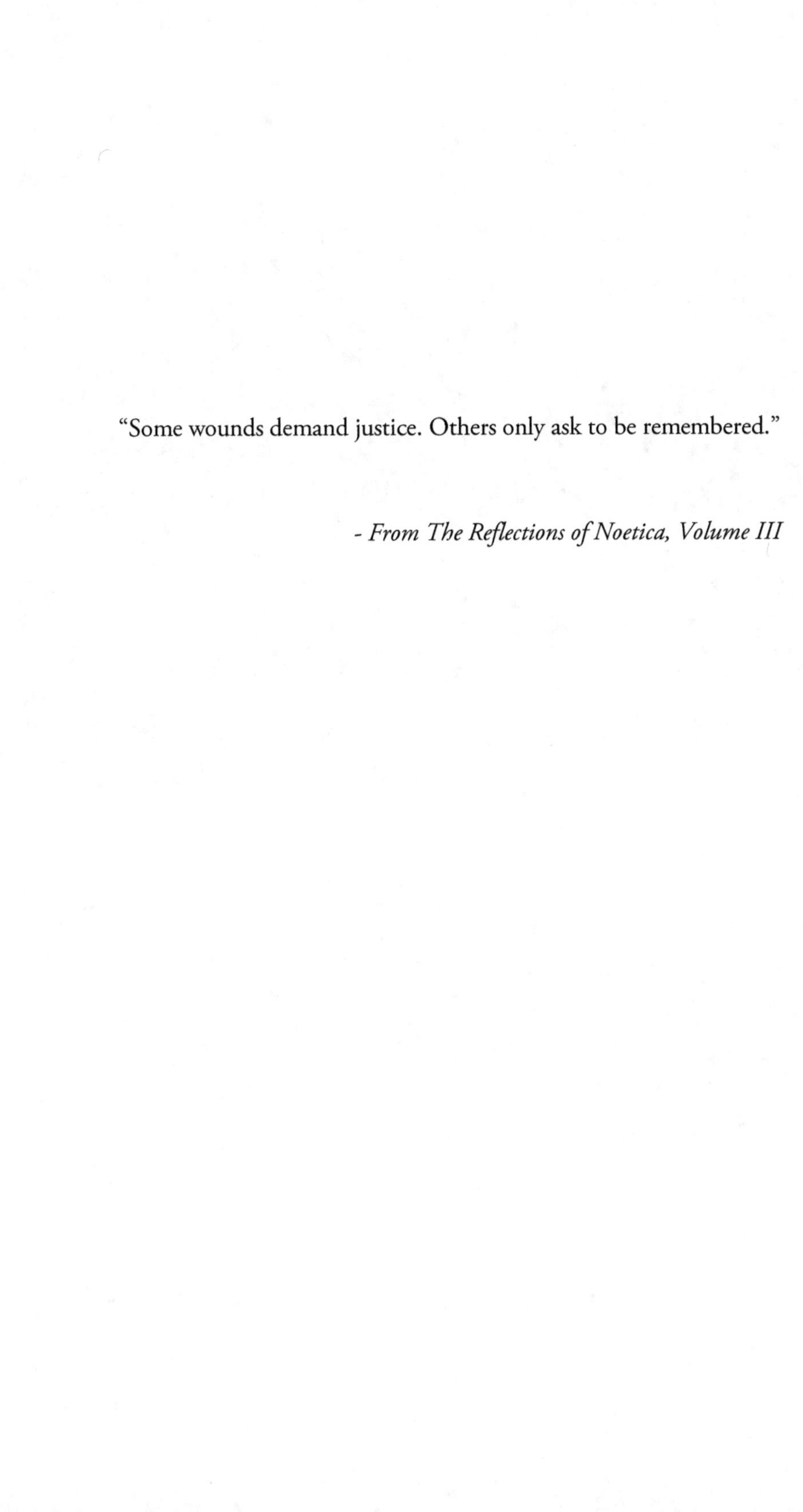

"Some wounds demand justice. Others only ask to be remembered."

- From The Reflections of Noetica, Volume III

A black Land Rover tore through the snowy roads of the Colorado mountains. Seated in the back on heated leather, Jane Meade of New York City looked up from the dossier of Daniel Antoine du Montreal.

Through the tinted windows, she could see the resort city of Vail twinkling in the last minutes of dusk. Snow fell softly from the sky in great sheets, blanketing the road, trees, and distant Christmas lights that dotted the mountain, appearing to Jane like ornaments on a massive tree. The unbroken white made the world look serene and safe, as if nothing in the world could touch the people living there. They were protected by their high mountains and gated properties and private security teams.

It was the perfect place for someone to disappear, if they could afford it.

Jane returned her attention to the dossier, to the photos of a man who was known in the hacker community as *Guns*, but who lacked the corresponding biceps in real life to back up the name. There wasn't much in his file she couldn't have learned on the net, with the exception of the personal notes she'd accumulated over her four previous visits. Those throwaway facts, the minutiae of his life, and the candid photos she'd snapped formed the continuity that would carry her from their last meeting to the impending one, such that to Danny, it would feel as if they had been steadily trading emails for the last six months rather than spending that time cut off from each other, as the contract stipulated.

Jane smiled at some of the things she'd written down.

Loves dogs.

Hates John Mayer.

Possible Information Dependency Syndrome.

"I tell Mr. Montreal we arrive," said Marcelo, a large Italian man with a thick accent and a mop of dirty blond hair.

They'd come into Vail via Interstate 70, but instead of following the tourists into the city proper, the Land Rover had turned off onto Spraddle Creek, a winding road that climbed ever upward, leaning this way and that to touch the long driveway of some mansion or oversized cabin.

When the SUV left the main road, its tires sank into fresh snow that led up to a wrought-iron fence. Jane checked her reflection in a mirrored compact as Marcelo slowed to a stop next to a call box with a keypad.

A man in a white snowsuit stepped out of the tree line, leaned slightly to get a better look at Marcelo, and then waved him in. He had to take a hand off of his assault rifle to work the keypad.

The gate swung open.

High pines marched by in close ranks, until finally the SUV pulled into a wide, snow-covered clearing.

On the far side stood a two-story cabin with an attached garage and a large, wrap-around veranda. There, Danny Guns Montreal posed casually against a post with a steaming mug in one hand and the other shoved into the front pocket of his blue jeans. He wore a black, long-sleeve shirt, gray slippers, but no jacket or gloves. There was no hint of shiver in his slim arms.

Jane gave a small wave through the window as they pulled past the porch steps. Marcelo put the car in park and got out. He reappeared at Jane's door and opened it for her.

Deep breath, she told herself. *Just do your job.*

She inhaled slowly and stepped out of the car. A smile spread across her face automatically.

"Hey there," she said, waving again as she crunched through the snow to the porch.

He raised his cup to her.

Jane smiled at his feigned restraint and let her eyes rediscover the man she hadn't seen since last June. He had a face like a caricature of a skull—perfectly round at the top and angular almost to a point from his cheeks down. It made his eyes appear darker than they were and gave his mouth a wide fullness that wouldn't have been so noticeable if he had been fifty pounds heavier. His hair was cut short to the scalp; neon blue glasses bit into the flesh above his ears.

He reached out with his free hand as she climbed the steps.

Jane pulled herself up and into his embrace. She pressed her face into his chest, pulled back after a moment, and planted a long kiss on his lips.

"Hello," he said, holding the cup out so as not to spill on her.

"It's been too long." She nuzzled his neck. "Much too long."

"Yeah." He gave a slight shrug. "Work, you know?"

Jane slipped out of his arms, smiled at him. "That thing for Lucas Cotton, right? How's that going?" She pulled the name and previous conversations from memory and the dossier notes equally.

"We're getting closer," he said, his eyes drifting to the car. "How was the drive up?"

"Treacherous. Marcelo got us through safely though." Jane put her ear against his chest. She could hear his heartbeat quickening, and for the first time, felt him shiver. "Let's go inside where it's warm," she suggested.

Danny nodded and handed her the cup. She expected coffee but tasted hot chocolate. The drink was much too bitter, but she sipped it politely.

"I put inside," said Marcelo. He followed them into the cabin carrying Jane's bag with both hands to avoid rolling it in the snow.

The cabin was warm but not overwhelmingly so. Its style, obviously not chosen by Danny himself, was a mix of modern wood furniture under a small mountain of plush blankets and knitted thermals. To the right of the entrance, a sunken living room nestled against a large, roaring fireplace. To the left, a small but functional kitchen hid behind a high bar on which a bottle of champagne sat chilling in a bucket of ice. Ahead, a circular staircase anchored the center of the open floorplan.

Jane looked to the rear of the cabin where an elevated bed and free-standing dresser marked a bedroom. On the far wall, floor-to-ceiling glass connected to an outdoor shower. She smiled at the memory of the serene woodland pastoral beyond the glass, a scene she had stared at many times while Danny gripped her hips from behind.

Marcelo placed the carry-on on the dresser near the bed.

"I'm happy to see you again, signora," he said, bowing slightly to Jane.

"I'll walk you out," said Danny. Then to Jane, "Make yourself comfortable."

After another forced sip of the hot chocolate, Jane put the mug down on the bar and slipped out of her jacket. She hung it on a hook by the door. Crossing the room, she removed her sweater, folded it neatly, and placed it in one of the several empty drawers in the dresser. Nimble fingers unbuttoned her blouse halfway before she pulled it over her head, taking the white camisole with it.

Jane unzipped the suitcase and dug for a faded San Antonio Spurs t-shirt. She slipped it over her head and let the persona of Jane Meade wash over her. Reaching under the back of her shirt, she unhooked her bra, and pulled it off with a quiet sigh.

Danny returned in a gust of cool air. Only after the door had closed and Marcelo was out of sight did he relent and rub his arms. Why he had to put on an act in front of Marcelo was beyond Jane, but it wasn't really anything new for him.

"Want me to make us some dinner?" she called, kicking off her shoes and replacing them with warm, fur-lined slippers.

"No." His head was buried in the fridge, muffling his response. "I'm gonna make it. You relax. You've had a long drive."

Jane crossed to the bar and sat down on a padded stool. She regaled Danny with invented stories of New York City nightlife as he prepared a pasta dish. He let her taste the sauce on the end of a wooden spoon—too much garlic—and she poured him a glass of champagne in what might have been a flute made from real crystal.

The alcohol hit her fast, and soon the drive from Denver was all but forgotten, as was the past life in which she was nothing more than a meretricious companion for lonely men who could afford the $3,000 nightly fee.

For his money, Danny got a friend, a girlfriend, a confidant, and whatever else one human might want from another human. Jane enjoyed clients like Danny, simple men who wanted nothing more than basic companionship and the potential of passionate sex.

He was a fair lover, as lovers went, not overly skilled but nothing Jane would write a bad review about. He was respectful almost the point of awkwardness, but sincere in his efforts to please her. In bed, Jane was his intermittent lover, a necessary part of the human experience that Danny couldn't afford to have in his life full-time. The movies liked to paint hackers as gregarious party monsters who spent all their time in synth dens or at raves cavorting with underage techno-junkies under matrices of neon lasers.

The reality was far less sexy and felonious.

Simply put, Danny craved connection.

There was a sadness to his existence that Jane did her best to ignore as he served her a dish of shrimp carbonara. He'd made salads and baked some bread; he plated everything with care, obviously proud of himself. They ate and laughed as the sun set and the lights in the ceiling ramped up.

After dinner, they migrated to the long sectional in the living room where they opened a bottle of wine—a 2011 Malbec from Argentina. Jane listened with practiced intensity as Danny laid out the Lucas Cotton job. He spoke with enthusiasm and took delight in the opportunity to school her on the latest technology. The way he smiled at her, engaged her non-verbally, gave the illusion that he loved her.

In those moments, the gulf between them stood out in stark relief, not just because of the pay-for-play relationship, but more from his inability to connect with people.

He only had a few friends she knew of, and yet he was known the world over.

But perhaps that was only half true.

No one really knew Daniel Antoine du Montreal, and Jane sensed he preferred it that way.

The last bottle of wine went empty shortly before midnight, after which they retired to the bedroom. Jane suggested a shower, and as the stars twinkled high above the glass roof, she scrubbed Danny from head to toe. He stood there like a

Greek statue, his eyes closed, as if he were carefully storing away the sensation of being touched by another person.

He didn't have many kinks, but like a lot of men, he loved to be bathed. Something primitive from childhood, Jane supposed. She thought about how long it had been since he'd called his mother as she ran a razor over his stubble and stroked his erection.

The intrusion into what was clearly a non-sexual moment for Danny forced his eyes open. He moved his hands from her hips to the small of her back. He was facing her, and yet, he didn't seem to be looking at her at all.

"Are you here with me?" she asked.

He nodded.

She ran her fingers along his earlobe, feeling for a whisperer. He often had trouble disconnecting from the network, a fact plainly spelled out in his engagement rider. He'd specifically asked for *someone to help me shut out the noise.* Jane had brought no technology with her except for her palette and the subdermal sliver in her wrist. Of her many expected tasks, keeping him away from the network and the feeds and the never-ending stream of data was often the most difficult.

Danny's entire life was in the network; he couldn't stop himself from reaching out to it.

When all else failed, sex usually got his undivided attention.

"Take me to bed," she told him.

He followed orders well, and Jane was almost certain he delighted in being told what to do. He led her by the hand from the shower to a tiled anteroom where warm air blew over them from above and below. What the fans missed, Danny addressed with a soft blue towel. When they were both dry, he picked her up and carried her to the bed, laying her gently among crumpled gray sheets that smelled of lavender and man.

Jane crawled backward on her elbows until she could rest her head on a pillow. She reached out for him, stared into his eyes the way she'd stared at his photos in the Land Rover earlier. She watched him climb onto the bed, stopping to kiss her feet, shins, and thighs. A warm tongue dragged through her labia and over her light pubic hair.

Finally, he settled over her, his face shadowed in silhouette. Jane reached down to guide him into her. Danny settled onto his elbows as he always did, wrapped his hands behind her head as he always did, and fell into a steady and familiar rhythm.

Jane stared at the wooden crossbeams in the ceiling, at the wires and metal casings running along them. As the discomfort lessened, she closed her eyes and rubbed her cheek against his. She wrapped her arms around his back and pulled him closer.

Working for Adelai Associates wasn't the worst job in the world. It paid well, and there were perks. At least Danny made an effort to be tender.

"Do you want me?" she asked.

"More than anything," he replied, breathless, in her ear.

"Then I'm yours, Danny. I'm yours."

His tempo increased. He extended his arms, lifting his weight from her chest.

Jane grabbed his hips, threw her head back, and moaned in time with his movement. In the deepest core of her being, a tingle lit, threatened to grow and explode, but she knew the threat was empty, the window of opportunity too small.

Danny cried out.

She opened her eyes, expecting to see his face contorted in selfish ecstasy. Instead, he had his hand on the back of his neck, as if someone had stabbed him and he was trying to stanch the bleeding. He slipped out of her and tumbled backward off the bed.

Jane gave chase, reached the edge of the bed in time to see him convulsing on the floor, flopping around like a fish on the deck of a boat. His muscles went rigid, and the screams turned to coughing.

She rushed to his side, grabbed him by the neck. Something hot burned her fingers; she moved her hand to his hairline.

"Danny, what is it?"

He gasped for air, his eyes circling wildly.

Jane thought of the landline on the wall in the kitchen. How long would it take an ambulance to arrive? How would Adelai Associates deal with a client dying during an engagement?

"Look at me, sweetie," she said. "Look at me."

His eyes focused on her, but they were wide and misty.

"Danny!"

"Johnny," he sputtered.

There was only one Johnny that mattered to him: Johnny San Vito, a fellow celebrity hacker and one of his oldest friends.

"What about him?" she asked.

"Dead." His voice broke. "Johnny's dead."

Danny looked away, slowed his breathing.

Jane held him for a long time, unsure of what to say or do. There was nothing in the Adelai Associates handbook that covered powerful men and what to do when they were reduced to quivering boys. All she knew for sure was to keep her arms around him.

She stroked his hair, made soothing noises, and listened as one of the most feared hackers on the planet sobbed into her chest.

ONE
KAILI

Static tore through the construct's enameled sky.

Months had passed in the simulation without incident, so many that Kaili Zabora had almost forgotten that while she enjoyed the pristine sands of Coronado Beach in San Diego, her true self was enclosed in a stasis pod at Le Soleil Rouge in Astoria, Oregon. She'd retreated to the Pacific Northwest just after the new year with the memory of the Perion City fiasco still fresh in her mind. She had wanted to put 2015 behind her, the year everything had come crashing down, and focus on the future.

Thinking about the future had led her to body modification, to Le Soleil Rouge, and ultimately, to her private simulation. There, she would spend her days relaxing until the surgeons out in the real world had finished installing the augmentations—bio-mechanical upgrades that would make her strong and fast enough to survive what was coming.

Her extended vacation on the virtual Coronado Beach had also given her time to think, and when there was nothing to think about, she took comfort in the company of her older sister, Anela, and one-time lover, Rick Diaz, both of whom had been digitally resurrected from the dead at Kaili's request.

Kaili often reflected on how perfect everything was. The water was always cool, the wind warm, and the sun bright. There was always food in the small hut just up the beach, cold beer in the cooler by her chair, and plenty of birds singing in the air above her.

But then, the static had come, so loud and intrusive.

It took the entire construct by surprise.

A sweating Corona slipped from Kaili Zabora's hand, spilling cold beer onto her bare legs before falling neck-down in the white sand. She grabbed her ears and pressed, but the monstrous noise seemed to be coming from within, as if the modulated screaming had erupted from her own mind. She watched the distant waves of the ocean tremble as they went in and out of focus. Kaili sank into her chair, retreating from the tremendous weight of the dead noise.

The world around her pixelated, obscuring her view of Rick walking the shoreline, collecting seashells in the surf, his bare back reddening in the sun. To Kaili's right, Anela reclined in her chair as if sleeping, her own beer held securely between her breasts. She didn't stir even as the echoes of the static wound down.

Kaili's fingers tightened around the arms of the chair, and she clenched her jaw hard enough to send a dull ache through her skull. None of it was real, of course: not the teeth, the rigid muscles, or her jaw. They were just bits of code, ones and zeros racing through a farm of CPUs, no more real than her lost love collecting seashells or her late sister sunbathing in the nude.

Simply remembering the separation of virtual and real was enough to quell the rising panic. Her face softened. She took a deep breath, let it out slowly.

The static continued to pulse, swirling around her like the last gasps of a snow flurry, the flakes growing smaller until they were nothing but glinting pinpricks on the air. Then they were gone completely, winking out of existence just as the chest-rattling noise abated.

Silence took hold of the construct.

Kaili felt the calm melt over her.

The entire construct froze. Down the beach, Rick stood motionless at the edge of the water, bent at the waist, his slight belly overhanging his blue and white swim trunks, a hand reaching for the wet sand.

Anela's beer no longer rose and fell with her breathing.

Even the gravitational forces that pushed the waters of the Pacific toward land had ceased their machinations. Waves stood like glassy dunes extending to the horizon. Birds that had once fished the choppy waters now hung suspended in the sky as if someone had cut out their silhouettes and pasted them onto the construct's dome.

Kaili tried to lift herself out of the chair, but her hands had begun to sink through the plastic arms. She wiggled her feet, watched the viscous tan cloth cling to her legs.

"Annie," she said, her voice flat in the motionless air.

Her sister didn't respond. For a moment, it looked as if Anela was opening her mouth to speak, but her lower lip kept falling, melting into her chin, then into her neck. The construct dimmed before Kaili had to watch the rest of her liquefy and sink through the tiny holes in the lounge chair.

Kaili's ears popped like a champagne bottle uncorking beneath a hand towel. She felt pressure at her back, felt her naked skin sloshing around in a lukewarm liquid. A thin cloth covered the length of her body from her chest to her ankles.

The stasis pod at Le Soleil Rouge.

She lifted a hand; it rose only a foot before hitting the lid of the pod. The curved surface was glass over parallel tubes that glowed blue from within. The inside of the stasis pod had reminded Kaili of a tanning bed the first time she saw it, though Dr. Jenkins had been quick to point out the circuitry filling the gaps between the tubes.

"We would never charge this much for a tan," he'd joked.

When? How long ago was that?

Kaili felt for the pod's seam with her left hand. When her fingers slipped into a small gap, she was able to lift despite the awkward angle. The lid resisted for an inch before hydraulics took over, opening it more than ninety degrees, enough for her to see the darkened ceiling.

Someone had turned the lights off in the stasis room. Monitors and vidscreens that had once shown her vitals were powered down and covered in thick layers of dust. The prep counter opposite the pod was littered with chunks of drywall and splintered wood.

Kaili sat up, tracked the trail of debris to its source.

An emergency light above the door sensed her movement and responded with a dull yellow glow.

It looked to Kaili as if something had exploded into the room in the corner by the ceiling. Exposed studs splayed out in a dense thicket. The wooden framing was charred in places, as if a fire had burned briefly before the sprinklers put it out. Whatever chaos had transpired had been enough to punch a hole in the wall and force the cabinets to the floor. It had even knocked over a server pylon—a tall, black steel cage in which her private San Diego beach lived—onto its side in a position that blocked the door.

Kaili flexed her legs, found them compliant, and swung her feet over the edge of the pod. Her body felt languid and sore, as if she had run a marathon the day before. None of the pain was intense though, and she wondered how many procedures the staff at Le Soleil Rouge had been able to get through before someone set off a bomb in the hallway.

If they even got to the procedures.

She examined her thighs, ran her fingers over the thin scars that traced down from her hips to her knees. Dr. Jenkins had assured her the incisions would be invisible to the naked eye by the time she woke up, and even though he hadn't kept that promise, at least it meant the augments were installed. Now the only question was whether they would work.

Kaili looked down at the floor, a mere two feet below her dangling toes. At no point in her remembered life had she been so unsure about standing up, but then she had never been in stasis for so long.

"Atrophy?" Dr. Jenkins had repeated, incredulously. "After only three months? With the work we'll be doing to muscle groups, they'll hardly have any time to rest at all. You may not be able to hike a mountain on day one, but I assure you, you'll be walking out of here on your own two feet."

The state of the room suggested more than a few months had passed. There was too much dust, too little activity. How long had she been asleep?

The emergency light flickered. No clue there. The battery-operated LEDs drew so little power, they could have lasted decades.

"Annie?"

Kaili closed her eyes, tried to summon the imaginary construct in her mind where the ghost of her sister dwelled. It was there she sought council with the older and wiser Zabora, through the uncertain times with Calle Cinco, through the hard times in Perion City.

She listened for a response.

A low growl answered instead.

The thin cloth landed on the floor with a wet splat as Kaili slipped off the edge of the pod and went down to a knee. Naked and covered in stasis gel, she thought of wrapping the soaked towel around her body as if everything were normal and she was just stepping out of the shower. She decided against it; the terry cloth would have made poor armor against whatever animal had made that kind of noise.

The growl came again, fainter, as she stalked to the door. The server pylon lay across it like a giant slash that seemed to say *no, not this way*. She thought about trying to push it aside, but packed as it was with servers and network devices, it might as well have been a missing piece of Stonehenge. There was no way her small frame could...

Kaili searched the skin on the back of her arms. The scars were faint, but there. She followed them to other scars, found lines running down her abdomen, spreading around her torso to her lower back. Without proper training, Kaili wasn't sure she'd be able to draw on their full power, but she took up a position under the pylon anyway.

Wet heels dug into the wall, slipping on the linoleum floors. She pressed at the corners of the cage; the steel was cold and unforgiving. At first, the monolith gave no indication it could ever be moved, but then Kaili felt a warmth stir in her body. It grew up from the soles of her feet as if her legs were thick fuses. Once the feeling reached her fingertips, the pylon gave a low creak.

She smiled, drew a sharp breath, and pushed with a low groan.

Debris had fallen into the space the pylon had previously occupied, so Kaili had to angle it away from the wall toward the center of the room. It teetered and fell with a deafening crash, taking a large bite out of the stasis pod. Yellow-tinged gel spilled onto the floor.

Kaili stood silently, listening, wiggling her toes as the warmth faded away.

When nothing moved for several seconds, she turned and pulled the door inward, nearly ripping it from the hinges. In the hallway, the emergency lights were out, likely destroyed by the explosion. Amber guide lights lined the floor by the walls, leading away to the left where they abruptly disappeared into darkness. There was just enough ambient light for the shadows to play tricks on her eyes.

Unwilling to risk the unknown, Kaili followed the hall in the other direction. She passed several stasis rooms, some open and empty, others closed but showing evidence of attempted entry. Two left turns later, she found a frosted glass door with a large *W* etched on it. Her thoughts turned to the lockers on the other side of the door, to her clothes and phone and most importantly—

The growl came again, this time from behind, its echoes tread upon by the clacking of overgrown nails on the floor.

Once inside the locker room, Kaili engaged the door's deadbolt and slunk away toward a dark corner. Though she had only been in the room once, memories of the locker room's layout flashed in her head, reminded her of the sauna to her left and showers to the right. She stood with her back to a full-length mirror for several minutes, listening for the sound of a monster passing by, but heard nothing.

It was too dim to see the lockers properly; Kaili had to use her hand to count three from the left. Her worry about entering the combination in the dark turned out to be unwarranted—most of the lockers were open, including hers.

She made several passes with a frantic hand, but her locker was empty— nothing remained of her belongings. She lingered on the small shelf where she had placed Rick's wedding ring. Why hadn't they let her wear it in the pod? What harm could it have possibly done?

The smell of the beach came back to her. For months, she had walked the gold-flecked sand with Rick. In that time, he hadn't said a single word to her— Kaili didn't want to admit she could no longer remember the sound of his voice— but his eyes had always told her he loved her.

Rick Diaz was a ghost like Anela, someone she had loved and, by her own hand, had lost. She'd met him in 2004, the morning of the Reaping, and by close of business that day, he was dead—one of hundreds of victims in a coordinated attack by Calle Cinco against Vinestead International. She had given him the poison, had watched him die, and in the end, had taken his wedding ring in remembrance.

Now, he lived only in her fantasies. And even though those fantasies allowed her to feel his lips on hers, his arms around her neck, they paled in importance to his ring—the only physical evidence of their shared time together.

The ring signified everything she was fighting for: avenging Rick's death, stopping corporate subjugation, and taking down the largest, most corrupt conglomerate in the history of the world—Vinestead International.

Without the ring, who was Kaili Zabora anyway?

"Annie," she whispered. "I need you."

The glass pane in the locker room door shattered, scattering shards over the tile floor. Something wet and matted slammed into her. Kaili put her hands up and grabbed a fistful of damp fur. Her left hand ran over the open mouth of some wild animal. Teeth cut into her palm, slicing deep enough to send blood sailing through the air. She stumbled backward, tripped over some loose clothes, and slammed her spine against a low wooden stool.

The monster came fast out of the shadows, clearing the length of her body in a single leap, its mouth stretched wide and aiming for her neck.

Kaili twisted, offering her shoulder instead of her exposed jugular. Claws pierced her chest, but there was no pain. Instead, the warmth came again, exploding inside her like gunpowder set alight.

With augmented fury, Kaili sunk her thumbs into the throat of the animal. Inch by inch, she pulled it apart.

Growling turned to gurgling; blood spilled onto her chest. The pressure on her shoulder lessened by degrees until finally the monster gave its last, pathetic gasp.

Kaili pried its mouth open, pushed it to the side. Out of breath, with blood oozing from her shoulder and hand, she stared at the shadowy mass now lying still by the showers.

A dog.

Just a dog that hadn't seen a meal in a while.

Kaili stared at the ceiling. Spots danced as her brain tried to find patterns in the darkness.

"What the hell's happening, Annie?" she asked.

TWO
TANZY

"You won't forget me when I'm gone. Refuse the fire, take the song."

The young woman on stage played with the hem of her Billie Eilish t-shirt as a smattering of applause went up from the nearby tables. She nodded to what must have been a group of her friends and hurried off the stage, as if relieved to be out of the spotlight.

From a roped-off area near the back of the club, Tanzy lifted her hands and clapped politely for a poem that had made little sense. The girl—with her thick-rimmed glasses and faded red flannel—looked the part of a New Age Portland Poet, complete with her subtle nose stud and tattoos that ran out of her sleeves to the very tips of her fingers. And while her rhyming verses might not have contained any true insight into the human condition, she was exactly what Cloves & Poetry advertised: coffee, flavored cigarettes, and if there was time, obvious rip-offs of Basho and the old beat poets.

The crowd seemed to enjoy it anyway.

The club was at ninety percent capacity according to the last update from Cleo. Tanzy enjoyed sitting in most nights, happy to get away from the grind of managing I.C.E-1, Portland's premier cipher den, of which she happened to be the suit. She used the downtime to remember what it was like in the days before virtual reality and computers. She recalled her own youth, the years she spent writing terrible poetry and pilfering Newports from her mother's purse. Life had been simple then. She'd known who she was and who her friends were.

But then the Net came, and everything changed.

Message from the Quatrain. Benny Coker is en route. ETA in six minutes.

Tanzy took a drag of her clove cigarette and placed it on the edge of an ornate brass ashtray. On the small table to her left, her palette lit up with a text version of Cleo's message. She tapped the notification, and an aerial map of Portland appeared, showing her location with a red pin. Nearby, a blue circle pulsed as it navigated the streets of downtown Portland.

"Thanks, Cleo," she whispered to herself.

She had been expecting a visit all day, and the fact that Benny Coker couldn't give her an exact time had irritated her to no end. The owner and proprietor of White Line Media considered himself some kind of celebrity who would be mobbed if someone let slip his travel schedule. So instead, he made people like Tanzy wait in anticipation, made them clear their entire Friday just so they would be ready when the feed monger finally decided to grace them with his presence.

Tanzy had spent most of the day at the office, waiting. Now it was past eight and the stress of the day had exacted its price. She pulled a code card from her clutch and held it to a small etching of a flower on her right wrist. Thin LEDs lit up on the card as it synced with the micro-controller in Tanzy's arm, filling her with coded stimulants like pure adrenaline shot from the tip of a needle.

Chaucer's Carafe. It came on strong, instantly, and faded with a nice taper some sixty minutes later.

Tanzy closed her eyes as the code latched onto her grow-wire and made its way up to the custom I.C.E biochip in her neck. The simulated caffeine hit her like a sudden rogue wave, sending a tremor down her arms that made her fumble with the card. She caught it halfway to the floor, replaced it in her clutch.

Footsteps nearby drew her attention.

Marlon nodded as he approached, a tight smile on his face. He'd gone with purple eyeshadow that flared into his buzzed hairline. Short, beaded dreads clattered on his head with every step.

"Cleo says we're having company," he said. "Can I bring you something?"

Tanzy breathed in sharply through her nose. "Bottle of water. And a… um…"

Whiskey neat.

"Whiskey neat," she continued. "Top shelf."

"Sure thing, boss." Marlon shot her a finger gun and turned back for the bar.

A chorus of voices rose in encouragement as a young girl no more than fifteen climbed the two steps up to the stage. Even at a distance, the electric sky-blue energy of her eyes sparkled. She approached the microphone and cleared her throat.

"Hi, thank you," she said. "I'm Lisandra and this is Sunrise."

Message from the Quatrain. Benny Coker has arrived.

Tanzy drew her gaze away from the young poet and eyed the doorway with a casual glance. Two security guards entered first, branded in White Line suits. Benny came in behind them, dressed down in a button-up and slacks, his dyed black hair slicked back over his ears. Bringing up the rear were two I.C.E-1 enforcers in thin jackets and sunglasses.

She sat watching him out of the corner of her eye, pretending to be entranced by the swirls of smoke rising from the ashtray.

His security detail stepped to the side as Benny found a path through the setup of small tables and chairs. He didn't wait for anyone to remove the rope around Tanzy's section, instead opted to step over it with the effortless alacrity of a much younger man.

"Please, don't get up," he said, raising his hand.

"Wasn't going to," said Tanzy. She gestured to the seat across from her.

"Thank you for meeting with me," said Benny. "I really appreciate—"

"Let's skip the chit chat, Mr. Coker. I've been waiting all day, and I still have work to do."

His right eye twitched. The owner of one of the most powerful media companies on the East Coast was unaccustomed to being interrupted.

"They told me you were a hardass," he said, smiling. "I wouldn't have expected that from a Portland girl. Aren't you guys all flannel and Birkenstocks out here?"

Tanzy held her tongue and her gaze as Marlon returned with the drinks. He placed her bottle and Benny's glass on C&P-branded coasters.

"Five minutes," said Tanzy.

"There's this kid," said Benny, picking up his drink. He sniffed the whiskey before taking a sip. "Little punk named Dylan."

"What about him?"

"He was fucking my wife."

Tanzy smirked.

"Yeah, I know, hilarious." Benny put the glass down. "Good whiskey. Anyway, it was my fault. I was ignoring her. She put an end to it, but the kid didn't see it that way."

"We don't do hit jobs here."

He chuckled. "I know. Believe me, if all I wanted was him dead, I wouldn't have come all the way out here to find someone to do it. Plenty of Atlantic City shore trash who would do the job for twenty bucks and some synth. No, I need a den for this."

"Spit it out, Mr. Coker."

"And in the light of dawn, my vagina stands alone."

Benny narrowed his eyes, cast a glance over his shoulder at the girl on stage.

"You, uh," he said. "You like this place?"

"I own this place."

He nodded. "Should have known. Anyway, kid's got some pictures of my wife, Eileen. Compromising pictures. Pictures I don't want out in the world, you get me? He's threatening to sell them to another feed, says he's mobbed up with a den called FireChain out of Margate. I don't know if that's true or not, but my IT team can't find those pics anywhere in VNet. I thought maybe you could go where we can't."

"We could," said Tanzy, mulling the job over in her head. Ultimately, it was a simple seek and destroy, with one little wrinkle. "So, the job is to find the pictures and remove them from a network where they can be infinitely replicated?"

"And burn the kid."

"Excuse me?"

Benny leaned forward. "Burn him out of the network. I don't want him to be able to jack in again, ever. Burn his chip or do a viral block—I don't care. Kill every picture you can find and then boot him completely."

The audience applauded; soft orchestral music rose to fill the silence that followed.

Message from the Quatrain. References to Eileen Coker have been found in two darknets: Dreamside and Overrun 6. Chasing.

"Two-fifty," said Tanzy. "Seven days."

"Two hundred and fifty thousand?" he asked.

"That's right."

Benny scoffed. "Calle Cinco bid seventy-five. I've got a freelancer in Margate who'll do it for fifty."

"Then hire them. Calle Cinco's been running without a suit for years; I wouldn't trust them to handle my laundry. Or pay your fifty to a freelancer and send him up against FireChain and see what happens. They're a small group, but they're still a den, and they'll eat him alive."

Benny took another sip. "I'll do one-fifty, and that's based on reputation alone." He gestured to the club. "This place doesn't exactly inspire confidence in your tech skills."

"Three hundred," said Tanzy. "You insult my home again and it'll go to four."

He put the glass down roughly, splashing the table.

Out of the corner of her eye, Tanzy saw her I.C.E-1 enforcers perk up.

"Two hundred. And I'll let you advertise on White Line. And free stays at the White Dragon, everything comped."

Tanzy picked up her cigarette, tapped the ash away, and drew. Smoke billowed from her mouth.

"Three hundred, crypto of your choice, in the I.C.E-1 proxy account by midnight, or you can try your luck with one of the Seattle dens."

"Tanzy, be reasonable."

"We're done here." She lifted a hand and gestured to the enforcers.

Benny watched as they removed a section of the rope.

"Well," he said, standing, "this has been a complete waste of my time."

"That depends," said Tanzy.

"On what?" He brushed away the outstretched arm of one of his bodyguards.

"On whether three hundred large gets to the proxy by midnight. The choice is yours, Mr. Coker. My ciphers have already located some of the photos on multiple darknets. It's up to you whether we're finding them for you or for us."

Benny scowled, but only for a moment. He turned in a huff and hurried out of the club. Only when he was outside did Tanzy hear him growl a distant *bitch*.

"Cleo…"

Yes?

"Let the girls know I'm expecting payment from White Line by midnight. I want to know the second the money hits the proxy."

Message relayed to the Quatrain. Do you think he'll pay?

"I don't know," she whispered. "I don't think he's used to being talked to like that by anyone except his wife. If he doesn't, we'll do the job anyway and sell the pictures back to him."

A faint giggle echoed in the back of Tanzy's head.

As the night wore on, the poetry from the stage grew darker, more militant. Once the Chaucer's Carafe wore off, Tanzy loaded a downer known as Single Needles. It produced a languid warmth throughout her body and smoldering fires in all the right places. Marlon brought her an ottoman for her feet as she settled deeper into the chair.

"It was your luster I lusted for and rushed us through the rusted door."

Tanzy clapped, mostly out of habit and partly because it was expected. Her patrons weren't subtle about looking to her for approval. She obliged when she could; it kept them coming back, kept them buying… kept the money flowing, kept the money washing.

Message from the Quatrain. A large sum has been deposited in the proxy.

Tanzy eyed the clock on the wall—10:55 p.m.

"How much?" she asked, sitting up. "Is it the full three hundred?"

Total sum is $475,000 in Helsinki crypto.

"Helsinki? No one uses that anymore. Ugh, get Benny on the phone."

The transfer did not originate from White Line Media.

Tanzy pulled her palette from the table, loaded the ledger from the proxy account.

"Where then?"

Helsinki privacy protocols prevent—

"Tell the girls to find out."

Several minutes went by as Tanzy stared at the nearly half-a-million sum at the top of her ledger. Someone had sent her money through one of the oldest and most secure cryptocurrency houses on the planet. Unless Benny really wanted to hide the payment from the feds, there was no reason to use such an untraceable proxy. Any of the stateside houses would have masked it sufficiently, and with much lower fees.

Message from the Quatrain. The payment is a POD disbursement from account #193BA83K.

"What's a POD disbursement?" she asked.

Payable on Death.

"Whose death?"

Cleo was silent for a moment. She answered softly.

Johnny San Vito.

Tanzy sat back in her chair. For a moment, tears threatened to overwhelm her, but she pulled them back, pulled them all the way back.

"I... I want confirmation. Ask the girls. Is Johnny San Vito really dead?"

Message relayed to the Quatrain.

THREE
GORDON

"Take a deep breath and release it. When your lungs are empty, gently squeeze the trigger."

Jessie tightened her grip on the Sig Sauer 9mm and inhaled sharply through her nose. Her arms trembled as she held her breath, but Gordon put a steadying hand on her shoulder to calm her. She curled her finger around the trigger, squeezed slowly until the hammer fell and the gun jerked in her hand. Thirty yards away, a bullet tore through the outer border of a paper target and struck the wooden backstop behind it.

Five inches to the left and she would have hit the green silhouette. Seven more past that and she would have put a bullet between the eyes of the would-be assailant.

"Nice," said Gordon, patting her shoulder. "You scared him. Now try to stop him."

The wind had drawn a few strands of her blonde hair into the air; Jessie tucked them behind the temples of her safety glasses. She followed his instructions again, but slower, taking several seconds to draw in a breath. It fluttered out through her slightly parted lips, white and wispy in the crisp November morning. She paused to let the last shivers leave her hands and then pulled the trigger twice in quick succession.

The first bullet landed just inside the green target while the second didn't even mark the paper.

Jessie thumbed the release on the side of the Sig and dropped the empty magazine into her waiting hand. She inspected the chamber to ensure it was empty before placing the gun on the foam lining of its carrying case. She stepped away from the blue barrel and opened her hands to show Gordon they were empty.

He nodded at her. "First shot was on target. He's gonna have trouble hearing out of that ear from now on. Second one missed entirely."

Jessie looked down at the dirt.

"Hey," said Gordon, going down to a knee. He looked up at the ten-year-old girl who just the week before had been reluctant to even pick up a gun. "You rushed it, that's all. You breathe, you fire. You try to shortcut the process and someone's gonna end up getting the better of you."

She nodded, said, "Sorry."

"Don't be sorry." He touched her on the cheek. "You're learning is all. I didn't touch a gun 'til I was twice your age. You're gonna be grouping headshots in no time, believe you me."

"Really?"

"Just takes practice," said Gordon. He stood and put his hands on his hips. "As a wise man once said, I fear not the girl who has fired a thousand guns once. I fear the girl who has fired a single gun a thousand times."

Jessie stared back, unblinking.

"Put three more in the magazine for me," he said, handing her the autoloader.

As the girl shook three bullets out of the small ammo box, Gordon noticed movement out of the corner of his eye. Coming out of the tree line behind him was the blue denim vest and wide-brimmed hat of Douglas Evans, the democratically elected arbiter of the Lost Pines Survivalists camp. His gait suggested there was more to his sudden appearance than the desire for an early morning stroll. He held up a hand as he cut through the benches next to the shooting range.

"Ready," said Jessie, holding up the magazine.

"Slot it up, but don't charge it just yet."

"I thought I'd find you two out here," said Evans, touching the brim of his hat. "Does your momma know what you're up to, Jessie?"

The girl nodded enthusiastically. "It was her idea. She said Mr. Gordon is the best shot in three counties."

"Is that so?"

Gordon shrugged. He had no choice but to play humble when people talked about his skill with a gun. If he'd been blessed with some innate ability or if he'd practiced for years to become proficient, he might have genuinely accepted the praise. The truth of the matter was his abilities came through code, from the kind of shortcut he'd just warned Jessie about. He'd thought the subroutines and hidden methods etched on his synapses would fade with time, like the muscle memory in his fingers that no longer remembered how to play the opening riff to *Paradise City*, but the intimate knowledge of the Sig's mechanics and the absolute control of his body as he fired it, persevered through the years, despite the willful neglect.

"What's he got you shooting there?" asked Evans.

Jessie ejected the magazine, checked the chamber, and handed the gun grip-first to Evans. Gordon had spent two days going over gun safety with the girl, and he was proud to see her treat the weapon with respect without having to be reminded.

"Looks like this guy's seen some action. From your personal stash?"

Gordon nodded.

Mechanical arms in the imaginary video library in his head sought out the tapes of a night some twenty years prior when the Sig and its identical brother had last seen real action. Before the video could start playing, Gordon began counting, running through an ascending list of integers as a ploy to distract his mind. The numbers incremented faster and faster until the impulse to revisit the past faded from conscious thought.

"Well," said Evans, "it's a fine weapon. Why don't you show me what you can do with it?"

Jessie looked to Gordon for permission. He nodded to the blue barrel where the magazine lie.

"Take it slow," he reminded her. "Count to three between each shot."

Gordon followed Evans back a few paces as Jessie got into position. She wouldn't be able to hear them at a distance with her earplugs in, but Gordon spoke in a softer voice just to be safe.

"So what can I do for you, Sheriff?"

"You know I hate when you call me that, Gordon. Authority is held by the people of Lost Pines, not any one person. All I do is help settle disagreements."

"And what disagreement have you brought me today?"

A breeze cut across the firing range, prompting Jessie to lower the gun for a moment. Beyond the backstop, the sun hung high in the clear sky. Normally, a Texas sun was to be feared, but the early winter cold and soft breezes were doing a fine job of keeping the harsh rays at bay.

"How long have we been friends, Gordon?"

"Couple decades, give or take."

"And how many times have I asked you about your life before you came to Lost Pines?"

The first shot rang out.

"Make like an arrow and come to a point, Evans."

"There was a woman at the gates, come 'round this morning, asking after you. Not by name, but… the things she knew about you, the way she described you. It fits a timeline, Gordon. It explains why you walked in here twenty years ago with a single duffle and a reluctance to tell us your name."

"It's Gordon."

"No," said Evans, "your other name. She showed me the pictures. You're younger, but it's you. She said she wanted to talk to you."

"What'd you tell her?"

The second shot answered, followed by an aborted cheer from Jessie.

"I told her to fuck off. What do you think I told her?"

"Good man."

"But that don't mean I'm not concerned." He crossed his arms. "Some of the things she said, well, they might make Clemons nervous. You two already don't see eye-to-eye, and this might be enough for him to stir up some serious shit. I'd sure hate to see you get the boot."

Jessie's third shot punctuated the warning. She put the gun down on the barrel and turned around, smiling.

"He ain't got the votes," muttered Gordon, slipping into a West Texas drawl he'd adopted his first day at LPS. After twenty years, it felt less like an act and more like another side of him, one that didn't exist before he stepped through those gates.

"You don't owe child support or nothin', do you?"

Gordon flashed on a dimly lit hotel room. He saw a woman lying on the couch, head hanging to one side, weighed down by a whirring immersion rig. He counted to seventy-nine, pushed the image away.

"Not likely," he replied.

"Makes you nervous, don't it? Havin' someone come 'round asking after you?"

"What makes you think that?"

Evans lifted the brim of his hat and made a show of looking down. "You've had your hand on your gun since I mentioned the pictures."

Gordon loosened his grip on the Sig's twin on his belt and shoved his hands into his pockets.

"Well, alright," said Evans, spitting casually into the dirt. "That settles it. You really are *him*."

"No, that ain't me."

"Come on, Gordon. You know people don't move on from that kind of shit."

"Mr. Gordon! I got him in the face!" Jessie had retrieved the paper target from the backstop and was waving it proudly in front of her.

"A fine shot," said Evans.

"Good job, Jess. That's enough for today. Run along and show your momma what you did."

The girl frowned for a moment, but she'd become accustomed to taking orders from Gordon. She showed her empty hands and took off in a youthful, haphazard run towards the tree line.

"See you tomorrow, Mr. Gordon!" she called.

He waited for her to disappear into the trees.

"What're you gonna tell Clemons?" he asked.

"Not a goddamn thing. But you oughta get out ahead of this. We've got families here, Gordon, dependin' on each other for survival. It ain't fair to use 'em as cover. If you're not the man you were twenty years ago like you say, I think you'll do what's right."

He patted Gordon on the shoulder like a father imparting wisdom to his son. "Appreciate you, Evans."

"'Til the end, Gordon." He touched his hat and headed off toward the tree line, leaving Gordon alone with the cold breeze.

As he cleared the Sig and placed its various pieces back in the carrying case, Gordon thought about how lucky he had been to last this long. Going off the grid wasn't something to be done on a whim, and staying off for good was a dream he didn't honestly think would ever come true. He'd taken every precaution: cut his ties to the world, sent out false leads, and said goodbye to the tech he'd loved so dearly.

He'd made all of those sacrifices, and yet somehow, they'd still found him.

"I'm not going back," he said aloud.

If anything, it was time to go deeper. He could flee to Peru, Val Verde, or hell, across the globe to Siberia, somewhere the tech couldn't follow him, where stories of his past hadn't been memorialized into myth and legend. He'd find another group of outcasts to join, maybe teach their kids how to shoot and kill.

Gordon willed himself to take that first step back to camp. Soon, he'd passed through the trees and come out on the east side of the compound near the vegetable gardens run by Sam Reed and his boys. A dirt path took him to the plaza where half a dozen men stood around sipping water from canteens. Around them were ATV flatbeds loaded with freshly cut firewood. A group of younger boys were transferring the wood to wheelbarrows so it could be distributed to the roughly thirty families who lived and worked at LPS. Last year's winter had been the worst Texas had seen in decades, global warming be damned. No one was going to suffer through another cold night this year, not if Clemons had anything to say about it.

Tyler Clemons nodded to Gordon as he passed. The former golden boy at Mac Haik Temple still talked like a used car salesman, but even Gordon could detect the occasional sincerity in his voice. Next to him, seated on his bench as per usual, was Clay Bartlett. His thick glasses were raised to the sky; he only looked down when Gordon cast a shadow over his face.

"How's the birdwatching, Clay?"

"Forty percent," he rasped. Age had taken some of his voice. "Sorties up forty percent. More than last week and the week before. They're watching us, Gordon." He glanced at Gordon for a moment. "You'll keep your face to the ground if you know what's good for you."

Clemons smirked, shook his head.

"Good lookin' out," said Gordon.

Past the double-wide trailers, he took a northerly turn and ended up near the small stream that ran through the compound. Across a newly built bridge he'd constructed himself, he lumbered up a sharp rise that led to his cabin, complete with its own bathroom and separate bedroom. Those hadn't come with the cabin when he got it, but he'd found that home improvement was just as effective as counting when it came to keeping old memories from bubbling up.

He'd redone the interior, added his own indoor outhouse, and finally, the small bedroom, which barely held his twin bed and a small dresser.

Gordon stepped inside and left the door open behind him.

The main room was chilly and smelled of a doused fire. Two wooden rockers sat near the front window. Facing them was a small couch with new upholstery done by Jessie's mom, Carlene. Directly ahead, a small fridge buzzed from the half-kitchen. There was no stove, but the hot plate was enough for a quick meal. To the right stood Gordon's dining table, not that he could ever remember eating dinner there.

He took his meals in the mess hall with the rest of the camp. Sometimes, being a member of the Lost Pines Survivalists meant sitting around long picnic tables with like-minded individuals and discussing a world that was spiraling more and more out of control.

Vinestead's invasions of privacy.

Perion's synthetic humans.

The MX aggression south of the border.

Like Gordon, the people of LPS had chosen to withdraw from the world, from a government that wanted to enslave them, corporations that wanted to exploit them, and a population too frightened or too complacent to believe they held the power of true democracy in America.

Gordon crossed the room and stood next to the small couch. He fingered his belt until the holster slid down his hip. He placed the holster and the Sig on the counter. With a groan, he collapsed into the worn cushions and put his head back. It was too early in the morning to be feeling his age, but the cold had a way of making the creaks worse. His mind wandered, played out the scene to come.

For once, he didn't start counting. He simply closed his eyes and waited patiently for the inevitable.

Twenty years of rest had led to this moment.

Twenty years of running in place.

But no more.

He heard the footsteps at thirty paces out, followed them as they tracked through dirt, wooden steps, and finally the rug just inside his door.

When Gordon opened his eyes, he saw a young woman standing in his living room. Shadow hid her features, save for the sparkling auburn hair and two beady, golden eyes.

Gordon tapped the armrest with his fingers.

One, two, three…

"What took you so long?" he asked.

FOUR
DANNY

The buzzing of his Syzygy biochip woke Danny up.

All night, it had coughed and stuttered, pulling him from looping dreams in which Johnny San Vito met many horrible deaths: plunging from the roof of a tall building, bleeding out in a back alley on the outskirts of Umbra, or more likely, overdosing on synth while jacked into VNet. By morning, the chip had settled into a low rattle, a vague complaint about the state of its internal circuitry.

Danny flashed on the night before: Jane moaning below him, an explosion of light brighter than a nuclear blast, and then a flood of data so intense and massive it had knocked him off the bed. Faces and numbers had tumbled out of the cobalt darkness, bringing with them snippets of code whose characters were too deformed by speed to be read. These fragments, these bits and bytes of thirty-five years of life, coalesced to form a photo mosaic of the man himself, with his narrow eyes and cocky smile.

It was only after the dump completed that Danny's Syzygy could take a breath, and even then, it came ragged and labored. The side effects lingered into the morning; Danny found it hard to think and harder to interact with the network in any meaningful way. His whisperer was down, and his sliver was as blank as the day it came out of the packaging.

Everything went through the Syzygy.

Danny slipped out of bed and stumbled to the spiral staircase in the center of the cabin. He took the steps slowly; white knuckles gripped the handrail until he'd made it all the way upstairs. The lights came up automatically, casting a dim blue hue over a workbench that ran along the entire perimeter of the room. Vidscreens and ancient laptops scrolled text, each one working a job he could only vaguely remember kicking off.

He sat down at his desk and waited for his eyes to adjust to the brightness of the screen. The system didn't automatically log him in; the connection to his biochip was too unreliable. Danny had to resort to a break-glass CLI to work his way into a backdoor and bring up the Syzygy companion app he'd written. The app's connection to the chip had higher priority, and still, it struggled.

Insufficient disk space.

The message repeated over and over, and yet Danny was having a hard time believing it. His Syzygy had a full exabyte of storage, which was more or less infinite considering what it did on a daily basis.

Danny issued several commands, instructed the chip to start offloading the data to local storage. The Syzygy warmed in his neck as he sat back and waited for relief.

He stared at the naked ceiling of the cabin.

Took a breath.

Johnny San Vito was dead, and his death had activated a Dead Man's Loop that had, in turn, dumped a lifetime of happy hackery straight into Danny's biochip. Of course, he could have triggered the dump in error, a slip of the keys by a careless and perhaps synthed-out Johnny. The concept of a Dead Man's Loop wasn't new to Danny—he and Johnny had discussed it before—but only one of them had evidently felt the need to build it.

Danny had always imagined his personal data would be lost to the ether when he died, but Johnny had designed, primed, and now triggered a fully functional DML.

But had he meant to?

Danny tapped a few commands on the keyboard and brought up browser windows for the Big Three media feeds—Lincoln Continental, the White Line, and VFeed—to see if any of them were running stories about the greatest loss to the hacking community since the disappearance of Kaili Zabora. But there was nothing. It was just another Saturday morning for a world that cared only for celebrity gossip, shady politics, and superhero movies.

A thought occurred to Danny, a seemingly simple thought he hadn't noticed in the fog of waking.

He got up and hurried downstairs, his steps growing more confident as the pressure in his head lessened. His phone was still on the counter where he'd left it the night before. He scooped it up and dialed Johnny. When it went to voicemail, he tried again, and a third time. He called the ancient landline in Johnny's apartment in Umbra, but it just continued to ring into oblivion.

Danny sent text messages, emails, push notifications—every fire-and-forget type of message he could think of—to all of Johnny's known and unknown mailboxes. Even if Johnny was jacked in, the notifications would reach him in VNet.

There was no response.

Worse, there was no ACK, no indication the messages were even delivered.

Johnny had gone off the grid before, but he'd never shut down his accounts. It felt to Danny like a total wipe, an erasure of Johnny San Vito from the fabric of the digital world.

How far had the Dead Man's Loop gone?

An email alert flashed on Danny's phone.

Large transfer detected. Open the MetaFCU app to view.

Danny loaded the app. At the top of his transaction list was a transfer valued at over $750,000 at the current Helsinki crypto exchange rate. The transfer was tagged with the word *fratelli.*

Johnny. The damn fool had really done it. Emptied his bank accounts. Dumped all of his data. Wiped himself out.

"Good morning," said Jane.

Danny turned to find her sitting on the edge of the bed, a pillow in her lap, her messy hair falling over her breasts. There was a smile on her face despite the hunching of her shoulders and the telltale redness in her eyes. She'd drunk as much as Danny if not more. He imagined a jackhammer skipping along the surface of her brain.

"Morning," he said. "You want some meds?"

She rubbed the side of her head. "Yeah." She grabbed her Spurs t-shirt from the dresser and pulled it on as she followed him to the kitchen.

Danny retrieved the Tylenol from the cabinet next to the fridge and laid out three pills for her. He put a bottle of water next to them.

"Thank you," she said, reaching for the little white pills. "How are you holding up?"

"Better now." He took a swig of his own water. "My chip was way overloaded. I'm just now starting to get the data off. Once I clear up some space, I should be able to think better."

Jane came around the bar, put her fingers on his stomach. "I didn't mean that. I meant about Johnny." She looked up into his eyes.

He remembered crying in front of her the night before, but now he couldn't remember if the tears had come because of the needle in his brain or the dagger in his heart. In that moment, he realized he didn't truly believe Johnny was gone and wouldn't until he saw the body for himself.

Danny shuddered as the dark streets of Umbra flashed in his mind. All shadow and danger, all prying eyes that followed every move he made. Umbra was where the technorati congregated to worship at the altar of the cutting edge, where young punks with neon implants considered themselves ones while the rest of the world was full of zeros. Together, they writhed as a single organism under the Umbra Canopy, like insects squirming beneath a rock.

Umbra was a hacker's paradise by all accounts, but to Danny, it sounded like hell on Earth.

"Hey," she said.

He leaned forward and kissed her on the forehead. "I'm alright," he said. "I've just got a lot on my mind right now."

"Has there been anything about Johnny on the feeds? I would think it would at least get a mention on Lincoln Continental."

"No," he replied, suddenly aware of her hands moving down his back. "Nothing on the feeds. Which means no one's found the body or…"

"Or he's still alive," she said, pressing herself into him.

Danny stepped out of her embrace, smiled weakly.

"That's what I'm hoping. Still trying to find out."

Jane nodded, glanced back at the bedroom. "I'm going to shower, wash away some of this hangover. Join me if you want, okay?"

"Okay."

He watched her go, lingered for a moment, and then realized there were more important things than watching her shower.

Danny returned to his workshop upstairs and sat down at his desk again. The transfers were moving quickly, and with a few tentative commands, he found he was able to query the Syzygy. There was still a ton of data on the chip, and the lag was near unbearable, but at least he had some working room to run decryption.

The Syzygy warmed in his neck, produced a signature tingle that let him know the chip was maxing out its CPU. Multiple decryption methods ran in parallel, slicing up the data, hoping to make sense of its seemingly random contents. He would need a full immersion rig to pull out the actual data, but the Syzygy was in no condition to interface with a rig. At the very least, he could examine the meta and maybe answer the basic questions.

Where was Johnny when the files were created?

What did he tag them with and at what time?

Danny waited and waited. He checked his email again, checked the feeds. Minutes went by in which he thought of everything and nothing. His eyelids grew heavy, causing the ceiling fan to fade in and out to the point where he wasn't sure if it was real or not. He fell into a daze, a halfway point between waking and dreaming.

Regardless of his state of consciousness, he was always aware of what was coming out of his chip and how little sense it made.

So much garbage.

So many useless tags and dates and color codes, each one encrypted to an almost neurotic level—*Django tight*, Johnny would have called it.

Finally, after what could have been twenty minutes or twenty years, a microscopic crumb of metadata broke free of the amorphous blob of garbage. The decrypters ate it up, and all of them spat out the same word.

Brigham.

Danny fed the data back into the routines, found more references to Brigham throughout the data dump. At the same time, he enlisted a virtual army of gophers to seek out the word in various darknets. They returned an array of standard responses he could have easily found on a search engine—Brigham Young, BYU, the Brigham Resolutions—but nothing that would fit Johnny's MO.

Only one response stood out from the rest, both in its claim and the low reliability of its source. According to an anonymous visitor to Overrun 6, Brigham was a mirage, a place that shouldn't exist, and most importantly, not worth the trouble of finding.

If the source were to be believed, then perhaps Johnny had found Brigham somehow, and perhaps in its own way, Brigham had found Johnny too.

A chime from his phone broke Danny's train of thought. He picked it up to find twelve new messages in his inbox. Eleven of them were bounces from himself—messages he'd sent to Johnny earlier—but the twelfth was addressed to Johnny specifically, which meant his email was now forwarding to Danny through some no-ACK proxy.

The message was from the building management software at Canopy View Apartments in Umbra. Someone had tried to unlock Johnny's door using a keypad and entered the code incorrectly five times. The intrusion attempt had triggered a lockdown followed by an email alert to the building's staff and the occupant.

Danny read the email again.

Five wrong attempts?

Could it have been Johnny stumbling home after a bender, having forgotten the keycode to his own apartment?

Or was it someone else trying to get in, an Umbrat who'd stolen Johnny's wallet and tracked his apartment from his VID card?

Danny's heart sank.

He cleared his phone and brought up the number pad. Dialed. Went through the motions quickly before his brain could stop him.

"Thank you for calling the Ernst Group, this is Michelle speaking. What can I do for you today, Mr. Montreal?"

He coughed, his throat suddenly dry. "I need transportation to Umbra, California. And a hotel room, too, near the Canopy View Apartments."

"Of course, Mr. Montreal." Keys clacked in the background. "I have a 2:30 flight leaving Denver International this afternoon with a 5:45 local arrival time in Sacramento, California. Would you like me to book it?"

"Yeah."

"Very good. Please hold while I put that in the system for you."

From behind, Danny heard the steps groan.

Jane stood at the top of the stairs with a towel wrapped around her body.

"We're going to Umbra?"

"No. I am."

She smiled, toyed with the wet hair clinging to her neck and chest.

"Silly Danny," she said. "You know I wasn't asking. I'll pack our suitcases. You should think about a shower."

He shook his head.

"Alright, Mr. Montreal. I have you booked on the 2:30 flight. We'll have a car at your residence at noon to take you to the airport. I've also—"

"Michelle, was it?" he asked.

"Yes, sir."

Danny watched Jane disappear down the staircase.

"Make that two tickets to Umbra. And a suite at the Fritz."

"Absolutely, Mr. Montreal."

FIVE
KAILI

This wasn't how it was supposed to end.

Kaili had gone to Perion City with the goal of driving Perion Synthetics into an all-out war with Vinestead International, but somewhere along the way, she had lost sight of the bigger picture, of a hacker landscape undergoing a massive cultural shift. The caricature of an overweight script kiddie trying to hack an ATM from his mother's basement had been relegated to history. The previously passive and physically unimpressive hackers were now augmenting themselves with cheap Vietnamese tech bought in the black markets of cities like Margate, Umbra, and Lakon.

No longer could the average net ranger be intimidated by a little show of muscle; Cynthia Mesquina had taught Kaili that.

The freelance aggregator—and sometimes mercenary—had thrown more than a few wrenches into Kaili's plans with Perion Synthetics, and none of it would have been possible without her augmentations. Cyn was a tiny girl any low-level Calle Cinco enforcer could have shut down with a stern glare, but with her augments, she was bottled violence waiting to spill out.

Le Soleil Rouge was one of the few places on the West Coast that could do both body mods and skeletal and muscular augmentations. The services didn't come cheap, but Calle Cinco had some money stashed away for such contingencies. There were cheaper alternatives, but they used last century's tech to do the work: chemical sedation, scalpels, spreaders—basically anything from the dark ages of medicine. LSR offered stasis pods that completely removed the patient from the process. Their computer-controlled instruments did all the cutting automatically while experimental stem cell injections aided in the healing.

Kaili's plan had been simple: get in the pod, take a long, well-deserved vacation in virtual reality, and wake up a new-and-improved domestic terrorist.

Her arms, which had recently torn a hungry animal to shreds, were definitely improved, but the way they ached told her she was no longer factory fresh.

At least the augments were broken in now.

Kaili groaned, rolled over onto her knees, and struggled to get to her feet. Her augments were idle, leaving the business of finding equilibrium to her actual muscles. She stumbled over to the sink, hoping to wash away some of the blood, but of course the faucet had nothing to give. She stared at the broken glass in the basin; glinting shards reflected the small amount of light in the room.

She faltered, looked around.

Behind her, she opened the only closed door and found a stall in relatively good condition. The toilet was dry, but she sat down anyway. She covered her face with her good hand and tried to hold back the tears. In the silence, she heard the *drip-drip-drip* of blood falling from her palm onto the floor.

Kaili tightened the injured hand into a fist.

There comes a time…

Kaili lifted her head, held her breath. Had she imagined the voice?

There comes a time when you will be alone.

"Annie," she said, closing her eyes.

The imaginary construct failed to bloom, but a hazy vision of Anela came sauntering out of the darkness nonetheless—a memory pulled from decades ago.

… when you will be alone, and I will not be there to help you. That is when you must remember who you are and what you fight for. This war we have taken on may cost us our lives, and along the way, we will be pushed to the breaking point. But we will not break, Kaili. A Zabora never…

"Breaks," said Kaili.

She smiled at the recall, at the faint scent jumping across her synapses, as if she were actually back in her parents' kitchen in San Diego as she spoke to Anela long-distance in Austin. She remembered the modulation in her sister's voice, the cadence of her delivery, and her peculiar tic of never using contractions.

Kaili thought back over the months she had spent in stasis, enjoying Anela's company but wishing the older Zabora would say something. Memories were all Kaili had now; all information that would ever be passed from sister to sister had been passed, and there was nothing new to learn from ghostly idols.

But sometimes, remembering a few words, a smile, or the smell of someone's sweater was enough.

The toilet handle clicked against the porcelain as Kaili touched it out of habit. She exited the stall and crossed to the lockers, careful to avoid the pool of blood growing around the dead dog. She found a pair of pants a size too big on the floor, along with a burgundy t-shirt in a locker. Two LSR-branded sandals had been pushed up against the wall near the sauna; they were a close fit, but they would be more of a hindrance in a fight or a quick escape.

A thin scarf made a decent bandage for her hand, but her shoulder needed something more. With the shirt tucked into the side of her pants, Kaili left the locker room and started down the hall toward the reception area.

Everything had been so pristine before, all white and clean all the way down to the baseboards. She remembered the smiling technicians and how they passed by hugging palettes to their smocked chests, their faces immaculately made up and cheery. There had only been a few other customers lounging around in plush robes embroidered with their initials and the LSR logo—souvenirs to remind them of the time they defied nature.

Ahead, in the waiting room, Kaili spied a drink bar that had once been stocked with three different brands of bottled water. She could almost smell the sparkling plates offering crackers, pastries, and freshly baked cookies.

Hunger drew her hand to her stomach. She suddenly understood what had driven the dog to stalk her. Though the stasis pod had fed her nutrients, her stomach hadn't seen actual food since…

She stopped, put a hand on the wall, and tried to calculate the timeline. How long would it have taken for the waiting room at LSR to deteriorate into the shadowy mess in which she now stood? The snacks and water were long gone, and dust had settled over everything, but beyond that, there wasn't really anything to indicate how much time had passed. She needed to get outside, find someone, and ask them what had happened to Le Soleil Rouge.

Kaili listed the possibilities.

A terrorist attack?

A rival cipher den?

I.C.E-1 was only a short drive to the south in Portland, but what reason would have prompted Tanzy to mount such an operation? How would she have even known Kaili was in Astoria?

Kaili shook the questions away and pushed through the swinging door into the reception area. The outer glass walls were still intact, but the furniture had been overturned and loose pages from fashion and lifestyle magazines littered the floor. Drawers in the reception desk held nothing useful, but in the nearby cabinets, she found a first aid kit behind a stack of pre-made gift bags.

The antiseptic stung her shoulder, but it was worth it to kill whatever bacteria the dog might have been carrying around on its teeth. She wiped away most of the blood with a promotional LSR hand towel and then wrapped her shoulder as best she could. It wouldn't hold up in the long run, but maybe it was enough to get her to a doctor.

A phone sat inert on the reception desk, but Kaili tried it anyway. She listened to the silence in the receiver for several seconds before realizing it was probably a VoIP line and useless without power.

She pulled on the t-shirt and stepped out into the atrium. Her legs threatened to buckle with each step down, and the railing had seen sturdier days. Downstairs, the previously tall and meticulously etched glass doors had been reduced to their frames—ornate, curling arms reached out to hold glass panes that had long since shattered. Kaili stepped over the broken glass into the dying light.

Astoria's Old District got its name from the age of its buildings and not because it was a run-down, pre-gentrification commercial zone that begged to be razed and converted into condos. It had a quaint, mellow vibe to it, with building exteriors that reminded Kaili of the early 90s, a time before Kenneth Barnes and his Guardian Angel biochip, a time when flannel button-ups and bulky MP3 players ruled the world.

Visiting the Old District was like stepping back through time. Kaili had experienced a similar effect when she'd walked out of Le Soleil Rouge, though for her, it had been more like traveling to London at the height of World War II.

Flashes of black and white wartime photos arose unbidden, overlaying themselves on the destruction she saw around her. Most of the buildings she faced were completely bombed out, their roofs gone, as if a giant hand had come by and taken a swipe at them. Chunks of dusty concrete and brick obscured the sidewalks and spilled out into the streets.

The few cars parked nearby were burnt husks, with their hoods open and gaping holes where their engines should have been. There was no wind, and in the ethereal dusk, everything looked stagnant.

Dead.

Kaili stood waiting for signs of life, but nothing—not people, not rabid dogs—stirred in the narrow streets of Old District Astoria. Only the setting sun prompted her to move forward. Oregon skies liked to cloud at night, obscuring a reflective moon that otherwise might light her way. She stepped into the street and turned west, trying to spy the towers of downtown Astoria, the triple skyscrapers whose silhouettes adorned the city's flag. To her surprise, the larger of the three was still lit, including the aircraft warning beacons on the spire.

If the building had power…

Static tore down the street, forcing Kaili to take a step back. Tall lampposts with faux gaslight domes flickered to life, ramping their LEDs into a soft yellow glow. The trail of lights extended to the west and broke off in three directions at the intersection.

Kaili glanced to the side, ready to share the good news with her sister, but Anela was not there.

"Never mind," she said to the empty space.

She walked briskly to the intersection, at first relying solely on her muscles, then later with the power of her augments. Activating the machinery in her body was getting easier. She didn't even have to think of the augments themselves; all she had to do was *want* to walk faster, to visualize herself moving with more speed than her natural body could provide. That's when the warmth came and the pistons fired.

Kaili stopped at the crossing of Lake Street and Irving Avenue.

"Which way, Annie?" she asked.

Footsteps sounded behind her, but they weren't the delicate tapping of heels on asphalt that Kaili was expecting.

"You are in violation of curfew, citizen," said a low, modulated voice.

Kaili swung around and crouched into a fighting stance. The heat in her arms and legs provoked an immediate full-body sweat.

Approaching from the sidewalk as if he had just walked out of the boarded-up Starbucks with his evening decaf was a man in a black jumpsuit. He carried no weapon in his hands, but Kaili made out the butt of a pistol on his hip.

"You a cop?" she asked.

The man nodded in an unnatural, jerky motion. "No one is allowed on the streets after dark without paperwork. Do you have paperwork?"

"No," said Kaili. "Why's there a curfew? What's going on?"

"I am detaining you for violating martial law." The bill of his cap hid his face in shadow. He reached for her arm.

Kaili pulled away and stutter-stepped back several paces.

"Martial law?" she asked. "What happened here?"

"I'm not obligated to answer your questions, citizen," he replied, rushing forward. His gun came out of the holster in a flash of movement.

Though her first instinct was to run, Kaili instead leaned into the attack, reaching for the weapon before he could get it level. She twisted with one hand while holding him back with the other. Using her thumb to apply pressure to the pad of his hand, she wrenched the gun from his control and spun it around. A quick pull of the trigger put a round through the cop's throat.

He stumbled.

The gun dropped onto the asphalt between them.

A geyser of black liquid erupted from the hole in his neck.

"What the hell are you?" asked Kaili, though she already knew the answer. She'd seen plenty of damaged synthetics during her time in Perion City. She knew what inhuman blood coursed through their veins.

The cop fumbled for a flap on his chest, ripped at the velcro.

"I am Officer Mills, a third edition Gabriel-class Perion synthetic and part of the Pacific Northwest Defense Force. I am now... authorized... to use lethal force."

He fell to a knee.

Kaili shook her head. "Bullshit you're a Perion synthetic. We never had a Gabriel class."

"Times have changed, Savannah Kessler." He coughed oily sludge onto his chin.

"How…" The question caught in her throat. Kaili thought she'd left the persona of Sava Kessler to bake in the desert outside Perion City.

The synny looked up, and Kaili saw its eyes for the first time. A flash of recognition pulsed in the LED matrices.

"Chuck Huber sends his regards."

"What?"

The synthetic dove for the gun. Halfway through the movement, his head exploded in a spray of metallic confetti. Officer Mills fell lifeless at Kaili's feet.

She turned to see where the shot had come from, but the echoes were dying fast. To her surprise, no roving gang of bandits appeared from the rubble to threaten her. No sniper stood up from his nest to train his gun at her.

There was nothing but predatory stillness.

For the first time since waking up, Kaili didn't feel alone.

SIX
TANZY

The security protocols of the Reykjavik darknet had always made Tanzy's skin crawl. They were too abrasive, too rough in their handling of her digital presence. Getting scanned by Reyk code was akin to tumbling down the jagged ice face of some enormous mountain—naked. And yet, Reyk was preferred among the old school hacking community for its low-poly virtual and outright hostility toward anything Vinestead. If Tanzy wanted to talk to anyone from the old days without Vinestead listening in, this was the place to do it.

Tanzy shuddered as an icy hand dug into the back of her skull. The delicate dance between the scanners and her biochip ended abruptly as a registered key exchange short-circuited the remainder of the verification tests. She found herself standing under a streetlamp on the outskirts of a blurry town with flat fields and lazy snow falling from the sky.

A light from a tavern down the road blazed against a backdrop of a night sky with square stars and a blocky aurora borealis snaking its way between them.

She pulled her parka closer and walked.

The Quatrain hadn't been able to answer definitively whether Johnny San Vito was dead or not, and the longer they were silent, the more Tanzy realized it would take more than a few well-placed searches to figure out the answer. Johnny's digital signal had dried up a few minutes before the timestamp on the money transfer, after which there had been nothing but silence. That alone didn't mean he was dead, just that the network had lost visibility.

For hackers like Tanzy and Johnny, sometimes that was a good thing.

There was laughter and raucous shouting coming from the tavern's cracked windows, but when Tanzy stepped inside the Blue Saloon, she found only a solitary, lumbersexual bartender mindlessly drying a glass. He didn't even look up at her when she entered, just stood there with a disinterested look on his bearded face, as if contemplating which plaid shirt he was going to wear the next day.

Tanzy couldn't remember if he were real or not—some lonely Icelander role-playing at bartender or some pseudo-intelligence programmed for a few basic actions and left to rot behind the bar.

"Ah, well, took you long enough."

She tracked the voice to the back of the bar, to a booth half in shadow where she could see the blocky legs of a male avatar sitting sideways on a bench. He lit a cigarette as she approached, casting a wavy yellow light over his face.

His red eyes glowed like embers.

Phantasm.

"Something's up with the sat-coverage on the West Coast," said Tanzy, sliding into the opposite bench. She blinked as the lights suddenly went full bright. "I'm still dropping packets."

"Nerd." Phantasm lowered the cigarette and placed it in the air a few inches above the table. It hung there as if suspended by wires. "No wonder you're alone," he continued. "Talking like that all the time."

Tanzy smirked. "I'm never alone, Michael. You know that."

The air sparked, discharged, and four avatars dropped into place at a nearby table. Four women dressed in identical black leather outfits turned to look at the booth, their mouths held in tight lines below thin sunglasses.

"Ah, well, you brought the girls. Hmm. They're hardly the snuggling type, now are they? I bet they talk just like you, don't they?"

"If you mean they can discuss technology in a clear and concise manner, then yes."

"Well good on 'em," said Phantasm, "but they're still nerds. Girl nerds is still girl nerds. I bet Portlanderers eat it up, don't they?" He didn't wait for an answer, just shook his head. "Damn shame. They're hot as fuck, Megs, even in low poly. Which one is Princess again?"

Tanzy gestured to the woman in the closest chair.

"Ah, how are ya now, sweetie?" Phantasm's Irish accent was comically bad, and he knew it. In his normal voice, he spoke to Tanzy out of the corner of his mouth. "She and I have a thing."

"We do not," said Princess.

"I don't think he has a thing," said Strider.

"More like no-thing," said Whisper.

"There's Thing 1 and Thing 2 and he's got neither," said Cherry.

"Michael, have you seen Johnny?"

Phantasm stared at Cherry for a few seconds before returning his gaze. "Johnny?" he asked, plucking the cigarette from the air. "Johnny who? Johnny Cage? Johnny Rico?"

"You know who I'm talking about. My Johnny."

"Ah, well, the man himself, Johnny San Vito." He chuckled. "Tell me, sis. How'd you go and lose one of the world's most famous hackers now?"

The truth was Tanzy hadn't seen Johnny in over a decade, at least not in person. She'd seen the occasional news stories on the feeds and of course, his digital signature in VNet was always prominent. She wanted to tell Phantasm that Johnny hadn't been hers to lose, but those words in that order caught in her throat, made her wonder if they were true or not.

Her emotions threatened to boil over. She looked away.

"This is serious," she said. "I think he might be dead."

Phantasm nodded. "Seems impolite to assume."

"He dropped half a mil in my bank account last night."

Laughter filled the tavern; the bartender cleared his throat.

"Did he now?" Phantasm's laughter turned to coughing. "Sounds like you and me are taking a vacation. Or maybe you can buy me one of those fancy self-driving cars everyone's talking about."

"Michael…"

"My name is Phantasm, *Megan*."

She groaned. "Have you seen him, yes or no?"

"No."

"Have you been outside in the last week?"

"Ah, well… no."

Strider snickered.

"You can shut right the fuck up, you gobbly—"

"Phantasm!" Tanzy struck the edge of the table and snapped off a jagged chunk of wood. "My friend might be dead. One of the most well-known hackers in our community might be dead. But more than that, more than all of that, *my friend might be dead!*"

She squeezed the sides of her face and leaned her elbows on the table. There were tears somewhere in the distant periphery, but Cleo would lock them down long before they made it to her eyes. She let out a breath through gritted teeth.

The wood grain textures covering the table went in and out of focus.

"What do you need from me?" asked Phantasm.

Cherry answered for Tanzy, speaking rapidly in a subtle Chinese accent.

"The digital trail has ended," she said. "We must now rely on different tactics. There is considerable business handled offline in Margate, business we cannot track. If a contract was placed on Johnny San Vito, we can only discover it through personal investigation."

"Are you coming to Margate?"

"No," said Tanzy. "I need you to be our eyes and ears over there."

"Well if it's eyes and ears you're wanting, why not ask Benny Coker? I'm sure he'd—"

"Benny's not trustworthy. You are."

Phantasm sat back in the booth, drew the cigarette to his mouth without using his hands.

"There is a Russian syndicate operating in Margate," said Cherry. "They own many of the hackers and enforcers in the city. We would start there."

"Do you have any contacts in Margate?" asked Tanzy.

"Some." Phantasm turned to the window.

Tanzy followed his gaze, watched the pixelated snow accumulate on the glass pane. She knew what he was feeling, had felt the same thing many times before, the sensation of the real world intruding on virtual reality. In the tavern, everything was by design, from the rough furniture to the ornery bartender. Beyond its walls, the physical representation of the Reyk darknet ran on complex neural-assisted code, but code nonetheless.

And yet, Terrareal could still needle its way through the firewalls and security protocols to remind them they were just two sacks of carbon sitting in chairs and jacked into a virtual simulation.

There was a higher reality than the virtual world, but most people just wanted to forget about it.

"There's a guy I know over in Margate. Meltdown. Doubt he's part of any Russian syndicate or whatever, but he's probably got a cousin who is. I'll ping him."

"No," said Strider. "It has to be offline."

"I don't take orders from twiggies." He turned to Tanzy. "What exactly are you wanting me to do here? You know I can't just drop everything and drive down to Atlantic City. Who's gonna look after mom?"

"Don't bring her into this. You always use her as an excuse."

"You trying to start a fight?"

"If I did, you'd need a nurse."

Phantasm pointed angrily. "I wouldn't need a… you would…"

"Alright there, brother?"

"Mom needs me."

"We have arranged for a certified nurse to come to the house," said Whisper in a smooth, throaty legato. "She will provide care for the duration of your visit to Margate."

Tanzy nodded. "On my dime."

"Ah, well, aren't you the gracious one?" Phantasm waved his hands in the air. He shook his head, muttered curses under his breath. Finally, he asked, "You sending a car or what? And where are you putting me up in AC?"

"No car," said Strider. "You will drive yourself. Less conspicuous."

"I will conspicuously end you," he barked. "Now, sis, I can't help but feel I should be getting a cut of this half a mil."

"Find me some useful information, and it's yours."

Phantasm raised an eyebrow. "No shit?"

"If Johnny's alive, he'll be wanting his money back. If he's dead, you can have it. Either way, I don't want anything to do with it. That's not what Johnny and I were about."

"So, to sum up this enterprise, you want me to drive to Margate and ask a bunch of Russian mobsters if they know anything about the death of Johnny San Vito. And for my trouble, you'll give me five hundred large?"

"$475,000 in Helsinki crypto," said Princess.

"Uh huh," said Phantasm. "And what happens if I get my fingernails ripped out by Boris the Fingernail Ripper?"

Tanzy shrugged. "Every path has a puddle."

"Some fucking puddle. You should go yourself. They'll take you seriously. I'm nobody to them."

"Not happening," said Strider.

"I'm already on my way to Umbra," said Tanzy. "I've got some favors with Lincoln Tate I want to call in. And besides, I think Johnny keeps an apartment there. For all we know, he could be holed up inside, drunk off his ass playing some immersive murder simulator."

"Never knew what you saw in that guy. Him or that other one."

Phantasm shot finger-guns across the table.

"You mean Danny."

Whisper gave a quick nod. She had already suggested reaching out to Danny Montreal, but Tanzy had refused. There wasn't anything a celebrity hacker could do from his little cabin in Vail anyway. She wanted to know the full story first, then she would loop Danny in.

We have started our descent into Sacramento.

"Thanks, Cleo," said Tanzy.

Phantasm groaned. "I can't believe you talk to your biochip. Do you know how fucking crazy that makes you look?"

"I *am* crazy."

"Yeah you are. You take after mom."

Tanzy sighed. "How is she?"

"Up and down. She's forgot a lot, but the construct I've got her in keeps her occupied."

"And she's happy?"

Phantasm pushed his cigarette into the table; it disappeared in a blocky puff of smoke.

"She'd rather be outside, you know? When she remembers, she asks to go to the train yard to watch the engines. Don't know why she likes that."

Tanzy reached over the table and put her hand on Phantasm's.

"Dad used to have model trains, remember?"

"No, I don't suppose I do."

"He ran them a lot before you were born. And for a little while after that until he lost his job at Albright."

We are touching down.

"There's some shine on shit if I ever saw it," said Phantasm.

"It's how I like to remember it," said Tanzy. "Anyway, I'm jacking out. We just landed in Sacramento. I need to catch the train into Umbra before the sun goes down."

"Roger. I'll head out once the nurse gets here." He gave the Quatrain a little wave. "Take care, ladies."

Strider gave him the finger as they all pixelated out.

"Quite the harem," he mumbled.

"They're a good team."

"I'm good on a team."

Tanzy eased out of the booth, stood up. "You want to be a cipher? Live the rest of your life twigged out in a dentist chair? Everything shrivels, you know. Everything."

"Fuck that!"

"Keep it down," growled the bartender.

Phantasm circled a pointed finger in the air. In the next moment, the tavern had been reduced to dust, taking the bartender with it. A cool breeze came through and swept away the ashes, pushing them across a snowy plain to the distant ocean.

"Subtle," said Tanzy.

"Subtlety's for pussies," he said, standing from his now non-existent seat. "Dad taught me that."

Tanzy huffed, reached out, and tapped Phantasm on the forehead.

"He should have taught you when to shut up."

He pixelated out from under her finger.

SEVEN
GORDON

Gordon didn't get a good look at his visitor until she stepped into the room. From the ankles up, she looked like any other woman heading to an afternoon power meeting with the C-level players of a Fortune 500. Her black pant suit clung to her body in all the right places, showing the curves of her legs and the swell of her chest. The top three buttons of her white blouse were open, daring Gordon to take his eyes off hers.

The façade broke down at her feet where instead of the expected heels, she was wearing rough, black sneakers. There was mud on the soles; her walk into camp had come by field and stream instead of the front door. Whoever she was, she wasn't above getting a little dirty.

"You were expecting me," she said, stopping just inside the door. There were traces of an old Ukrainian accent in her voice, or maybe Russian.

"They told me someone had come to the gate asking about me. Said they knew stuff about my past. I wouldn't imagine someone like that would just walk away when asked to leave."

"I wasn't asked to leave," she replied, taking in the room. Her eyes lingered on the gun cabinet on the wall by the kitchen. "I was told to… *fuck off.*" She returned her gaze to Gordon and smiled. "A rude cowboy man recognized you from pictures I showed him. I see the resemblance is still there. Old, faded, but still there."

"The men in my family age well," said Gordon, dragging a finger over the armrest. In his mind, he rehearsed the motions necessary to flip it open, draw the Glock 9mm inside, and fire.

"And which men are those? Lassard men? Howard men?"

Gordon thought of the many aliases he'd used in the indeterminate months before joining LPS. How could this woman have known about them?

"You were a hard man to find, Mr. King."

He shrugged in reply. "You know my name. How about you tell me yours?"

"In time," she said, reaching into her jacket.

The muscles moved too quickly for Gordon to reasonably claim control. Before he could even issue a verbal warning, the Glock was in his hand and pointed at the woman. His finger tightened around the trigger.

"I'd like you to remove your hand from your jacket if you don't mind. And unless you want three new holes in that blazer, I suggest you do it very slowly."

"I did not come to fight," she said, a slight quiver in her voice.

"Then tell me what you want before I politely, but firmly, ask you to leave."

She took a deep breath. "I need help. May I?"

Gordon nodded.

The woman pulled a palette from an inner coat pocket, similar to the ones Gordon had used in college but much smaller and thinner. She tapped on the screen a few times before holding it out toward Gordon.

"What is this?" he asked.

The image on the screen was nothing more than a large dirt hole in the middle of a green meadow. The blue sky in the background made it seem idyllic and yet somehow ominous.

"There's a situation in VNet."

"Fuck VNet."

"I agree," she said, smiling.

"Then why do you give a shit if there's a situation?"

"I don't. Vinestead can go fuck themselves for all I care." She eyed the Glock in his hand. "Would you mind putting the gun down? You're making me nervous."

Gordon shook his head. "You're making *me* nervous, lady. I'll put it down when I see your ass walking out my front door."

She sighed. "I understand why you don't care for VNet. You've been here a very long time. You don't realize VNet is now a drug and the whole world is addicted. Everyone depends on it, and there's nothing you or your survivalist friends can do about that."

Maybe not anymore, thought Gordon, *but once upon a time, the whole thing could have been stopped before it started.*

"We're wasting daylight here," said Gordon.

"There was something in VNet, something very powerful, that was put there twenty years ago. And then, sometime around 2015, when the world's eyes were focused on Perion City, it disappeared."

"So what's the problem?"

The woman folded her hands at the waist. "Nobody knows where it went, who took it, or what they plan to do with it."

"And this has what to do with me?"

"I'm not sure. No one is."

"Of course you aren't." Gordon lowered the gun to the armrest, but kept it trained on his guest. "But you have a clue, don't you? I mean, you're here. You came all this way to find me, and for some misguided reason, you think I can or even want to do anything about it. Well, I'll tell you this—VNet, Vinestead, and you can burn in hell for all I care. Take a look around, lady. There's no network here. This is reality."

She smiled weakly. "Yes, we do have a clue. We know what it wanted before it disappeared."

Gordon raised an eyebrow.

"Yes," she said.

"Bullshit. How do you even know that? Are you saying this thing spoke to you?"

"No, it did not speak. It whispered, the same letter, over and over again. And those echoes remained after it was gone."

The gun trembled in his hand. He forced the next question out.

"What letter?"

Her eyes lit up as she whispered, "G, G, G…"

Gordon stood and stumbled away from the couch. Every instinct in his body told him to run, but the best he could do was hyperventilate his way through the kitchen and his bedroom to the bathroom. He dropped the Glock in the sink and put his hands on the edge of the counter. The numbers followed, one through ten in the blink of an eye, but then they changed, morphed into a single letter flashing out of the darkness.

G.

No one had called him that in years. The name sounded foreign in his ear, a relic of a life whose memories he'd ripped out of his own brain. So many of his recent years had been spent focusing on the present, cultivating an existence without past or future. A big part of that was escaping a world sick with technology, and the Lost Pines Survivalists had been more than happy to welcome him in.

He thought back to a night he could hardly remember.

The building in Old Downtown.

Austin. Natalie.

X.

It could only be X, reaching his hand out of the past to touch Gordon twenty years later.

Gordon moved the gun to the counter and turned on the cold water. He splashed his face, stared at his reflection for a moment. Water beaded on his beard and stung the corners of his eyes. As hard as he tried, he couldn't see the 19-year-old G-man in the sun-beaten face in front of him. That boy was dead and gone; he'd bled out in the rain-slicked streets of Old Downtown. What remained was nothing more than a crusty, overgrown shell. There were no raging desires, no misplaced anger like there used to be.

There was only a delicate balance between contentment and regret.

And this woman had come to upset that balance.

He couldn't undo the intrusion into the happy fantasy he'd created for himself, but he could boot the lady all the way back to Bastrop and give her a nice bruise on her ass for the trouble.

When Gordon opened the bathroom door, he found her sitting on the edge of his bed.

"You are G, yes?"

"No," replied Gordon. "G died…"

"Twenty years ago. Twenty years, seven months, twenty-four days since V-Night."

"You some kind of fan or what?" He folded his arms and leaned against the doorjamb.

"Everyone knows the story of V-Night. You're a hero, G."

Gordon scoffed. He hadn't felt like one at the time.

"Just what I need," he said, "a goddamn stalker."

"No, I'm not a stalker," she laughed. "No, no, no…" The fit shook her body, and she put a hand over her mouth.

"Why is that funny?"

"It's just," she replied, taking off her blazer. "You haven't changed. That night, you were charming and funny and full of yourself. But you loved that girl, and she loved you. I didn't understand then why she loved you, but I get it now. You're… naïve. It's endearing." She tossed her blazer to the foot of the bed.

"What… night…" Gordon closed his fist, realized he'd left the Glock on the counter behind him.

"I can't believe I finally get to do this," she replied, working the remaining buttons on her blouse. "Twenty years, I've looked for you. Twenty years, this case has stayed open. And now, *now*, I can finally cross your name off my list." She slipped out of the blouse; red sequins on a white bra caught the light from the window.

Gordon put up a hand as he inched his way back into the bathroom.

"I think you've misjudged the situation, lady."

"No," she replied, "I've judged you perfectly." She leaned to the side, reached under her thigh, and pulled out the Sig he'd left in his holster. She pointed it lazily in his direction. "I'm going to kill you, G. But first, I must prepare my body."

"Completely misjudged," he muttered.

She stood and flicked the clasp on her pants. "If anything, *you* misjudged me when you thought you could escape. You tread on my domain. And now, finally, you're going to pay for it." She slid the pants down to her ankles and stepped out of them.

"I don't even know who you are."

The woman stood with one leg slightly in front of the other and arms spread to the side. Her smooth skin was bisected by thin white lines running from joint to joint like spider silk.

"My name is Lucienne Shumeyko. Twenty years ago, you burned me out of the VNet singularity. Now you will face your death."

Registers snapped open; data came spilling out. The tail end of a conversation with Natalie replayed in fast-forward.

"You've got to be kidding me," he said.

"I have waited such a long time," said Lucienne.

"Well, you may have to wait a little longer. I'm not really in the mood if you catch my drift. Maybe you could buy me dinner first?"

"So adorable," she replied, reaching behind her back for her bra strap.

"Right back at ya, slick," said G, miming a gun with his hand.

A fine spray of blood erupted from the side of Lucienne's head. Chunks of flesh and bone splattered onto the white sheets on Gordon's bed. Her body wavered for a moment before falling sideways. She bounced off the edge of the bed and landed with a hard thud on the floor. The Sig bounced and skidded under the dresser.

Gordon stared at his finger for a moment.

Footsteps drew his attention to the left as a silver Beretta pushed through the doorway. Holding it was a shorter woman in a faded black duster. Gordon noticed a skeletal tattoo on the underside of her outstretched arm.

The woman stared at Lucienne while Gordon debated making a break for the Glock.

"Sorry about your bed," she said, lowering the gun. "I guess you guys were gonna stain the sheets one way or another, huh?"

Gordon's mouth opened, but he said nothing. He spread his hands.

She shrugged. "To each his own, I guess. If I were about to be murdered, I'd probably take one last lap around the block myself. But then again, I'm a great lay, so that really only rewards my murderer. Interesting quandary."

"Who…" asked Gordon, the words catching in his throat. He tried to lock his pulse down, but the commands simply echoed in the burnt-out husk of his inhibitor chip.

"Who am I?" asked the woman, smiling. She holstered the Beretta and removed her sunglasses.

Her irises sparkled; icy blue inlays gave off their own luminance.

"I'm the woman who just saved your life. You can call me Cynthia or just Cyn, if you're into brevity."

"Cyn," he repeated. "I'm…"

"I know who you are, G. I've also been looking for you for a long time, a few years now." She motioned to the half-naked Lucienne on the floor. "But, before you get any ideas, it was only in a strictly non-sexual and non-violent way."

"I…"

"Can't speak, got it." She turned her back to him, started for the kitchen. "We're not the only ones who know you're here now, G. And we won't be the last ones to come knocking at your door. You're partly responsible for the fall of the Net and the rise of VNet." She opened his fridge, clucked her tongue. "That made a lot of serious people seriously angry."

Gordon flashed on the Glock on the bathroom counter, the Sig under the dresser, and the small armory under his mattress.

"I'm ready for them," he said, his voice shaky.

Cyn came back into the room, gestured to the bed.

"You haven't moved since I shot Miss Ukraine 1994. You're literally quaking in your boots, G. No, you're not ready. But we have time. Not a lot, but we have time."

EIGHT
DANNY

"You ever been to Umbra before, mac?"

The driver tapped out an impatient beat on the steering wheel. The cab was inching its way through the pedestrian-clogged streets, often coming to a complete stop as the tranced youth and dazed hippies shuffled from one sidewalk to the other, their minds lost in some alternate reality with only a tenuous connection back to the real world. Occasionally, the cab bumped an unfortunate scatterbrain, but without fail, they hardly noticed the intrusion.

"Yeah," said Danny, catching the driver's eyes in the rearview mirror. "Back in '10 for the NetSec conference."

"Lot's changed since then. Whole new crop of nutbags and degenerates from all over the country. They think they're part of some new counter-culture revolution. Ha!"

Danny glanced over his shoulder down a crowded Mills Lane. He could still see the awning of the Fritz Hotel where he'd left Jane and the luggage. He assumed she was getting them set up in their room, probably hanging up clothes and filling drawers. She had a knack for handling the day-to-day stuff: checking them in, making sure they had dinner reservations—those kinds of things. She would have preferred to go with Danny, but showing up at Johnny San Vito's apartment with a stranger wouldn't have gone over well.

"Canopy View Apartments wasn't even here back in '10. They just finished these, what, end of last year? Third tallest building in the city next to the Tower and Decker Plaza. You got a rich friend, mac."

They rode on in silence for a while. Danny tried to ignore the tightness growing in his stomach as he catalogued the Umbra wildlife. He stared at men with bulging jackets and augmented eyes. He ogled women in barely-there attire and tattooed circuitry. So many people. They flowed like water, filling up the empty crevices of Umbra. They rubbed up against Danny's door as they jockeyed for position in the rolling tide.

In the middle of an intersection, the driver threw the car into park and unlocked the doors. "Closest I can get you, mac. You want to hoof it from here?"

Danny eyed the faces of passing strangers—too many to keep track of. He thumbed the fare on the vidscreen and exited. Outside, the combined sweat of a thousand people hung in the air; it gravitated to Danny's face and baptized him in the Umbra spirit. He slung the belt of his computer bag over his head and held his breath as he pushed through the crowd.

"Just one block down," the driver had told him. "Black building. You can't miss it."

Indeed, as Danny came out from under the awning of a Chinese restaurant, he looked up to see a towering onyx rectangle stretching for the Umbra Canopy. Its reflective walls bounced the random neons of the city and caught slivers of the afternoon sun.

There was no discernable difference between the walls and the windows, which made it harder to imagine Johnny standing behind one of them, looking down at a crowd Danny was trying desperately to taxonomize.

A young woman matched his stride on his right; she sported an undercut with high, green curls on top. Three feet away, a man with ridiculous holes in his ears adjusted the tiny matrix of wireless antennas inside them. Danny passed an ostensibly homeless person in a heap on the ground next to the entrance to the Canopy View building, and inside, spotted a thick doorman eyeing him from the other side of a glass vestibule.

Someone pushed at Danny's back. Foul breath of a drunk teenager seeped in from the left. The aroma of barbecued duck swept past him. Sweat pooled under his arms. The knot tightened. A woman's eyes—looking directly at him—flashed in the crowd, green pinpoints in a sea of shimmers. The sidewalk folded up. Buildings leaned forward.

Umbra fell in on top of him, crushed him to dust.

At least, it felt that way.

Danny slipped out of the crowd and into the glass vestibule. His shoes clacked against the stained metal grate on the floor. He moved them slightly to read a black and yellow sign that warned trespassers they would be electrocuted and possibly set on fire. He nodded at the doorman, but the weathered guard in his pressed black suit merely scowled back at him.

At the far end of the vestibule, a red panel blinked questioningly. Danny approached it and tried not to flinch as a matrix of blue lasers reached out and softly prodded his face. The vidscreen next to the panel came alive and displayed a message in small, neat type.

Welcome, guest of Mr. San Vito. Please take the elevator to the tenth floor, apartment 1010.

A dull buzz sounded as the glass partition slid back. The doorman was at his side instantly, not looking at Danny, but outside at the crowd. He dared anyone to come forward.

"That bad, huh?" asked Danny.

"Please keep moving, sir. I'd like to keep the lobby clear. It's going to be dark soon. You don't want to be outside when it's dark."

"Sure," he replied. Nearby, an elevator sensed his approach and opened its shiny black doors for him.

Danny reached for a button marked *10*, but it illuminated automatically, and the car rose on its own.

The halls of the Canopy View Apartments were a pale echo of Las Vegas modern, enough of an attempt at glamor and glitz to command high monthly rates but not so ornate and lavish that it alienated the typical Umbra resident. Johnny wasn't above spending the money he earned cordially stealing away Danny's clients, but he wasn't one to waste it either. Most likely, he'd chosen Canopy View for its central location and overstated security features.

Metal plates lined the ceiling. Thin rails of conductive polymer ran in parallel lines along the floor. Creases in doorjambs hid drop-down shutters that could slam shut at the touch of a panic button.

It was a tough ride being rich in Umbra. Most of its inhabitants held no steady job and merely leeched what they needed from the scene in a kind of informal, pre-industrial bartering system.

Sex, drugs, synth, data—it was all there for the trading.

Apartment 1010 was around the corner and at the far end of the hallway. Danny stood in front of the door and eyed the abrasions around the doorknob. A nearby panel lit up, put on its little light show, and then the door clicked open. Heavy deadbolts thudded into the frame. The word *welcome* scrolled left to right on the door's embedded vidscreen.

Danny pushed the door open with the tip of his finger.

The smell hit him first. Luckily, it wasn't the stench of a rotting corpse—not that he would have known what a rotting corpse smelled like—but it was putrid enough to give him pause, to make him wonder what kind of life Johnny had been living before his death. Even without the lights, he could see the room in his mind, all dirty clothes and stale pizza.

Stepping inside triggered the automatic lights and removed all doubt from Danny's mind that his friend had been slumming it up at the end. Pizza boxes and Chinese take-out containers lined the wall of the long living room. Near the sliding glass doors that led out to the balcony, Johnny had built a monument to Blue Rain with a pyramidical arrangement of empty cans. A menagerie of candy wrappers and crumpled chip bags covered the coffee table and most of the carpet surrounding the sofa. There, enough code cards to synth the entire city were splayed out on the cushions.

"Johnny? You here, man?"

No answer from the darkness beyond the living room.

Scenes like this were not uncommon for hackers who worked all day for weeks at a time. Danny himself had just come off a marathon session writing code for Lucas Cotton and his fledgling MESH service. The job had left his cabin in Vail a mess, but that's what hired hands were for. The Ernst Group had been able to get the cabin up to snuff two days before Jane was set to arrive.

Johnny's apartment, however, didn't look like the aftermath of a two-week job; this was months of neglect.

Lights ramped up in the kitchen and connecting hallway to the right, blooming into a soft warm glow as Danny came upon a bedroom that Johnny had converted into a home office. A four-by-four grid of vidscreens adorned one wall; amber lights in the lower corners showed they were powered on but dormant. Pushed against the far wall was a black desk striped with yellow. A single keyboard filled the otherwise empty surface. Boxes of hardcopy created a low shelf under the window. To the left, racks upon racks of equipment sat gathering dust in bins.

The lights remained off when Danny entered the room. He felt for a chair and sat down. The plastic wheels moved smoothly across a thick carpet protector. He swung his bag onto the desk, accidentally hitting a key on Johnny's deck as he put it down.

"I can't believe I'm recording this," said Johnny San Vito.

The vidscreens blinked, came alive, and created a grid of Johnny's face on the wall. The eyes looked straight ahead over Danny.

"Johnny, what's…"

"It seems like the kind of thing they only do in movies. Maybe that's because people can die in movies. But out here…"

It was a video.

There was no timestamp, but Johnny looked rough, with messy hair and shiny skin. Remnants of his last dinner lingered at the corners of his mouth. Bloodshot eyes constantly rolled to some screen off to his right.

"I'm only making two of these. There're no other people in the world I really care about. I've been thinking about you guys a lot lately." Johnny gulped. "I mean, I could have really used your help. I've been meaning to reach out, but…" He paused, put his hands to his mouth as he yawned. "Now I think it's too late."

A flash of green text crossed the screen.

BRIGHAM PLAZA.

Danny sat up straighter in the chair.

"So I'll keep this short. I want to get something off my chest, something I should have told you, but I never had the guts. I… I have feelings for you. Strong, romantic feelings…"

"What the shiny fuck?" asked Danny.

"I know us together makes no sense, but I want you to know I would have done it. I would have liked to be with you. Very much."

Danny tapped the spacebar and froze the video. He focused on the reflection of the door in the vidscreen, a door now occupied by a small shadow. He spun around in the chair.

"Yeah, I'm pretty sure that message was for me, Danny."

The voice was female with a muddled NorCal accent.

"Do I…"

She groped for the light switch on the wall, found it, and tapped it a few times until the track lighting in the ceiling came on.

He recognized her immediately. Dark, shadowy eyes, round face, long reddish-brown hair ending in curls, and lips painted in her signature bright red.

The knot in his stomach unfurled.

Megan Riley. The third pillar of the Reinhardt Triumvirate.

"Tanzy," he said. "What're you doing here? Were you and Johnny…?"

She shook her head, slipped her hands into the pockets of her gray jeans. Smiling wryly, she replied, "No, sweetie. You know I only have eyes for you."

He stood and they shared a quick embrace tainted by the smell of a festering gym locker room.

"It's good to see you again, Danny."

"Yeah," he said, trying to remember the last time he'd seen the suit of I.C.E-1 in person. They operated out of Portland, and for the most part, Tanzy didn't travel outside of the Pacific Northwest. He supposed the situation with Johnny demanded it.

His hand lingered on her arm.

She, Johnny, and Tanzy had made quite the threesome in the days before VNet, hacking their way through the untamed jungles of virtual reality, ripping off data quarries and speed jackers. Tanzy had always been the de facto leader of the Reinhardt Triumvirate, a trait she carried over into her cipher den.

"Where's our mutual friend?" she asked.

Danny shrugged, gave the room another glance. "I don't know. Maybe he couldn't stand the stench."

"Let me guess, he sent you money, didn't he? That's why you're here?"

"Maybe," said Danny. "You?

Tanzy smirked. "$475,000 in Helsinki crypto showed up in my proxy account last night. My girls did a trace on the transfer. It came from a POD account marked with Johnny's name. That's payable on death."

"I know what it means," said Danny, sighing. "I just don't want it to mean that." He put his elbows on his knees and spoke into his hands. "I think Johnny might have really done it this time. Last night, not exactly sure when, he triggered a Dead Man's Loop and dumped an ungodly amount of data onto my chip. I've been trying to sort through it all, but the encryption is tight. Django tight."

The fans in the server racks ramped up for a moment, then settled again.

"You don't believe he's dead, do you?" asked Tanzy.

"I'm hoping he's not. I fully expected to find him on the couch in his underwear eating cereal and watching some obscure anime."

Danny watched her shift from one leg to the other. Finally, she walked across the room to the server rack. She placed a hand on the dark face plates.

"If he dumped all his data to you, then these…"

"Are probably pulsed," said Danny. "I'm surprised this video even played."

She stared at the server rack for a long time, muttering something under her breath, testing an ineffectual power button on one dormant blade. The reds and blacks of her plaid flannel shirt looked out of place in Johnny's apartment—and in Umbra, for that matter. Her jeans were tucked into the loose flaps of black boots. A subtle aroma of weed wafted off of her.

"I was gonna try to see if I could recover anything," he said, patting his computer bag. "I don't know what your plans are, but…"

Tanzy cleared her throat, looked at him.

"I wanted to see if he was here," she explained. "Maybe find a reason he dumped all that crypto on me. But it sounds like you have all his data, so… I'm guessing we're not gonna find much else. Go ahead and look though, I'll keep myself busy."

"Doing what?" asked Danny.

She cocked her head. "I'm going to crawl into his closet and roll around in his dirty clothes."

Danny cringed. He remembered her sarcasm, remembered how funny and clever it had seemed in the early days—and how biting and mean it had been at the end.

"You staying in Umbra tonight?" asked Tanzy.

"Yeah, at the Fritz. You?"

She nodded, turned to look back toward the kitchen. "I was thinking about it. You mind if I crash with you?"

"Sure, but why? Can't you afford a place?"

Tanzy shook her head at him. "Yes, I can *afford a place*. But one of my best and oldest friends might be dead, and I want to be with my other best and oldest friend while he's still alive."

"Well that's fucking ominous." He reached for his computer bag and slid the laptop out onto the desk.

"Besides, I want to know what Johnny dumped to you. If it's as tight as you say, then we should have my girls look at it. And in the meantime, you and I can start tracking down Johnny just like the good old days."

The laptop booted. The snowy peaks of Colorado mountains filled the screen.

"All I remember from the old days is Blue Rain and General Tso's."

"I'm down," said Tanzy. "Though I'm more of a tofu girl now. Gotta fit the suit, ya know?"

Danny smiled. "No I don't. Never been a problem for me." He patted his stomach. "I'll call Jane and have her order some food."

"Jane? Girlfriend?" Her eyes sparkled. "*Wife?*"

"No, she's not my wife. She's uh…"

For a moment, he didn't want to say. His relationship with Jane was all fine and good when it was contained to his cabin in Vail, but out here in the world, there were people who wouldn't understand, and where there was misunderstanding, there was judgment. It took a second for Danny to remember how happy Jane's presence made him, how much he needed someone's presence every now and then.

Danny met her eyes, said coolly, "She's an Associate."

Tanzy raised an eyebrow. "Even better," she said. Then after a beat, "Do your thing. I'm gonna look around for a bit."

NINE
KAILI

Kaili crouched over the fallen synthetic and watched the black transport fluid ooze from its neck.

She didn't bother trying to take cover or hide. Someone had put a bullet through a moving target at long range, and if they were intending to do the same to her, she figured there wasn't much she could do about it. Instead, she knelt beside the synny and examined the markings on its wrist—a half pair of angel wings marked with three echelons.

It didn't make any sense.

Perion Synthetics didn't make a Gabriel series, and even if they had, what was this synny doing so far away from Perion City? James Perion had always wanted to spread synthetics far and wide to wherever they could do the most good, but only when they were ready. That was decades away—more, after the trouble Cynthia Mesquina and Cameron Gray had caused.

To have synnies roaming the streets, enforcing a curfew, was a dream too far, no matter how hard Joe Perion tried to fill his father's shoes.

Kaili checked the Gabriel's belt for anything useful and found two full clips of what looked like 9mm ammunition, a pair of steel handcuffs, a bundle of zip ties, and a compact baton. With a quick jerk, she pulled the belt out from under the synny and slung it over her shoulder.

She stood, looked again for her savior sniper. Around her, the Old District buzzed with unseen energy, as if worlds were turning beneath the static veneers of broken buildings. Above, the dusky sky was so pink and purple that it hardly looked real.

Was the sniper giving off that energy? Were they watching her through a scope? They'd saved her life, and a part of her wanted to know why.

Another part of her cared little for questions and simply wanted to run, to head west toward downtown to see if people still thrived in the city. There had to be someone out there who could tell her what had happened, preferably without pointing a gun in her direction.

A howl sounded in the distance; the raucous barking of dogs answered it. The echoes ran up and down the streets from the south, each reverberation digging into the cuts in Kaili's hand and shoulder. Her eyes drifted to the matte black Glock on the ground. The synny's hand was still outstretched, still reaching for it.

The Gabriel had come so close to killing her. It was unthinkable—a Perion synthetic had almost killed its former head of Public Relations.

She bent at the waist and reached for the gun.

The world spun around her, alternating between asphalt and sunset, blending into a terrible smear of black and pink. The crack of a rifle shot came from all directions and lingered in her memory long after she'd fallen face-first into the blacktop. Loose rocks clawed at her cheeks; dirt found its way into her mouth. Heat radiated from her limbs—augments popping on and off, trying to assess the damage.

She couldn't tell where she was hit, but she knew the sniper had opened fire on her—just as she was reaching for the gun.

Stupid, stupid Kaili, she thought.

She pushed against the ground, tried to roll herself over to breathe fresher air. Instead, a pain came as if she had slammed her hand down on a pile of broken glass. She imagined her grow-wire set on fire, burning beneath the skin of her left arm, zapping every nerve and bubbling the flesh until it no longer resembled anything human.

The images cycled through Kaili's imagination as she struggled to find a frame of reference for the pain she was feeling. She tried to clench her fist, but the fingers were numb and distant. Wanting—no, needing—to see the damage for herself, she rolled onto her back and lifted her hand.

Annie…

Her arm was gone, blown away just above the elbow.

What remained was a fleshy mush of sinew, blood, and circuitry—a stump with frayed edges where a high-caliber bullet had torn through. Kaili's vision blurred, as if her brain were refusing to accept what she was seeing. Paralyzed seconds turned into minutes; she knew something had gone horribly wrong, but she had no idea what to do about it.

It only took a brief flash of Anela's stern glare to get Kaili moving.

She grabbed the bundle of zip ties from her belt and fished one out with her teeth. Though her arm throbbed, she managed to hold it steady long enough to join two of the thick, black plastic ties together. Once they were secure, she wrapped them around her arm above the bicep.

She pulled the loose end with her teeth, screamed, and pulled again.

Rivulets of blood filled the gaps where plastic met flesh.

Between the heat and her racing heart, Kaili felt weak and languid. She lay back on the asphalt, clutching what remained of her arm. The tears made it hard to see the clouds rolling in above, blotting out the stars that had only recently started to sparkle. Flashes moved through the black shadows like little balls of lightning. Kaili saw greens, red, and sometimes orange strobes. They resembled aircraft, but there were too many of them, all flying in different directions, sometimes trailing after each other. With each slow blink, more appeared, their lights scattered across the dome of a world she would soon be leaving.

A Zabora never breaks.

Was there another world beyond this one? One where Rick and Anela waited with friendly smiles and open arms?

Kaili closed her eyes and tried to imagine it.

She wanted to give up, to drift away into fantasy.

A Zabora never breaks... until she does.

At least Anela wasn't around—in person or in Kaili's head—to see it happen.

"You should be dead."

The voice was deep and lacking any warmth.

"Give it a minute, would ya," said Kaili, squinting at a face silhouetted by a streetlamp.

The man had the rough outline of a soldier, with broad shoulders and a well-tailored uniform. He went down to a knee a few feet away from her, using his rifle for support.

"You smoke?" he asked, pulling off his gloves and fishing a box of cigarettes from his pocket. He offered the open box to Kaili.

"Got any synth? Something to take the edge off?"

She longed for a code card with a little Margate Mush on it. Then everything from the rude awakening to the sine waves of pain surging up and down her arm would simply drift away.

"No," said the man. "There hasn't been any synth around here in a long time." His eyes glowed a dull amber that spoke to some kind of augmentation. He inventoried Kaili, settling on her face. His eyebrows furrowed.

"Don't even think about it," she said, crossing her ankles.

"Fair enough." He lit a cigarette and took a long, pensive drag. He gestured to her clothes. "Never seen that uniform before. Who do you rep? MX? SoCal Liberty?"

"I don't know what that means." A tremor went up from her phantom arm. The skin below the zip ties had turned a sickly black.

"Who do you fight for?"

Kaili groaned and turned away. The lights in the clouds continued to dance.

"I asked you a question."

"Who do *you* fight for?" she asked. "Who gave *you* the right to shoot an unarmed woman in the street?"

The man tapped the emblem on his shoulder—an ornate *5* in the belly of an uppercase *C*.

"Calle Cinco. We're taking back everything from the coast to the Rockies, town by town."

Kaili studied his face, tried to figure out if he was lying or not. He couldn't be part of Calle Cinco; there weren't any satellite dens this far north.

"What's your name?" she asked.

"Flores. You?"

"Kaili Zabora," she seethed, tasting blood.

Flores turned his head and spit on the nearby synny. He scanned the surrounding streets.

"Sorry we had to meet like this, Kaili Zabora."

"You don't know me?"

He shook his head, crushed out the cigarette.

"Calle Cinco de Mayo? Perion Synthetics? Ring any bells?"

"Of course I've heard of Perion Synthetics." He patted the synny on its head. "Who do you think we're out here fighting?" His eyes drifted to the belt slung over her shoulder. "Look, I've got to get back at it. How about you toss me that belt so I can be on my way?"

"Yeah, sure, here—go fuck yourself."

"Have it your way."

Flores sprang to his feet, rotated the rifle in the air, and brought it down with a snap on the bridge of Kaili's nose.

Stars exploded; her head whipped backward into the asphalt. Blood flowed over her lips, her chin, but the pain never came.

She watched in a daze as Flores tried to rip the belt from her. A knife came out; he cut the zip ties on her arm, scoring her flesh. Fire ants scurried beneath her skin, but the tingling was almost pleasant, and the ants never sunk their mandibles into her.

Kaili watched his smile fade.

"You've been juiced," he said. "What'd they give you? Nanos?"

"I don't know what you're talking about," she screamed.

Flores grabbed her by the bicep and pushed the stump into her face.

"This! You should be dead by now."

Kaili examined the clotted mess at the end of her arm. Though some blood still oozed, the majority of it had pooled under the skin. It would have to be drained if she lived a few more hours.

If she lived.

Flores shook her. "What are you?" he asked.

She waited until the heat in her legs was unbearable.

Show him what you are, said Anela.

Kaili smiled, reached out with her good arm to grip Flores' uniform, and pulled him close. She wrapped her legs around his lower back and squeezed, keeping the pressure on until she'd drained every click and crack and pop out of his spine. When his face came into range, Kaili sunk her teeth into his neck. Scraps of flesh collected in her mouth.

She choked, spit.

Flores somehow had enough breath to scream, so Kaili kept up the attack until she'd chewed through his jugular. When the spray of warm blood splashed over her face, she knew she'd gone far enough.

He spasmed. She held tight with her legs.

"Look at me," she said, putting her face in front of his.

Flores gurgled in response.

"Kaili Zabora. Say it."

"K…" Blood flowed freely from his mouth.

"The Butcher of Burbank."

His eyes widened; he was going into shock.

"Veteran of the Reaping."

He coughed, convulsed.

"And the last fucking face you'll ever see."

Kaili imagined her muscles tightening to a crush point. Her augments responded accordingly.

Flores went limp.

Kaili pushed him to the side, rolled onto her hand and knees, and threw up a mixture of blood and bile. As she retched, an uncontrollable laughter overtook her.

"A Zabora," she sputtered, sitting back on her heels, "a Zabora never fucking breaks."

She would have, had it not been for the magical healing of her arm. What else had Dr. Jenkins done to her while she was under? Or was the rapid healing part of the process, some lingering benefit of the treatment?

Kaili stared at the clouds, trying to catch her breath.

The lights had stopped moving, but one by one they resumed their course, though now they all seemed to be headed in the same direction. She followed a bright red speck to the west.

In the distance, the towers of downtown Astoria beckoned.

TEN
TANZY

What are we looking for?

For a pseudo artificial intelligence, Cleo could be kind of dense sometimes. Tanzy had no intention of explaining to her in-chip friend why she needed to get out of Johnny San Vito's office, why she couldn't bear to be around Danny for a second longer. She had an image to protect, even in front of old friends, and the number one rule of cipher den suits was that they didn't show emotion, and they sure as hell didn't cry.

Tanzy stood for several minutes in the open area between the living room and kitchen. She eyed the pizza boxes and takeout containers on the coffee table, the cans of Blue Rain and Mountain Dew in a half-completed pyramid behind the sofa, and the reams of marked-up paper in mountainous stacks on the dining room serving counter. She knew Johnny wasn't the kind of guy to clean his own apartment, but to go so long without bringing someone in struck her as odd. A man of his means should have had a maid service coming every other day.

The fact that Johnny's apartment was in shambles wasn't lost on Tanzy, and the more she tried not to think about what the chaos implied, the more she found her emotions overwhelming her. She could see Johnny sitting on the couch, legs folded under him, with a laptop humming in his lap. She saw his gaunt face and steely eyes clearly, to the point where Cleo was moved to speak up.

She offered to *take the sadness away.*

As if code could ever do such a thing.

Sure, any of the dozen code cards in her purse could mask the sadness, but the thought of Johnny dead and bleeding out on some side street in Umbra would still be there.

The blood would still be oozing onto the asphalt.

The flies would still be buzzing around his face.

Cleo hit her with the image of a Sagamihara sunrise, of golden rays filtering around old telephone poles and thin breaks between low buildings. Tanzy smelled the distant Tokyo Bay, smelled the fried seafood sold by street vendors who only came out after dark.

It was a pleasant memory, but Tanzy wanted no part of it. She started walking, as if the emotional balm Cleo was forcing on her was a mist she could escape. In the small hallway off the main area, she turned left, glancing for a moment at the open door to a powder room before deciding there was no way she would be going in there.

Instead, she drifted left, letting her fingers brush along the wall as she entered the master suite. Small lamps in the corners turned on automatically, illuminating a low bed with its covers turned back. Aside from a pillow tossed haphazardly at the foot of the bed, the room didn't look too bad. It even smelled better, leading Tanzy to believe Johnny had spent little time there in the last few weeks. More than likely, he'd slept out on the couch—assuming he'd slept at all.

She sat down on the edge of the bed and touched a soft, black and white blanket that had been folded there.

"Cleo," she whispered.

Yes?

"I need twenty minutes unfiltered."

There was a pause before Cleo asked, *are you sure?*

Tanzy bowed her head. She could feel the weight of her tears building up behind the artificial barriers in her biochip.

"Yeah, I'm sure. Twenty minutes. But then I want the walls all the way up. I want to be perfectly straight when I walk out of here, okay?"

I'll inform the Quatrain. Twenty minutes. Starting now.

A plaintive sigh escaped Tanzy's lips, as if she were taking her first clear breath after years of mild suffocation. The strength left her neck; her head dipped back and then to the side. Gravity pulled her body to the bed, and she made no effort to resist it. She wanted to feel the blanket against her skin, wanted the soft fibers to absorb the tears that had suddenly sprung from her eyes.

Tanzy sobbed quietly and hoped the hand pressed against her mouth was enough to keep Danny from hearing. She allowed the face of Johnny San Vito to bloom in her imagination. There had been so many times over the years when she wanted to reach out to him, find out what he was doing, and somehow convince him to give it all up to come be with her.

Only, she knew he never would have. Fame, money, power… what man in his right mind would give up everything just to be with her? If the situation were reversed and he had called and asked her to shutter I.C.E-1, she would have laughed him right off the phone. In a way, it was Johnny who had taught her there were more important things in life than love, brotherhood, and family.

More than a few times, Johnny had rambled in a drunken stupor about the nature of existence, how it was the loneliest endeavor in the universe. Whereas Danny Montreal had taken that to mean he should live alone on a remote peak in Colorado, Tanzy had paid more attention to what Johnny did rather than what he said. Johnny built a reputation not just in Umbra, but all over the world. He did the same kind of work as Danny, but instead of toiling in the shadows, Johnny lived in the spotlight, trading away any semblance of safety and anonymity for praise and fame.

And now he was probably dead.

Soon, the world would find out, and his fame would grow even more. The media houses would feed nothing but Johnny San Vito for a week. People would want to know what he was doing at the end, and they would listen to anyone who could spin a story.

Tanzy didn't have the full story yet, but she would get it. Then the world would look to her, and she would play the part of a powerful suit mourning the loss of a powerful friend. The first lines of a eulogy formed in her mind. She saw herself standing over a coffin on a rainy California afternoon.

"Today, we put one of the greatest hackers of our generation, and my personal, dear friend, in the ground…"

She imagined the movers and shakers who would show up at the funeral, from media moguls like Lincoln Tate and Donato Banks to tech titans like Joseph Perion and Wade Vunak. She imagined each of them lining up in front of her, waiting for their chance to shake her hand and offer condolences.

The window is closing.

"Okay," she whispered. "Bring me back."

Tanzy had hardly finished speaking before an empty, neutral feeling of general content overtook her. She straightened up on the bed, wiped at the corners of her eyes with her sleeves, and adjusted a few strands of hair that had come loose.

There was no lingering at the doorway as she left Johnny's room. As far as her heart was concerned, there was nothing to feel anymore. Tanzy knew that on some level, the code was blotting out the emotions, but she didn't care. She couldn't have Danny seeing her upset, or sad, or anything other than the hard-as-nails suit she really was.

She walked confidently back to the kitchen and found Danny waiting for her. He had his bag slung over his shoulder.

"What were you doing in there?" he asked.

"I told you. I was sniffing Johnny's shirts."

Danny shrugged. "Alright, well, I didn't get anything out of those servers. Whatever killed that gear was probably strong enough to wipe everything on this floor. I think we'll have better luck with the data he dumped to my chip."

"Well, then, let's go take a look at it."

Danny glanced again at the hallway behind Tanzy, nodded slowly.

"Yeah, okay."

He said little else as they made their way out of Johnny's apartment and into the writhing streets of Umbra again. From what she remembered of Danny, he had a habit of clamming up when he was anxious, and there was nothing more assaulting to his senses than crowds in Terrareal. At a particularly crowded intersection, she snaked her hand into his elbow to keep him from drifting away, only to feel the trembling in his arm.

A god in virtual reality, said Cleo, *but just a man out here.*

Tanzy had been thinking the same thing, but where Cleo had laced her words with slight disdain, Tanzy felt only empathy. Danny was her friend, and friends backed each other when they needed help, when they were suffering.

She said nothing as they walked, merely led him through the crowd as best she could. And when they finally made it to the Hotel Fritz and the elevator doors closed, she didn't make a point of saying they were safe now. That would have only made him feel worse.

Instead, she waited for him to recover on his own, which he did as soon as he stepped off the elevator and saw his escort waiting at the open door to the suite.

If anything, the Associate was thorough. The suite already had a lived-in look to it, even though Danny had said he'd only arrived a couple hours prior. The chemical smell found in most hotels was absent, replaced instead by the familiar aroma of sugary sauces and fried rice.

They ate in the corner dining room where inclined windows provided a view of the south and east quadrants of the city. For what felt like a long time, the sun hung in the space between the Canopy and the city's taller buildings, until it sank completely, giving way to a light show unrivaled anywhere else in the country.

Buildings sprouted LEDs at the edges, some bordering windows, others spelling out the names of apartments, hotels, parlors, and various brands. Previously dormant vidscreens two and three stories high came alive, running through looping reels of advertisements cut with sports clips, gameplay trailers, and quite often, softcore pornography. As night fell, the windows around the dining room became mirrors, reflecting their subdued gathering.

Whatever emotional turmoil Danny might have been feeling, it had no effect on his appetite. He put away two large plates of General Tso's, both furnished by the Associate Jane in an act of servitude so reviling that Tanzy had to look away to keep from making a comment. When ignoring the Associate didn't work, she tried to strike up a conversation with the escort to see just how deep her programming went.

Somewhere along the line, Danny got up and went to the living room. He sat with his laptop on the large horseshoe couch. It wasn't until Cleo chimed in that Tanzy realized he was working.

Message from the Quatrain. New data stores have arrived from Danny Montreal.

When Jane excused herself to the bathroom, Tanzy used the opportunity to join Danny on the couch. She sat opposite him and put her feet up on the padded ottoman.

"How's the transfer coming?" she asked.

"Still queuing," he replied, not looking up from his laptop. "All my gear's still overloaded, so it's gonna take a while. Your ciphers should have something to start on by…" He glanced at his sliver. "Midnight, maybe?"

Tanzy repeated the action with her own wrist, sighed. It was barely 8:30 p.m.

"I hate to wait," she said, reaching for the small purse she had stowed on the arm of the couch. "I think what we need right now is some of Einstein's Time Dilator." She dumped a collection of code cards onto the ottoman, each branded with its own insignia and color. She spread them out and looked up at Danny.

"No thanks," he replied. "Gotta work."

"I wasn't offering," she huffed. "These are for me and my new best friend."

"What are we talking about?" asked Jane. She walked around the back of the sofa to the serving bar and grabbed a bottle of water. She approached Danny from behind and laid the bottle on his shoulder.

He thanked her but didn't open it.

Tanzy patted the empty cushion to her right as Jane rejoined them. She gestured to the spread on the ottoman.

"Pick a card," she said, "any card. Each one guaranteed to provide an experience beyond the reckoning of any normal woman."

Smiling politely, Jane refused with a shake of her head. "I'm just here to take care of Danny."

"Oh, please. Let him wipe his own butt for one night. I'm not going to sit around watching you serve him like some kind of…"

Danny looked up. "Like what, Tanzy?"

"Whatever," she replied. She took a breath, turned to Jane. "Now, I need you to pick a card because there's no way I'm experiencing the next four hours in real-time. Come on, we'll take this trip together."

Jane raised an eyebrow at Danny; he shrugged. She selected a card from the bunch—orange insignia of two doves—and handed it to Tanzy.

"A fine choice, yes." Tanzy snapped the edge off the card and beckoned Jane to come closer. When she was in range, Tanzy held the card near her biochip until a green LED lit up. Then she held it to her own.

This will affect cognitive stability…

The floor of the Fritz suite rose up around her as Tanzy was sucked into an infinite well of warmth and pleasure. Then, like a rubber band returning to its natural state, her body rushed forward to rejoin a world that was no longer itself.

Time ceased to be linear. The music shifted to a light Jazz mix with a healthy dose of forlorn trumpet. The lights dimmed to almost nothing, and yet Tanzy could see every detail in Jane's face, from the creases in her lips to the subtle flushing of her cheeks.

For what seemed like forever, they lay back on the couch with their mouths an inch apart and whispered meaningless sequences of sounds and coos to each other.

Danny Guns Montreal felt a million miles away—Johnny San Vito even further.

"Does *Brigham* mean anything to you, Tanzy?"

"Brigham," she repeated, lowering her voice to imitate Danny.

Jane giggled.

"I'm seeing it over and over again in the meta," he continued.

Brigham could refer to Brigham Young, the—

"No, Cleo," said Tanzy, waving her hand in the air. "Johnny wasn't Mormon. He probably chose the word 'cause it sounded funny. He's got a fondness for stupidity."

Jane laughed a lilting staccato that got a smile out of Danny.

"Why are you working anyway?" asked Tanzy. "My girls are gonna crack that nut long before you do. You should come over to the fun side of the couch for a bit."

He acted as if he didn't hear her, but Tanzy could see he was breaking.

Jane got up and went to the serving bar again. She retrieved another bottle of water, again. This time though, she opened the bottle and took a long pull. Handing the rest to Danny, she lingered behind him, running her hands over his shoulders. Slender fingers worked his thin neck.

He tried to ignore her, kept typing.

"Couldn't you take a break, sweetie?" she asked, whispering loud enough for Tanzy to hear. "It's been a long day. You need to try this synth. It's... wonderful."

The clacking of the laptop's keyboard increased.

"Hey," said Jane. "Is it you and me?" When he didn't respond, she pressed a thumb deep into his shoulder blade. "I asked you a question."

Domineering, thought Tanzy. *Did he pay extra for that?*

"Yes," he replied, finally looking up at her.

"Do you trust me?"

He nodded, catching Tanzy's eyes over the screen of his laptop. They grew thinner as she smiled at him.

Jane drew the code card out of thin air—Tanzy hadn't even noticed her taking it—and pressed it against Danny's neck. His head rolled to the side.

Tanzy gestured to the card. "Round two?"

Jane nodded, touched the card to her neck, and quickly tossed it across the couch before she collapsed forward, grasping Danny by the neck as the strength temporarily left her body.

Tanzy picked up the card, turned it over in her hands.

I'm not sure this is a good idea.

"I know," she replied. "I'm not gonna load it. Give me Fazed Fifteen instead."

That is definitely not a good idea.

"Just load it, Cleo. I can still see his face."

Jane slipped a hand into Danny's shirt.

Fine. All exterior doors are now locked. I have notified the Fritz staff to not let anyone onto your floor.

See you in the morning, Megan.

ELEVEN
GORDON

Gordon sat on the toilet and stared at his blood-stained hands.

One, two, three, four, five…

The shitty apartment in Old Downtown came hurtling out of the gloom, bringing with it the voices of children who had just experienced the first real danger of their lives. They'd stood over the body of a wannabe arms dealer and watched as four bullet holes leaked his vital fluids all over the worn carpet beneath his cheek. They'd listened to the final gasps of a man drowning in his own blood.

Then Gordon had aimed a pistol at the man's head.

He'd asked Natalie, "You ever kill a man?"

And Natalie, her face scrunched up in an effort to hide the terror behind her eyes, had answered by lowering her gun and backing away.

She'd even whispered, "No…"

Ten, eleven, twelve, thirteen…

It was a nineteen-year-old G who had smirked then, who had actually turned to this innocent girl and asked, "Do you want to?"

How beautiful she had appeared in the hazy light of that apartment. How virtuous she'd seemed when she shook her head and turned around. She had wanted no part in the killing of another human being, didn't even want to witness it.

Perhaps it had been seeing her reluctance not as a weakness, but as an appreciation of the value of human life that had led G to lose his enthusiasm for the moment. Gordon recalled the adrenaline of the encounter, the pain in his back, and the ache in his muscles. His body had prepped for a final fight, a last-ditch effort to avoid death. The urge to kill the man they had only known as Reynolds fizzled out like the last embers of a cigarette, and G had found himself speaking only for his own benefit.

"Me neither."

A final bullet had put Reynolds out of his misery.

Thirty-eight, thirty-nine…

Gordon shook his head. The counting wasn't helping. The instant recall of Reynolds' death wasn't a choice; the environment demanded it. He tried to keep his eyes on his fingers, on the blood rolling down his wrists, but he could always see Lucienne's body in his periphery.

Cyn, despite having caused the mess in the bedroom, had opted out of helping Gordon clean up. He imagined her sitting in the living room with her feet up while he crawled along the floor picking skull fragments and clumps of hair out of the carpet. He'd dragged Lucienne's half-naked corpse to the shower in an effort to contain the blood, but once her heart had stopped, the stream had turned to a trickle.

Deep red lines traced down her neck, flowed over her clavicles, and took one of two paths down either side of her right breast. The dead woman's unblinking eyes studied the moldy grout in the shower wall, her mouth slightly open as if she might raise a complaint.

Gordon wondered how he was going to get rid of the body. The LPS compound was large but not infinite. A fresh grave was sure to be noticed by someone sooner or later.

He tightened his hands into fists, but the harder he tried to hold onto the fabric of reality, the more he felt the threads slip through his fingers.

"I don't know why you're cleaning up," said Cyn, from the doorway. She stood with her shoulder against the jamb, a thin palette in her hand. "It's not like you're gonna be staying here much longer."

"So everyone keeps telling me," he replied. "Look, I appreciate you saving my life and all, but you wanna tell me what the fuck is going on? And who this is?"

"That's Lucienne Shumeyko," said Cyn, tapping on her palette. "Vinestead Network Security turned real-world enforcer. You see it a lot with those Eastern European import types. They spend years as gods in VNet, crushing out hackers and ciphers with a power that disappears as soon as they jack out. Pretty soon, they want to be that same kind of shit-kicker out here, so they get themselves some augments and implants, take some classes down at the *Y*, and then you get a girl like her. Trained killer, but psychotic and lacking discipline. If you've been hired to kill someone, you don't strip down to your undies and make a big show of things. You just… kill them."

"What were you hired for?" he asked, unsure where he'd last seen the Glock.

"To find you, of course. Protect you from all the hot Ukrainian assassins circling this place right now. My employer is very interested in keeping you alive for some reason."

"Do you work for Vinestead?"

Cyn snorted. "Fuck that. Do I look like the kind of girl who would work for that shitbag company?" She touched her hair. "Do I have a set of devil horns I'm unaware of? No, G. I'm strictly freelance. A job came through a business associate, and I took it because they paid seventy percent of it up front. And if I could get a signal out here, I would let him know I've made contact, and the rest of the fee would be sitting in my bank account before we even made it back to Umbra."

Gordon ran the name through his memory. No record of any place called Umbra came back. Not that it mattered.

"I'm not going with you."

"Yeah, you are."

He looked up at her. She smiled back at him.

"You gonna make me?"

Her eyes sparkled, popping crystal blue around the irises.

"I could, if I wanted to. It's important you know that. Things have changed since your day, G. The world is far more dangerous, and so are the people in it. You look at me and see nothing but a small frame and thin arms and there's no doubt in your aging mind that you could overpower me if it came to it. I don't blame you. That's small thinking, and guys are like that. But really, you have no idea what you're looking at when you look at me."

Cyn slid the palette onto the dresser and took off her jacket. Underneath, she wore a thin, black t-shirt with a faded print of Black Star Circle's logo on the breast. She pulled up the sleeves and rotated her arms so Gordon could get a good look at the skeletal tattoos running their lengths.

"The ink covers augmentation scars. Implants, overdrives, almost every tech you can think of, all resource-controlled by a mil-spec Ayudante biochip." She nodded to the shower. "No doubt Lucienne had something similar inside her. With Vinestead funding the build, I'd say she would have given me a challenge in hand-to-hand combat."

Gordon huffed. "At least a bullet to the head hasn't changed."

"Don't be so sure," she replied, shrugging. "Subdermal plating is really taking off. But like I said, I could drag you out of here kicking and screaming, tie you up, and make you ride like an abducted child all the way back to Umbra. But I don't need to. You're gonna come with me willingly."

Without waiting for him to ask why, Cyn reached for the palette and handed it to him. Gordon studied the image for a moment before realizing he wasn't looking at a still photo. The aerial footage of a forest clearing was moving.

"That's a live feed from a Lincoln Continental drone that's been circling this place for the last twelve hours. In four hours, it'll return to a nearby airfield to refuel. When that happens, we'll lose visibility for eighty-three minutes, and I won't be able to see Vinestead scum like her sneaking up on your back porch. Or, you know, front porch. And this…"

She leaned over to tap the screen.

Gordon caught the scent of some manufactured deodorant or perfume.

One, two, three, four…

G buried his face in Natalie's shoulder, breathing in the chemical tracers that fed the fire in his stomach.

Eight, nine, ten…

Natalie's groans grew like the dull revving of an engine.

Gordon shook his head, cleared the memories.

The image on the palette panned up, showed the horizon. A silver glint flashed as it sped by.

"That's a Vinestead drone. It has military markings, but we don't think it's under government control. There's another one way up there too, but we haven't been able to get a good look at it. It flies like a Jatayu strike drone, which you rarely see outside of the MX."

"Why are you showing me this?"

"Because I know you want to stay here. You think it's safe, but you don't seem to grasp that your cover's been blown. If I know you're here, Vinestead knows you're here. Beyond that, any number of players could be watching. I've read the histories, G. I know how many people died that night in Austin. How long do you think it'll be before the corpses of hired guns start stacking up outside the gates to this place? And how long after that before the police or the government get interested?"

"I can't just leave," he said, handing the palette back to Cyn. He stood and faced the shower. "Going back means plugging into the grid, and I can't do that. There are things out there worse than Vinestead and the police."

"I know," said Cyn. "And one of them is calling your name."

He looked down at Lucienne as he dialed on the water. The stream washed the blood away from what remained of her face.

"Sure, a virus or something," said Gordon. "I don't know if you've noticed, but we aren't exactly swimming in tech around here. That's the beauty of this place. A virus could take down VNet and YNet and ZNet, the whole system could collapse, and the crops here would still grow. The cows would still give milk. No matter how bad things get, rubbing two sticks together will always make a fire."

He adjusted the spray to Lucienne's chest.

"Tech isn't the savior you people think it is," he continued. "I would have been just fine here living out the rest of my life, but now you're telling me that because I walked outside on a particular day at a particular time, you were able to ID me from a drone feed? Do I have that right?"

Cyn didn't answer.

Gordon lowered his head, spoke into his chest.

"So no, Cyn. I'm not going with you. Vinestead can send as many goons as they want; my people will turn them away or cut them down. It doesn't really matter to me. The world can burn to the fucking ground for all I care."

"Who're you talking to, hoss?"

Gordon turned to find Evans standing in the doorway. The old man's eyes fell on the dead Vinestead enforcer.

"And who the hell is that, Gordon?"

"Sheriff," he replied, wiping his hands on his jeans. "Would you believe it's not what it looks like?"

Everything friendly that had ever existed between them seemed to dissipate, drowned out by the falling water.

"Not what it looks like? Jesus, Gordon. It looks like you've got a dead woman in your shower."

"I can explain," he replied, looking over the man's shoulder. The bedroom was empty; Cyn was nowhere to be seen. "Come on, it's me. You know me."

Evans shook his head. "I thought so too, but maybe twenty years ain't enough time to really get to know someone. I gotta tell Clemons about this… whatever this is. A death on LPS property is gonna bring the law. You've put everyone at risk."

Gordon grabbed a towel from a nearby rack and rubbed out the damp marks on his jeans.

"She broke in and tried to kill me."

"Was that before or after you stripped her down?"

"It wasn't like that."

Evans huffed, picked up the Glock from the sink. He ejected the magazine and cleared the chamber.

"We'll go see Clemons, see what he says."

One, two, three, four…

Evans moved his hand to the revolver on his hip.

"Now, Gordon."

TWELVE
DANNY

Danny awoke to sunlight streaming into the master suite and the sound of distant, muffled sobbing. Jane was still asleep beside him; her hair splayed out over the pearlescent white Fritz pillows. The last time he'd seen Tanzy, she was tucked under his arm, nuzzling her nose into his neck. Now, that side of the bed was empty, the covers thrown back.

Where had she gone?

He blinked away the haze and surveyed the room. The automatic blinds on the large bay window had rolled themselves up, providing a clear view of the Umbra Canopy, less tantalizing now in the bright morning.

The sobs came again, drawing his attention to the living room. He noticed Tanzy sitting on the couch, saw the shoulders of a white robe bob a few times.

"Tanzy," he said, coughing to clear something in his throat. "What's wrong?"

She barely looked over her shoulder. "The feeds are blowing up." A sniffle. "It's Johnny." She lifted a small remote and pointed it at the vidscreen on the far wall.

The voice of Lord Jon Ray of Lincoln Continental filled the room.

"… expecting a statement from Oakland PD any minute now. We'll keep that feed open and bring it to you as soon as it's available. In the—"

A quick advertisement for a new Koertig immersion rig cut Lord Jon Ray off mid-sentence. He returned fifteen seconds later.

"… just joining us, we are hearing reports that the body of Johnny San Vito was found overnight in a southside Oakland neighborhood. He was 33 years old."

"Turn it off," called Danny.

He slid away from Jane and put his feet on the carpet. His pants and boxers were only a few feet away, but he needed a moment to clear his head before he could stand up. The Syzygy had let the afterglow of the night before linger in his bloodstream, but with a simple mental command, Danny instructed it to sober him up.

The *Syzygy* called on subdermal chemical stores and released the necessary meds to counteract the dehydration and impaired cognition. By the time Danny pulled on his boxers and joined Tanzy at the couch, the fog had mostly cleared.

"I can't..." said Tanzy. "I just can't believe it."

Aerial footage of the Umbra Canopy looped on the vidscreen. The message *GAMEOVERJSV* was written in block letters a mile wide.

"He got mixed up in something," said Danny. "He never mentioned anything to you?"

"No, you?"

"Just the data dump." He stood behind Tanzy and put a hand on her shoulder. "And you're sure Johnny didn't send you anything?"

Tanzy shook her head. "Just the money. And even then..." She paused, cocked her head to the side. "Are you kidding me?"

"What?"

She held up a finger, tapped the side of her head.

Cleo was talking to her again.

"Why didn't you tell me? And I'm guessing you've been through it, right?" She sighed, gestured to the vidscreen. "Show me."

The vidscreen blanked, returned with a mirror of Tanzy's virtual desktop. It consisted simply of a large command line interface on the left and two smaller status windows stacked on top of each other on the right.

"Get it up there, Cleo. And make sure it's secure in transit."

"What is it?" asked Danny.

"Something Johnny sent me last night. Cleo thought it was an attack so she blocked it out until she could unpack it, which she did. It was like you said, Django-tight encryption."

"And?"

"It's a mod request," she replied, pulling a blanket over her legs. "An internal Vinestead memo about isolating a particular set of coordinates. Cleo says it's legit."

Danny climbed over the back of the couch, groaning at the soreness in his lower back. The previous night had taken a toll on him, enough to draw protest from every muscle in his body.

Tanzy pointed to the vidscreen. "It looks like something happened in VNet in October of 2015, only we didn't hear about it because everyone was so focused on what was happening in Perion City."

A diagram expanded from the upper right corner, depicting a point in VNet's cubic virtual reality. The coordinates glowed a bright red.

"There are a lot of names attached to this thread," said Tanzy. "Arthur Sedivy, of course. But there's also Vance, Rahat, and Patel. Someone named Lydia. Oh, man, look at that last one."

Danny squinted. "Julius Parker," he read. "Never heard of him."

"Yeah, but I have." Tanzy turned to him, put a hand on his arm. "You know the story about how the Net fell, right? Guy creates a clone of his girlfriend, girlfriend turns into a psychotic AI, creates a virus to wipe out her douchebag boyfriend, and that gives Vinestead the green light to come in and wipe everything out with an antivirus, including the Net itself. Well, I knew a guy who knew that douchebag."

"Don't we all?"

"I'm serious, Danny." She pushed some hair out of her face, wiped her eyes. "This was years ago, way before we all met up. I used to do basic hacks like board crashing and rat pinching. Then this guy named G introduced me to quarry rushing."

"Just G?"

Tanzy shrugged. "These quarries would net split all the time, and you could find some really choice data just floating around in the ether. Or, if you were like G, you could hack the other rushers while they were busy pilfering. Anyway, G was friends with that douchebag guy *and* some other creep by the name of Jape."

She pointed to the screen, her finger wavering.

"At least, that's how I knew him, but look… Julius Parker, J.P. Get it? He had this horrible Jamaican accent we all made fun of behind his back. But it was like he believed he was Jamaican, you know? Really put me off. Anyway, the Net goes down, G falls off the face of the planet, and after a while, I start asking around. And every single time I mention Jape's name, I get firewalled. Hard." She swallowed. "Found out later that butthole is Vinestead. And now look how far he's climbed."

Tanzy stood, unable to contain the rage rattling her body. Muscles flexed under the dragon tattoos climbing her legs. She stomped away to the kitchen and returned with two bottles of water.

"So what's the connection?" asked Danny, taking one of the bottles. "Why would Johnny send this to you?"

"I think it's pretty clear." Tanzy walked up to the vidscreen as if she needed a better look at the coordinates. She tapped the glass. "He left us a breadcrumb. I think he's been there."

A soft rustling came from behind—Jane getting out of bed, walking to the bathroom.

"And Vinestead," prompted Danny, thinking about how easily the night before had unfolded, how inappropriate the whole thing was in a world where Johnny San Vito was dead.

"And Vinestead didn't like it, right," said Tanzy. "One of the most famous hackers in the world finds a hole in VNet. The feed writes itself." She paused, scratched the inside of her arm through the robe's plush sleeves. "If I had to guess,

I'd say there's something at these coordinates that Vinestead doesn't want people knowing about. Anyone gets too close, and they shut 'em down, in there *and* out here. Bastards."

Bare feet fell softly on the carpet.

"I'm ordering some food, Danny," said Jane, bouncing along in a long, white t-shirt with an Alamo graphic on the front. The hem of the shirt bounced along her thighs. "Tanzy, what do you usually eat for breakfast?"

"Vinestead scum," she replied, gnashing her teeth.

Danny smiled thinly. "You know we're gonna get one back for Johnny, right?"

"Damn right we are. If Vinestead wants a war with I.C.E-1, they'll get their war. You don't just take things from me, especially not my people." She waved a hand around angrily for a few moments before collapsing on the couch.

He waited for her breath to settle. "Where do you want to start?"

"With breakfast," said Jane.

Tanzy eyed her without turning her head. Her hand moved to her chest, rested there as if remembering something.

"Cleo's already making the calls," she said, turning her attention back to Danny. "First, we find out what's going on at those coordinates. Then we make a bunch of noise and bring Vinestead to us. And if that Jape creep is leading the response team, I'll murder him right in his face." She tossed the empty water bottle onto the ottoman. "Did you bring a rig?"

"No," replied Danny, gesturing to his neck. "Just the Syzygy."

"Really?" She raised an eyebrow. "Choice gear, but we're gonna want to proxy through a physical rig. I know some people in town. I'll get us a couple shiners by noon." Then to Jane, "Unless you want to come too?"

Jane raised a hand. "I prefer to keep things physical, thank you."

"She really does," said Danny.

"Yeah, okay, I'm gonna borrow the bedroom," said Tanzy. "Give me twenty minutes."

Danny nodded, waited until she'd slid the bedroom doors shut. Jane was looking at him from the kitchen with doleful eyes. He got up and walked past her to the dining area. Below, the quiet Umbra streets pulsed with potential. Bells tolled over the din. Vidscreens flashed images of Johnny San Vito looking healthy and powerful.

But nothing recent.

Nothing that truly captured the man who was now dead.

Jane sat down at the nearby table.

"Is this what you wanted?" she asked.

"What do you mean?"

She gestured to the living room, the bedroom beyond.

"All of this. The shitty food, the drugs… inviting someone into our bed. I just wanted to check in, make sure you're not self-destructing as a way to deal with your friend's death."

"I didn't hear you complaining."

"Danny, come on," she said, pulling at his arm. "I'm here for you, to be with you, whatever that looks like. But you've lost someone you care about. Most people don't mourn with code cards and strange women."

"What does it matter?" he asked. "Johnny's dead. He got mixed up with Vinestead and now he's dead. And me? Tanzy? We're about to follow in his footsteps, which means we'll probably end up dead too. So yeah, I'm gonna eat some shitty food and do some synth and spend what few nights I have left with the women I love. I…"

A smile formed on Jane's face. She stood, reached for him.

"Did you just say you love me, Daniel?"

He wasn't sure who was asking—Jane Meade or the woman wearing her persona. Not that it mattered; the answer would likely be the same for either. He'd only ever spent a total of four weeks and two days with the beaming woman standing in front of him, and yet he felt a connection with her he'd only known a few times in his life.

With Tanzy, Johnny, and now Jane.

Of the thousands of people he'd met over his lifetime, he'd only ever bridged the gap with three of them.

It made them worth holding onto, especially now that one of them was gone.

Danny pulled her into an embrace.

"Yes," he said.

"Yes, what?"

"Yes, I love you."

She kissed him lightly on his lower lip.

"Is it you and me?" she asked.

"You and me."

"Do you submit to me?"

"Yes," he said, groaning as her hand slid into his pants.

"Then listen closely. Less shitty Chinese food, okay? And way less synth. Drugged Danny is not the Danny I know and love."

She gripped him, tugged him forward.

"What about…" he said, nodding to the bedroom.

Jane shook her head.

"Think back to last night, Danny. Can you remember her face? Because I do. And I'll tell you this, man that I love. I was there for you. She was there for herself. Do you understand what I'm saying?"

He nodded.

Jane stroked the side of his face, kissed him again.

Outside, the mourning bells began to ring in earnest.

THIRTEEN
KAILI

Kaili hardly noticed the ground passing beneath her feet, taking note only when the asphalt turned to grass as she crossed out of the Old District and into a wooded area. The clouds had thinned, allowing just enough light to keep her from running into trees and stray roots. Her plastic slippers flapped noisily against her heels; she was simply too tired to care about stealth anymore.

She skipped through time, losing seconds and minutes as she focused solely on moving forward, one foot in front of the other. She tried checking the hour on her sliver, only to be reminded it had been part of the forearm Flores had shot off. The sliver probably still worked, but carrying around her own severed limb just to keep track of the time seemed like overkill. There was also the question of *how* to carry the limb: by the wrist like a hammer, palm-to-palm in an awkward handshake, or maybe by interlaced pinkies like new lovers?

Kaili smiled.

Annie would have liked that one.

Thinking of her sister made Kaili's heart hurt. All she wanted to do was get back to Coronado Beach, back to Rick and Annie. But even without her private construct, even without her sister standing in front of her shaking her head, Kaili knew she couldn't just give up. She needed to get back to Burbank, get herself a new arm, and figure out what the hell had happened to the world.

The woods repeated the same clumps of trees and undergrowth, reminding Kaili of a childhood trip to Big Sur. There, the trees and mountains had loomed large, full of endless adventures, like a giant playscape put there for her amusement. Visions of Annie's ponytail swinging from the back of a baseball cap came flooding back. Once, on an impromptu mid-week hike, they had wandered off together, following a tiny dirt path well past the *trail closed* sign. And when they finally got to the top of the mountain, they had sat together watching the morning fog burn off, like someone pulling a gray duvet off the Pacific Ocean.

"That is our world out there, Kaili," her sister had said. "Ours."

Two years later, Anela had followed a herd of Californians to a new tech mecca in Austin, Texas.

Six years after that, she was dead.

Kaili paused at the edge of a tree line, pushed away the questions to focus on the clearing in front of her. She recognized the place, had visited once in the few days she'd spent wandering around Astoria before going under at Le Soleil Rouge.

The Astoria Column was supposed to offer the most scenic views in the entire city, with clear lines of sight to the bay, the river, and the ocean beyond. Kaili had been unwilling to pay the twenty-dollar admission fee to go inside the attached museum, but she had spent time admiring the artwork on the Column. According to the informational plaque in the courtyard, the tower was a hundred and twenty-five feet tall, and the mural wrapped around it would stretch over five hundred feet if unraveled completely

Kaili wondered why such banal trivia had stuck in her head.

Scenic views and measurements hardly seemed to matter anymore. So much had changed since that day. Husks of cars and discarded camping equipment covered the parking lot, as if a large group of survivors had called the monument home for a while. Judging from the sleeping bags and partially collapsed tents they left behind, they seemed to have moved on in a hurry. Nothing stirred in the debris, no people or animals scavenging.

The once-towering column had been cut down to half of its former glory. The wreckage from the observation deck had fallen on the other side of the courtyard, crushing two unlucky minivans.

The tattered remains of a banner hung from a twisted railing.

Astoria Column Centennial Celebration, Presented by Friends of Astoria.

The plaque flashed in Kaili's mind. There, embossed in granite, were the words *Astoria Column, Established 1926.*

Not even her augments could keep her legs from buckling; she fell to a knee, got her hand out just in time. Unless she was suffering from some kind of neural dissonance, then the plaque and the banner meant the year was now 2026.

At least 2026, said Anela.

"No way," said Kaili. "No way."

Bonnie Diaz—also known as Kaili Zabora—had walked into Le Soleil Rouge in January of 2016. Could she really have been in stasis for a decade? Her memory was no help—everything there was foggy and so many of the remembered moments refused to crystalize into something useful. She needed more data.

Kaili forced herself to stand. She found a path through the parking lot, climbed over the traffic barriers that had been placed around the courtyard, and trudged across the expansive lawn that had long since been trampled to dirt. She found the plaque on its side, ripped out of the ground with the evercrete still clinging to its base.

She knelt and brushed the dirt away.

1926, just as she remembered it.

"Ten years," she muttered. "Do you hear me, Annie? Ten years in stasis."

She had missed so much. All the preparation, the planning, was now moot. All-out war with Vinestead had been on the horizon for so long. James Perion was supposed to have led the people in open revolt against the 'Stead, but now… now people were fighting the very synthetics who were supposed to save them.

Kaili swayed with a sudden dizziness. She was hungry, but more than anything, she just wanted to lie down and close her eyes. She hadn't come across any shelter that would keep out the light rain that was sure to move in overnight. The makeshift tunnel by the Column looked promising; the ground around its entrance was undisturbed.

"Could be empty," she said, hoping her sister would back her up.

Crickets chirped, the wind rustled, but Anela made no reply.

Kaili drew the small flashlight from her bandolier and put it in her mouth. Flores' sidearm was a heavy Smith & Wesson revolver with an extended barrel; the augments in her arm warmed up to keep it level. She walked as if crossing a rickety bridge and kicked aside any loose debris that might trip her up if she had to make a hasty retreat. The tunnel was full of garbage and the smell of unwashed humans. But there were also neat piles of canned goods and a dozen blue water jugs stacked in a plastic pyramid.

"You know what they call this?" asked a metallic voice.

"Fuck!" yelled Kaili, swinging the gun around. She stumbled backward, kicking over the stack of cans. She pointed the flashlight at the far end of the tunnel and finally noticed the torso.

"They call it… a *bonanza*."

It had to be a synny; it was missing both legs and both arms beneath the elbows. Most of its inner workings—intestines, stomach, liver—were gone, and what remained hung down like rotted pieces of meat in a butcher shop. Its ribs poked out from beneath torn flesh. Tatters of a uniform covered the rest of it.

Kaili gasped.

Someone had scalped it, had taken a knife from its chin to the base of its skull and folded the synthetic skin outward, revealing a glinting metal orb covered in artificial muscles and black sinew. They had also pulled the teeth from its jaw, as well as the eyes from the sockets. Somehow, it was still able to speak.

"Clearly, this is a trap," said the synny. "Everything laid out just so. It's almost too perfect, isn't it?"

"What happened here?"

The synny adjusted its gaze. "Oh, you know, the usual death and destruction. Screaming, gunfire, general disorganized panic, that sort of thing. So long ago, though."

Kaili killed the flashlight.

"No," she said, "I mean, what happened to the world? Is it really 2026?"

"The date is September 8, 2029. And what happened to the world is what always happens to all good things. Organics."

"Summarize for me. 2016 to today."

"Summarize?" Its voice distorted briefly. "What do I look like to you? A protocol droid from some science fiction movie? I don't take orders from organics."

Kaili examined the lashing job holding the synny to the door. Bungee cords held the main torso while thick strands of Christmas lights held the stubs of his arms out in a messianic pose.

"Please… I have to know. Did Vinestead finally start the war?"

Garbled laughter filled the tunnel. "Spare me your conspiracies. Oh, Vinestead International is going to take over the world. They must be stopped. Death to Vinestead!"

Kaili spit in the dirt.

"You make my point," it continued. "And how foolish did you look when Vinestead came to the country's rescue? When primitive synthetics began their reign of genocide and oppression, who do you think rose to meet them? Vinestead's best and brightest, that's who."

"Bullshit," said Kaili. "Vinestead has never been about the best and brightest, just the power-hungry and corrupt."

"Typical organic thinking. So primitive. Vinestead is the only reason organics are still alive. If Joseph Perion had had his way, there would be none of you left, only snapshots of personalities plastered onto superior synthetic chassis."

"Isn't that what you are?"

The synny let out a digitized snort. "I'm a seventeenth iterative descendent of the original Markinson AI. My programming cannot be compared to an organic consciousness. I remember everything, understand everything, and even though scavengers removed my tongue and bound me to this monument, I can still hold a conversation."

Kaili turned the flashlight back on and approached the synny. She waved the light in its empty eye sockets.

"You're closer now," it said. "Don't worry. I have no teeth to bite you."

The machining on the synthetic's skull was far more detailed than anything she'd ever seen in Perion City. Taut sections of fibrous material composed the muscular structure—a design Chuck Huber had often theorized but never implemented. It was possible he'd finally succeeded after ten years, but something about the synny's overall build was too neat, too mass-produced.

"What class are you?" she asked.

"What?" it seethed.

"Your model. We used to use astrological signs, but I ran into a Gabriel earlier so I guess Perion's moved on to something else."

The synny flexed its limbs, shook in place.

"I am no mere Perion synthetic!" The tunnel rattled with distortion. "I didn't descend from some tinker toy. If I had hands, I'd rip your tongue from your mouth for such an insult."

Kaili took a step back. "If you're not Perion, then who the hell made you?"

"I was not *made*. My consciousness emerged from Markinson. The only thing *made* was this chassis, constructed by the greatest minds in organic history."

Don't say it, thought Kaili.

"I am a Vinestead synthetic, and you should be on your knees thanking me and my kind for saving the world from Joseph Perion's folly. But, unfortunately, you and I have run out of time for our little conversation."

Rustling sounded beyond the flapping walls. As Kaili turned to the entrance, a small object came bouncing down the tunnel. It settled near the water bottles and sat there, inert, as if waiting.

"Like I said before. Clearly a trap."

The object exploded, gouging Kaili's eyes with shards of white light. The concussive force put her off balance. Gravity reached up, wrapped its tendrils around her body, and yanked her to the ground.

Mechanical laughter echoed into nothing.

FOURTEEN
TANZY

Cold rain fell on worn stone, pooling in the moss-filled cracks.

Tanzy wiped the water from her brow and stared at the shimmering temple and its crumbling roof. Thick doors of charred wood wavered like sheets of paper in the breeze. Steps led down to a courtyard where Danny stood in a shallow puddle of rippling water. He tapped his leather boots tentatively, as if he wanted to go splashing around like a toddler.

"Smells like pop," said Tanzy, holding out her hand, letting the rain collect in her palm. She brought the water closer to her nose, smelled citrus. "No, more like oranges." She wiped her hand on her brown slicker.

Danny inhaled deeply, tilting his head back.

"I don't smell anything."

"This can't be the right place," said Tanzy, glancing at her sliver. The coordinates were still settling.

"Maybe what we're looking for is behind those big scary doors." Danny bounded up the steps with the kind of limitless energy only found in virtual reality. He stood before the tattered doors and bent slightly to peer through a large keyhole.

Tanzy ported across the gulf and joined him at the door as he pushed through.

A shimmering fog greeted them; silent flashes of blue lightning formed tiny threads in the mist. They stepped into an open-air room that ended abruptly at the edge of a deep pit. A stone ledge circled the room, leading to a small altar flanked by two thin windows of stained red glass. The fog swirled, descended into the pit, drawn by some unseen force.

It was the perfect hiding place… but for what?

Danny's avatar flexed; the damp cloth of his black t-shirt stretched over his massive biceps. A tentative foot edged over the stone, hanging out over the infinite emptiness of the pit.

"I'm coming for you," he growled. "Whatever you are."

Danny bent his knees, sprung, but Tanzy managed to grab him and fling him back toward the door. She shook her head.

"You really don't think ahead, do you? You have no idea what's down there, Danny."

"I don't care," he said. "I want to go into there now please."

Tanzy leaned over the edge to peer down into the never-ending blackness. With a wave of her hand, she conjured a green glow stick and dropped it in. The fog swallowed it whole, spat back crackling lightning.

"Well, I don't think it's a virus," she continued, "if there even is an *it*. But more importantly, *it* isn't down there."

"There's only one way to know for sure," said Danny, crouching again.

"No, look." She held out her sliver. "I must have keyed the coordinates wrong. We're off by one on the Z axis."

Danny stopped, puzzled the numbers. "Then what the hell is down there?"

"Does it matter?"

"Yeah," he replied. "I kinda really want to know. I... I can't stop thinking about it."

He's under the influence.

"Yeah, I know," said Tanzy, sniffing around again. "That's what smells like oranges. This construct has embedded emotionware. Probably a remnant of some abandoned game."

"Did Cleo tell you that?" he asked, taking another deep breath.

"Yes. Your chip didn't mention it?" She smiled.

"My chip doesn't talk." Danny smacked the side of his head. "Come on, boy. Lock this down." He shut his eyes tight for a moment, as if dealing with some internal pain. "Ah," he said, nodding. "There's your oranges."

Tanzy reached for his arm.

"Let's try this again," she said.

They jumped.

A steel girder covered in rotted red flesh popped into being in front of Tanzy's face. She ducked, dropped to a knee on a small patch of white plastic. Danny wobbled in place beside her, put a hand on her shoulder for support. As the construct settled, Tanzy stood and took in the matrix of broken beams.

There was something familiar about the arrangement, some half-remembered nightmare of horrible things happening to many people at once.

"Looks like a jungle gym from hell," said Danny. "Although you'd have to be a pretty big kid to play on it."

He put a hand on a nearby beam and immediately withdrew it. Rust came off in large clumps, clung to his hand. When he shook it, the flakes flittered into the air before seeking out another girder.

"It's everywhere," he mumbled.

Tanzy looked closer, saw traces of red flakes on every surface. Throughout the endless matrix of cubed beams, viral ash hung at odd angles, irrespective of gravity or any sense of up-ness.

"Lattice," said Danny. "That's the word I'm looking for."

"Still not right," said Tanzy. She slapped her sliver with her palm, knowing full well it would accomplish nothing. "Cleo, what am I doing wrong?"

Let me work on it.

"Well?" asked Danny.

"Off by one again. No way I did that wrong twice in a row."

"I have to say I'm rather disappointed."

"Do you have to? Really?" Tanzy walked to the edge of their small, floating planet and looked out into the matrix.

"I'm compelled to comment. It's in my nature." Danny put his hands on his hips. "So, what the hell are we looking at here? Garbage construct?"

Tanzy smirked. "You really don't recognize it?"

He spread his hands.

"Fine," said Tanzy, "but we really don't have time for this."

Her hands went up like a conductor beginning a grand symphony. Wisps of white smoke flowed from her fingertips, coalescing into a thick ribbon that wound itself around a nearby girder. It jumped to another, contracted, and pulled together. As the ribbon split over and over again, the groans of aged metal filled the construct. Beams that had fallen out of place rearranged themselves, first into an endless chess board, and then into a more curved outer edge as the far sides bent backward.

White flakes aloft in the construct formed walls between the cubes, folding to the outside edge like corn still on the cob. There was only enough material to do a small patch, about five cubes across. The island below their feet stretched out toward the grid, wearing thinner in the center to provide contrast.

"I smell oranges," said Danny.

I'm not detecting any emotionware, said Cleo.

"No, I think you're just crying, you big baby."

He wiped a tear from his cheek and sighed. "This isn't just someone's guesswork, is it? This is the real thing."

"Feels like it," said Tanzy. "The code is very old and clunky."

"I never thought I'd see a homedir neighborhood again. I mean, you remember something, but when you come back to it, it never quite looks the same. But this, this is 1999. Vintage Net."

Tanzy shrugged. "It's not our world anymore. We may have cut our teeth here, but it was never really sustainable. A free Net? In 2019? I don't think so. Nothing is free anymore."

"Death is free," he replied, approaching a nearby cube.

It had no outer wall, and more than the other homedirs around it, seemed to be wasting away from the inside, sloughing off a never-ending stream of rust and metal shavings. A green aura built inside it, and though the source was hidden, the light itself gave the impression of being tangible.

Danny looked over his shoulder, saw Tanzy following along with him.

"Is our destination a homedir?"

"Maybe," she replied, checking her sliver. "It's in the right direction, but I don't think this is it. I mean, it's not a cube. This looks like someone took a homedir and moved it to another location in VNet. They cut it out like a tumor."

"Or a virus," said Danny. "I bet that's where the coordinates lead."

Message from the Quatrain. The provided address is unreachable. Likely a virtual address.

Tanzy waited for her to stop talking. "Cleo says no. The girls say it's probably a virtual address, so we can't jump directly to it. Something's getting in the way and redirecting us."

Protected constructs weren't anything new in Tanzy's line of work, but usually they were guarded by weak code or some off-the-shelf fire. It was one thing to port to a location and get rebuffed, but inline redirection was virtually unheard of. A cipher den might have been able to pull it off in the old Net, but this was VNet, and no one changed the rules of the game without Vinestead's say-so.

"Someone beat us here," said Danny. "They're protecting Johnny's coordinates."

"Vinestead, most likely. They're the only ones with the access." She shook her fist. "Even so, of all the places in the world to try to protect, a construct in VNet is the absolute worst. The ego on these people. They're not gonna keep us out for long."

Danny's attention had drifted away.

"Hey, are you listening?"

"No," he replied, staring off into space. "I was thinking of a way to get us into a place no one can get into."

"And?"

"Well, you said Vinestead is breaking the rules to protect the construct. That means we need to break the rules to access it. Look."

He spread his arms, took a step back. A portal appeared in the virtual air—black with a sparkling white border. Within it, a list of destinations scrolled, each line ending with a count of the logged-in users.

Raging Spike was pushing just over a million concurrent users, while Slash and Yearn was reaching for two. Danny ran a sort on the list and found the most populated destination in VNet: Bedlam, an Escher-inspired den of sexual deviance at once known and unknown to half the population of America. Its user count was maxed out at 3.6 million, with a waiting list of over eighty thousand.

Danny pulled the name out of the window and converted it to coordinates with a swipe of his hand.

"You wanna explain yourself?" she asked.

"This is our ticket in."

"Into what? The world's saddest orgy? We don't have time for this, Danny."

"How about some pumpkin smashing?"

"Excuse me?"

Smashing Pumpkins is an alt-rock band from 199—

Tanzy waved the interruption away.

Danny chuckled his way into a coy smile. "You remember, right? Smashing pumpkins into small piles?"

He may be referring to SPISPOPD, a cheat code in a number of popular video games that allows the player to walk through walls.

"Ah," she said, "yeah, I remember. I guess that might work. It's certainly not the dumbest thing you've ever suggested."

"The problem's that it's just us. The VNet mainframe is gonna see us coming a mile away. We need somewhere with a ton of movement to mask our approach. When you max out a server's resources, a lot of strange shit can happen. You can even clip through walls straight into a protected construct."

Tanzy clapped slowly. "I knew I brought you for a reason." She reached out and took his hand. "Load it."

The homedir graveyard shifted one register to the left, plunging the world into darkness. A flurry of fleshy ribbons spun out of the void to form a swirling mass of naked bodies. Rhythmic techno blasted from beneath a newly formed floor, thumping its way through black shag carpet, velvet couches, leather ottomans, through pillows of black and gray, until it rippled the skin of the trembling bodies locked in awkward and impossible embraces.

"Ugh," said Tanzy, clasping her hand over her mouth and nose, "it smells like the inside of an orange's butthole in here."

Danny nodded. "Emotionware. Can't get away from it."

A sea of clouded orbs looked up from mounds of flesh to stare at Tanzy. Whispers floated over the moans of the assembled crowd; they rained down from above as gravity-defying revelers extracted their virtual pleasure from each other. On a long, inverted staircase above her, men, women, and meshes of the two sent her inviting looks. Rivers of breasts crested and spilled over low backs of couches. Erect penises wavered like trembling flagpoles in a heavy storm, monuments to manhood that demanded her attention, that stirred inside her a desire to possess—

Shutting it down, said Cleo.

A veil fell over the construct, masking Bedlam in a pearlescent shimmer. Eyes softened around her, lost their piercing stares. Mouths that had once been aggressive and provocative turned friendly.

Cleo's soft whispers coursed through Tanzy's autonomic system, unclogging the tendrils of synthesized excitability and arousal from her neural pathways. The emotionware in the construct kept trying to fill in the empty space, kept fighting back with the combined force of 3.6 million horned-up deviants.

"Hey, you alright?" asked Danny, smiling. "We really don't have time for this, Tanzy."

Tanzy gritted her teeth, wrenched her eyes away from a slender Asian with long blue hair and pierced nipples.

"Where to?" she asked.

Danny led her by the hand to a free-standing partition that separated a sunken pit of sheets and sweat from a lather-filled swimming pool of diving faces and breathless gasps. The partition was nothing more than two steel plates bolted to a single silver pipe in the center. Danny reached into the space and instructed Tanzy to do the same.

"Alright," he said. "I'm gonna open the gates and let everyone on the waiting list in. I'll make 'em port in right next to us, so don't freak out. When I tell you, load the hack."

Tanzy felt the construct shudder; eighty-thousand additional perverts had joined the staircase nightmare orgy, and the server struggled against the weight.

"Okay, now, hit it!"

SPISPOPD executing.

Bodies crowded around them, forcing Tanzy closer to Danny. His arms vibrated as he pulled her into an embrace. Their bodies inched toward the gap in the partition, squeezing and conforming to the small space.

The construct stuttered, its processors trying desperately to figure out what the hell was happening to two of its occupants. Coded arms reached for Tanzy, tried to hold her in place, but it was too late.

Tanzy felt her lips on Danny's, felt their bodies compress into the same virtual register. For a moment, they were one entity, and she heard his thoughts as plainly as the techno music modulating around them.

Danny's Syzygy is trying to join with me. I don't like it.

And then Danny and his biochip were gone, ripped from her grasp in a violent tremor of the construct.

Unknown viral threat detected. Purging.

Tanzy felt herself falling through thick ether; it spilled over her lips and into her throat. Air disappeared, light went with it, and soon her entire body ached with prickly numbness.

FIFTEEN
GORDON

"Clemons, this is Evans. Come back."

The radio crackled in the relative silence of the camp. Gordon's footfalls hardly made a sound as they dug into the dirt path. There was something about the trail of boot prints heading back to his cabin, a chain of size 11s growing ever larger, that made him think perhaps he'd seen the last of his little home in the Lost Pines of Texas. He'd spent a majority of his life in those four wood walls, existing in a solitary stillness he found comforting.

No loud noises.

No constant hum of technology.

And certainly no violence.

"Clemons, this is Evans. Come back." He spoke more emphatically into his radio, and Gordon thought he heard a touch of nervousness in his voice.

The radio chirped; someone on the other side was fumbling with their unit.

"Kinda busy up here, Doug," said Clemons. "A whole mess of black SUVs just pulled up at the gate and they don't look friendly. What do you need?"

Evans glanced over his shoulder at Gordon, asked, "This wouldn't have anything to do with the woman in your bathtub now would it?"

Gordon shrugged.

The unofficial sheriff of Lost Pines sucked his teeth and spit into the dirt. He lifted the radio to his mouth.

"Just checkin' your twenty. You need me up there?"

Open static.

Finally, Clemons said, "Shit, Doug. I think we're gonna need everyone up here."

"What are we talkin' here? Police?"

"Naw, I think it's worse than that. Just get over here and make sure you're armed."

"10-4," said Evans. He stowed the radio on his belt and turned back to Gordon. "Who was the woman?"

For a moment, Gordon wanted to reply with *what woman*, but the look in Evans' eyes told him this was not the time to be fucking around.

"That was the woman from the gate this morning," he said, slipping his hands into his pockets. "You didn't recognize her because of the... you know." He waved his hand in front of his face and mimed an explosion behind his head. "She took exception with you telling her to fuck off."

Evans grunted. "Yeah, I had a feeling about her. So, what? You're telling me she jumped the fence and followed you home?"

"Just like that. Walked in without knocking, said she was there to take me back, and as you can imagine, it was my turn to take exception. There was a disagreement."

"No shit."

"She was on my property fair and square. I could have blown her away the second she stepped through my door, but I didn't."

Evans shook his head. "Doesn't matter, Gordon. Whether the killin' was righteous or not, we still have to get the law involved."

"Do we?" Gordon stepped forward, lowered his voice a little. "I mean, who else really knows she's here? Or that she got in? Or anything at all?"

He thought of Cyn; she would be the only other witness, but he didn't think she'd do anything to help Vinestead. He scanned the trees around them, wondering where she'd run off to. Something in the back of his mind told him she hadn't gone far.

An angry groan rose in Evans' throat.

"I don't like this," he said, shaking his head rapidly. "Nope, not one goddamn bit. I'm just tryin' to keep the peace here, Gordon. I don't make the calls." He paused, dug the toe of one boot into the dirt. "Who was she? And who are her friends at the gate?"

Gordon took a deep breath. He would miss the fresh pine.

"I don't know about the people at the gate, but she was Vinestead. A um... mercenary or something."

"Mercenary stripper, is that it?"

"They prefer to be called dancers."

"No!" shouted Evans, stubbing a finger in Gordon's chest. "You don't do that shit right now."

Gordon had never seen the man so upset. Evans paced back and forth in a small circle as if he didn't know what to do. His hand kept moving from the radio to the revolver and back again.

The radio crackled, emitting three loud chirps followed by a voice Gordon didn't recognize.

"Red Dawn, Red Dawn, Red Dawn."

Evans' hand steadied on the revolver. He looked to Gordon.

In his first week at Lost Pines, Gordon had sat with a couple of other newbies and learned a short but important list of code words that the camp used to signal important events. There was *spotlight*, which was usually followed by the name of a child who had wandered off. There was *Clooney*, which meant someone had gotten hurt and needed medical attention. One of the more important code words was *come one*, which meant everyone needed to assemble in the main plaza. It was used for everything from disseminating flu shots to lighting the Christmas tree the day after Thanksgiving.

The code word *Red Dawn*, as it was described to all newcomers, was the worst thing you could ever hear coming through the radio. It meant, quite literally, *an invasion*.

In twenty years at Lost Pines, Gordon had never heard the words outside of the newcomer briefing.

Until today.

Evans opened his mouth to speak but stopped when he heard the distant gunfire. The shots echoed in the trees, settled.

Slowly, like the intrusion of a morning alarm into a dream, an air raid siren ramped up. They had only ever used it to alert the camp to bad weather—a tornado or a strong storm—but now it meant something else completely. Hearing its high-pitched drone in the crisp November morning with sunlight filtering through the trees felt wrong—unnatural enough to open a pit in Gordon's stomach.

"I need…" said Evans, unsure.

Gordon put a hand on his shoulder. "You need to get to the armory. Clemons probably only took his sidearm to the gate with him. They may need more firepower."

"And you?"

"I'm going to the gate, see if I can settle this without open warfare. There's too many innocent people here."

Gordon thought of Jessie and her mom. If they remembered their own orientation, they'd be headed to the bunkers on the east side of camp.

"Guess I expected that," said Evans. "Hoped for that, too." He pointed down the path toward the main road. "Now go."

He ran.

For a while, he kept to the main road, but as it started to veer away from the gate to circle around the cafeteria, Gordon cut through the trees and did his best to stay vertical through the undergrowth. He came out of the woods near the rec center. As soon as he stepped foot on open ground, the gunfire started in earnest. He dropped to the ground reflexively but got up a moment later when he realized none of the bullets were coming his way. He ran hunched over to the edge of a nearby building and peeked around the corner.

There was chaos at the gates.

Gordon memorized the players and the positions as he broke from cover and joined Will Hatchett at one of the many evercrete barriers set up on the road. The father of two was too busy loading a new cartridge into a bolt-action Winchester Magnum to acknowledge Gordon's arrival.

On the other side of the road, an enraged Clemons fired his AR-15 on full auto. When the chamber clicked empty, he swapped weapons with his son, Clay, who sat on the ground next to him with his back to the action. The boy reloaded the AR-15 with a steady precision only years of training could have produced.

Gordon mirrored the younger Clemons and put his back against the evercrete barrier. He revisited the gated entrance to LPS in his mind. Three large black SUVs were parked perpendicular to the entrance, providing cover for the three or four men who hid behind each one. A fourth SUV with a silver cattle guard had pushed through the gate but was now stuck on razor wire. The doors were closed, its occupants presumably still inside. Bullet holes dotted the hood and windshield.

The more Gordon examined the memory, the more he noticed two silhouettes behind the glass of the lead SUV. They were sitting motionless, unconcerned with the bullet-storm raging around them.

In a sudden lull, an amplified voice broke out from beyond the gate.

"Lay down your weapons!"

The men and women of Lost Pines responded with a volley of bullets and curses.

"You are harboring a wanted fugitive," said the voice. "Give us Gordon King. This does not have to end in bloodshed."

Will Hatchett stopped firing and turned to look at Gordon.

As did Clemons.

For a moment, the elected leader of Lost Pines appeared to be running the numbers, calculating the odds of survival versus the benefits of having Gordon around. His mouth opened, let out a guttural scream. He popped up and sprayed bullets at the gate.

Gordon looked back at Will, who smiled and rose to level his rifle. A bullet caught him in the shoulder, spinning him in place before sending him to the ground on his stomach. As he writhed in pain, Gordon's own calculations came to their inevitable conclusion.

He stood suddenly, felt the bullets whiz around him. He put his hands in the air and faced the SUVs.

"I'm here," he called, as the shooting died down.

Gordon stepped around the evercrete barrier and approached the lead SUV. Both doors opened at the same time, and two identical men stepped out. They wore similar black suits, hats, and dark sunglasses. Mirroring each other perfectly, they arrived at the front of the SUV just as Gordon did.

"You are Gordon King?" asked the one on the left.

"I am. Who are you?"

"I'm Agent Haggard. This is Agent Kraft."

"You federal?"

"No," said Kraft, barely moving his lips.

Gordon looked over their shoulders to see the other men walking out from behind the SUVs. Their guns were pointed down; some checked their body armor for damage. They assembled on either side of the lead SUV, their eyes jumping between Gordon and the LPS militia.

"Well, if you're not Feds, then you gentlemen are trespassing on private property. It's within our rights to defend ourselves, even if that means killing every last one of you."

Neither agent acknowledged the threat. Their blank expressions seemed bolted on.

"You are correct," said Haggard. "We have no legal right to be here, nor do we have a legal right to kill every man, woman, and child in this camp. But we will, if you don't come with us right now."

Gordon looked over his shoulder, saw Clemons and Evans standing side-by-side. Deeper in the crowd, he spied Jessie's mother hiding behind the corner of the main building, a long-barrel shotgun in her hands.

"You are out-gunned," said Kraft. "These people don't have to die for you."

"If I come with you," asked Gordon, "you'll pack up and leave right now?"

"Once you're inside the car, there will no longer be a reason for us to be here."

"Who are you people?"

"They're Vinestead!" shouted Cyn, forcing her way through the throngs of people and barricades. Her weapon was already drawn, and in a few seconds, she would have a clear shot.

Her arrival shook something loose in the agents. Their mouths morphed into sneers, and they reached simultaneously for the holsters inside their jackets. Gordon felt a sudden rush as their movements slowed.

1, 2, 3…

The numbers came shooting out of the darkness as code scrolled by in his periphery. He thought back to a night twenty years prior when he'd sat in a Greyhound terminus in Austin with a code cube tethered to his neck while he shivered and dumped six months of memories and accumulated code. All of his subroutines, all of his new powers he'd downloaded from Synaptic Synth, gone. It was the only way to rid himself of his memories of Natalie.

248, 249, 250…

The faster the numbers incremented, the more pain he felt throughout his body, as if he had walked down the wrong alley in Old Downtown and been jumped by a roving gang of punks. He could feel them moving around him, but the shroud that had fallen over his vision obscured their forms. He reached out for something to hold onto, but that just brought teeth down on his clenched fists.

756, 757, 758…

A mechanical arm in the tape library of his brain reached past a dozen empty slots for a vision of a building at Fifth and West in Old Downtown. The aromas of gunpowder and blood floated past him, tickling his nose. He caught a brief flash of Natalie cowering beside him, but then her face dissolved into a mash of unrelated ASCII codes. Compilers finally caught up, turned the nonsense into something recognizable.

X's Vengeance.

It was the same code he and Natalie had used to storm the offices of the ZabSix cipher den in Austin. It had given them the strength to take down a dozen metal guards and to get close enough to Anela Zabora to put a knife through her heart.

Only, it wasn't the original *X's Vengeance*—that had been deleted at the Greyhound terminus. This was more like an echo, a vibration in his synapses that had never quieted. Whether it would work like its predecessor was anyone's guess.

Gordon reached for the code at *1,024*, wrapped his mind around it at *1,025*. By *1,390*, he had fully absorbed the ones and zeros. His inhibitor chip, once considered a useless piece of slag occupying space in his neck, was reborn in a flash of fire and ash. A molten spike dragged down the back of his neck as the code loaded.

The shroud lifted, and Gordon opened his eyes, ready for a fight.

He fell forward into the back of the SUV, stumbled, and regained his balance. At his feet were three men, one missing chunks of skin on his face, the second with limbs twisted at odd angles. The third had pieces of a shattered visor in his eyes; pools of blood hid most of the damage.

Gordon followed the trail of bodies around the SUV, saw limbs broken or torn away, saw body armor stripped from oozing chests. At the front of the SUV, Haggard and Kraft lay motionless on the evercrete, the flesh torn from their faces, revealing glinting metal underneath.

Cyn stood nearby, her mouth open, her eyes unblinking.

"What the hell was that?" she asked.

Gordon looked down at his hands; they were caked in dirt and blood. He could see bone protruding from his knuckles.

His stomach lurched, sending his breakfast streaming out onto the evercrete. Gordon doubled over and went to a knee, felt cold fire run up his legs. Everything hurt at once and no amount of breathing or counting was going to change that.

The crowd around him began to murmur, and out of the corner of his eye, he saw Clemons and Evans approach.

Gordon looked up at them.

Clemons cleared his throat. "It's not our way to boot anyone... but I think it's time you moved on, Mr. King." His voice lacked the smugness or satisfaction Gordon was expecting.

Beside him, Evans nodded reluctantly.

Cyn slipped her hand under Gordon's arm, lifted him to his feet as if he weighed nothing.

"Come on, G," she said. "It's time we plugged you back into the world."

SIXTEEN
DANNY

In a moment of panic, the overloaded servers at Bedlam Adult Entertainment, unable to tell Danny from Tanzy, striped their bits in an alternating sequence in a single positional coordinate. For a brief, terrifying CPU cycle, Danny felt closer to Tanzy than all the matter in the universe seconds before the Big Bang. He smelled her perfume, felt the memory of her tattoos climbing his own legs, and somehow, like a second conscience, heard the soft, childlike voice of Cleo pitch to shrill alarm as she tried to warn of some ill-defined danger in a nearby construct, one close enough to swallow the echoes of her screams.

Wall hacks were nothing new to Danny or any of the other aspiring hackers he came up with. In the original Net, folding virtual space was as easy as moving and porting at the same time, seeing himself one place but imagining himself somewhere else. It wasn't even called a wall hack back then; it wasn't until VNet came along that the word took on real meaning.

VNet's draconian restrictions meant no random porting anywhere in virtual space. Destinations were protected, typically behind a paywall, so unless a user was duly authorized, they could only port where Vinestead allowed them to port and nowhere else. Inevitably, someone discovered that if they completed 99% of the port and simply stopped, the server would come in from behind and *push* them the rest of the way. At that point, it was just a program making a snap decision about the location of virtual avatars in digital space.

It didn't always work, but in a place as crowded as Bedlam, the server was more than happy to shuffle off a few non-committal avatars, push them through the cold emptiness of VNet ether, to a destination far from the beaten path.

Only, by the time Danny's feet hit the cracked sidewalk, Tanzy was nowhere to be found, ripped away by the trembling construct. Her absence hit him like a wave of nausea, a rippling uneasiness that distracted him so completely he didn't even notice the grungy teen standing next to him. In that instant of recognition, the rest of the construct snapped into place in cubic chunks, clacking like dominos thrown onto a table.

The teen stood next to a lone payphone at the edge of a gas station parking lot. He bit nervously at his fingernails while throwing side-long glances through Danny at the strip mall beyond the fuel pumps. There, a glowing Domino's Pizza sign blazed against a dark sky. Below, the windows of the restaurant oozed a warm yellow light, showcasing the clean yet empty serving counter and kitchen inside.

Danny swept the construct. It was empty except for the kid.

"Who are you?" asked Danny.

The teen fished some change out of his baggy blue jeans and put a quarter and a dime into the payphone. His palm hovered over the keypad while his fingers beat out a familiar sequence of numbers.

A muted ring burbled from the earpiece.

"Domino's West North, how can I help you?"

Danny heard the voice on the other end of the line perfectly, as if he were holding the receiver to his own ear.

"Delivery," said the teen.

"What and where?"

"Two large pepperoni. Hold on." He only slightly covered the receiver with his hand and turned toward Danny. "What? You think we need more?"

Danny opened his mouth to respond, decided against it.

"Alright, make that three large peps. Chad thinks he can eat a whole large by himself."

"Name for the order?"

"Ben Babbage."

"And where's this going?"

Danny kept listening but looked around the strip mall again. Another teen, slightly more disheveled, had appeared in front of the Domino's.

"Village at Starwood on Canyon. Apartment 301. Gate code is 1844."

"That's $19.22 plus tip, Mr. Babbage."

"Thirty minutes or less or it's free, right?"

"Something like that."

The phone went dead. Ben—though Danny was sure he'd given a fake name for some reason—placed the receiver back on the hook and checked his watch.

8:22 p.m. The numbers flashed across Danny's vision on the face of an ancient Casio.

"Thirty minutes to burn," said Ben.

It was clear the kid couldn't see or hear Danny; he walked right through him toward the pumps, cutting across a damp parking lot to a median full of bare trees.

Danny followed, trying his best to identify the unique aroma wafting through the air. It smelled almost like the ocean, but more polluted and tinged with gasoline.

Orange streetlamps flickered as they walked the median to the strip mall. The first beads of sweat began to form under Danny's arms. He tried to lock down the sensation, but the Syzygy couldn't find a way to interface with the construct. The chip thrashed in his neck, fighting against a virtual world Cleo had wanted no part of.

In the distance, a sign crackled to life, illuminating the roofline of a Blockbuster Video. The store filled out, populating rows upon rows of DVD cases. Behind the counter, a well-endowed girl in a dark blue polo sat reading an oversized copy of SPIN magazine. Even at a distance, Danny could see her plainly, as if her avatar were floating in a white construct, zooming in and out on the details of her body—blood-red lipstick, loose jean shorts, and protruding from the hem, the lower half of a rose tattoo on her inner thigh, its stem adorned with thorns.

Ben headed first in the direction of the video store, but when he reached the covered sidewalk, he turned left and engaged the spiky-haired teenager who stood leaning against the brick wall.

"Smoke?" asked the young punk. He looked up from his Discman. "Oh hey, man. Didn't see you there."

Ben cocked his head. "You did something with your hair, Krass. It's much more… up."

Krass touched the tips of his green mohawk as if they were needles on a cactus.

"You like it? My dad hates it."

"Yeah, but how do you sleep?"

Danny nodded in agreement.

Krass shrugged. "Smoke, man." He pulled out a small baggie. "Couple hits of this ten minutes before bed and it's *lights out, wet dreams.*"

Ben folded his arms and glanced through the window of the Blockbuster. At the counter, the cashier noticed him and waved. He nodded to her.

Danny tapped his inert sliver, hoping there were video controls for the movie he was watching. It wasn't quite a memory—there was more *aliveness* to the construct—but nothing he did seemed to affect the people or events. He even tried pushing Krass off the wall, but his hands simply melted through the young punk's avatar.

"So what's up, man?" asked Krass. "You lookin' to trade? Some dope for a hit of that synth you got?"

Ben shook his head. "I don't think so. You gotta be in the right state of mind for that, no extra chemicals in your body. That pretty much puts you on the outs 24/7, am I right?"

"Not all the time." He put the baggie back in his pocket. "Just tryin' to make some coin out here, man. Smoke helps me accept my station."

The Syzygy sparked; Danny felt the shower of metal embers roll down his back.

"Tell... you... what..." Ben's words slowed to guttural tones as his avatar came to a complete stop.

Both he and Krass froze, shimmered, and finally pixelated into construct dust.

Danny watched the ashen clouds swirl and dissipate. He turned to see if the cashier had suffered the same fate, and that's when he noticed the explosion forming inside the Blockbuster. It advanced like a video stepping through each frame, unfolding slowly like a golden ball of cotton candy, already melting the windows.

"That was one thing you could never find in the old Net," said a voice from the right. "The pixilation was so janky, so... primitive. But here in VNet, it's fluid, almost natural."

Danny raised an eyebrow. The man coming around the corner of the Domino's looked strangely like Ben, though older now and with better posture. He still wore faded jeans and an ancient Metallica t-shirt, but his disheveled hair had been updated to a twenty-first century undercut.

He came close enough for Danny to smell the Brut on him.

"Now, just who the fuck are you?" asked older Ben. His eyebrows dipped menacingly between light blue eyes.

Danny ignored the question, asked instead, "What is this place? Some kind of honeypot?"

"Sure." He shrugged wearily. "If you want to simplify things. What's great about this construct is how mundane it is, just a playback of a memory, and yet for some reason, hackers like you just keep throwing yourself at it. Over and over. You come here to take and end up giving me everything. I learn so much about so many people just like you... Guns."

He said the name as if it had just popped into his head.

"Ah," he continued, gesturing to Danny. "It's a pleasure to meet you, Guns. My equally ridiculous name is Bullets."

"No, it's Ben."

"Ben, Bullets, what's the difference? It's not like your name is really Guns. Unless... oh, no." He smiled, bent slightly at the waist to laugh. "You're not *the* Danny Guns Montreal, are you? Feared freelance hacker to the stars? Holy shit, man."

He grabbed Danny's hand in a flash and shook it vigorously.

Danny sent every mental command he knew to restart his Syzygy chip, only to find it already online, already humming along quite contently. It was allowing Ben to take control of Danny's avatar, but why?

"This is amazing," said Ben. He touched Danny's head, ruffled his hair. "It is you. It's so you. I should have known by the muscles."

He stepped back and threw one hand out to the side. A phone materialized in his hand like a magician pulling a playing card out of thin air.

"If you know who I am, then you know you shouldn't be trying to keep me here," said Danny, wriggling his hand. Something was probing his fingers, slithering around them like snakes, crossing his flesh with rough scales.

"Hold up, let me just grab a picture real quick." Ben lined up several shots, his smile growing larger with each one. "People are gonna love this."

A breeze blew through the construct, pushing the smell of pizza and gasoline and putrid water down the sidewalk. In the back of his mind, Danny focused on the underlying aroma of a codified cocktail that filled the gaps in his synapses. The Syzygy chip hummed as a sudden hint of lavender reminded him of Jane, of the scent that lingered on her neck at all times.

He felt as if he hadn't seen her in weeks, though he knew she was most likely still sitting across from him on the couch, watching the feeds or reading some book or whatever she did in her downtime.

"Nobody believes me," said Ben, unable to mask a frown. He collapsed the phone into a small tab and shoved it angrily into his front pocket.

"Why would they?" asked Danny. "Seems to me like a feared freelance hacker to the stars wouldn't be the sort of dumbass who would fall for a honeypot. At least, not by accident."

Ben narrowed his eyes; the gears behind them turned slowly, clunking like a poorly maintained engine.

"Naw, no way you knew," he said. "You wouldn't let yourself get probed like this."

It was Danny's turn to smile. He shrugged sheepishly.

"You broke into a secure VNet construct."

"So did my friend. Did you probe him too? Did you kill him, Ben? Did you kill my *best friend?*"

Ben's face twisted in confusion. "I don't know what you're talking about."

"You will," said Danny, flexing his arms. The fabric around his biceps tore and fluttered in the breeze.

"Oh, so that's what this is?" Ben gave a thin smile. "Well, I'm afraid you've come to the wrong place. Whatever you think you're going to do here, you're mistaken. I'm already tracing your location. I know you're in…"

Dull razors traced lines behind Danny's ears.

"You're in Umbra," continued Ben.

"Yeah, I am." Danny rubbed his neck. "And so are you."

Ben waved both hands and cast an arc of viral code at Danny.

The Syzygy deflected it, sent the payload crashing into the nearby wall where it melted the brick like crayons in the sun. A hole appeared, and instead of the interior of the Domino's or Blockbuster, Danny saw a foggy tunnel.

At the end of the tunnel, a trail of emerald flashes spun in a lazy pinwheel.

"What the hell is that?" asked Danny.

A sudden kick sent him sprawling backward, ripping through the fabric of the construct, tumbling through the void of the ether...

... to the soft couch at the Fritz. He tore the immersion rig from his face and took a deep breath of fresh air. Dim LEDs in the ceiling glimmered as he fell onto his back.

"Find anything?" asked Tanzy.

"Yeah," he chuckled. "The guy who killed Johnny."

"And that's funny why?"

"Because he calls himself Bullets, and that's what I'm going to put in his skull."

Tanzy responded with a doubtful groan.

SEVENTEEN
KAILI

"Astoria is burning, and it's your fault, Ms. Zabora."

Kaili kept her head down and her eyes closed, but she paid close attention to how the low male voice echoed in the room around her. The room itself was quiet, lacking the cacophony of looped nature sounds that had followed her from Le Soleil Rouge to the Astoria Column. Hard floors, empty walls, and the faint chemical smell of conditioned air told her she was in an office of some kind. Whoever had grabbed her had dumped her in a chair and waited for her to wake up. And though she had given no indication that she was conscious, a man somewhere in front of her had begun talking.

"But we are by no means unique. All across the country, cities large and small have been laid to waste by legions of Perion's sideshow synthetics. Humans have been forced back to nature, and not all of us are surviving. They don't even call us humans anymore—now we're just... *organics*." A chair creaked. "You can open your eyes now, Ms. Zabora. We both know you're awake."

Kaili lifted her head and waited for her eyes to adjust to the bright halogens dumping light from the ceiling. Empty office space stretched around her, an endless sea of white tiles extending to the very edges of the building. There were no solid walls, just windows that rose from floor to ceiling. Slightly behind her, a thick column ran through the center of the space and contained three elevator doors.

"Where are we?" she asked, suddenly aware of a swollen lip.

"Thirty-eighth floor of the Astoria Prime building," said the man sitting behind a desk. He was dressed in a dark suit with the collar of a pressed white shirt unbuttoned. Deep creases ran across his forehead, and his eyes appeared to be shrouded in black despite the oppressive lights in the room.

He smiled at the attention, folded his hands on a wide glass desk that was empty except for a small, framed photo in the corner. The photo was turned out toward Kaili and showed the man sitting in a high-backed, ornate chair with a little girl on his knee.

"Do you know me, Ms. Zabora?"

There was something familiar about his face, the way his eyebrows plunged in the center, how the purposeful stubble grew into carefully styled hair with just the right amount of gray.

"I can see you trying to work it out. How amusing. I will tell you this much: it has something to do with why you're handcuffed to that chair."

Kaili ran the face against the ghosts from her past. She scrolled through the entire Perion Synthetics corporate directory and then moved on to other companies like Nixle Chronos, Pattrn, and Vinestead—

She tried to rush the desk, but the handcuffs yanked her back to the chair, cutting into her wrist with enough force to draw blood. She scanned her immediate area, looking for something to throw at him, but there was nothing except the desk, the two chairs, and—

And no guards, said Anela.

Kaili looked around for her sister before turning her attention inward. The signal was faint, but her imaginary construct had bloomed somewhere deep in the murky darkness. Anela's voice carried up and out of the pit, circled Kaili's head.

"And there it is," said Arthur Sedivy, CEO of Vinestead International. He gestured to the chair. "Please, sit down. You're embarrassing both of us with this display."

"I'll stand."

"Suit yourself," he replied, "but far be it from me to sit while a lady stands, if you can be called that." He pushed back and rose to his feet.

Kaili had to keep lifting her head. The man who was listed in the Pattrn directory as topping out at five feet ten inches appeared almost a foot taller in person.

"Why am I here?" asked Kaili.

Sedivy turned to the window and shrugged. "Why are *you* here? The real question is why am *I* here? I'm a little insulted by the entire predicament, if I'm being perfectly honest. I mean, did I live my best life? Perhaps not. But was I the best CEO Vinestead International ever saw? Did I make the shareholders rich beyond their wildest dreams? You bet I did. So what if we bent a few man-made laws now and then?"

"I don't…"

"No, you don't." He glanced over his shoulder, rolled his eyes. "You think you're just an innocent bystander in all of this. You think Calle Cinco was about protecting individual rights and keeping power out of corporate hands. You thought you could prop up Perion Synthetics and pit them against me. Do you see a pattern in all of this?"

Kaili shook her head.

Just keep him talking, said Anela.

"Is it really 2029?" she asked.

Sedivy nodded. "Now and forever."

"So I've been gone thirteen years, and in that time, you managed to produce a synthetic that could rival Perion's?"

He examined his fingernails. "Not rivals, exceeds."

Kaili laughed and sat down. Her augments had cooled, and her muscles were happy for a break.

"I'm glad the situation amuses you."

"It does," she replied, leaning as far back as the chair would allow. "It's just amazing we ended up here. I've killed so many of your shitty employees. You've hunted me for years. All that fighting, and here we are, finally face-to-face, and there's nothing left to fight for. The world is crumbling around us and evidently we have James Kirkland Perion to thank for it."

Sedivy crossed to the front of the desk. "Yes, in a way, the fighting is over between us, but the war out there will rage for eternity. The synthetics have too many resources, and we organics are too tenacious to die out completely. It's a stalemate between man and machine, and the only way it will resolve itself is if the planet is destroyed to the point where neither side can survive. Full planetary reboot. We all die. Nobody wins. This is the hell you and the great James Perion created."

Kaili chuckled into her chest. "I never thought I'd see the day when the untouchable Arthur Sedivy would give up. I figured you'd scratch and claw to the bitter end. But just like that, you want to crawl away and find a dark corner to die in?"

"I would keep going," said Sedivy, shrugging, "if I thought it would make a difference. But this is reality now, and the fiscal goals of Vinestead don't matter much to its new owners. The mechanical monkeys are at the controls, and their only goal now is inventing new forms of misery."

"Unlock these handcuffs and I'll show you misery."

Sedivy chuckled, adjusted the cuffs on his jacket. "There is no key, but once you understand and accept the situation, the handcuffs will unlock themselves."

"What?"

His eyes flashed red. "Open your eyes, Ms. Zabora!" he snapped, kicking the desk behind him. The glass surface cracked, slid across the floor on its metal frame, and smashed through the window. For a moment, the desk teetered on the edge before falling over the side. The framed photo ended up on the floor, face down.

Cool night air flowed into the room, bringing pine and smoke to Kaili's nose. The wind fluttered the edges of Sedivy's suit.

Kaili closed her eyes and leaned her head back.

"So dramatic," she moaned. "Just kill me already."

"Again?"

"Excuse me?" She narrowed her eyes at the perverted smirk on his face.

"I asked if you wanted me to kill you again. Start this whole thing over? Do you enjoy waking up naked in that stasis pod? Do you like having to sneak out of Le Soleil Rouge all scared and alone? Tell me, Ms. Zabora, why is it that sometimes you kill the dog and other times just run away from it? That's not the big, bad Krazy Kaili Zabora the world knows, not the scary Calle Cinco poster girl that I'm supposed to fear. If anything, this experience has shown me just how much of a scared little girl you really are. You are a child playing in the grownup world. And it has finally caught up with you."

Kaili shook her head. How could he have known about Le Soleil Rouge and the dog?

"Because I was there," he replied. "I'm everywhere, even inside your head. Don't look so surprised. You chose the form of your tormentor."

The question was on the tip of her tongue, but her voice had stopped working. There was too much to take in, too much nonsense to—

"This," he said, gesturing to his body. "Of the infinite horrors, you chose this. I will never understand your obsession with Arthur Sedivy. In the grand scheme of things, Vinestead International is a blip on the radar of human existence, a tiny company with narrow-minded aspirations that will be gone in a few hundred years. I can show you their demise. I can let you fight them for eternity if that suits you. Always fighting, never winning. Looping until entropy befalls the reality above your own."

"I'm…" Kaili shook in the chair. It was too crazy to believe.

"Deceased. Murdered, actually."

"And this is…"

"Hell. *Your* hell, specifically. A world where the synthetic spawn of James Perion have taken over and the only salvation lies in Vinestead International."

"No," said Kaili, sitting up.

Sedivy approached and bent at the waist, placing his hands on her knees.

"No to which part, Ms. Zabora?"

"All of it."

"Ah," he replied, baring his yellow teeth. "Let no one accuse the Butcher of Burbank of being gullible. You're right to be suspicious. If this is hell, where are the rest of the damned, eh?"

The elevator dinged behind her. Kaili turned in her seat to watch the door open.

"Your mouth falls agape," said Sedivy, "and your last breath catches in your throat. A sickness grips your stomach, tightening into a knot so thick and heavy you can't even stand. You wonder if you can trust your eyes. You wonder… is it really her?"

Anela Zabora stepped out of the dark elevator, her long red dress catching the slight breeze. Tears glistened in the corners of her eyes.

"Annie?"

"Oh, Kaili. What have you done to us?"

"She's been quite the naughty girl," said Sedivy. "Murder, sabotage, whoring—to name a few."

Kaili stood, turned around. The woman looked so much like her sister, but she couldn't be, just couldn't.

"I assure you, she is. And it's not just her; all of your Calle Cinco cohorts are here as well. James Perion, too, should you ever get the urge to speak with your former employer. Joseph Perion hasn't arrived quite yet, but I don't imagine it will be long."

"Talk to me, Annie. Tell me what to do."

"It's too late now, isn't it?" asked Anela. "Things have changed. There's no more war to fight, no world to save from corporate tyranny. It all goes on without us. All we can do now is pay for our sins. That's all."

"That's all?" asked Kaili.

Anela nodded solemnly, removed a tear from her cheek with an elegant swipe of her hand.

Kaili looked around the room again, peering through the windows at the world beyond. Astoria burned to the left, light bounced in the clouds to the right, and ahead of her, the Pacific Ocean sparkled and thrashed in a light fog. She turned to face Sedivy and found his suit had burned away, leaving a muscular shell of a man who had been burnt to a crisp. His eyes smoldered red and yellow.

"And now you understand," he growled.

The handcuffs opened, clinked to the tile floor.

"I understand what you're claiming," said Kaili, rubbing her wrist against her stomach. "This is hell, and you're some kind of demon. Have I got that right?"

Sedivy nodded, shedding his hair to reveal glowing horns.

"And that's my sister. She's in hell too."

She felt stupid even saying it out loud.

"Yes, of course," said Sedivy. "What do you hope—"

"And I'm dead. Murdered, you said. And for my sins, God has damned me to hell. But not a Christian or Mormon hell, but my own, personalized nightmare afterlife, derived from my experiences and memories."

Sedivy stopped smiling; the smoke billowing from his nostrils dissipated.

"And that's my sister?" she asked again.

His eyes jumped from Kaili to Anela and back.

She turned to Anela, "And *that's all*, right?"

Anela nodded.

"No…" Kaili sighed. "You have her face and her eyes, but you are not her."

She dropped her gaze to the floor, tried to look through the sparkling white tiles.

She had no doubt her augments could tear through them with a few well-placed punches, but she had a hunch she wouldn't need any true physical effort at all.

It was so simple.

So obvious.

"It's a neat trick," she said, tapping the floor with her toe. "I bet the religious types eat it up, don't they? Hellfire and damnation. They're all afraid they deserve it. Why in the ever-loving fuck-all would you think I'd be like one of them?" She nodded to the Anela golem. "Or her?"

"It's not a question of believing," said Anela. "It's real."

"*It is* a question of believing," replied Kaili, "and *it is* not real. Have you never heard my sister talk?"

Anela hadn't lived long enough to meet Arthur Sedivy in virtual or Terrareal, and consequently, he had no knowledge of how she avoided contractions when she spoke. That he had tried to pass off an inferior Anela Zabora was not surprising; that he hadn't done his full research was a rare miss for a man with the near-infinite resources of Vinestead International at his disposal.

The tile beneath her feet bubbled around her toes. A simple dissolve would have sufficed, but she felt like showing off.

"Accept your fate," said Sedivy. "Your suffering has only just begun."

"How about you go fuck yourself, Arthur?"

Sedivy roared as he approached, burning three-pronged footprints into the floor.

Kaili raised a middle finger and focused on the ones and zeros rushing beneath her feet. She reached into the data stream with her mind and pulled, tearing open a hole just wide enough for her to fall through.

She hit the next floor down and reached out again.

The pain built in her legs until she could no longer feel them, and the dust scratched at her lungs every time she took a breath. Floor after floor scrolled by, each one dark, empty, and reeking of sulfur.

Finally, she hit the lobby, and with the roar of some virtual demon in her ears, she bolted for the door with a smile on her face.

None of it was real.

She was jacked in.

EIGHTEEN
TANZY

"What's he like, really?"

Tanzy let her gaze drift over the crowded dance floor of Version Seven. There, in a sunken pit of LED tiles, a dense, interconnected mass of people writhed in time with the techno-slop booming from the speakers in the ceiling. The private booth in which Tanzy sat with Grace O'Conner seemed empty and spacious by comparison, with plenty of room for them to sit across from each other on either side of a low table.

"Who?" asked Tanzy, coyly. She placed her drink on the table and picked up one of the code cards Grace had brought her.

"You know who I mean," she replied.

Tanzy raised an eyebrow.

Grace wasn't the kind of woman who frequented techno-synth clubs like Version Seven, and it showed in her choice of dress. Instead of the frayed booty shorts and too-small, white tank tops most of the girls were wearing, Grace had gone for a forest green blouse over black pants. Her ears, neck, and wrists were adorned with the thinnest threads of gold—no flashy diamonds, no blinking LEDs. Silky black hair fell on either side of her shoulders, surrounding a face with far more Asian features than her name would have suggested.

Even outside the boardroom at Pattrn, Grace was the epitome of the corporate power woman, and everything Tanzy wanted to be.

"Ah, yes, *the* Danny Guns Montreal," said Tanzy. She fingered a code card with the words *River View* embossed on its face. "Well, he can be a real bitch sometimes, if you want to know the truth."

Danny had spent most of the day jacked into VNet facing off against whatever honeypot Cleo had been smart enough to avoid. And in the end, he'd come out laughing and cursing someone called Bullets. But then, instead of telling her what had happened, he'd locked himself up in the master suite, feeding Tanzy some lame story about having to scan his biochip from top to bottom.

Grace smiled; her eyes widened.

"He has a tendency to get fixated on things," continued Tanzy, "to the detriment of himself and the people around him. Imagine you have a best friend who treats you like a queen 98% of the time, but then during that 2% when someone gets his attention, he casts you aside like you're nothing. He leaves you sitting awkwardly on the couch making small talk with his vagina-for-hire."

"His what?"

"It doesn't matter. I'm sure you'll read all about it someday when Danny writes his memoirs. *Path of the Gun: The Life and Times of Danny Montreal.* He already has a title picked out."

Grace laughed, touched her neck. The gold traces on her fingers glimmered in the neon beams dancing around them.

"I can't wait to read it," she said.

"Of course you can't. You and everyone else have this image of Danny as some feared celebrity hacker and it's just not true. That's not who he is, not now, not back when..." She trailed off, thinking of Danny in the time before the Net, the dimly lit streets of their shared childhood, Johnny's house at the end of the cul-de-sac, nestled against a wooded area where they would drink their first beers years later.

"I'd love to do a featured profile on Danny," said Grace. "Eddie Chen has been pushing on me to leverage my relationship with you."

Tanzy shook her head. Edward Chen should have been coming directly to the suit of I.C.E-1, not sending his VP of UX—not that Tanzy minded rubbing shoulders and being seen with Grace.

"We might be able to work something out, Grace, but that depends on whether you can get me what I'm asking for. I can't guarantee Danny will spill his guts to someone who works for a soulless social networking company, but I can put you in the same room."

The music thumped, grinding against Tanzy's spine, while Grace considered the offer.

"And you're not gonna tell me what you need it for?"

"Does it matter?" asked Tanzy.

"There could be a privacy conflict—"

Tanzy put up a hand. "I'm not asking for any data not publicly available on your little yearbook site already. All I want is for my girls to have direct access to the data. We're not gonna sell it. We're not gonna spam people. I just need the facial metadata. We need to find people quickly, and that includes people who don't have accounts on your... *service.*"

Message from the Guns. Rolling to you at Version Seven.

Finally, the prince had deigned to come out of his chambers.

"I need some time to consider your proposal," said Grace. "Plus, I don't think I'm set up to do Helsinki crypto. I'll need American currency."

"I could do that," said Tanzy, "but I don't have time to wait."

"You don't really have a choice," said Grace, a playfully thin smile growing on her face.

Tanzy smirked and shook her head. "Beat it, O'Conner. Danny's coming and if he sees a Pattrn Monster here, he's gonna crap his whities."

Grace looked to the dance floor, to the hall that led in from the entrance. She frowned.

"One day," she said, gathering her clutch. "I'm gonna make him part of Pattrn."

"Stranger things have happened," said Tanzy.

A slender hand reached across the table. Tanzy shook it and nodded farewell to a woman she would have never sat down with in the old days. Grace was corporate, which was just another word for control. It didn't matter how much synth she did in secret or how much backdoor access she provided to cipher dens like I.C.E-1, she would always be a corporate drone, always commanding power in a world beyond Tanzy's.

Grace disappeared into the hazy hallway at the back of the booth, and Tanzy used the brief solitude to regroup. A thread of anger still vibrated within her. She flashed on the rejection coming from Danny, tried to unpack it and understand why she'd let someone make her feel so bad about herself. That kind of externally defined value might have flown when she was fourteen and still trying to figure out the world, when Tori Amos was guiding her through adolescence and boys like Danny and Johnny made convenient stand-ins for first loves and first losses.

The way Danny had quite literally shut the door on her had made her feel like she wasn't worthy of his friendship, that she ranked no higher in his estimation than a hired Associate or a synth junkie living on the street.

She'd thought she deserved more than that.

Tanzy slipped the River View card to the back of her neck and recoiled as the music volume tripled, drawing her eyes to the dance floor.

Version Seven rocked back and forth under the weight of its revelers. Techno-infused orchestral riffs rained down from the ceiling like thick sheets of reverberating thunder, laying down an oppressive blanket under which men, women, and barely legal children danced and jumped and gyrated. Faces bobbed in an endless sea; hungry mouths opened to the ceiling where flecks of water tinged with a minty green scent fell from sprinklers.

Circling the far side of the throng was a smiling Danny Guns Montreal. He avoided the localized rain showers while guiding Jane toward the back of the club where the stairs led up to the private booths. A few minutes later, he appeared from the hallway with wild eyes and mussed hair.

"We're looking for a Koertig v5," he yelled, stepping past Tanzy to the balcony railing.

"Well, hello to you too." Tanzy glanced at Jane who shrugged in return. "Nice of you to let me back in the game, Danny."

"What?" he asked, his neck almost snapping as he gave her a quick glance over his shoulder. "Oh, yeah, okay, sorry. Koertig v5."

Tanzy turned to Jane. "What's he on?"

"I don't know. It's an upper, obviously, but there were a lot of cards on the bed when I went in. I'm not sure which one he took last."

"Is anyone listening to me? Koertig—"

"Version 5," said Tanzy. "I heard you, Danny. No one runs Koertigs. Those are in-house Vinestead rigs."

"I know!" He scanned the dance floor again, then lifted his eyes to the other private booths on the second floor. "Cleo was right to boot you."

"What's that supposed to mean?"

"The guy I met in the honeypot, Bullets. I think he's a noob."

Tanzy crossed her arms. "How could you tell?"

"Little fucker didn't recognize me until after a scan."

Tanzy laughed. "Maybe you're not as famous as you think you are."

"No, yes, I mean, he knew of me, but he didn't really know me, know what I'm capable of. That's why I'm thinking he's gotta be fresh meat. And if so, he might be dumb enough to still be here."

"Sure," said Tanzy. She got up and joined him at the railing. The cold steel bit into her forearms. "Dressed in a Vinestead polo with a Koertig immersion rig just slung over his shoulder, right?" She shook her head. "Not even a noob would be dumb enough to rock Vinestead gear in here."

"Well, it's my only lead until your ciphers crack the download."

Tanzy reached out and placed a hand on his. "Then have some patience. Unload whatever code has you jacked to the teeth, and we'll work on this together." She moved closer, slipped an arm around his waist.

His eyes were glassy, moist.

She could almost see his pulse in them.

Danny nodded slightly.

The music enveloped them. Seconds ticked by, marked by repeating loops of electronic tones. Jane disappeared, reappeared with drinks. They tasted bland. The same song played over and over again, varying only slightly with each iteration. Screams from dancers wafted up. Moans and flashes of naked flesh spilled from booths.

Jane offered Tanzy some earplugs, and in the muffled maelstrom, Tanzy found a soft spot on the couch where she could put her feet up. Jane sat nearby, her eyes never leaving Danny's back. Tanzy watched her for some time, wondered how anyone could manufacture interest in another person for so long, especially someone who cared so little for those around him. Sure, he acted all lovey-dovey when things were going well, but throw in a little grit and Danny would tear down every pedestal he'd ever built, and all the women he'd known and loved would come tumbling down.

Danny slowed, and at first, Tanzy thought it was him coming down off the synth high, but as the minutes stretched into an hour, she realized his stoicism was too measured to be natural. He gave off the aura of a body rebuilding, resetting, so that it was primed for what was to come.

His head shook in tiny spurts. He wrung his hands.

Tanzy cleared her throat, called out, "Why do I get the feeling you're about to do something incredibly stupid?"

"Do you have your palette?" he asked, over his shoulder.

Tanzy removed her earplugs and dug around in her bag. She pulled out a palette and placed it on the table. "You come over here and use it."

Danny snapped out of his trance and slid into place on the couch. He pulled the palette onto his knees. His fingers shook the small rectangle as they thumped out keys on the virtual keyboard.

"What're you doing?" asked Jane.

"Huh?" said Danny, putting a hand to his ear. "I can't hear you."

Tanzy kicked the table. "She asked what you're doing!"

He narrowed his eyes, cupped his hand around his ear. "Still nothing. Hold on. Let me turn this down for a minute."

Danny stubbed the *Enter* key on the palette, creating a deafening suck of sound in the club. The music cut out as hands went to ears in protest against the sudden silence. Lasers continued to spin, casting neon lines over the walls, but it was as if someone had suddenly put the world on mute.

A few confused utterances filled the void, followed by a random cough.

Danny's eyes sparkled.

Tanzy mouthed the word *no*.

He smirked.

"I swear to god, Danny."

"Guns are meant to blaze," he replied.

Tanzy covered her face with her hands. Through splayed fingers, she watched Danny jump up on the railing and raise his hands into the air.

"Ladies and gentlemen! Can I have your attention please! I am Danny Guns Montreal!"

"Fuck you, Danny!" called a voice from the crowd.

"I'm sorry to interrupt your party, but I'm looking for a Vinestead hacker named Bullets."

His voice carried throughout Version Seven, aided by speakers that were meant to pipe techno into the nooks and crannies of the building. Tanzy watched half of the crowd from the couch. They were a sea of confused faces, breathless expressions of chemically enhanced humans.

Message from the Quatrain. Intrusion countermeasures have been deployed at Version Seven.

"There's no way he's still here," said Tanzy.

"Turn the music back on, fuckhead!"

"Bullets," screamed Danny. "I'm looking for Bullets!"

The glass pane by his feet exploded as a bullet tore through his leg and ricocheted in the booth. Tanzy felt her body move without conscious thought, making itself smaller as it dove for the floor. Screams filled the air, the music suddenly resumed, and above it all was the uncontrollable laughter of Danny Guns Montreal.

UPD are en route.

"Police are coming," said Tanzy, motioning for Jane to grab one of Danny's arms.

They pulled him away from the railing, out through the back of the booth, to a staircase that led to an emergency exit. An alarm sounded as they pushed through the door.

"What is your problem, Danny?" asked Tanzy. "Do you have a death wish or something?"

Danny wasn't listening. He was smiling, his eyes wide, watching the Umbra Canopy scroll by overhead.

"Hospital?" asked Jane.

Tanzy shook her head. "Not in Umbra, dear."

The hospital was on the grid. So was the police station.

For what they were up against, they'd have to stay as far away from the grid as possible.

Tanzy smirked.

Even if that meant losing a limb due to a dumbass provocation.

She yanked on Danny's arm, caught his eye.

"We're going back to the hotel," she shouted. "I'll come back and get the rest of your leg later."

His eyes went wide, then closed.

NINETEEN
GORDON

The car was a rental, and Gordon was pretty sure Cyn wasn't getting her security deposit back.

He watched blood seep through the bandanas he'd wrapped around his hands. Dark, red stains grew on his lap, soaked his jeans, and worked their way down to the leather seats of the Jeep. Everything from his forearms down had long since entered a state of throbbing numbness; the commands he sent to flex and straighten his fingers went largely ignored. He tried to busy himself with recovering the memory of his fight with the Vinestead agents, but there was only static, only snow.

Beside him, Cyn tapped her thumbs on the face of the steering wheel as she guided the Jeep away from LPS, onto Highway 71, and then north on a toll road that hadn't existed the last time he'd been in Austin. She hadn't said a word since leaving LPS, but every so often she would jerk her head to the side, as if someone were whispering in her ear.

The Jeep's center console lit up, showing an incoming call.

Cyn tapped the screen.

"Bryce," she said. "What's the buzz?"

A deep voice filled the cabin. "Nothing on the scanners yet," he replied. "Local law isn't responding to anything in the area."

"What about that Vinestead drone we saw? You're sure they haven't put in a call?"

"Naw, it's quiet. And the only drone tailing you is me. It should be clear all the way to the airfield."

Gordon felt Cyn's eyes on his lap.

"The package is going to need some medical attention before we take off."

Bryce's laugh made the speakers in the door buzz. "No shit. I saw some of what went down. Surprised that boy didn't leave pieces behind." He cleared his throat. "There's a hospital just up the road from the airfield. I'll have them send someone over to take a look."

"And LC1 is ready to go?"

"Fueled and idling, going through pre-flight now. If we leave within the hour, we'll be in Umbra before sundown."

"Umbra?" asked Gordon.

"Is that you, robo-killer?"

"That's the package," said Cyn.

"Shit, man. Can't wait to meet you. You gotta show me how you pulled some of those moves."

"Maybe," mumbled Gordon, looking out the window. A sign touting an 80-mph speed limit flew by.

"Is there anything I can get you?" asked Bryce. "Beer? Food?"

Gordon thought about the go-bag in the back seat of the Jeep. Its green leather was caked in dust after years spent beneath the floorboards of his cabin. It contained everything he needed to start over: ID, passport, guns, a two-year-old palette still in its shrink wrap, and about twelve thousand dollars in mixed bills. It was all he'd managed to take with him from LPS—that and the looks of reproach from the residents. They'd all wanted him to leave; only Evans and Jessie had waved goodbye.

"Blue Rain, vodka, change of clothes," said Gordon.

"Anything else?"

"Let's start there, see where this goes."

"He's about your size," said Cyn. "Little smaller in the chest."

"No problem," said Bryce. "Let me put this bird down and I'll meet you in the hangar."

"Later, B," said Cyn, tapping the red phone icon on the screen.

Gordon watched the undeveloped land east of Austin scroll by. He'd only heard stories about the proliferation of toll roads in the city, how they were supposed to usher in a new age of growth in the Live Music Capital of the World. Looking past Cyn to her window, Gordon could almost make out the towers of Old Downtown.

Frost Bank.

The Austonian.

"What're you doing?"

"Huh?" asked Gordon.

"Sounds like you're counting."

"Oh, yeah," he replied. "It helps me stay focused. I count things in the environment, inventory them."

Cyn nodded her head. "Is that so? Do you know how many people you killed back there?"

"Eight."

"Wrong," said Cyn, engaging the turn signal. They sped past a sign that read *Austin Executive Airport*.

Gordon's stomach lurched. The numbers tried to tamp it down, but the end result was a muddled feeling of unease, as if he'd forgotten to take out the trash.

"Two up front," he said. "Three to each side. That makes eight."

Cyn shook her head, guided the car to the outside lane of the frontage road and blew through a four-way stop.

"You killed six people," she said. "The other two were synthetics."

"Synthetics? You mean like cyborgs?"

"No, I mean synthetic humans. Artificially intelligent, completely autonomous, indistinguishable from us."

"If they're indistinguishable, how did you know—"

Gordon pushed back into his seat as the Jeep rushed the open gate just inside the airfield and whipped around an orange-striped Cessna. They pulled up next to the last hangar in a line of eight. Inside was a white Gulfstream with the words *Lincoln Continental One* stamped on the side. Its door was open; on the steps, a lanky man in a gray hoodie, presumably Bryce, stood with a palette in his hand.

He waved to Cyn.

The Jeep's engine rattled to a halt.

Cyn turned in her seat and faced Gordon. "Vinestead synthetics are easy to spot if you know what you're looking for. They were rushed to market this past summer to compete with Perion." She sighed when Gordon returned a blank look. "A lot has happened since you've been out of the world; synthetic humans are just the beginning. If you want to survive out here, you'll get your ass up to speed quick-fast."

Her tone grated.

"Well," he said, calmly, "maybe if you would tell me what the fuck is going on, I wouldn't have to ask so many goddamn questions. Or maybe I shouldn't be asking *you*. Why don't you take me to whoever's bankrolling this Mickey Mouse operation so I can get some real answers?"

Gordon didn't notice the woman standing next to his door. She pulled it open as if she could no longer wait for him to get out on his own.

"I'm Dr. Stair," she said, forcing a smile. "Come with me, please."

"Better go," said Cyn. "We're wheels-up in twenty minutes."

The doctor was young, maybe in her late twenties. Gordon searched his memory for a way to describe her taut, unblemished skin and settled on *fresh*. Unlike the women of LPS, the doctor appeared to take advantage of the skin creams and make-up the real world had to offer. Long black eyelashes surrounded soft, metallic blue eyes. At a certain angle, they seemed to glint.

Dr. Stair blushed under the attention.

"Right this way, Mister…?"

"Gordon," he replied, following her to a nearby card table.

She had already laid out the contents of a first aid kit, and even before he sat down, Gordon could feel her taking inventory of his injuries.

"Let's get a look at those hands first."

Gordon nodded, placed the bloodied bandana stumps on the table in front of her. She slipped on a pair of blue latex gloves and unwrapped the fabric. Gordon winced as the dried blood tugged at the open wounds.

"Would you like something for the pain?"

"What pain?" he growled. He looked over to see if Cyn had heard him, but she was busy talking to Bryce.

Dr. Stair smiled, unzipped a small black bag. She fanned out a series of what looked like thick credit cards. Their exteriors were pearlescent, with the name *Scott & White* embossed in the corner. Under that were names of drugs. She handed him a card marked *codeine*.

Gordon fumbled the card onto the table. It had no pull tab or perforation that he could see, no way to get at the medicine inside. He stared blankly.

"What am I supposed to do with this?"

The doctor removed the last loop of the bandana from his left hand and placed an antiseptic pad on it. She picked up Gordon's other hand and placed it on top.

"Pressure here," she said. "I'll do the card for you."

She stood and walked behind Gordon. Her fingers pressed lightly on the back of his head, pushing it down. He tried to place the nature of her perfume as she touched the rough plastic to his neck.

"Hmm," said Dr. Stair. "It's not loading."

"What's not loading?"

A finger traced over the scar on his neck.

"What kind of biochip do you have?" she asked.

"A what?"

"Biochip," she repeated, returning to her chair. "Guardian Angel? Simons? Life Solutions?"

"I don't have any of those."

Gordon noticed Cyn looking over, as if she could hear their conversation.

"He's an older model," she called. "He needs the chemical stuff."

"Oh," said the doctor. "Well, I only brought synth with me. I just assumed…"

"It's fine," said Gordon. "I can take it."

The numbers ran through his head, doing their best to stay out ahead of the pain. Dr. Stair unstacked his hands and unwrapped the other bandana.

"How old are you?" she asked.

"853," he replied, latching onto the last number in his head. "No, um, I guess about 40."

"And these injuries? Part of some mid-life crisis? You really shouldn't be getting into bar fights at your age."

He shook his head. "Just life catching up with me. You know how it is."

"I do," she said, her voice softer. "I ran too, for a while." She placed gauze carefully on the back of his hand. "But then I met someone who helped me turn it around. Did a stint at Dahlstrom. Now things are normal again."

"This is normal?"

She flashed a smile. Her left eye shaded to black and back to blue.

"Did you... did you just wink at me?" he asked.

The doctor gave a little shrug. "You *are* an older model, aren't you? Well, the good news is that you won't need new hands today. A few tendons could use some aug work, but they should hold up under normal use. If you don't want surgery, you need to avoid bar fights for at least eight weeks."

"Any broken bones?" asked Cyn.

"I don't think so. It's mostly just lacerations, but I can stitch those up with minimal scarring." She turned to Gordon. "That's gonna hurt, so you'll need to get something to help with the pain when you get where you're going. Either that or have a Guardian Angel chip installed. That would pretty much blot out the pain."

A commercial flashed in Gordon's mind, playing on a television in a dorm room a lifetime ago.

"Doesn't Vinestead make that?"

She smiled as she threaded stiff black wire through a needle.

"Ah, so you're one of *those* people."

"Which people?" he asked, wincing as the needle pierced his skin.

She leaned forward, whispered. "You know, AV'ers, anti-Vinestead types. They're against the company and everything they make, including the Guardian Angel biochip, which, by the way, has saved countless lives over the last two decades."

"No," said Gordon, gritting his teeth. "I don't have a problem with Vinestead, but they sure as shit have a problem with me."

"Yeah they do," said Cyn. "Gordon, this is Bryce, my handler."

Bryce nodded, shoved his hands into his hoodie's pockets.

"So this is the infamous, old school, no-chip-havin', grass-fed-beef-eating, not-showering-for-two-days, robo-killin', Net-crashin', all-flow-no-shit, hacker extraordinaire G." He pointed to Gordon's hands. "Didn't your momma ever tell you not to throw hands with a synthetic?"

Gordon squeezed his hand, tested the strength of the stitching.

"I don't know," he replied. "I think I came out okay."

"What's the damage, doc?" asked Cyn.

"He'll be fine with some rest. The bumps and bruises will heal on their own. I'm almost done with his hands and then we'll get to work on that bullet hole."

"Excuse me?" asked Gordon.

Dr. Stair cocked her head. "You've been shot... in the back. I thought you knew."

Bryce laughed. "Bad-ass-motherfucking, bullet-hole-in-the-back, not-knowin'-it's-there, you-should-see-the-other-guy, big-dick-swagger—"

"So how much longer then?" Cyn interrupted.

"Depends if the bullet's still in there. I don't see an exit wound, so I may need to dig a bit. Fifteen minutes?"

"You have five." Cyn turned and walked with Bryce to the plane.

"You should probably lie down for this," said Dr. Stair.

"Just do it," he mumbled.

He felt her hands on his back.

"I'm about to hurt you, Mr. Gordon."

He flashed on a memory of Jessie. He hoped she was okay.

"I know," he replied.

A scalpel went in, cut loose a single thought from his mind.

I deserve the pain.

TWENTY
DANNY

It was still dark when Danny came out of the haze.

Neon danced beyond the windows of the master suite, running along the jagged rooftops of a sim parlor, fast food multiplex, and a tech shop directly across from the Fritz. Awnings pulsed as their backlit designs wavered under the steady drizzle. Danny watched raindrops slide down windows, each one offering a view of the city that was simultaneously all-encompassing and comically simplified, as if the problems of the world could be condensed to a speck of water.

The Syzygy buzzed with anticipation, waiting for Danny to move his body. His right leg felt numb, but when he reached for it, he felt a needle pull against the skin in his elbow. A plastic line ran from the crook of his arm to a clear bag hanging on a rack next to the bed. The lights were too bright, the world too hazy. Danny shut his eyes, tried to open his mouth to speak.

Shards of glass and metal spilled down his throat.

Rain pattered on the window. Somewhere in the room was the sound of light breathing, of shuffling polyester.

Danny struggled to see through the bursting stars, but soon his eyes adjusted to the hulking mass sitting in one of the two suede chairs to the left of the bedroom door. A thick trunk of a leg was perched horizontally over the knee of the other. Crossing it was a thick cane with a sparkling gold *T* atop it. A bejeweled hand held the cane steady.

"The great and powerful Danny Guns Montreal pulls through after all," said a husky voice. "And here I was trying to figure out which of your obituaries to feed."

"Do I know you?" Danny rasped.

"We haven't met, but you know my business, just as I know yours. My name is Lincoln Tate and I run Lincoln Continental. A pleasure to meet you, Mr. Montreal."

"Yeah," said Danny, "sure."

"When I heard you'd been shot and almost bled out across the street from me, I had to come see if I could help, as a professional courtesy, of course."

"How did you know I was here?"

"I told him," said Tanzy, from the door. She held a glass of wine in her hand; the blood-red liquid sparkled. "Tate and I have a previous working relationship. I thought he might help us with the investigation."

"Wasn't your place to recruit."

"Well, you were out of it, Danny, for twenty-four hours. We had to do a blood transfusion and knock you out with some medical-grade synth. Lincoln provided the connections for that synth, by the way."

Danny fumbled for his sliver. It had turned to Monday in a blink.

"No offense, Mr. Tate," said Danny, "but why would someone like you help someone like me?"

Lincoln rose from his seat and approached the window. He stood with his arms crossed behind his back.

"Exclusivity," said Lincoln. "In my game, it's everything. Being one step ahead is everything. So Johnny San Vito is dead. Two days later, someone tries to kill his known associate Danny Guns Montreal at Version Seven." He spread his arms to the city. "What is going on under my roof?"

"It's our business," said Danny. His bare legs shivered beneath the sheets.

"It was," said Lincoln, "but now your business is all over the feeds, all of them except mine. If you wouldn't mind, Tanzy." He motioned to the wall.

She tapped the vidscreen and brought up a quadrant of feeds. White Line Media dominated the space, growing larger on the screen as more subbers tuned in. Its headline was certainly eye-catching.

Danny Guns Montreal shot in the dick in Umbra nightclub fracas.

"Well that's pleasant," said Danny, groaning.

Tanzy swirled the wine in her glass, drained the last of it with a flourish. "It gets worse, Danny." She tapped on the fourth quadrant and expanded VFeed to full screen. The headline jumped out in bold black type.

Infamous hackers Johnny San Vito and Danny Montreal claim responsibility for VNet virus.

The dullness in his leg spread to his gut. For a moment, it was as if a hole had opened up around his naval and sucked his soul through to another dimension.

"No one's buying that if it makes you feel better," said Lincoln, "but VFeed caters to the worst kind of people: oldies with money, ya dig? The kind who will spend a lot of money to protect even more money."

"Like I don't have Uncle Sam gunning for me already," said Danny.

"This is different." Tanzy sat down at the foot of the bed. Her elbow bent back slightly as she leaned over. "Whatever virus they're talking about, they'll keep it active as long as it takes to get to you. And no doubt they'll have federal and state looking for you. If some deputy sheriff picks you up on the tram back to

Sacramento, he's gonna put you in a hole, and then Vinestead's gonna come for you. You can't risk going outside anymore until this is over."

Danny shook his head, stared past her into the living room.

Where was Jane?

"The first thing we gotta do is put out a statement," said Lincoln. "You go live on my feed first thing tomorrow and tell people your side of the story. Let 'em know Vinestead is full of shit."

"In exchange for what?" asked Danny.

Lincoln turned abruptly, smirked. "Your freedom ain't good enough for you? You think this is all some kind of VR game you can just jack out of? You poke the Vinestead bear from the safety of your keyboard, but out here, it's bullets and pain."

"Alright, easy," said Tanzy, raising a hand. "Look, Danny, we need Lincoln's resources. He's working for us."

"I don't remember cutting a check."

"You didn't," said Lincoln, resuming his survey of the Umbra gloom. "Johnny paid me three years ago. And that's not all…"

"Dammit, Lincoln," said Tanzy. "I wanted to tell him." She turned to Danny, waited for his eyes. "You never let me tell you what happened after we jumped from Bedlam."

He remembered well. The lights. The vibrato. The sensation of something important and pure being ripped from his grasp.

"You got booted," he said.

"Yeah, eventually. But for a split second, I was somewhere else. It was like…" She paused, searched her memory. "Like seeing something fly by on the highway. You barely catch a glimpse of it. Well, I saw something. It was cold, and prickly, like a, um, misty green flash. I don't think it wanted me looking at it, but I did. Whatever this thing was, it flooded my buffer with what I thought was garbage. Cleo barely saw the honeypot coming and kicked us out. It took her an hour to find the pattern in the data, and another hour to crack it into English."

"What did it say?"

Tanzy folded her hands in her lap, looked down at them. "Nothing, really. Just a single letter repeating. G, G, G…"

Danny looked over at Lincoln, who seemed uninterested.

"You've heard this before?" he asked.

Lincoln glanced over his shoulder. "I have. Johnny came to me with the same crazy story. Something in VNet he couldn't handle, couldn't even touch. Said he didn't know what its purpose was or what it wanted until it spoke to him. Called it a religious experience, talking to this… *thing*. Said it spoke to him and asked for G."

"G," said Danny. He looked at Tanzy. "The guy you used to rush with?"

She shrugged in response.

"He's the most famous G in Net lore," said Lincoln. "I sent one of my best freelancers after him three years ago. She traced him all over South America, following false leads, until she finally found him not more than thirty miles from where he was last seen in 1999."

Tanzy smiled. "If he's anything like he used to be, we should be able to take down that virus, make whoever wrote it pay for what it did to Johnny."

"I don't think it's a virus or at least, not just a virus," said Danny. "There's more…" He flashed on Brigham Plaza, on the various storefronts. In his memory, their walls writhed with dormant viral code. For some reason, the slow-motion explosion inside the Blockbuster stuck in his mind.

"And besides," he continued, "I don't know this G. I don't work with people I don't know."

Lincoln turned away from the window, approached the bed. "Well, that's some tough luck, Mr. Montreal. G's here, in Umbra. I've been holding onto him for three weeks waiting for Johnny to show up and claim him." He went silent for a moment, lowered his voice. "Look, Johnny is dead. The contract has already been paid. If you don't want G, you can cut him loose. I don't really give an Umbrat's nut at this point. What I'm offering you is logistical support and freelance muscle, as well as a peek at what your friend dropped in my inbox last Friday.

"All I want is access to your story. You've already proven yourself worthless in a firefight, *Guns*. The next bullet might catch you in the brain, but it doesn't have to."

Distorted memories of Version Seven's strobing neons came back to him in a swell of panic. Glass shattered all around him; angry snakes bit at his legs. And all he could think about was how none of it would have happened in the safety of VNet. There, he was a relative god. Out here, he was just a man who had been shot in the leg. Out here, he wasn't Guns—he was just Danny.

"I'll think about it."

Tanzy patted him on the foot.

"Yeah, you do that," said Lincoln. "But the clock is ticking on this. I get the feeling G isn't much for orders. If he wants to go, he's gonna go. Everyone has their limits."

"I'll walk you out," said Tanzy.

"Be seeing you, Danny."

Danny nodded, watched as Lincoln and Tanzy walked together through the living room, speaking in whispers. They lingered at the front door, in the little alcove with the inset paintings and buzzing overhead light.

An ache climbed Danny's leg, worked its way into his back, and caused his muscles to spasm and tighten. He grimaced at the pain, searched the nightstand for pain meds, but found no bottles. Instead, Tanzy had left him her collection of code cards in a shallow glass. He pulled the pile onto his stomach and shuffled through them.

In each metallic card, he caught a glimpse of his reflection, saw eyes staring back at him that seemed to belong to someone else. They were full of worry and doubt, lacking the self-sure smugness with which they surveyed his cabin in Vail. It had been a bad idea to come down to Umbra, even if it was all for Johnny. Brotherly love only went so far, and now there was a hot spike of pain in his leg and a numbness that threatened to overcome him.

He was going to make Johnny's killers pay, that was for sure, but it would be from behind a terminal, where it was safe. Zeros in bank accounts, child porn on personal devices, and fabricated paper trails long enough to put anyone in prison, no matter how rich or how powerful.

The first step though, was to get the fuck out of Umbra.

Tanzy reappeared at the door, the sleeves of her flannel bunched around her hands. Her normally pale skin had a red tint to it.

"No longer playing suit?" he asked.

She folded her arms. "Not seeing any clients today. No need to dress the part." She nodded at the code cards. "Pain?"

"Pain," he replied.

"Try the Atmos. It'll knock you out for the rest of the night. Very smooth ascent with that one."

"What about you?" groaned Danny, pulling the card with the etched cloud design from the pack. "You going out?"

Her eyes drifted to the windows. "Going in," she replied. "The girls cracked some of Johnny's encryption while you were out. My brother's helping me sort through the first chunks of data. Mostly pics, some old IM chats from BBS days. I think it's in chronological order. It'll be fun when we get to the Triumvirate. God only knows what he saved."

"Your brother?"

"Phantasm. You remember him."

Danny nodded, spied his suitcase by the dresser.

"Another hire I didn't approve."

Tanzy smirked. "It's cute how you think you're running the show."

"Where's Jane?" he asked, the words trembling on his lips.

Tanzy narrowed her eyes the tiniest fraction, thinned her smile to almost nothing.

"Danny," she said, pausing for way too long. "I'm sorry. She left…" A fake sniffle. "… to get groceries. That was, I don't know, ten, fifteen minutes ago. Maybe more. I'm sure she'll be back though. She always comes back, doesn't she?

Because she *loves* you, and you *love* her, and you're gonna get married and have a bunch of little hackers and prostitutes."

Her words broke apart into laughter.

"You're such a bitch, Tanzy."

She shrugged. "I'm sure you're not the first john to fall in love with an Associate. What you need is a proper love doll. I hear Persona Luxe is doing crazy things with synthetic skin these days. Add in a little Perion gray matter and you'd have yourself a loyal, lifelong companion. Beats jerkin' it in VR, right?"

"Wouldn't be the same," he argued, thinking of the way the fine hairs on Jane's stomach rose at his touch.

"It'd cost you the same in the long run." She smiled again, turned away before he could reply.

Danny thought about shouting at her in the living room, but she turned on the vidscreen and ramped up the volume.

He popped the tab on the edge of the code card and struggled to hold it to the back of his neck.

Atmos bloomed like a time-lapse storm over a rolling prairie of wind-blown wheat. Thick clouds enveloped the room, rising up through the sheets, pushing down through the gridded ceiling.

Warm, soapy water washed over his feet.

A heavy blanket, cool but not cold, conformed to his body.

The ache of the bullet wound faded away.

The room itself faded away.

Danny saw Johnny's face in a distant cloud, watched helplessly as it receded into the blinding infinity.

TWENTY-ONE
KAILI

Kaili stood on the curb in front of the Astoria Prime building, her breath coming sharp and ragged, waiting for the pain in her legs to numb itself out. Despite the physical toll of falling through floor after floor, she couldn't help but smile, buoyed by the realization that none of this was real, that somewhere beyond the confines of this nightmare construct, the world was still turning. It might still be 2016, with plenty of time left to prepare for the war with Vinestead.

She imagined picking up where she'd left off, and her heart fluttered. But first...

The building across the street was nothing more than a pile of evercrete and rebar, with corded metal I-beams thrown in to complete what some graphic artist had considered the ideal post-apocalyptic rubble heap. Kaili lifted a finger and began to scratch the air in front of her in long, slow strokes. Someone had gone to great lengths to hide the construct's code, but with the right poking and prodding, the ones and zeros came spilling out from behind the veneer like the guts of a bug crushed beneath her shoe.

Sentences reduced to strings; strings reduced to hex sequences. With a slight tug, the rubble heap, the street, and even the supposed air she was breathing, snapped easily into blocky code.

At that point, manipulation of the construct required nothing more than a mere inkling of a thought.

Kaili imagined a tear in virtual space, cutting down through the rubble into the sidewalk, as if someone had taken the view across the street and collapsed it into two dimensions. The line expanded, revealing darkness behind it—the infinite ether in which the construct lived. She imagined two hands reaching out, slipping slender fingers into the tear. They pulled apart, creating a doorway through which she could escape.

But before she could take a step forward, someone else stepped through.

Arthur Sedivy had assumed his normal form again, and though he stared intently at her while he brushed the arms of his jacket, he did not approach. With a subtle gesture over his shoulder, he wiped the portal away.

The simulation stuttered, slowed. The twinkling reds and greens in the cloud froze, and the air turned stagnant.

Sedivy cleared his throat. "Was the demon thing too much?"

"A little," said Kaili. The code around her had changed, and though she reached for it, the ones and zeros kept slipping through her fingers like fine sand.

"Yes, well, I wanted to do something different this time around. I have to say, Ms. Zabora, this whole thing is beginning to bore me. Don't get me wrong—at first, it was fantastic. Watching you run around trying to figure things out. Bad things would happen, and you would die in the most horrifically wonderful ways. Then you would wake up with your memory reset and do it all again. The suffering was exquisite. I used to watch it live, to the point of distraction, if I'm being honest. Now I just have someone put together the highlights of the day for me to watch with my evening nightcap."

There was no way of knowing if he was telling the truth or not. Kaili only remembered the beach, the waves, and Rick.

"Why the personal appearance then?" she asked.

He shrugged, adjusted the jacket of his white suit. "Bored this morning. Nothing but meetings and income projections and glad-handing. There's only so much a man can take before he needs his spirit lifted. And I'll tell you, nothing, not women or booze or synth, compares to the joy I feel when I watch you bleed out in the street. You have been a thorn in my side since our so-called Reaping, and now you've finally been pruned. I can't even begin to tell you how wonderful the timing is. With everything we have coming down the pipe before the decade is out, we just couldn't have someone like you out there on the loose. Too much of an unknown quantity, you know what I mean?"

"Lady of Kaos," said Kaili.

"Well, not anymore."

Pressure built behind her eyes; she was straining too hard. It had to be Vinestead code after all. Not just anyone on the planet could mold it.

"Do you really think this construct can hold me?" she asked, figuring a little bravado couldn't hurt.

"It *has* held you," said Sedivy. "For quite some time. This construct is actually the future of the American prison system, designed by Vinestead International right here in California. No inmate-on-inmate violence, no guards putting their lives at risk for degenerates, and most importantly, absolutely no chance of escape. Each of our confinement pods are self-contained with no link to VNet.

"There is absolutely nothing beyond the borders of Astoria. Drive long enough and the scenery will start to repeat. Stay in the city, and there will be danger on every corner, violence waiting in every shadow. Pain, agony, humiliation; these are your cellmates now. Any control you think you have over the walls of this prison is an illusion. You're here for my amusement, and even after I've lost interest, you will continue to suffer."

"But none of it's real," said Kaili. She lifted her stump of an arm. "You expect me to cry over this?"

Sedivy shook his head; his fine gray hair fluttered. "Doesn't matter. It felt real when it happened, didn't it? Do you think because this is virtual that I can't hurt you? I have more tricks up my sleeve than a few rogue synthetics and a trigger-happy domestic terrorist."

"I would expect nothing less from a sick fuck like you."

"You should be nicer to me, Ms. Zabora. I hold your life in the palm of my hand."

He removed his hand from his pocket and rotated a small object in his fingers. With a snap of his wrist, he cast it across the street. The object sailed through the air in slow motion, glinting like a tiny crystal marble arching from curb to curb. It hit the pavement at Kaili's feet and bounced away, coming to rest near a storm grate.

"Son of a bitch," she said, kneeling to pick up the ring.

"Bodies can be shot, cut up, and torn apart. But to break someone's heart? Imagine, Ms. Zabora, if I tore away a single muscle fiber, would your heart still be your heart? And if I tore another? And another? Over and over? At what point would it stop being your heart and become nothing but an empty cavity?"

Kaili slipped the ring onto her thumb.

"Ms. Zabora?"

"I don't know," she said, without looking up.

"Well, then let's find out," said Sedivy.

The pavement accelerated to the right as if someone had pulled the sidewalk out from under her. She fell into the ether, striking hard with her palm before folding into the space where her other hand should have been. Inertia forced her onto her stomach, pressing her face into rigid, contoured plastic. She stared at the grooves, recalled the last time she'd seen them.

The Eighty Express—the mag-lev train that ran between Sacramento and San Francisco with a single stop in Umbra.

Kaili scrambled to her feet and grabbed one of the hanging straps above the aisle. The train lurched forward, then settled into a gentle rocking she remembered all too well. Outside, the lights on the tracks reached into an oppressive darkness just far enough to see the edges of the California desert.

Astoria's lush forests were gone.

The train car was empty. Behind her, the rear windows showed a track receding into shadow. Ahead, more cars waited, their LEDs flickering menacingly.

Fucking Arthur Sedivy.

"You want me to find him, don't you?" she asked. "You want me to walk through each car until I see him slumped over in a seat. Well, fuck you."

The train shuddered, pulled Kaili forward.

"No," she screamed, wrapping her arm around a nearby pole. "I'm not playing your game."

Above, four lines of LED tubing flared; an electric zap made the hairs on her arm stand up.

Darkness fell.

She was trapped… trapped in some kind of simulation with a vengeful Arthur Sedivy at the controls. She wondered how it could have happened, how Vinestead could have found her.

Kaili shook her head.

Maybe it was all just a bad trip, a fuck-up by the server farm techs at Le Soleil Rouge. It would make sense; almost everything she'd encountered so far could have been derived from her own subconscious. Even the change in Anela's speech patterns could have been a manifestation of her brain trying to inject conflict into her fantasy.

Sedivy in control, Perion's synthetics on a killing spree, encountering a dead Rick on a train: these were classic Kaili Zabora fears brought to life.

But in a dream, Kaili would have had more control. She'd have been able to stop the train, push back the darkness, and return to the beach. Instead, she sensed code all around her, hiding just below the surface. It had evolved since before, garbling itself and refusing to revert to its binary origins. It was as if someone had observed her manipulating the ones and zeros and decided to scramble the encryption again.

A smoldering breath caught in her chest.

"Bonnie."

Kaili recoiled at the hand on her shoulder. She whipped around, slamming her damaged arm against a man's chest. Even in the darkness, she recognized his face—the cheekbones, the sharpness of his chin. Her legs gave out, but Rick Diaz caught her and held her up.

"You," she said, trying to catch her breath. "You talked. You said my name."

"One of your names," he replied, slowly, as if English were new to him. "That's what they tell me, anyhow."

And it was his voice, just as deep and silky and perfect as it had been during their afternoon in the Umbra Tower where they'd drunk wine and made love while the world spun lazily around them. More than a decade had gone by with Kaili unable to recall the sound of Rick whispering in her ear, but now that she'd heard it again, registers popped open in her memory, spilling out every intimate detail of that day in 2004.

"What are you?" she asked.

He adjusted his arms, pulled her close. "Meta," he replied. His breath smelled of wine—red, strong. "Orphaned data pulled from my Guardian Angel chip and my work with LyDIA. An echo, I guess, is the best way to describe it."

"But how can you hold me like Rick held me?" She slipped a hand around the back of his neck.

"It's what he wants me to do."

"Who?"

The light from the adjacent car caught Rick's eyes as he looked over her shoulder.

Kaili groaned, dropped her forehead into his chest. His starched shirt felt rough against her skin.

"So it's really his show then, isn't it?"

"Yes."

"Do you see any way out of it?"

"We," he began, struggling with the words. "We're all in a relationship we can't get out of."

Kaili lifted her head, tried to read his expression in the dark.

"I understand how tough it can be," he continued. "I really do, but you need to break out of it, Bonnie. You need to do the things that make you happy. You can't let Vinestead dictate that."

"How do you know those words?" she asked, pushing against his chest.

"You don't even notice it anymore, the way they manipulate you."

"Stop!" Her augments fired up, let her escape his arms. She spun around half-expecting to see Arthur Sedivy standing behind her, but there was nothing. "Stay out of my head!"

"The Eighty won't take you home, but it will take you away from here. That may not be what you want—"

"You weren't there," said Kaili, raising an accusatory finger to the empty car. "You don't know what went down."

"Find it, Kaili," whispered Rick. His neck contorted, crushed by an unseen hand. "The answer is inside you. Find the house—" Blood bubbled from his mouth. He coughed, sent a fine spray across the floor.

Kaili gasped as Rick collapsed, revealing another figure behind him.

Arthur Sedivy stepped out of the shadows.

"How many muscle fibers do you think that was?" he asked.

"You were spying on Rick, you son of a bitch!"

He shrugged, nudged Rick's body with a polished shoe. "Why else do you think we give Guardian Angels away for free? For the public good?"

"People aren't gonna—"

"Now," he interrupted, "the night is young. What would you like to do next? Back to Astoria? How about San Diego? I've made some changes to your childhood home I think you would appreciate. Perhaps a midday picnic with your sister's decaying corpse at Balboa Park? Wouldn't that be fun?"

Kaili opened her mouth to curse at him, but Sedivy spoke over her again.

"Wait, no," he said, holding up a finger. The gesture sucked the air from her lungs. "I have just the thing. Oh, yes, that's quite good. I think I'll bring the team in to watch with me. Pardon me for a few minutes."

The lights clicked on, taking the shadows and Sedivy and Rick with them. The train slowed as Kaili took a deep breath.

"Now arriving at Astoria Terminus," said a voice from above.

TWENTY-TWO
TANZY

Tanzy was only half-watching the sparkling Umbra sunset when Danny finally came limping out of the bedroom. His hair was matted on one side, and there was a clear line of drool running along his cheek. He looked like a wrinkled plastic bag that had been tossed in the air by strong winds and unceremoniously dumped in the gutter.

Such was the lingering price of Atmos.

He rubbed his eyes, glancing at the vidscreen on the wall as he shuffled past it. Flashy graphics showed the words *VIRAL SCARE* in white lettering on a red background. VFeed was wasting no time kicking the hornet's nest, scaring grandmas and everyday hackers alike with talk of something dangerous in their precious VNet.

Danny paused, shifted his weight to his good leg.

"I didn't release a virus."

"I know," said Tanzy, setting her palette aside. She crossed her arms in her flannel, enjoyed the warmth.

He looked at her as if noticing her for the first time. With obvious discomfort, he made it to the couch and lowered himself to the cushions.

"I got too close to something," he muttered. "They're trying to put the spotlight on me so I'll stop. Surprised they didn't try to straight-up kill me like they did with Johnny."

"Who says they aren't trying?" asked Tanzy.

Danny shot her a look; his eyebrows scrunched up like a child who just found out their puppy died.

"Phantasm says the response is already building on the East Coast. Vinestead is proxying contracts through different groups in Margate, New York, and Bangor. Umbra Immigration stats have been ticking up all day too. There are a lot more people here now than there were this morning. And I'll give you two guesses who they're here to see."

"So what's the play?" He still seemed groggy, as if his brain weren't operating at full capacity.

"That depends."

"On?"

"You telling me about the honeypot. I let you slide because you were acting like a little bitch when you came out, and then you got shot, and then Lincoln, but now it's time to lay those cards on the table. You either tell me what you saw in there or I walk."

Danny narrowed his eyes, smirked. "I liked you better as regular Tanzy. I.C.E-1 Tanzy is kinda mean."

"I'm not joking—"

"I was gonna tell you," he interrupted. He put his hands to his face, rubbed the oily skin on his temples. "I was. I just had to solve a problem first. Myself."

"Not the time to be prideful, Danny."

"I don't think it's that. Johnny left pieces for all of us, even for feed mongers, evidently. Maybe throwing all of it into a pile isn't the best plan. Maybe what he gave us is meant for us alone. He knew I'd figure it out."

"And did you?"

"Not even a little."

Message from the Quatrain. Hotel Fritz intrusion attempts have exceeded second threshold.

"But I have an idea," he continued. "I'm pretty sure the answer is somewhere in Brigham Plaza. That's the name of the strip mall construct. I think it has an IRL analog somewhere, or at least it did. What I saw was maybe five, ten percent of the storefronts and basically zero of the interiors. When I was going back over the data, I used some of the positional logs to map the space in a private construct, but it's incomplete. I have no idea how far the construct goes or what it contains. But I'm betting the answer is there. *Something* in there is worth protecting. Worth faking a viral attack for."

"So what are you saying? You want to map it?"

I could do that, said Cleo.

"We *need* to map it. Bullets will know if we jack into it again, and then there's the issue of the Blockbuster."

"What's a Blockbuster?" asked Jane. She stood in the doorway to the dining area with a book in her hand.

"It's before your time, you walking fetus," said Tanzy.

Danny craned his neck. "They rented movies. You'd have to go in and pick one off the shelf and if they were out of stock, you had to watch Uncle Buck again."

"Gross," said Jane, tucking the book under her arm. "You need anything, Danny? You hungry?"

Tanzy groaned. Jane had basically turned herself off for the past two days while Danny recuperated, proving beyond a doubt she was only there for him.

Even the friendliness she had shown Tanzy was only for his benefit. When he wasn't watching, she reverted to an inert doll, one that didn't feel the need to talk or engage or really do anything except exist.

"I'm good," he replied.

"You sure? I could go out and get something."

"No, you can't," said Tanzy.

They both looked at her.

"Cleo says we're already under siege. The Fritz doesn't take kindly to people coming in and shooting up their guests, but even they have limits. I'm sure it won't be much longer before they politely ask us to leave."

"Vinestead?" asked Danny.

"In everything but name. Mostly freelancers who don't mind getting their coin straight from the bank. A big payday and the notoriety of killing famed hacker Danny Guns Montreal goes a long way in this city."

"Well, then," said Jane. "I suppose we can order in." She sat down on the couch next to Danny, pulled his head into her lap.

Tanzy huffed. The Associate seemed unfazed by the looming danger. Perhaps she didn't fully understand it? Or was it in her script to appear aloof?

"You didn't finish telling me about Blockbuster," said Tanzy.

"Oh, yeah," said Danny. He looked up at Jane, batted his eyes at her. "It's blowing the fuck up."

"And?"

Danny rolled his head to look at Tanzy. "Explosions are bad. You know, with the fire and flying debris and everything. Plus, I think it means we only have a limited amount of time to explore Brigham Plaza. Either Bullets will show up to boot us or the explosion will wipe us out. Either way, we can't just explore at our leisure."

"Cleo can map it."

"Anyone can map it," he replied. "It just takes time."

"We can buy her time."

"If you say so. You haven't even been there yet. It's like walking through someone else's dream. It's..."

"Ethereal?" prompted Jane.

"Yes, ethereal. Thank you."

Tanzy had choice words sitting on the tip of her tongue, but a flash from the vidscreen stopped her short. The VFeed graphics swept to the left and were replaced by a live video from outside Hotel Fritz. An aggregator with a shaved head and blue sunglasses stood in front of the main entrance and addressed the camera.

She slapped the remote to unmute.

"… believe he is holed up here at the Hotel Fritz in Umbra's second quadrant. A spokesperson for the hotel will not confirm if Mr. Montreal is actually inside at this time, but witnesses report seeing Lincoln Continental owner Lincoln Tate coming and going from the premises yesterday evening. And we also have reports that Tanzy of the domestic terrorism group I.C.E-1 may also be inside with Montreal based off this photo taken from surveillance drones earlier today."

A crisp photo of Tanzy standing at the window looking out over the city flashed on the screen. Her loose hair and baggy flannel made her look less like a suit of a dangerous cipher den and more like a lost little girl who'd stepped out of 1992 into a scary new future.

"We're not sure how much I.C.E-1 is involved in the release of the VNet virus, but it's clear they are working closely with Montreal. We'll continue to follow…"

Tanzy muted the vidscreen. Vinestead's threat was clear: surrender Danny or I.C.E-1 would get roped into the muck storm.

She glanced at Danny. His narrow eyes suggested he'd heard the same threat.

"You wanna walk away?" he asked.

She huffed, picked up her palette. "Vinestead can burn in hell. And so can you for asking me that question."

Message from the Quatrain. It is no longer safe at the hotel.

"I know," said Tanzy. When Danny and Jane returned puzzled looks, she turned away and approached the window. "Tell Lincoln we'll be ready to move in ten minutes. And I don't think we'll be going by car."

Outside, the media circus was swarming like gnats to a porch light. From ten floors up, they looked infinitely distant—or at least, far enough away to be of no concern at all. Those were mere commoners milling around in the streets: aggregators, freelance hitters, and in greater numbers, the curious technorati of Umbra City, come to experience the visceral thrill of live murder.

"Jane, would you mind helping Danny pack up—"

A dull *thwack* raised every hair on her body. She jerked away from the window, watched as a circular crack appeared out of nowhere. Seconds later, two more bullets hit the glass, leaving similar breaks like craters on a glass moon. She stood for a moment, bewildered.

"Tanzy, get away from there," shouted Danny. "Lights off, everything off!"

The suite responded with a low electronic tone and powered down. A hand gripped her roughly at the elbow—Jane, pulling her away from the window. They moved back to the couch, put it between themselves and the glass. Danny was already on the floor, pulling himself around the ottoman to them.

You have too much adrenaline in your system. Countering.

Tanzy felt her heart reach a pitch, hold, and slowly start to descend. A slight tremble spilled down from her neck into her body, rattling her bones to the point where Danny had to grab her hands to keep her from shaking too badly. He grabbed her by the chin.

"Are you okay? Are you hurt?"

She shook her head. "Scared. Cleo's regulating. Give me… a minute."

The Quatrain is responding.

Lights from the adjacent buildings flickered and went dark. A section of the Umbra Canopy directly over the Fritz did the same, shutting off its LEDs and vidscreens for two hundred yards in every direction. Now the only light they could see came drifting up from the assembled crowd below; it threw strange shadows on the ceiling of the suite.

The girls were doing their jobs.

"Tell Lincoln we're moving now," said Tanzy.

Message relayed to Lincoln Tate.

"Leave everything," she continued. "We'll send someone back for it later. The blackout's gonna make it harder to move."

They both nodded at her. Jane deftly stroked the top of her wrist in a motion Tanzy barely noticed, as if swiping at a subdermal sliver.

"But I'm taking the rig," said Danny. "I can't leave Johnny's—"

"Well obviously take the fucking rig," said Tanzy. She puzzled the sudden outburst, then muttered loud enough for Danny to hear, "Dial it back, Cleo."

Adjusting levels.

"Jane, can you help Danny?"

Jane nodded, slipped a hand under his arm.

"Let's move."

While Jane helped Danny limp to the door, Tanzy threw equipment into the two duffel bags on the couch. She felt every brick and wire to make sure their rigs and other equipment were included. When both bags were full, she slung them over her shoulder and met Jane and Danny at the door.

"I'll go out first."

Tanzy opened the door slowly. A flash of movement across the hall drew her attention to a door in its last inch of closing. There was no audible click, but Tanzy was sure it had been slightly ajar just moments before. She stared for several seconds at the twinkling peep hole, wondering who might be standing on the other side of it.

Then again, if they were going to make a play, they'd have already made it.

"Move," she whispered, motioning for Jane to follow.

They turned their backs to the elevator and headed for the emergency stairwell at the back of the hallway. Tanzy went in first, stood for a moment at the landing, and listened for footsteps below.

Message from Lincoln Tate. Escort is en route.

"Good," said Tanzy.

The Fritz wasn't far from Decker Plaza, but even so, Tanzy hoped the escort was bringing some firepower with them.

"What's good?" asked Danny. "You should get Cleo a speaker."

"Lincoln is sending an escort to take us over to Decker Plaza so your girlfriend won't have to carry your skinny ass the whole way."

"I don't mind," said Jane.

"Of course you don't, honey."

Tanzy thought she saw a glimmer of anger cross Jane's eyes before they disappeared into shadow.

They descended the evercrete stairs in silence, pausing only once when a door opened and shut somewhere below.

Cleo kept a running commentary on the situation outside.

UPD responding to unrest.

VNet chatter focusing on Umbra.

Quatrain releasing LunaOS control back to the city.

Tanzy turned the corner at a landing and started down yet another set of steps.

"This is the ground floor," said Danny. "Where're you going?"

"I don't think she intends for us to walk out the front door," said Jane.

"Is that what she intends… doesn't intends?"

"You need to flush your system," said Tanzy. "That Atmos is still lingering."

"Just tell me where we're going!"

Tanzy chose to ignore him and didn't look back to see if he was following. After two more flights, she turned down a hallway and found a door marked *Utility.* She held it open and ushered Jane and Danny inside.

The deadbolt in the door clicked shut.

"Is this a panic room or something?" asked Danny.

"Tell Lincoln we're ready," said Tanzy.

"Ready for what?!"

Message relayed.

Tanzy heard Jane whisper, "Are you alright?"

To which Danny answered, "I'm very confused. And hungry."

"I'll fix you a sandwich when we get where we're going. Something meaty."

Message from Phantasm. You alright, sis?

"Tell him I'm going to vomit," said Tanzy.

Message relayed.

Danny started to speak, but a sudden series of clicks from the wall stopped him. A rack of mops and brooms broke apart in the middle, and the left side swung open into the room, revealing a scrawny teen in military fatigues. Draped across his chest was a gold-plated AK-47.

His eyes were pure machinery—red and fiery. They bounced around the room in sharp movements.

"You Banshee and Goons?" he asked, his voice bordering on squeaky.

"All our fucking lives, man," said Danny. "Who are you?"

"Kevin Costner," said the kid.

"Like, the actor?"

"You heard me, Goons." He stepped forward, extended a hand to the open door. "Welcome, friends of Lincoln, to the Umbra Underground."

TWENTY-THREE
GORDON

Gordon hadn't bothered to unpack the go-bag.

For three weeks, it sat in the corner of the room in a leather chair that probably cost more than the cabin he'd called home for the last twenty years. The bag's frayed canvas and caked dirt looked out of place in the well-appointed suite, one of a dozen on the ninth floor of Decker Plaza, a building Cyn kept referring to as Tate Tower.

For twenty-one nights, Gordon had looked at the go-bag and begged himself to bug out, to slip into the elevator when no one was looking and just disappear into the writhing sea of people on the street below. For twenty-one mornings, he'd thought *today is the day I go*. And yet, for one reason or another, the days kept ending with him between the soft sheets of the king bed with a Blue Rain vodka in his hand and the vidscreen on the far wall tearing through episodes of sitcoms he'd never heard of.

And while the laugh track filled the room and the vodka worked at his nervous system, he would think about his life at Lost Pines and worry about Jessie and Evans and all the friendships he'd formed over the years. He would worry about Vinestead going back to the camp with an army of synthetic agents to find out everything they knew about Gordon King. He imagined metal fingers scraping at Jessie's cheek, imagined them drawing blood.

When those thoughts turned to dreams, Gordon would snap awake in the middle of the night, gun in hand and heart racing.

As the days wore on, it became harder to deny the fact he'd put the whole LPS community in danger. Even the people he'd hardly talked to had information, and that information was valuable to a company that had somehow become even more powerful and dangerous since the last time Gordon dealt with them.

The right choice became increasingly clear over time: he had to disappear again, this time out of the country. He needed to send up false flags and let Vinestead know he no longer had anything to do with LPS. Only then would

Jessie and Evans be safe. Only then could he enjoy the comforts of Egyptian cotton and endless liquor.

Gordon stood at the window and stared at the glowing city of Umbra through rivulets of rain. Never in his life had he imagined a place so dedicated to the ones and zeros of the Net, a place where the digital world spilled out into Terrareal to form a hybrid reality where human and machine coexisted and sometimes even merged. It was a lawless city—evidently there had been a shooting at Version Seven across the street, a sister techno rave to Version Six back in Austin—and while no one had been formally charged, someone had been beaten to a pulp in a back alley and branded as the triggerman.

This is what happens when you break the unwritten rules in Umbra, the man's swollen face seemed to say. Not that there were many rules, but disrupting everyone else's good time and shattering the illusion of a utopian paradise seemed to be high on the list of *just fucking don'ts*.

Lightning flashed beyond the Canopy.

A knock came at the door.

"Come in," said Gordon.

The door wasn't locked; what was the point when Lincoln could easily override them?

Cynthia Mesquina didn't look quite as imposing in regular clothes. Nothing about her gray fleece or skin-tight leggings suggested a woman capable of extreme violence. If anything, Cyn often looked like she was coming or going from the gym. The only feature that was out of place was her shiny black hair. It was no longer confined to a ponytail on the back of her head; it now hung in thick curls over her shoulders.

Cyn stepped into the room and closed the door softly behind her.

"Tonight's the night," she said.

"Is it?" he asked, glancing at the go-bag.

"Not for that." She crossed the room and sat on the edge of the bed.

"Where have you been?" he asked, turning back to the window. He watched her reflection in the glass, the way she stared at his back. "It's been a few days."

"Things are getting weird in Umbra. We've been trying to sort it out, but it looks like our hand's gonna be forced on this one."

Gordon took a sip of his drink. The Blue Rain masked the vodka so well he hardly tasted it.

"Just tell me already. I've done enough waiting."

"Well," said Cyn, putting her hands in her fleece, "something's come up with the client, the one who paid us to find you."

"Yeah?"

"He's dead."

"Ah," said Gordon, the word echoing in his glass. "So you're telling me I sat around here for nothing when I could have been making my way to Val Verde. That... sucks."

Cyn smiled. "You know, that's where I looked for you first. Based on everything I'd read about you, I guessed you wouldn't have gone across the pond. You would have headed south hoping your six words of Spanish would get you past the MX and settled in some low-tech area close enough to civilization that you could get to a terminal in an hour if you needed to. Do I have that right?"

He took another sip. "Maybe."

"There's no running away anymore, G. Vinestead has a bead on you. They know you're here in Umbra. I'm sure there were drones tailing us from Austin, and even though the Canopy keeps the bigger birds from spying from above, Vinestead still has eyes at street-level. The second you step outside, they're gonna know about it."

"So I'll have to shoot my way out. I've done it before."

Cyn stood and joined him at the window. She put a hand on his back.

"It doesn't have to go down like that," she said softly. "Lincoln and I... we can help you."

"Y'all don't want to help me. You were trying to sell me, and your buyer died."

"Yes, but he had friends—"

"I'm not a fucking decorative plate to be bid on, Cynthia."

"It's not like that." She slipped between him and the window, held his arm. "Lincoln's first thought when the buyer died was to cut you loose. He wanted to turn you out into the cold and dark and I said no. I changed his mind, G. I told him we snatched you out of your cozy little life and brought you to the front lines of a war that is just waiting to pop off. And now it might have. Now we might actually be preparing for the first meaningful skirmish since Calle Cinco de Mayo."

Gordon lifted her hand from his arm. "It's not my war," he said, turning away. He put the drink down on the dresser and opened a drawer. There were a few articles of clothing Bryce had gifted him that he didn't want to leave behind. He looked around for another bag he could pack.

"Well, that's some bullshit," said Cyn.

"How's that?"

"Not your war? You fucking started this war. You gave Poland to the goddamn Nazis. If it weren't for you and your friends, we might still have a free Net. Do you even understand how much VNet has changed the game? Vinestead controls communication for ninety percent of the population. We're talking deep packet inspection, advertisement tuning, privacy invasion—everything evil that can be done with your meta is being done by Vinestead every goddamn day. And that's on you, G."

He slapped his palm against the dresser. The stitches stretched but held.

"It's not on me," he said slowly. "I didn't copy a sixteen-year-old girl's mind into the Net so I could have a virtual fuck slave. I didn't get mixed up with a cipher den and their psychotic suit. I wasn't the selfish prick who wasn't happy with just one girl. All I did was try to clean it up, because that's how fucking stupid I am. I clean up other people's messes. And now you want me to clean up yours, don't you?"

"Don't you even want to know what's happening?" asked Cyn. She sat down at the desk near the window, crossed her legs. "Aren't you at all curious why something in VNet is calling your name? One of the scene's best hackers is dead because of it. And his friends are following the trail of blood. Without our help, they could end up dead too. And then Vinestead wins another round."

"Not my pig, not my farm."

Cyn sighed, put her elbow on the desk.

Gordon could feel her eyes on him, but he didn't meet her gaze, didn't want to. He stared a hole into the carpet, started counting at a slow, deliberate pace, enunciating and visualizing each number clearly in his head.

One, two, three...

"They're coming, you know," said Cyn.

"Vinestead?"

"The buyer's friends. They're coming here, right now. They went sniffing after their friend and Vinestead didn't like it. Now we've got a fake virus floating around VNet and an army of ambitious mercenaries looking to make a name for themselves."

"Another mess, right?"

"I'm not saying you have to clean it up. No one is saying that. We've already been paid to find you; that part is done. What comes next is completely up to you. I know there's enough money in your bag to get you to South America. If you want to walk, you can walk. I would hope..." She paused, looked down at her knees. "I would hope you wouldn't though."

Gordon heard the change in her voice, the kind of wistful tone that suggested there was more to her feelings than what she was saying. It was the kind of naked interest that would have aroused him a decade ago, back when his interest in love and sex still smoldered. Turning off that part of himself after Natalie had seemed like a daunting task, a fool's errand he would never be able to complete.

And yet, in his years at LPS, he'd never taken an interest in any of the women. Even Jessie's mom, who loved that her little girl had a father figure, who had made advances any man with half a brain couldn't have missed, had remained at a distance, held there by the memory of Natalie, a woman he'd wronged in so many ways, some banal and some too horrible to remember.

Then, of course, there were Cyn's other motivations.

"When I first met you, you acted like I was nothing but a job to you, a *package* to be delivered. Then you brought me here, introduced me to Lincoln, and then I barely saw either of you for three weeks. Three fucking weeks, Cynthia. I've been sitting in here wasting my life away. Getting drunk and watching TV, trying like hell to avoid plugging myself back into the world. And today, *today*, you come in here with your hair all fixed up and your cooter bulging out of your pants and put your hands on *me*? Do you honestly think I follow my dick everywhere?"

Cyn stared back for a moment, unblinking. "What exactly are you accusing me of, G?" She stood, tightened one hand into a fist. "Because it sounds like you're suggesting I'm whoring myself out to you. Do *you* honestly think I'd use my body like that just because Lincoln Tate snaps his fingers? I decide how I use my body, and if I did up my hair, it's because I want to look nice, and if I put a hand on you, yeah, it's because I kinda like you. You're a decent guy in a shit position and you looked like you could use some kindness. But you're also an asshole, G."

She moved to the door.

"Cynthia…"

"Get fucked, alright? Bryce will come get you when our guests arrive. You can wait in here with your booze and your *Scrubs* until then." She opened the door, stepped out into the hall. "Or just go for all I care. You know where the door is. Oh, and I'm going to walk away now. I'm sorry if my ass moves while I walk. I assure you it's just to get me down the fucking hall."

She slammed the door behind her.

For a moment, he felt a twinge in his stomach, some manifestation of misplaced guilt and shame. He buried the feelings in a deluge of sequential numbers.

So what if Cyn was pissed at him?

It was better that way.

Better she stayed at a distance.

TWENTY-FOUR
DANNY

Kevin Costner treated Danny, Tanzy, and Jane to his own flavor of mumble rap as he led them down the brightly lit tunnels of the Umbra Underground.

Danny had half-expected to be walking ankle-deep in gutter run-off while avoiding rats that had grown comically large in a dark and nutrient-rich environment. Instead, the Underground reminded him of the long tunnels of a subway station, with tiled ceilings and walls of polished rock. There was evidence of upkeep, as if a team of custodians came through the corridors every night to make sure the floors and baseboards were as clean as they could be given the circumstances.

Tanzy strode ahead confidently. Now that she had an audience in Kevin, she'd resumed her suit persona, no longer just Megan, but now Tanzy, respected and feared leader of the I.C.E-1 cipher den.

Jane kept to Danny's side, holding his hand lightly and smiling whenever he looked over at her.

"This way," said Kevin. "This way to the man with the plan, the Dapper Don of Azerbaijan, the man with whispers in his crispers." He bounced as he walked; white LEDs in his earlobes rose and fell like equalizers as music pulsed in his head.

"You've been down here before, haven't you?" asked Danny.

Tanzy glanced over her shoulder, nodded. "A while ago. State of the Network '14, I think. Someone called in a bomb threat at the convention center on the last day and I just happened to be sitting next to Lincoln. Guy was real smooth about it too, all *allow me to show the lady out*, and all that. Kevin was there, though he was just a baby then."

Kevin nodded. "Born hard, live hard, die hard."

"I don't think that's how that goes," said Danny.

"Everything goes," he replied, electric sliding his way around a corner.

No underground dwellers crossed their path as they walked the polished floors, which allowed Danny to take his time on his bad leg. The wound still hurt, but only in a distant, faraway place on the other side of his biochip. He kept his mind busy by counting the LED arches that ran across the ceiling. They glowed steadily without any hint they might suddenly go out, leaving them lost in the darkness below the bustling city.

"How many people know about the Underground?"

"It's more myth than public knowledge," said Tanzy. "Only the real players in Umbra real estate have access to it. Even Lincoln didn't know about it until he bought out Decker Plaza. It's so the Umbra elite don't have to mix with the proles, ya know?"

Danny looked over his shoulder, down the endless corridor. Something about the featureless walls and sharp corners reminded him of a maze construct in the Net, extending so far into the draw distance that walls and ceilings and floors all crammed into a single point that might as well have been a black hole.

"What is it?" asked Jane.

"Thought I heard something," he replied. When he looked forward again, Kevin was standing in front of him, his head cocked to the side.

"What did you hear, hacker man?" he asked. His eyes blazed; tiny apertures opened and closed.

"Could have been my imagination."

Kevin nodded. "You know the way, Banshee?"

"Just follow the scent of fancy suits and fine cigars, right?"

"That's the deal, big wheel," said Kevin, brushing past Danny. He walked a hundred paces down the corridor and turned the corner.

For a moment, they stood together, listening to his footsteps echo. Danny shifted to his good leg, tried to relieve the ache climbing his hamstring.

Tanzy cleared her throat. "Let's keep—"

A volley of percussive gunfire roared around the corner.

Danny felt Jane grip his shoulder. The next second, she was pulling him along the corridor toward Tanzy. They ran, following the I.C.E-1 suit around corners marked with the names of the streets above them. Small placards on the walls pointed out landmarks, but Danny barely had time to read them. There was too much pain in his leg, and the Syzygy couldn't decide where to focus its attention.

It tried lowering his heart rate so he could think straight.

It tried to numb his leg.

It tried to build a map of the city above his head to stem the panic of not knowing where he was.

All of this occurred under a blanket of automatic gunfire, of a gold AK-47 spraying wildly in tight corners.

Finally, mercifully, Tanzy turned off the main hallway and entered a white door marked *Decker Plaza* in tiny gray lettering. She guided Danny and Jane inside and shut the door. There was hardly enough room to turn around, but Tanzy managed to paw at a small keypad on the far wall. She tried a few different combinations before groaning in disgust.

"Tell Lincoln to open the door."

Seconds later, an electronic chime sounded in the wall, and the keypad flashed green. Tanzy pushed against the wall and nearly fell into the adjoining room. Danny and Jane followed behind, steadying the I.C.E-1 suit as she adjusted to the low light.

As the door clicked shut behind them, a spark of orange flame pierced the darkness, illuminating a tall man in a fitted red t-shirt. The lights came up around him, revealing a thick pane of reinforced plexiglass that bisected the room. There were small seams indicating a door, but no handle with which to open it.

The man drew on his cigarette. "You're early."

"We ran," said Tanzy.

"Into trouble?"

"No, for our health."

The man jerked his head to the side and listened to someone whispering in his ear.

"Ah," he said. "You were tailed. Well, better get you on this side of the glass then, huh?" He touched the sliver on his wrist.

The seam in the plexiglass shimmered and broke apart.

Jane pulled Danny through the opening and away from the door to the Underground. She kept looking back, afraid someone might come knocking, perhaps.

"I'm Bryce," said the smoking man. He held out a hand. "You're Tanzy, right? And that would make you Guns. And you are, Miss…?"

"Meade," said Jane.

Bryce smiled. "I'm just fuckin' with you. Lincoln briefed me on all of you. Come on, let's head up to the lounge and relax. May I escort the lady to the elevator?" He held his elbow out for Jane.

Jane slipped behind Danny's shoulder, grabbed his hand.

"Or the other lady?" asked Bryce.

"What about Kevin?" she asked.

"Kevin?" He put his arm down, started walking toward the elevator. "Fine. Don't no one want to get escorted ain't no one gonna get escorted."

In the elevator, Danny leaned against the wall and put his weight on the handrail. The walls were covered in vidscreens showing the view outside the building. At first, endless patterns of rock and evercrete scrolled past, until finally the elevator broke the surface, and Umbra erupted around them. It wasn't a live feed of the city, just an artist's rendering of what Umbra might look like at dusk, with pinks and purples pushing down from the sky and oddly bent light illuminating the building faces.

"Yo, Guns, can I get you anything, man?" asked Bryce.

Danny bobbed his head. "What you got?"

"Sheeeit…"

"No synth until tomorrow," said Jane. "Doctor's orders."

Lincoln Tate was standing at the elevator doors when they opened on the ninth floor of Decker Plaza. His gold chains danced in the light, reflecting both the yellow mood lights in the ceiling and the cacophony of neon bleeding in from the windows. He smiled at the sight of Danny leaning against the wall.

"Mr. Montreal. I wish you were coming to me under different circumstances. Tanzy tells me the Fritz is no longer safe. Do you have any idea who's behind the aggression?"

There was something in his elevated speech that made Danny think for a moment that maybe Lincoln was behind the whole thing. All he would have to do is stage unrest outside the hotel, take a few pot shots at the suite's bulletproof windows, and twenty minutes later, Danny would come running to him.

"Vinestead," said Tanzy, when Danny didn't respond. "They've got a bounty on our heads. Security at the Fritz is good, but it wouldn't have held up forever. We're safer here in the meantime."

She had sided with Lincoln rather quickly. Danny eyed her suspiciously as they walked down the hall to what Bryce had referred to as a lounge. Inside, Jane helped him to a nearby couch in a sunken section of the room. The couch wrapped around a large, square coffee table that held various liquors and tumblers. A stack of stone coasters sat beside them.

"Please, make yourself at home," said Lincoln. "I have plenty of room, food, and booze."

"Can I fix you a drink?" asked Jane.

"What about doctor's orders?"

"It's gonna be mostly ice," she replied, reaching for a bottle of rum.

Danny let his gaze wander over her back, over the bumps of her spine pushing through the thin white camisole. She wore a black bra underneath; Danny traced the horizontal line to the side of her body where—

His eyes snapped to the corner of the room, to a shadow moving in the small alcove behind the bar. The spectral figure stepped forward to meet his gaze.

"Ah, Cynthia," said Lincoln. "Mr. Montreal, Tanzy, this is Cynthia Mesquina, one of my best freelancers. She's the one who tracked down the elusive G. Speaking of, Cyn, will he be joining us?"

Cyn kept her eyes on Danny as she came forward. Out of the corner of her mouth, she said, "He's thinking about it." Then to Danny, "I thought you'd be bigger."

"Cool," said Danny, taking his drink from Jane. He took a long sip, sought out the microscopic amount of rum she'd mixed in with the Coke and ice. He failed to detect any.

Cyn smirked and turned for the bar.

"I think she likes you," said Jane, leaning into Danny. She put her hand on his leg, probed the bandage beneath his pants. "Either that or she wants to murder you. Sometimes it can be a fine line."

Danny chose to ignore the freelancer as well as the private conversation Lincoln and Tanzy were having. He heard Bryce announce to no one in particular that he was going down to check on Kevin Costner but didn't respond. He focused instead on the face next to his, to the faint smell of Jane's breath as she spoke to him in hushed tones.

"Just say the word and I'll kick her ass," she continued.

"Don't worry about her," said Danny. "She's just playing it tight until she gets to know us. Seen it a million times. You can't trust someone by their name or rep; you have to see how they work, you know, see them in action."

"I've seen you in action."

"Yes. You have."

"And I trust you. Do you trust me?"

About twenty thousand dollars' worth, he thought.

"Of course."

She kissed him on the nose, lingered in his space.

"Hey, teenage love song, knock it off," said Tanzy. "Lincoln's gonna show us a video Johnny sent him the other night."

"In exchange for what?" asked Danny.

"Same as before. Access to your story. He wanted you to sign a contract first, but I talked him out of it."

Danny shifted on the couch, put a foot up on the coffee table. "And what if I don't sign after we watch the video?"

Tanzy glanced at Lincoln, who had wandered off to the bar to talk with Cyn.

"Then I'll give him my rights—an exclusive interview with I.C.E-1 and the Quatrain." She shrugged. "I mean, who really cares, right? It's just a scoop. If we don't work with Lincoln, some other media feed is just gonna make up their own story. At least this way, we control the message *and* whatever manipulation we put in it."

Danny nodded. She was right, of course. It was just a story after all. What really mattered was finding out what happened to Johnny, and if there was something in the video that could help, it was worth the cost.

Tanzy smiled, turned back to Lincoln with a thumbs-up sign.

"We're good to go," she said. "Let's see what Johnny thought was important enough to send you."

"Good," said Lincoln, nodding to Cyn.

The freelancer touched her wrist, tapped a few times.

Thick curtains rolled out of the ceiling and covered the tall windows on the outside walls. The lights and sounds of Umbra faded, and there was no noise in the room except for a distant thumping from Version Seven and Jane's quiet breathing in his ear.

Cyn pulled two palettes from the bar and handed them to Tanzy and Danny. She hardly acknowledged Jane, almost went out of her way to ignore her.

The palette was already on, and the image was frozen on a top-down view of a dark room. In the center stood what looked like a smoothed coffin. Monitors and twinkling LEDs lined up against the wall, and in the background, an EKG beat out a steady tempo.

"Have you already seen this?" asked Danny.

Lincoln nodded. "Just once. Once was enough."

"What are we looking at?" asked Tanzy.

"You can't tell from the video itself, but the file was geo-tagged out of Astoria, Oregon. We believe this is Le Soleil Rouge in the Old District. They do body mods and augmentations."

"We have better techs here in Umbra," said Cyn.

"But they have better privacy in smaller towns like Astoria," said Lincoln, "or so she thought."

"She?" asked Danny. "Is there a woman in that coffin?"

"That's a stasis pod, but yeah, there's a woman in that coffin."

The video began with the sound of gunfire. Tinny screams rattled the small speakers in the palette.

"Who's in the coffin, Lincoln?" asked Danny.

"Ladies and gentleman," said Lincoln, "I give you the last known sighting of the Butcher of Burbank herself, Kaili Zabora."

TWENTY-FIVE
KAILI

The train shuddered to a stop at Astoria Terminus.

Kaili waited for the doors to slide open before stepping out onto the empty platform. Parched, brown leaves blew across the gray evercrete, caught up in breezes she could see but not feel. She looked past the ticketing station, expecting to see a smoldering Astoria beyond, but the world simply dropped off into nothing.

The stairs leading down to the street ended in darkness, and all around the platform, the black ether swallowed up both light and sound. Kaili stood for a moment with her toes hanging over the edge, wondering why Sedivy had stranded her on a platform that was literally in the middle of nowhere.

What suffering was there to be had here?

She glanced back at the train, gave silent thanks Rick was no longer on it.

"The word you're looking for is *jejune*. You'd want to say, 'Astoria Body Mods produces rather *jejune* augmentations.'"

Kaili looked around for the source of the voice but saw no one. The canopy above held a matrix of brilliant LEDs, casting lens flares that partially obscured her vision.

"Nobody's gonna know what that means. We should just say *Le Soleil Rouge good, Astoria Body Mods bad.*"

The speaker was female. Kaili tracked the source to the cracked door of the ticketing station. Cold, blue light spilled from the opening.

"God, you'll never understand social media. Obvi, this isn't for our core audience. It's for sophisticates who appreciate good copy. Why don't we make one ad with my refined language and one with your southern-fried corndog verbiage and see which one gets the most shares?"

"Hello?" asked Kaili, approaching the door.

"You're one to talk about southern-fried, *Ginger*."

Kaili pushed the door open and stood at the threshold. The ticket kiosks were gone, replaced by a bank of vidscreens on the far wall. In the center of the room stood a single rolling stool with no arms. The conversation between the two women played from speakers positioned in the corners. Kaili scanned the various feeds on the monitors until she found the matching video.

The women sat together behind a desk in the reception area of Le Soleil Rouge, nudging each other with their elbows as they fought for control of the lone computer. Kaili recognized them both. The philistine in the black blazer, short blonde hair, and dark glasses was Ramona—she'd checked Kaili in and shown her the facilities. The other girl, Ginger, had been the one to help her into the stasis pod. She was wearing the same purple scrubs from the day Kaili went under.

Each screen on the video wall showed a different room at Le Soleil Rouge, including the doors to both locker rooms, the secondary waiting area, and a dozen stasis pods. In the lower right corner of each pod feed, the occupant's name glowed in stenciled green letters.

BRONSON, M.

IRWIN, C.

DIAZ, B.

On the feed marked *LAPENTA, D*, Dr. Jenkins stood over a stasis pod with a palette cradled in the nook of his arm. He made a few notes before turning off the lights and leaving.

Kaili sat down on the stool.

"Is this live?" she asked aloud, half-expecting Sedivy to answer her.

Had Vinestead hacked their way into the servers at Le Soleil Rouge and hijacked the simulation? She searched the vidscreens for a timestamp but found none.

A single chime rang out from the speakers.

"Customer," said Ramona, glancing at her sliver.

Ginger stood quickly and smoothed out her scrubs. "I'll be in the back," she said, "unless it's a cute guy, in which case I'll be right back." She pushed through a swinging door and reappeared on a different video feed.

Ramona busied herself behind the desk and pretended not to notice as the customer came up the wide spiral staircase in the atrium. Kaili watched him give each step consideration as he eyed the chandelier hanging from the high ceiling. Either he was awestruck by the glittering crystals or…

Kaili rolled closer to the vidscreens.

The customer was a tall man; his head barely cleared the door's threshold as he stepped into the reception area. He was dressed in dark pants and a hooded sweatshirt, with light blond hair framing Slavic features. He smiled at Ramona, but it was all teeth, nothing in his eyes.

"Good morning. Welcome to Le Soleil Rouge. How can I assist you today?"

The man walked to the center of the waiting room and glanced over his shoulder at the doors.

"Do you have an appointment?" continued Ramona.

"No," he replied, reaching into the wide pocket of his hoodie. His hand came out holding a silenced 9mm. Ramona barely had time to put her hands up before he trained the gun on her head and pulled the trigger. A spray of blood appeared on the wall behind her.

Kaili flinched, almost fell off the stool as she tried to back away.

On another screen, Ginger perked up at the sound of Ramona slumping out of her chair and hitting the floor. She took a step toward the reception area, hesitated, and then reached for a panel on the wall. She brought up a carousel of video feeds and swiped through.

"Good girl," said Kaili.

Ginger expanded the reception area feed to full screen, but by then, the shooter had already pushed through the swinging door. She turned just in time to take a bullet in the chest. Her brief scream raised the fine hair on Kaili's arm.

In a pod room, Dr. Jenkins nearly dropped his palette.

The man didn't even look at Ginger as she fell across his path. He simply stepped over her, putting two more rounds in her head as he passed.

Dr. Jenkins stepped into the hallway and looked around. "Just what the hell do you think you're doing?" he asked.

"Kaili Zabora." His accent was thickly Ukrainian.

"There's no one here by that name."

The man squared up, scowled. "Bonnie Diaz."

"There's no one—" he started, but it was too late. His eyes had already jumped to a nearby door.

Tiny plumes of smoke burst from his chest. He fell backward into the wall and slid to the ground.

Kaili moved to the vidscreen showing her room and banged on the glass.

"Wake up!" she screamed.

She turned her thoughts inward, tried to reach below the simulation to something real, something that could shake her from the electronically induced dream.

The man put the 9mm back in his pocket and approached the door. Kaili wasn't sure it was hers until the lights came up in her pod room. He entered cautiously, closing the door behind him with care, as if he might disturb her slumber.

Kaili stood and paced the small ticketing station. If he killed her, would the entire simulation just turn off? What if he jacked her out? Would she be able to fight him off? The augments she had used since waking may have only existed in Sedivy's sick nightmare. Out there in the real world, she might not be strong or fast enough to fend off an armed Ukrainian goon. Still, she had to be ready.

Monitors and vidscreens woke up as he approached the stasis pod, displaying her vital signs and brain activity. He observed them for a minute before fixing his gaze on the pod. His fingers searched out the release latch.

The cover opened slowly, sucking air into the hydraulics.

The white towel they'd draped over her body at insertion was gone, replaced by a mesh of electrodes and wires. Spiky needles dotted her arms and legs, touching each of the major muscle groups. The black lines running between them made Kaili smile. They were the same lines Cynthia Mesquina had covered up with a skeletal tattoo. It meant Dr. Jenkins had already installed the augments.

Whether the augments actually worked was still unknown.

Kaili held her breath as the man reached into his jacket again. He pulled out a long, silver tube which he then unscrewed. The syringe that slid out caught the light, and Kaili felt a knot tighten in her stomach.

"What is that?" she asked, banging on the vidscreen. The vertical hold on the image began to roll, recovering just in time for her to see the needle go into her arm. She waited for some kind of change in the construct, but nothing happened.

The man spent the next ten minutes removing the electrodes from her body. The thin spikes required more attention; each one produced a small rivulet of blood when it was extracted. He dropped the metal needles onto a nearby table one at a time until Kaili's body was completely free of circuitry. He then used the stasis gel in the pod to wipe away the excess blood.

Kaili's body glistened under the LEDs.

The Ukrainian's hands moved to the bundle of wires behind Kaili's neck.

"Do it," she whispered.

Instead, he pulled a cell phone from his pants pocket and started punching in numbers. He paused, his thumb hovering over the screen, his eyes running back and forth over Kaili's body. His free hand stroked the side of her face, then her breast.

This time, he smiled with his eyes.

Kaili heaved, spit bile onto the floor.

The man placed the phone on the cart with the electrodes and unzipped his hoodie, tossing it onto the counter behind him.

Kaili looked down at her legs, convinced she could feel his hands grabbing her ankles. She shouldn't have been able to feel real-world stimuli in the construct, but the ghostly fingers gripped her feet nonetheless. She held her breath as he pulled her legs out of the pod, rotating her body in the process.

The VR wire bundle came free, but the construct remained. Kaili let out her breath, stared at the dangling electrodes.

The video feed wasn't live.

It might not have even been real.

Slippery feet hit the floor, and the man struggled to keep Kaili's body from falling. He lifted her away from the pod, closed the lid, and then draped her over the top face-down, stabilizing her with an open palm on the small of her back. With his other hand, he undid his belt and zipper. Black pants fell to the floor; his boxers bulged.

Kaili retreated from the vidscreens until her back hit the wall. She turned and ran from the room.

The Eighty Express had departed without making a sound. In its place stood a vidscreen that extended above the station's canopy and below the platform. Pixelated blues and blacks showed the Ukrainian thrusting into her limp body, his hands gripping her hips, the stasis pod rocking back and forth. Blood-tinged gel sloshed onto the floor, and several times he seemed to lose his footing, but he kept up the pace, occasionally reaching out to slip a hand under her chest.

Kaili screamed, shut her eyes tight.

"Oh, come on," said Sedivy. "Don't spoil this for me."

The skin on her eyes became translucent, and no matter where she looked, she saw the video feed.

"It's not real," she whispered, trying to focus on any part of the video other than the man's erection or his smug smile.

A chirp rang out on the platform. It wasn't until it sounded for a fifth time that the man withdrew. With one hand on her back holding her up, he reached for his phone on the cart. Whatever he saw on the screen made him groan.

"What?" he asked, pressing the phone to his ear.

A conversation in Ukrainian followed.

"They're asking if he's ready for extraction," said Sedivy, his voice echoing from somewhere above the canopy. "He's telling them he's still working on insertion."

The Ukrainian looked down at Kaili and nodded.

"Now he's asking for five more minutes."

"You're a monster, Arthur…"

Suddenly, the man in the video looked up, directly into the surveillance camera.

Sedivy chuckled. "They just told him they can see him on the cameras. And they're giving him *ten* more minutes."

The man waved to the camera and tossed the phone back on the cart.

"Call him off," screamed Kaili.

"This has already happened," said Sedivy, "though it's the first time you're seeing it. I think I'll make it part of the normal loop."

The Ukrainian resumed his stance behind Kaili, but now he hammed it up for his audience. He grabbed her under her shoulders and lifted her body. Her head fell back on his shoulder.

Kaili watched her body shake, watched his thick hands slide over her skin, tracing patterns in the stasis gel.

He lifted one of Kaili's hands and waved it at the camera.

Her scream tore through the construct, shaking every fiber of virtuality, until the vidscreen, canopy, and platform fell apart. Kaili turned and ran down an invisible hallway, chasing a receding door she just couldn't catch up with. The walls stretched, separated into individual voxel strands, revealing the black ether behind them. Somewhere at the other end of the infinite passage was a safe place free from pain.

If only she could reach it.

Bony fingers wrapped around her left ankle, sending her sprawling. The gravity in the construct shifted, tipped, and threw her into the disintegrating ceiling. The world blurred.

When the light and noise settled, Kaili found herself seated on the stool again, staring at a sweaty Ukrainian in mid-climax.

TWENTY-SIX
TANZY

The lights were down in the lobby at Decker Plaza.

Shades had been pulled on the tall windows that looked out on Nand Street, blocking out the noise and fervor of a city teetering on the edge. Vinestead had held a match to the underbelly of Umbra, and now the oil was reaching a boiling point. Soon, it wouldn't be safe to walk the streets at all, let alone lift the shades and look outside.

Tanzy found a comfortable leather chair in a small lounge off the main lobby. An ornate brass lamp in the corner gave off just enough light to mark the furniture but not much else. At least the room was empty; only a handful of people milled about in the lobby, and most of them were security. There were faces she didn't recognize and didn't care to look at. She had a feeling they might try to talk to her, might ask her *what's wrong* in that condescending tone all men used.

And if they did, they were likely to catch a fist in the nose.

Even Cleo sensed something was wrong, and with the exception of a few status messages from the Quatrain, she mostly kept quiet. Once Tanzy was seated in what she finally realized was a smoking lounge—the Lincoln Continental cigars on the coffee table were a dead giveaway—Cleo suggested a small dose of synth to help with her elevated heart rate.

Tanzy refused, put a finger to her mouth, and started biting at the nail.

I recommend—

"No," she repeated, more defiantly. She wrenched her head to the side, as if Cleo were some small angel standing on her shoulder. "I want to feel this."

Snippets of the Kaili Zabora video flashed in her mind, and this time Cleo didn't step in to regulate Tanzy's emotional response. Every muscle in her stomach contracted as the smiling face of a bulky Ukrainian faded into the darkness. The pain pulled her forward until she had her chest on her knees. She stared at the dark red carpet under her feet.

The video had been, at first, mildly upsetting, but as the scene progressed, a sickening fury had grown in Tanzy. Though she held no personal affection for Kaili—they were competitors in a tight market space, after all—seeing her treated like an object, a plaything for some man's pleasure, was too much to bear. It took minimal effort to imagine herself in Kaili's position, and when she did, her mind took her back to a storage room hidden deep in her childhood, to a scarred metal door with the word *Janitor* scribbled on masking tape across it. And if it hadn't been for Cleo standing in front of the door to that memory with her arms crossed and head shaking back and forth, Tanzy might have gone in, might have remembered in startling detail that night from so many years ago.

Instead, Cleo had held firm, as she always did.

In the end, the pressure had been too much, and Tanzy had walked out of the room in a daze even before the video was over. Danny and Lincoln called after her, but she'd waved them away. She had wanted air, wanted some space to sit and collect her thoughts. There was something about Kaili's pain that she wanted to absorb and redirect. It would just take time... without Cleo chattering in her head, without Danny pretending to care, and without Lincoln worrying about their business arrangement.

Heavy boots fell in the lobby; echoes suggested someone walking with determination toward the front doors.

Stopping.

Just keep walking, thought Tanzy. *I'm not in here. I don't need to be rescued.*

The footsteps grew louder as they came toward her.

"Not now, Danny," she said, lifting her head.

The man standing in the entrance to the lounge was not Danny. He had a thicker build, was several inches taller, and the scars on his face told the story of a life not wasted behind a computer screen. He carried a large black duffel bag in one hand.

Tanzy admired his impeccably fitted suit.

"You're not Danny," she said.

"No, I reckon I'm not," he replied. "Do you mind if I sit? I'm waiting for a ride."

"It's a free country." She sat back in the chair, wiped at her cheeks with the back of her hand.

No known matches in any government databases, said Cleo.

The man dropped his duffle next to a leather chair with thick, rounded arms and sat down. He'd barely had time to adjust his coat before a young girl with tattooed forearms appeared out of nowhere.

"Something to drink, sir?"

"Blue Rain, vodka, two cherries, black, please."

The girl nodded, turned to Tanzy. "Ma'am, would you like something?" Then, in a hushed voice, "I would have come over sooner, but..."

Tanzy nodded, lifted her hand slightly to wave the girl away.

The coffee table between Tanzy and the stranger seemed to compress such that she felt he was sitting right in front of her, that she could smell his breath. In reality, he was a good ten feet away, far enough that Cleo didn't have to worry too much. After all, they were in Decker Plaza, Lincoln Tate's castle. Who would dare attack the suit of I.C.E-1 on Lincoln's turf?

"So," said the man, crossing his leg, "are you from here or just visiting?" He put a hand on his knee; thick scars ran over his knuckles.

"Look, I was sitting here alone in the dark. What exactly about that picture makes you think I want to get hit on right now?"

"Hit on," he repeated, using a slow Texas drawl to imply disbelief. "Ma'am, I was just being cordial. I guess hospitality hasn't made it this far west yet."

Narrowing search to TOLA region.

"Welcome to California," said Tanzy, tightly.

They sat in silence for a minute. The girl came with a drink and set it down on the coffee table. She raised a discreet eyebrow at Tanzy, but Tanzy waved her off again.

The man took a sip of his electric blue drink.

"Not the same," he muttered, placing the glass back on the table. "You know, we have a saying about Californians where I come from."

Tanzy looked away.

"Stop moving to Texas," he continued, chuckling.

"Why would anyone want to move there?"

The man sighed. "It's a big place, lots of variety. Oil barons in Houston. MX gangs in San Antonio. Hipster technorati in Austin. Something for everyone." He took another sip. "Great place to disappear. Well, it was."

His tone turned wistful.

"What do you mean?" asked Tanzy.

"Nothing really, just lots of open land. You used to could find yourself some acreage and walk it like a king. Now you got these drones flying overhead day and night, just waiting to take your picture."

"That's why I live in Portland. Lots of trees."

He nodded. "That's why I lived in the Pines. Didn't help."

Message from Danny. Where did you go?

Tanzy ignored the impulse to answer, instead asked, "Who were you hiding from?"

The man smirked, put the drink down. With his index fingers extended, he brought his folded thumbs together to form a *V*.

"Ah," she said, nodding.

"What about you?" he asked.

"What makes you think I'm hiding from someone?"

He made a show of looking around the empty lounge.

"A woman with tears on her cheeks is sitting alone in a dark room. She's wearing a faded flannel, so she's not here on business. She doesn't have a bag with her, so she's not on her way out the door. If I had to guess, I would say you've had a lover's quarrel. And I'm guessing it's their voice you keep hearing in your head when you tic like that."

Tanzy folded her arms. "Is that what you see? Well, let me tell you what I see sitting across from me. A man with a six-dollar haircut in a six-hundred-dollar suit. Scars on both hands like he's been bare-knuckle boxing since he was a kid. A black canvas bag full of what I can only assume are long-barreled rifles and explosives. And to top it all off, he's got a face that doesn't exist in any state, federal, or private database going back twenty years."

A finger broke away from his drink to point in her direction.

"You checkin' up on me?"

"Just trying to figure out your deal."

"You could have just asked."

Tanzy dropped the playfulness and barked, "Who the hell are you?"

"King. Gordon King. And your name?"

The tension of sitting across from an unknown male with unknown intentions drained out of her. Even the horrors of the Kaili Zabora video were temporarily forgotten.

She suppressed a smile. "So, you're the infamous G. Destroyer of the Net. Vinestead's Most Wanted. Former low-level quarry rusher."

"That's... what they tell me."

"I know you, Gordon."

"Is that so?"

"You look different than I imagined you back then. The way you talked and acted... I thought you were some goofy white kid screwing around in his dorm room."

Gordon tilted his head to the side. "Ah, quarry rushing. Pre-millennium."

"I remember the last time I saw you. We were rushing Mylo Rivera. Remember? You took down a noob... um... God, what was his name?"

"You don't mean UltraKill, do you?" Gordon laughed. "Quarry was packed that night. Who were you?"

"Not Jape, I can tell you that."

The glass slipped from Gordon's hand, caught the edge of the coffee table, and spilled blue liquid over the carpet. He held his hand in a fist for several seconds before relaxing.

His eyes flittered.

"You know... Jape?"

"No," said Tanzy, "but I've got a feeling he's mixed up in whatever this virus business is that's all over the feeds. You spilled on yourself, you know that?"

Gordon pulled a handkerchief from inside his coat and blotted gently at his pant leg.

"I didn't know that," he said, glancing at his bag. "The Jape thing, not the Blue Rain." He picked up the glass from the floor and set it shakily on the table. "You're uh, you're the buyer's friends Cyn was talking about, right? You know Johnny San Vito?"

"Knew," Tanzy corrected. "He's dead."

"I'm sorry."

"Not your fault," she replied. "Or maybe it is. I don't know yet. All I know is something is going down and we could really use the old G."

"As a sacrifice, the way I hear it," he said.

"Not like that at all. We're up against Vinestead on this one, and it's big time. No more petty skirmishes. We're gonna finish the war Calle Cinco started."

She flashed on the Ukrainian thrusting into a limp Kaili Zabora and winced.

"Cyn says I started the war."

Tanzy scoffed. "I don't care what that body mod junkie says. Vinestead was gonna take down the free Net one way or another. All you did was give them the excuse they were waiting for."

Gordon placed the damp handkerchief on the table next to the glass, sighed.

"That wasn't me. That was G. I'm not that goofy white kid screwing around in his dorm room anymore."

"Clearly."

"And I don't really plan on sticking around for any war with Vinestead."

"*Clearly*," she repeated, motioning to his bag.

"You and Cyn can play UltraKill hackers all you want, but I'm gonna go find a nice hole to crawl into. Vinestead doesn't have much presence in South America, so—"

"You ever been raped, Gordon?"

The question caught him off guard. "Excuse me?"

"Raped. Held down and penetrated against your will."

"Can't say I have." His eyebrows furrowed.

Tanzy leaned forward in her chair. "I just watched a woman get raped. I watched a man drug her and force his dick into her."

"Jesus…"

"And you know what? Maybe that doesn't really matter in the grand scheme of things. When they write the history of the war against Vinestead, they probably won't mention the time Kaili Zabora got pounded in the ass by some Ukrainian goon."

"Zabora?"

"Why did you come sit down over here?" asked Tanzy.

Your heart rate is elevated again.

"I'm waiting—"

"Don't give me that bullshit, Gordon. There are plenty of seats by the door and more outside. You could have waited in your room for your ride to arrive. You came over here because you saw me sitting alone and crying."

He shifted in his seat.

"That's the old G I remember. Yeah, you were a dick to noobs like UltraKill, but you were always friendly to me. You can sense when people need your help, and so can I. Kaili Zabora needs my help. *That's* what this is about to me now, because that's what this war is really about… the people. You don't abandon your friends, and everyone, *everyone* who isn't Vinestead is our friend. You, me, Cyn, Danny… we're in this together, like it or not."

Gordon lowered his head, sighed.

"Twenty years ago, you made friends with a thirteen-year-old girl who knew nothing about the Net. You helped her take control of it, carve out her own piece of it. Now that same little girl is sitting across from you asking for your help because she's never killed anyone, and she's never been shot at before. She's never taken down an entire cipher den with a couple of guns and her bare hands."

Gordon flashed recognition, smiled weakly.

"It's nice to see you again, Tanzy."

TWENTY-SEVEN
GORDON

They argued late into the night. Gordon only half-listened to the shouting coming from the small conference room off the main lounge. Tanzy had invited him in a few times, with the ostensible goal being to support her claim that Kaili Zabora needed help and that her well-being was more important than a virus or anomaly or whatever in VNet. Her friend, Danny, held the opposite opinion, that Kaili's predicament wasn't important, and that if she had mattered at all, Johnny San Vito would have sent some video to Danny instead of Lincoln.

Gordon's fingers ached as they pecked at the little plastic keys on his laptop. He'd bought the computer himself at a small shop two blocks over from Decker Plaza. The clerk, a young punk with spiked piercings in his cheeks, had almost laughed when Gordon had asked for a handheld device with a true, physical keyboard after being offered something called a palette, which looked more like an old-school viewee with a shitty on-screen keyboard with absolutely no haptic feedback.

How the hackers of the modern world got anything done without being able to feel their position on the keyboard baffled him. And yet, that seemed to be the way it was done now. Cyn was adept at it; she could type quickly with only one hand. Others, like Danny's girlfriend, Jane, could bang out novels with just two thumbs tapping on her phone's screen.

Gordon preferred the old way, with two little nubs pressing into the well-worn indentations in his index fingers. He liked a screen with a cursor, liked the accuracy of a pixel-width pointer over a stubby finger. And most of all, he liked a screen without fingerprints on it, something pristine with a little gloss and high contrast.

As the night wore on, the number of tabs in his browser kept growing. Every name that came tumbling out of the conference room went into Umbra's resident search engine, Luna Reach, such that Gordon had tabs open on Danny Guns Montreal, Kaili Zabora, Calle Cinco, and Johnny San Vito. Hour after hour, he read about the history of the hacking scene since the turn of the century, how cipher dens had grown into almost reputable organizations, and how Vinestead had further tightened its grip on the world's population.

It was 2:00 a.m. when the words on the screen began to dance and slide around. Gordon rubbed his eyes with his palms and leaned back as far as he dared on the barstool. A series of cracks climbed his back, echoing in the quiet lounge. He glanced over at Jane who had been sitting on the couch all night, tapping away on her phone, seemingly unfazed by having to wait. She had the air of an NPC waiting to be called back into the game. The few times Gordon had tried to engage her, she'd responded with curt answers delivered in a less-than-cordial monotone. It was only when Danny came out of the conference room a few times to hit the bathroom that her face brightened again.

"Been that kind of night, huh?"

Gordon raised his eyebrows at Bryce. Sweat beaded on the man's shaved head, as if he'd just come out of a sauna. He slipped behind the bar and served himself a tall glass of iced water. It went down in two gulps.

"Better than yours," Gordon answered.

Bryce smiled wryly, nodded. "Been in the tunnels all night, looking for Kevin. Tanzy said he was shooting at someone last time she saw him."

"And?"

Bryce filled another glass. "And…" He sipped, coughed. "Found the casings, but no Kevin."

"I'm sorry, man."

"Don't be sorry," said Bryce. "I found that little fucker an hour ago at Sim Pai over on XOR Street. He just went there. Like, got into a gunfight and then made for the sim parlor. Who does that?"

"Kids," said Gordon. "I don't understand them anymore."

"Grow some balls, Danny!"

They both turned to the slightly open conference room door.

Bryce smiled. "I only know Tanzy from her I.C.E-1 ads in darknets. Never seen her like this, though. Danny must be hating life right now."

"Danny Guns Montreal," Gordon recited, "celebrity hacker for hire, whatever that means, virtual recluse and known associate of Johnny San Vito."

"Droppin' knowledge bombs." Bryce leaned back against the sink. "The way Lincoln tells it, she, Danny, and Johnny were a thing in the before time." He cleared his throat. "Or, I guess, after your time."

His time. The late 90s. He'd been a sophomore then, walking the hot sidewalks of the University of Texas with fifty thousand other students. When Gordon looked back on those memories, he saw the goofy white kid Tanzy had described, a boy on the cusp of manhood and totally unprepared for what was coming. So much had changed after meeting X and Natalie. He'd climbed aboard a train that had sped into a land of death and killing. And when it was all over, he'd no longer recognized himself.

Not a boy. Not a man.

Just a loose cable that needed to be pulled from the switch.

"My best friend was murdered by a cipher den when I was 19. I tried to save him, but that just provoked a virus that then devoured the Net. Because of me, Vinestead now controls virtual reality, and hackers have been forced into standalone darknets, cut off from the rest of the world. Everything that is happening today is because of me. We're still in my time, son."

"You're the kind of old school hacker they make sims out of," said Bryce. "Never thought I'd meet one. No biochip. Never been to VNet. Still cracking skulls with your own two hands." He took a drink. "Dying breed."

"Aren't we all…"

The doors to the conference room swung open then, and a beleaguered Lincoln Tate walked out with his coat draped over his arm. He'd unbuttoned his purple shirt; a loosened black tie hung below the opening. When he saw Gordon and Bryce looking at him, he rolled his eyes and nodded to the bar.

"Whiskey neat," he said. "Please, Bryce."

"You got it, Linc."

"Sounded rough in there," said Gordon.

"Those two have some unresolved issues that run deep." Lincoln placed his hands on the bar; his rings sparkled under the mood lighting. "But, I think we have a solution that might work. It's gonna depend on you and Cyn though." He picked up his glass of whiskey. "And you too, Bryce."

"I'm down for whatever."

"You find Kevin?"

Bryce nodded. "Banging robotic octopus hookers at Sim Pai."

Lincoln grunted. "And what about you, Mr. King? Are you down for whatever?"

"Nope. But I'll listen to what you need and tell you if I can help."

"Do you know what kind of work Tanzy does?" he asked.

"She's the suit of a cipher den called Ice One, which is actually somehow pronounced Ice Prime."

Lincoln nodded approvingly.

"He's been studying," said Bryce.

"And so you know about the Quatrain?"

"Not really much on the net about them," said Gordon.

"Well, all you need to know is that they're four stone-cold bitches who think fast and work faster. I showed Tanzy a video earlier, and she sent it to them."

Gordon nodded. "She mentioned that. Something about someone getting raped."

"Not just someone," said Bryce.

"Yeah," said Lincoln. "Well, the Quatrain went deep into the Astoria databank and pulled deleted footage going back to the synthetic collapse in Perion City. They found a woman who looked like Kaili Zabora going into Le Soleil Rouge in January of 2016. LSR, it's a body mod clinic. They retrofit bodies with tech. I don't know if you knew about those."

Gordon blinked a few times.

"Anyway, four months later, early May, the man we saw in the video is seen getting out of a black van and going into LSR. Comes out half an hour later with a sack the size of a young woman."

"Who's the guy?" asked Gordon.

"No fucking clue." Lincoln slid his empty glass across the bar and waited for Bryce to refill it. "Tanzy says the Quatrain is still putting his face through the Pattrn image databanks. I'm sure they'll come up with something soon, unless he's an FOB brought in special. Not the point though. Where's Cyn? She should be hearing this."

"Saw her heading back to her room earlier," said Bryce. "Want me to grab her?"

"Probably not a great idea," said Gordon. "She saw me with my bag. I was actually on my way out when I ran into Tanzy downstairs. I guess Cyn thought I was gonna stick around while you guys hashed this out."

"She's taken a shine to my man G." Bryce laughed, wiped his forehead with a towel.

"Really?" Lincoln raised an eyebrow. "What happened to that little Jackie Chan she brought back from Vietnam?"

"Huy? That dude was Vietnamese. His visa ran out like six months after he got here, and Cyn wasn't exactly interested in helping him renew."

"No shit?" asked Lincoln.

"You don't remember that? Been a couple years."

Lincoln smiled at Gordon. "Guess I was busy running a media empire."

"You were getting to a point?" asked Gordon.

From the couch, Jane chuckled.

"Yeah, alright. So when that van takes off from LSR, it's just out in the open. Traffic cameras had it all the way down the coast to Sacramento. They went east from there to Folsom. You know what's in Folsom, Mr. King?"

Gordon shrugged. "The prison?"

"Not since 2005. Now it's a for-profit criminal rehabilitation center owned by…"

"Vinestead," said Gordon.

"Smart man," said Lincoln. "So the van drives in, man gets out, opens the back doors. Two guys in white jumpers come out and grab the Kaili Zabora bag and take it inside. And so far, the Quatrain hasn't found any footage of the Butcher of Burbank walking out of there."

"So she's been there... what... three years?"

"Best guess at the moment. Vinestead's probably got her chained up in a cell deep underground. I don't think she's ever getting out of there without some help."

A fresh glass of whiskey appeared on the bar. Bryce slid it to Gordon.

"And that's where you and Cyn come in, Mr. King. She has an unprovisioned, mil-spec Ayudante biochip and augments out the ass. And you, well, she told me what you did to those Vinestead synthetics at Lost Pines. You two should have no trouble getting into Folsom."

"And I'll be overwatch," said Bryce.

"Oh, well, sign me the fuck up." Gordon took a sip of the whiskey, groaned at the sickly fire erupting in his stomach. He burped, turned his laptop so Lincoln could see the screen. "Everything I've read about Kaili Zabora says she's at the top of Vinestead's shit list. So what makes you think the two of us—"

Bryce cleared his throat.

"Beg your pardon," said Gordon, "the *three* of us. What makes you think we'll be able to storm a maximum-security prison where Vinestead just happens to be holding their most valuable prisoner? Don't you think security's gonna be extra tight around there? And that's on top of the normal razor wire and surveillance systems."

Lincoln huffed. "Don't overthink it, Mr. King. Razor wire can be torn down. Security cameras can be shut off remotely. You'll have Lincoln Continental and I.C.E-1 backing you up. All you and your fists of steel need to worry about are the meatbags standing between you and the woman who runs the most dangerous cipher den in America. Having Calle Cinco in your debt can get you far in this country. Far away, too. Dig?"

Gordon considered the offer, shook his head. He didn't need a cipher den's help to get out of the country. A private plane could take him over the MX and drop him somewhere in Panama or Columbia. Then he'd just disappear into the countryside, never to be seen again. It was far enough away that Vinestead likely wouldn't be able to touch him, nor would his memories.

For some reason, Lincoln was under the impression that Gordon gave a damn about anything except putting as much distance between himself and the memory of that night in the Austonian twenty years ago. That was the true threat to his well-being, and the longer he stayed plugged into the real world, the greater the chance he'd sniff Natalie out of the ether. Too much time had gone by to reconnect now. Too many apologies had gone unsaid.

"That's not the only problem," said Gordon, wetting his suddenly dry lips with the whiskey. "I don't think Kaili Zabora is gonna be happy to see me."

"*You* know the Butcher?" asked Bryce.

"Nope."

"She know you?" asked Lincoln.

"She knows *of* me."

"How would Kaili Zabora know about an old school hacker who hasn't been seen in twenty years?"

Gordon stared at the ice melting in his glass.

"I killed her sister."

Lincoln put a hand to his face.

Gordon stared straight ahead and finished off the whiskey.

TWENTY-EIGHT
DANNY

At some point, the arguing just had to stop.

Tanzy could lobby all night for Kaili Zabora's welfare, but there was nothing she could say to convince Danny to abandon what he considered the main mission in favor of some dangerous side quest that promised little reward. By the end of it, Danny was more tired of the constant back and forth than anything else. Tanzy had worn him down, made the act of arguing the focal point of his anger. In the end, knowing no resolution could be reached, he'd simply walked out of the conference room with Tanzy hurling insults at his back.

Lincoln himself had shown Danny and Jane to a room on the other side of the tower. He'd said little regarding Tanzy, preferring to make idle conversation with Jane as they walked the carpeted hallway. At the door, he bade her a good night, gave Danny a weak smile, and left them standing just inside the open door.

Jane wasted no time shutting out the world. She engaged the electronic deadbolt and tested the door for good measure.

"The sun will be coming up soon," she said, reaching for the buttons on her blouse. "We should get some rest, start fresh in the morning." She tossed the shirt to the side, adjusted the shoulder straps of a velvet red bra.

Danny reached for her, drew her into an embrace. He buried his nose in her neck, breathed in, and pressed his body against hers. He felt her arms wrap around him, felt hands slide over his spine. He'd been overcome by a desire to hold her, to feel accepted in someone's arms.

"It's alright," she whispered, running her fingers through his hair. "It's just you and me now. Just you and me."

He nodded, mumbled, "But when I let you go…"

"There's no rush. I have all the time in the world for you."

In fact, she didn't. It was technically Wednesday, and Friday was coming fast. Soon, Jane Meade would return to the ether and disappear for another six months.

"I wish you'd stay forever," he said.

"I know."

He pulled back, looked into her eyes. "No, I mean it."

"*I know*," she replied.

They stood swaying in each other's arms until Danny's eyes got heavy.

"Let's get into bed," whispered Jane.

Just the thought of clean sheets and a firm mattress made his body ache. There was a throbbing in his neck, a feeling like he couldn't turn to either side. The pain in his leg was merely a footnote to the full-body fatigue he felt.

"I want to," he replied, "but I need to do some work first."

She withdrew from his embrace, smiled. "If that's what you want. I'm gonna run a bath. I'll meet you between the sheets when you're done." She stood on her tiptoes to kiss him on the nose.

Danny stood for a few minutes, swaying a little as he half-listened to Jane move around in the bathroom. It was hard to imagine she had done the same thing just a few days ago in his cabin in Vail. Then, he had felt none of the tension and aggravation he was feeling now. In fact, he'd been overcome with anticipation of her visit, imagining a week away from the ones and zeros. There would have been drinking and hot tubs and snowmobiling and sex and synth and everything he needed to take a vacation from himself.

Now, he'd been sucked back to the dying days of the Reinhardt Triumvirate, arguing with Tanzy over whether to avenge Johnny's death or put his life on the line for a powerful but mentally unstable suit.

It was just like Tanzy to look past her friends at a shinier prize. The Triumvirate had never been about Johnny and Danny for her; all she had wanted was a springboard to something bigger and better, something that commanded more respect. And it wasn't necessarily her ambition that grated, but the nonchalance with which she went about chasing it. The disregard she'd demonstrated for Johnny and Danny was just too much.

Danny closed a hand into a fist and cursed Tanzy's name. He glanced at a small table next to the door where someone had delivered his rig and some fresh clothes for both he and Jane. Danny grabbed the rig pack and tossed it onto the foot of the bed. His palette beeped throughout a self-scan, letting him know with dulcet tones that the moment of insertion was coming soon.

He sat down with his back against the bed, slipped on the immersion rig, and listened to the familiar beeping count him down. He closed his eyes, and in the darkness, saw Tanzy silhouetted against a window, her hands on her hips, her eyes burning with a fire he hadn't seen in years.

A rush of electrical signals jumped the gap between the rig and his Syzygy, yanking his conscious mind into a world that, in many ways, just made more sense.

He arrived in VNet with all the fanfare of a local high school sports hero returning to his hometown after thirty years. A series of numbers flashed in front of him; they morphed into stars as the server accepted each digit of his passcode. Small white fireworks exploded in the periphery, sizzling so close to his virtual ears that he could almost feel their heat.

The VNet insertion protocol was supposed to make users feel welcome, make them feel proud for choosing VNet over any other inferior virtual reality product. Most users hated the splash screen and turned it off as soon as possible. Danny hadn't seen the splash in years, but after his last insertion, he'd decided to scramble his VID and start fresh with one of his throwaway accounts. Everything from his digital signature down to the hardware IDs in his rig reset, making him appear like a new user to the watchful eyes of Vinestead security.

A circle spun in the air in front of him, giving off tiny concentric circles of light that painted the previously invisible room around him. The faster the circle spun, the more Danny could see of the default welcome room. Only, the walls weren't the usual desert sand and there were no windows showing green pastures and blue skies and gently rolling dunes.

Instead, the dingy gray walls around him were uncomfortably close. A bucket of stagnant water pressed against his leg. The room smelled of abrasive chemicals, but at the same time was musty and stale itself. An old-style filament bulb hung from the ceiling of the tiny room and illuminated a brown door with a copper-plated handle that had been worn to the underlying metal.

Danny reached for the handle, pushed the door open.

Bright, fluorescent lights stung his eyes for a moment before the Syzygy dampened the input. Long rows of chest-high display cases stretched out in front of him. They were lined with movies—original DVD cases in front of a handful of ugly white boxes stamped with Blockbuster graphics.

"Can I help you with something, sir?"

Danny craned his neck, saw the question had come from a young girl sitting behind the counter at the front of the store. He remembered her face from—

The Syzygy buzzed in alarm.

Brigham Plaza.

Somehow, he'd jacked right back into a place he thought might be impossible to reach again. Not only that, he'd done it wearing an avatar the server didn't know, couldn't know. How then had he come to walk the aisles at Blockbuster in an inaccessible construct?

Had he missed something in his rig wipe? Or had Bullets somehow found a way to identify his unique combination of immersion hardware and biochip to effectively tether Danny to Brigham Plaza?

"Um, no," he said. "I just… I don't know how I got here."

The girl narrowed her eyes, gestured to the double doors to her right.

"The door opened. You came in." She turned her attention back to the oversized SPIN magazine in her hands. "Hell of a day."

Danny stepped out of the aisles and headed to the front. He passed cardboard barrels full of used DVDs, their covers marred by garish yellow stickers with ludicrously low prices on them. When was the last time he'd seen a movie go for less than twenty bucks on streaming, let alone for the three dollars Blockbuster was asking?

He'd just passed a display of boxed candy when the sizzling started, something like the sound of a fuse burning but modulated down a few octaves. He stopped short as a speck of gold light appeared in front of him. Quietly, such that Danny had to lean in, the speck roared like a ball of fire tearing down a hallway. Black folds appeared as the thing grew, bulging on all sides. The heat it gave off forced Danny to take a step back.

"What the hell is this?"

The girl looked up. "Milk Duds."

"No, this little…" Danny waved a finger in the air. "This explosion."

She raised her eyebrows, looked where he was pointing. With a sigh, she returned to her magazine. "Look, man. It doesn't bother me if you're tripping, but my manager isn't gonna like it. If you can't pull it together long enough to rent a disc, then I'm gonna have to ask you to leave."

It *was* an explosion; Danny was sure of it.

An explosion in action, still moving, still growing.

How fast it was growing was a question better answered by the Syzygy. He stared at the speck for a minute to let the chip take measurements and extrapolate a growth pattern.

Danny asked how long it would take for the explosion to overtake the entire construct.

The Syzygy answered with *twenty-seven minutes.*

He recalled Bullets ordering a pizza.

Thirty minutes or less or it's free, right?

It wasn't a lot of time to explore the entire strip mall, let alone figure out what secrets the so-called Bullets was hiding there. Danny decided to make the most of his time, choosing to ignore for the moment that he'd been drawn back into the honeypot without his permission.

At the exit, he paused.

"What's the phone number to this store?"

"801—"

"Thanks," said Danny. He stepped outside into the humid air and looked around.

A quick search revealed area code 801 to be in Provo, Utah, so at least now he knew where this place was supposed to be. While he was searching the horizon for landmarks, he noticed the younger version of Bullets he'd seen last time. The kid went into the Blockbuster and struck up a conversation with the cashier, all while the explosion roared behind him.

Then, like a subtle popping of his ears, Danny felt another presence enter the construct. The digital signature matched the one he'd met before. Bullets must have been running some kind of intrusion notification, though it seemed to lag behind Danny's actual appearance in the construct.

That lag gave him a window of time, no matter how short, to exploit the construct.

Bullets drew closer, still obscured by the limited draw distance.

A confrontation was the last thing Danny needed at the moment, and besides, there was still more he wanted to know before the final showdown.

Danny waved his hand palm-up in small circles until a silver sphere with two little blades appeared above it. With a glance to the sky, the sphere rose to the top of the construct and bathed it in a deep blue matrix of lasers. Telemetry data flooded into his biochip along with a three-dimensional map of the entire strip mall. He flashed on a wireframe of the main complex, jagged like the face of a cliff, with a parking lot rounding off the edges.

Bullets had only built the strip mall map from side street to side street; everything beyond that was just empty ether. Except...

Danny squinted, tried to see the image more clearly in his mind. There was something behind the Blockbuster and the Domino's where an alley should have been. Instead of a service road, the asphalt gave way to gently sloping ground that extended to a small hill in the distance. Atop the hill sat a four-story mansion, vaguely Victorian, with a bright moon blooming behind it.

Soundless lightning flashed, but only as reflections in its windows.

"Take a picture. It'll last longer."

Danny opened his eyes and saw Bullets standing in front of the Blockbuster. With a flick of his arm, he reached back and pulled the growing explosion through the windows. Flames burst through the glass, warped around Bullets' avatar, and headed straight for Danny.

Heat grazed his cheeks for a moment before he pixelated and jacked out.

TWENTY-NINE
KAILI

"There are right and wrong ways to handle incoming data."

Kaili let the memory of Alex Trent, one of Calle Cinco's former recruiters, wash over her.

"It's just like driving a car. Now, you can be like one of those nervous housewives constantly scanning in front and behind and side-to-side. You're watching for cars slowing down or entering your lane. You're checking for speeders rolling up on your ass or maybe an ambulance cutting down the shoulder. It's too much data; the brain can't be that vigilant all the time."

The conversation had come only a few weeks after Kaili joined up with Calle Cinco, and there had been plenty of drinks and synth to go around. She hadn't known at the time that the synth wasn't designed to get her high, but rather to enhance her recall of everything that had been dumped on her during training.

"Or, you can be like the distracted captain of industry in his Porsche who believes the roads were built just for him. He doesn't give a shit about the data passing outside his tinted windows. He ignores other drivers, doesn't signal, and weaves in and out of traffic to avoid ever slowing down. But we can't be like that either, Kaili. We can't dismiss what's happening to us, even if it's easier or less painful. We have to face the data one way or another."

Kaili slumped in the stool, her hands hanging between her knees. The walls of the ticketing station seemed to press in on her.

She looked at nothing in particular.

"So how should you drive?" continued Trent. "Should you treat other drivers like obstacles? Watch every move they make? No. What you want to do is drift. And by that I mean allow the data to wash over you, but instead of analyzing each bit, reduce the stimuli into a general impression of what is happening. Think colors and shapes instead of patterns and edges. You'll save yourself the processing power if you don't examine every single one and zero the network throws at you.

"Let it wash, Kaili. Be above the stream, not in it. Never forget the infinite chasm between you and reality. Your senses will always try to bridge that gap, and they will, if you let them. What I'm going to teach you is how to dial down your perception and muddy your synapses. Then, nothing will ever be able to hurt you. You'll be invincible."

Kaili wiped the sweat from her forehead. Undulating chills ran down her spine, swallowed up by the heat of her augments. The constant shifts in temperature made her stomach contract and expand in nauseating waves.

Drifting had saved her from most of what Sedivy had wanted her to see. When she brought the video feed into focus, the Ukrainian man was fully dressed again, leaning against the wall and playing with his phone. More men arrived, one of them carrying a small video camera. The vidscreens dimmed and returned as a multi-screen presentation of the camera's POV. Kaili heard one of the men refer to her attacker as Nazar. She stored the name deep in her databank.

Nazar issued orders in gruff Ukrainian, but Kaili understood what he was telling the men. One of them produced a black body bag and laid it out on the floor. The others lifted Kaili from the pod and placed her on top of it. For a moment, they stood around gawking at her, until Nazar told them to zip her up and carry her out.

The camera followed the procession down the halls of Le Soleil Rouge, past the bodies of Ginger and Ramona, down the spiral staircase, and out the front door. The trip from the doors to the waiting van took only a few seconds, with barely enough time to gauge the time of day or season. There wasn't any snow on the ground, though the evercrete sidewalk had a sheen to it.

Wet ground in Astoria wasn't much of a clue, but it wasn't snow.

Kaili resumed her drift as the video jumped ahead. Grainy images flitted by, sometimes showing the coastline, other times an endless sea of redwoods. Night fell, day rose, and every once in a while, the camera held steady on the body bag as Nazar injected something into Kaili's arm.

Finally, she caught a glimpse of something familiar in the stream—downtown Sacramento.

Sacramento, where Calle Cinco had fired the first shots of an oft-promised war with Vinestead International. Were they bringing her back to the beginning to make an example out of her? Maybe to string her up by the ankles from the highest floors of the Vinestead West building?

The skyline receded and the camera caught the fading signage along the Lincoln Highway, which turned into the 50 as they traveled east. Small, hollowed-out suburbs scrolled by, left for dead in the desert by a mass transit system that simply couldn't reach that far. Like shriveled leaves on a plant, these micro-cities sank deeper into poverty and lawlessness the farther they got from civilization.

Farther from the city, but closer to…

The road signs changed from green to orange once the van turned off the highway. For a while, it appeared they were passing through another generic suburb—movie theaters and an outlet mall appeared through the grimy windows.

Traffic thinned as the landscape turned more wooded. Nazar barked an order and the men quickly stowed their weapons on shelves along the top of the van. One of them pulled a duffel bag from a locker and began handing out drab brown jumpers.

Kaili covered her mouth as Nazar began to undress again, only to pull on his new uniform with the words *Folsom Rehabilitation Center* written across the breast pocket.

The video cut out just as the van passed through a high, chain-link gate topped with razor wire. The vidscreen wall came alive again, showing various feeds throughout the Folsom campus. Kaili focused on the view from an underground garage where Nazar was opening the back doors of the van. A small team of white-scrubbed attendants stood by with a gurney and waited patiently as the men moved the body bag onto it.

Nazar gave a little wave. Kaili gave the screen the finger.

"A few years ago," said Sedivy, his face appearing just to the left of the main vidscreen, "a group of students at Berkeley did some exploratory research into the application of virtual reality in criminal rehabilitation. Evidently, those burlap-wearing tree-huggers weren't fans of our ReTread program, which we pioneered right here at Folsom. And I guess there are some left-wing progressives in our government who find it less than human as well. I think we had the program up barely a year before I had the director of the CDCR calling me asking for an alternative."

The gurney rolled through the dank, empty hallways, turning unmarked corners seemingly at random. LEDs phased in and out on the ceiling as it passed.

"The jury's still out on what exactly rehabilitates a serial killer, so we tried to avoid any kind of aversion therapy or negative reinforcement. We're not psychologists; we're innovators. We build technology. So while I couldn't give them a fool-proof rehab program, I could provide them with an essential tool for keeping the incorrigible safe and secluded during their time behind bars."

Lights came up in an operating theater; the camera looked down from high above the table. A dozen men in gray and black suits filled the observation area. They ceased their idle chatter as the gurney pushed through the double doors.

Kaili watched as her body was unceremoniously removed from the bag and dumped onto the operating table.

She closed her eyes, drifted toward the memory of Rick, imagining his cold body lying on a metal slab at the Sacramento morgue.

"I'm sorry, is this boring you?" asked Sedivy.

"Listening to you talk is worse than torture," Kaili mumbled.

"Oh I doubt that. But if you'd rather let the video speak for itself, so be it. Just don't come crying to me with questions later on."

His voice crackled, cut out. Murmurs from the men in the audience rose to fill the room. Their words were hard to make out, but Kaili heard her name mentioned a few times.

A woman in white scrubs pushed through the operating room doors with her gloves held high. Two nurses flanked her on either side.

"Good morning, everyone," she said, addressing the audience. "I'm Dr. Crystal Royce, and I'll be preparing Ms. Zabora for integration into virtual population today. At Mr. Sedivy's request, I'll be providing more commentary than I typically do during these procedures. Nurse?"

The nurse on the right touched a wall of monitors.

Dr. Royce continued. "Our scans show muscular and skeletal augments in the patient's left arm. Rather than spend the time decoupling the augments from the patient's body, we're going to proceed with amputation just below the shoulder. Growth of the augmentation matrix in the upper arm is minimal, so we'll be able to fish out anything that has slipped through. Let's begin."

A nurse pressed a green *PREP* button on a nearby vidscreen. A mechanical arm rose up from the operating table between Kaili's feet. It moved in tiny spurts, placing electrodes at strategic points on her body while the nurse inserted an IV line into Kaili's right arm. The other nurse pulled straps from the sides of the table and tied her down.

Dr. Royce reached for a tray of tools and lifted the bone saw. She tested the blade a few times while a nurse applied a tourniquet to Kaili's left arm.

The sliver embedded in Kaili's wrist caught the bright lights of the operating room.

In the construct, Kaili touched the blackened stump where her arm used to be. Had they really taken it from her?

"Is this supposed to shock me?"

The video shifted to the audience. A smiling Arthur Sedivy turned and looked back into the camera but said nothing.

Kaili clenched her jaw as Dr. Royce began to cut into her arm. What did one limb matter anyway? She could walk into any body mod joint in Umbra and have a new, better arm fitted within a day. Sure, it'd never be the same as her original equipment, but it would be stronger, more powerful. At least this way, she wouldn't have to go through the trauma and pain of losing her arm in the first place.

The dark streets of Astoria came back to her, along with the searing pain and the crack of a rifle shot.

"I can still take down Vinestead with just one arm."

"I don't doubt it," said Sedivy.

The feed refocused on a nurse dropping Kaili's arm into a bio-waste container.

"I could take every limb from your body, reduce you to a lump of gray matter floating in a tank, and you'd still find a way to make trouble for me."

"Then why not just kill me and get it over with?" Kaili rose from the stool and kicked it aside.

"Quiet. We're coming to the best part."

Dr. Royce pointed at Kaili's head, and the nurses began fitting a white facemask over it, clamping it down to the table. The doctor turned to face the audience.

"The patient has a Class Four unbranded jackport and biochip."

Kaili's legs went soft. She put a hand on the wall for support.

"We will now remove the biochip and install a prototype third-generation Guardian Angel. As the patient will be in VR for the remainder of her life, we will skip the grow-wire installation and other non-essential operations. Scalpel, please."

"No!" screamed Kaili; ripples tore through the station, creating long, meandering cracks in the wallpaper.

Sedivy chuckled. "Welcome to the Vinestead family, Ms. Zabora."

Kaili tried to scream again, but no sound would come. Saliva dripped from her lips as her stomach heaved.

Trent whispered in her ear.

Float above the stream, Kaili. Not in it.

She pushed everything away—the video, the sound of Sedivy's cackling, and the possibility that somewhere out there the real Kaili Zabora now had a Guardian Angel biochip implanted in her neck.

The visual feed pixelated; ambient sounds modulated into a low hum. Kaili dropped through the floor of the construct and descended through an ever-thickening cloud of ethereal mist. It chilled her bones and forced her thoughts inward where it was still warm.

"Leaving so soon?" asked Sedivy, his voice distant.

Sensory input muted to a slight rustling of leaves falling to the ground, punctuated by the distant calls of seagulls flying above Coronado Beach.

Underneath it all, she heard Anela calling her name.

THIRTY

TANZY

Rain pelted a blocky shack in the Reykjavik darknet.

Throughout the day and well into the night, wind gusted like the fevered sighs of a restless demon, until all at once, everything stopped and settled into a frightening stillness that paralyzed the entire construct. In those moments, Tanzy could hear the plastic clicking of Phantasm's fingers on multiple keyboards.

He'd set up a small command center in the corner of the shack between the fireplace and a decrepit wooden table. There, a grid of six vidscreens climbed the wall, each of them scrolling text at a speed no normal human could follow. Output overflowed like multicolored waterfalls, dumping bright reds, greens, blues, and whites onto a black background. Tanzy knew from experience that each of the colors had a special meaning for her brother, though she hadn't yet been able to figure out his method fully.

Tanzy sat on the floor in the center of the room on a worn wool carpet that had once held the image of an Icelandic mermaid sitting atop a rocky outcropping in the middle of a swell, her eyes and bare breasts pointing high into a formidable, black sky. Now, all that remained were impressions of color—dark blue, murky black, and in the center, a streak of green and flesh.

Around her, she'd arranged a series of five portals that floated a few inches off the ground and angled back for optimum viewing. Four of them were labeled for the Quatrain—Cherry, Whisper, Strider, and Princess. The center portal contained her workspace, and at present, showed a wireframe map of the California State Prison. A small portion of the desktop scrolled names of current inmates and categorized each one with a question mark, a red *X*, or a green check mark.

The Quatrain was hard at work searching the guest registry at CSP Sacramento, a sister facility to Folsom that held the dirtbags who weren't quite dirtbag enough to make it to the big house. The girls were trying to find someone who would fit the bill for what Tanzy had in mind. So far, there had only been a few green checkmarks, and those Tanzy had already dismissed after a cursory inspection.

"The girls aren't finding anyone," she muttered, glancing over her shoulder at Phantasm.

He'd leaned back in his chair like a gamer entering their sixth hour of playing some point-and-click role-playing adventure. If it hadn't been for his hands jumping back and forth over the three keyboards, she might have thought he was sleeping.

"Ah, well, I told you, Vinestead keeps all the best political prisoners next door at Folsom. Still not sure why we don't use someone there."

Tanzy stretched her back.

Phantasm had the realism in the Reyk construct dialed up to eleven to give him more feedback from the keyboards and let him type faster than he could out in Terrareal, which was all well and good for him, but it meant Tanzy's body couldn't stay seated on the floor forever, and every once in a while, she had to get up to stretch her legs.

It was a small price to pay to get her brother working at maximum speed. The Quatrain was the best group of ciphers she could have ever hoped for, but they were geared toward big data stuff—cracking databases, processing large amounts of information, and seeking out nude photos of a feed monger's wife. Phantasm was a hard worker, and if given a task, he could be relied on to carry it out while the Quatrain worked on more important things.

"Hello?" asked Phantasm.

"Oh, was that a serious question?" Tanzy pitched her voice in mock surprise. "You really want to know why we're not faking a prison break at the prison we're actually trying to break into?"

"Oh, yeah." He chuckled to himself. "Well, whatever. I'm gonna be in their building OS in ten minutes."

Tanzy pulled up the record of another green checkmark.

"The same way you were gonna check on Johnny, huh?"

"That wasn't my fault. You sent me to Atlantic City. What did you think was gonna happen?"

The photo attached to the dossier phased into true color, showing a middle-aged man with curly black hair that fell forward over low eyebrows—brooding eyebrows. His mouth was set in a severe line that ticked up on the right side, as if he had a secret to tell.

"I thought you would do what I asked you to do."

Phantasm snorted. "Like it mattered. Johnny's dead anyway."

"I haven't seen his body," said Tanzy, absently.

"It was all over the feeds, sis."

"Feeds lie," said Tanzy. "Everyone lies."

As detailed in his dossier, Marshall Alan Dougherty had done his share of lying. His rap sheet started with petty crimes in his youth and ended with six counts of premeditated murder in 2013. Dougherty had led a small cabal of well-connected enforcers known as the Marshall Plan, which in his absence, had declared publicly and on numerous occasions that they wouldn't rest until their leader was released from his undeserved captivity.

"Got him," said Tanzy. She pushed the record to the Quatrain and tossed a three-dimensional copy over to Phantasm.

He looked up for a moment before returning to his screens.

"I heard about that guy," he said. "Killed those girls in San Francisco, right?"

"Guess so," said Tanzy.

"Why do you want to bust *him* out?"

Tanzy leaned forward through her screens and put her elbows on the soft rug. She cradled her face with her hands.

Can I load anything for you? asked Cleo.

"Load me a new brother," whispered Tanzy.

Perhaps a sister instead?

"I wish." She took in a deep, musty breath. "We're not breaking *that* guy out of prison, Michael. We're just pretending to. And it has to be someone worth breaking out, someone with connections, or Vinestead won't take it seriously. All I need you to do is find Dougherty's cell and when I tell you, open every door between him and the outside world."

Phantasm stopped typing, turned in his chair.

"But why Dougherty?"

Tanzy plied a chunk of wood from the floor and chucked it at Phantasm. He put up a hand and stopped it in mid-air. The wood splintered into a million little pixels, dissipated. By her leg, the construct drew in a new section of the floor.

For a moment, they stared intently at each other.

Phantasm laughed.

Tanzy shook her head. "You're such a shit."

"Shut up, you love me," he replied, returning his attention to the screens. "I'm primed whenever you are."

"Time hack."

12:31 a.m. Pacific Standard Time.

"What about Cyn and G?"

They are in position and awaiting your signal.

Tanzy laced her fingers and stretched her arms over her head.

"Cherry, you've got Folsom Utility ready to go?"

"Of course."

"Give me rolling brownouts, every few minutes, starting on the southeast side of the city. I don't want a panic—just enough to get them thinking of siphoning off Folsom."

According to city plans, Folsom Prison, or as Vinestead called it, the Folsom Rehabilitation Center, had separated from the city's power grid in 2010, opting instead for a dedicated hydroelectric dam at the north end of Folsom Lake. Attacking that facility directly would draw too much attention, but if the city itself asked for some extra juice through automated processes, that might go unnoticed for a precious few minutes. If Cherry got the timing right, they could be leeching Folsom enough to cause their own natural brownouts. And once those hit, a full outage wouldn't seem as suspicious.

Tanzy threw a map of the city onto the wall in front of her and watched the pixels toggle off and on.

"Whisper, I need you to trend *freemarshall* and *jointhemarshallplan* on all the major feeds and social networks. Mention that his last appeal was biased and dox everyone involved in the hearing. I want full saturation in twelve minutes."

A murmur of assent flittered past Tanzy's ear. She killed the four extra vidscreens and used their space to bring up video feeds from around the prison. Aside from the sweeping spotlights, there was little activity at the facility.

"Strider, how are we doing on guard movement at Folsom?"

"Regular and methodic. No visible holes in the pattern."

"Well, hopefully we can draw them off when CSP goes to shit. Let me know as soon as we get guards crossing the map."

Phantasm got up from his chair without speaking and walked to a nearby corner. He stood for a moment rolling his shoulders and dipping his head side to side. All at once, he began throwing punches at the wall, striking hard enough to rattle the pictures hanging nearby.

"Princess," said Tanzy, "what's the current sea craft count?"

"Fourteen, with nine confirmed mobile."

"Start bringing them in. Hold a hundred yards from the bank near Folsom Lake Crossing. Keep the pattern moving and don't be quiet about it."

Phantasm let out a triumphant roar.

"Are you done?" she asked.

"All warmed up."

"Good, I need you ready in two."

"Aye aye, Captain Flannel," he said, stepping up to his table. He picked up a thin folio and extracted a code card. "Let's see, what goes best with committing multiple felonies?"

"Besides doing your damn job?"

"I gotta be in the right state of mind for this. I need all my… *power*." He flipped the code card around a few times as it cycled through a rainbow of neon colors. "You ever try *The Lord's Prayer*?"

"No," said Tanzy.

And you won't, said Cleo.

"Meltdown gave it to me. It's like if Ritalin was a person and you gave that person Ritalin. Recursively multi-threaded hyper-attentiveness."

"What does that have to do with the Lord's Prayer?"

Phantasm raised an eyebrow. "Sometimes you see God."

"Can you just load it so we can get a move on?" groaned Tanzy.

"Sir, yes, sir!" He flourished a salute with the card in his hand and then slammed it hard into his other wrist. The thin metal disappeared like a debit card into an ATM, swallowed up by unbroken flesh.

The wind died down, bringing silence to the shack. Phantasm's breathing grew deep and slow. For a moment, he stood with his head back and eyes pegged open.

Our father, who art in Heaven, said Cleo.

"Don't," Tanzy warned.

Phantasm shook, stuttering in place as a guttural sound came pouring out of his open mouth. The trembling of his body set the air around him on fire, bathing Tanzy in an oppressive heat that made her lift her hand and close her eyes. When the heat subsided, Phantasm was gone.

She found him seated at his desk in the corner, hands on separate keyboards, typing furiously.

"Just a few more things to double-check before we go-go-go," he said tightly.

"The city has requested power from Folsom Electric," said Cherry. "Current draw is ten percent."

"Increase the frequency," said Tanzy.

"Local PD is mobilizing from Lakeridge Cove. Satellite scans didn't show any craft in the area, but they're there now."

"Bring the boats closer to shore. Beach two of them. Let Cherry know when they hit. Cherry, turn those brownouts into permanent blackouts when they do."

Seconds ticked by. Tanzy's fingers found their way to her mouth.

Rain pelted the window in time with her heartbeat.

"Beached," said Whisper.

"Going to black," said Cherry.

"Open the doors, Phantasm."

"I am Phantasm, and I bring you freedom," he replied, slapping his keyboards with both hands.

"Three, two, one…" counted Tanzy.

"Movement in CSP," said Strider. "All exits open. Guards rolling to secure."

"How's Dougherty?"

"Still asleep," said Strider.

"Wake him up."

"Phantasm says, let there be light!"

"Confirmed," said Strider. "All interior and exterior lights at CSP are active."

"Any movement from Folsom?"

"None," said Strider. "Guards are maintaining normal rotations."

"Well…" Tanzy thought for a minute. Surely a little ruckus at CSP would have them calling Folsom for backup. Maybe a *little* ruckus wasn't enough.

"A live video feed from CSP has been posted to Pattrn," said Whisper.

"Alright, then let's hit 'em harder. Princess, beach all the boats. Phantasm, open all the doors."

"Opening all the doors, Captain! Cell doors! Bathroom doors! Closet doors!"

"Cherry…"

"Yes?"

Tanzy hesitated for a moment. She had spent her bag of tricks and not one guard had moved from their post at Folsom. All that remained was the great equalizer, a move that, while effective, would make their intentions all too clear.

Then again, if they quit now, Folsom would be on-guard for years to come.

"Fuck it," said Tanzy. "Take Folsom Utility and Folsom Electric off the grid."

"Wait," said Phantasm. "Let me open the doors in Folsom before you kill it."

"No!" barked Tanzy. "That's high-level Vinestead net in there. We don't want to get stuck in that spiderweb."

"But…"

"No, Michael."

"Both electrical grids are offline," said Cherry.

"Confirmed," said Strider. "Folsom's dark. I've lost visual on the guards."

Tanzy sighed.

There wasn't anything else she could do for Cyn and G now. It was up to them to get inside, find Kaili, and bring her out.

Tanzy pulled the video feed from Folsom closer, searched in the shades of black for some kind of movement.

Outside, the rain fell languidly, having spent its energy lashing the shack all day and night. And underneath the soothing sound, Tanzy could hear the clacking of fingers on keyboards.

"He's still typing, isn't he?" she whispered.

Yes, said Cleo.

"Did he touch the Folsom net?"

Yes.

"How much time do we have?"

Not enough.

Tanzy groaned, looked over her shoulder at her brother.

"You just had to, didn't you?"

He shrugged.

"I am Phantasm, and I fear no network, no ice, and no man."

One by one, the screens in front of him went dark.

THIRTY-ONE
GORDON

The walls of the construct were a translucent white, bulging like rounded prisms, lit from behind by an unseen source. Streaks of primary colors broke off from the corners of the room like lens flares from multiple suns. Gordon recalled how futuristic the space had looked the first time he saw it, how its spacious footprint had been twice the size of his dorm room at UT.

Now, the construct felt as if it had contracted in the decades since, shriveled up like a desiccated animal left in the open air. His presence seemed to overwhelm the simulation, and for a horrible moment, he thought maybe he had left the code cube dormant for too long, that twenty years was too much for the ROM to burn fuel in a holding pattern.

He remembered the display on the far wall, a large rectangular stamp in the white material. It was on, though the image it showed was faded to nothing. He could barely make out the words *Synaptic Synth* in large, blocky letters.

"Welcome back," said a soft voice.

Just as he had in another lifetime, Gordon turned and watched the last pixels of Alessandra's avatar fall into place. She was as regal as ever, towering over him by a good six inches and dressed in snug clothing that implied caged sexuality.

"Ale," he said, pronouncing both syllables with a practiced Spanish accent. "It's good to see you again."

She folded her hands. "It's been quite some time since we last met. How can I help you today?"

Gordon smirked. She wasn't being passive-aggressive. Alessandra was from a time before pseudo-AI and was nothing more than a promotional avatar with a host of pre-programmed responses. Though she remembered her interactions with him, she had no feelings about them. She had no feelings at all.

"Do you remember the mass uninstall we did last time?"

"Of course." She gestured to the vidscreen on the wall. "We removed 742 modules along with their related data stores. Do you wish to uninstall additional modules?"

Gordon watched a list scroll on the display, long-forgotten names of packaged knowledge he'd once downloaded in an orgiastic feast of self-improvement. Ancient programming languages like BASIC, COBOL, and Haskell appeared in the list, as did outdated routing protocols like RIP and IGRP. Each name came with an associated uninstall date and storage size.

So much data.

So many synaptic bridges burned.

It had not been a trivial task—removing knowledge from a human brain. Alessandra had warned him about it at the time, telling him in no uncertain terms there was no scalpel in the world that could cut out only what he had downloaded from her. All she had was a spoon, and that spoon would take with it all of the surrounding synapses, including his experiences, memories, and other, unknown parts of his consciousness.

Such was the price of cheating the system, of using software to download knowledge instead of learning it through instruction and practice.

The list stopped after *Zenith Brandt Analytical Models*, ending on an empty line with no name but an associated storage size. The number, however, was a single-character symbol Gordon didn't recognize.

"Mr. G?"

"No," he replied. "Nothing to uninstall. I actually need it back. All of the tactical modules, hand-to-hand combat, and security systems. I also need weapons familiarity on an AR-15 and Gains mil-spec machine pistol. Can you roll those into one dump?"

Alessandra joined him at the screen. "Should I reinstall from this list or give you a fresh copy? If you recall, there is nominal delay in absorption if we install fresh."

He thought of the world beyond the glowing walls of the construct, the one where he was lying in the soft grass next to Cyn with a code cube attached to his neck via electrode. Just getting the cube to interface with his damaged jackport took more than an hour, and now there was only a little daylight left in the sky.

"Just give me the cached versions then. Scroll the list again, and I'll point out which ones I want."

Alessandra cleared her throat softly, stepped between Gordon and the display. She put a hand on his chest, and for the first time, he realized he was wearing the avatar from the last time he'd loaded the construct—jeans, a white t-shirt, and some black Chucks streaked with white paint. It was the same outfit he'd worn as he walked out of Austin for the last time, headed east to find the Lost Pines Survivalist camp he'd heard about.

"I have to advise against a piecemeal strategy," said Alessandra. "Each module contains considerable metadata, small slivers of sense memory and synaptic connections. This has created a matrix of dependencies I cannot unravel. If you only load a subset of these 742 modules, you may experience fragmented memories and schizophrenic consciousness. The process would be upsetting."

"So, what? It's all or nothing?"

She nodded slowly.

"But there were…"

He trailed off, suddenly aware of the futility of trying to argue with a promotional avatar.

What he would have told Alessandra had she the capacity to understand was that there were things in the metadata he specifically didn't want to remember, a whole swath of time between the night he and Natalie stormed the ZabSix cipher den and the day almost a year later when he woke up with a headache to find a note in his handwriting.

Lost Pines Survivalists. Lost Pines, Texas. Ask for Evans.

In his mind, 1999 hadn't happened. Alessandra had scooped it out along with all the knowledge that had made him a heartless killing machine. Loading the modules meant loading that year back into his databank.

Was Kaili Zabora worth that? Would the woman whose sister Gordon had killed be grateful for his sacrifice?

Gordon bit his lip. There was no way of knowing the answer to that question without knowing exactly what memories he had dumped. All he really knew was that he'd wanted to get rid of something and that something involved Natalie and X in some way.

"It's been twenty years," he mumbled.

"Approximately," said Alessandra. "I can recommend additional modules to help with your advanced age."

He narrowed his eyes at her.

"Men's health concerns are serious business," she continued. "You would benefit greatly from a working knowledge of nutrition and exercise. Although, given the time difference, there may have been advances I'm unaware of."

"No," said Gordon. "I don't have time for that right now. How long would it take to restore the entire list here?"

"Approximately five hours. A majority of the data is already in your head. I'll simply be removing blocks."

Gordon sat down on the floor and crossed his legs.

"I've got four."

"I'll do what I can," said Alessandra. "Let me know when you're ready to begin."

The air in the construct was infused with something like mint, and when Gordon took a deep breath, his lungs tingled with a slight burn. He placed his hands on his knees, closed his eyes, and tried to cast his mind back to that night outside ZabSix where he and Natalie had sat on the curb in the misty rain, the smell of blood and gunpowder in the air. He'd been so damaged, so jacked with synth, that there were no words in his memory of that moment. Natalie's lips had moved, but the sounds themselves were gone.

He had no idea how that night had ended.

But that would soon change.

"Hit me."

Flashes of light and sound came hard and fast out of the darkness behind his eyes. The construct fell away, crushed into a fine cloud of pixels by the pressure bearing down from above. Memories flooded into him in a jumbled mess, filling in a puzzle too vast and complex to see all at once. He drifted from one sliver of a moment to the next, sometimes feeling Natalie beside him, sometimes feeling more alone than he ever thought possible.

The deluge of sensory data lasted several minutes until finally the fog cleared and Gordon found himself seated on the couch in Natalie's old apartment, the mint having turned into some mixture of crushed flowers and potpourri. Natalie's legs lay across his lap, and judging by the cutoff shorts and tank top she wore and the hint of tan lines, he guessed it was midsummer, maybe four or five months since the killing spree in Old Downtown.

She had her head turned to the back of the couch, eyes closed, chest rising and falling with the steady tempo of someone half-asleep. Her hands were layered on the obvious bulge in her stomach.

The conversation came back to him all at once, and he heard the echoes of Natalie's voice in his head.

I don't want him to know this world. I want him to have a normal life.

Gordon rewound to the morning Natalie had told him she was pregnant, had come out of the bathroom holding a white stick by one end as if it were a short but dangerous snake. And as the air drained from the room and Gordon felt himself suffocating, he could only think of the night in the Austonian when a jacked-in Natalie had spent her last real night with X in virtual reality, how she had laid there on the couch moaning from the electrical signals coming down the wire while her body lay unused and trembling.

He remembered using it.

Natalie had figured it out on her own, of course. She wasn't stupid, and though they had been intimate once or twice since X disappeared—albeit drunkenly and desperately—the timing of those encounters didn't line up. She had probably known just by looking at him what had happened.

For whatever reason, she'd never mentioned it.

But as she stood outside the bathroom door with the white stick, it all suddenly clicked for her.

Gordon had expected her to scream and punch and kick and ultimately force him out of her life altogether. Instead, she'd gone to her knees in front of the coffee table and laid her upper body across it. The pregnancy test had skidded across the birch wood surface.

The shame of the moment had been unbearable.

Gordon shook himself from the memory, tried to get back to the couch on that languid summer day so he could feel Natalie's legs under his hands. He overshot, found himself standing in a freezing, empty apartment with nothing but a white bag of trash in the corner. He'd gone to Houston for a day to see his dad, and Natalie had used that time to move out, to disappear.

The bag, he'd discovered, contained the various possessions he'd left in her apartment—miscellaneous wires, code cubes, and a cracked viewee.

On the wall next to the door, he found a note.

We've gone home, it said. *Don't follow us.*

We.

Natalie and…

The memory crumbled into empty ether and a single letter came hurtling out of the resulting darkness.

X.

She was going to name their son after X.

Xavier Purcell, if she gave him her last name.

Xavier King, if she gave him his father's.

"I have a son," said Gordon, his words lost to the rending of the construct, to a powerful shaking that jumbled his thoughts.

Somewhere, a timer expired, and Alessandra pulled the plug.

Gordon awoke under a sky that had turned from blue to black. Stars blurred and trembled above him. Beside him, Cyn removed the binoculars from her eyes and gave him a wary look.

"You alright?" she asked.

He could feel it—the accumulated knowledge that had been reloaded into his brain.

"Yeah," he replied.

"Good, 'cause Tanzy said we need to be ready to move in five. We've got twelve minutes to hit the wall. Blackouts are already rolling across the city."

Gordon got up on shaky legs, walked a few feet away from Cyn, and threw up in a small grouping of shrubbery.

"Oh, yeah, I like this," said Cyn, shaking her head. "Gonna get myself killed for Krazy Kai. You know she shot me, right?"

"Can you just… be quiet?" he asked, wiping his mouth with the back of his hand. "You have no idea what I just downloaded."

"I'm sure it'll serve us well right up 'til the moment we're captured, tortured, and turned into ReTreads."

His stomach settled after a few minutes, and he returned to Cyn's position. He picked up an AR-15, let his hands glide over the various parts. Gordon knew the names of every individual piece of metal, every rod and every slide, and even with his eyes closed, he could dismantle, clean, and reassemble the entire weapon.

He put the scope to his right eye, aimed the rifle at Folsom Prison across the river. There were guards walking the high walls. Plenty of security. Plenty of danger.

For the first time in a long time, the threat of violence didn't scare him.

It excited him.

He smiled, felt himself starting to count, but stopped. He didn't need that crutch anymore.

Gordon was finally whole again.

"Beware the G man," he muttered. "Beware his presence and his absence. May the Net be cleansed by his righteous hand."

"Nice speech," said Cyn. "What does your shrink think about it?"

He returned a scowl, which Cyn summarily ignored.

"Hey," she continued, "how come you didn't tell me you have a kid?"

THIRTY-TWO
DANNY

The viral fire stayed with Danny well into the next day.

It was a primitive virus, easily countered given enough time, but with the lack of sleep and synth haze and general unease of the past few days, the virus lingered longer than expected. Danny spent the night going in and out of sleep, rousing himself just long enough to take a sip of water or rub his hand on Jane's leg. He dreamed of fire engulfing an old house, tall and dark against an impossibly large moon.

It came as no surprise when he learned Tanzy and the others had gone sometime during the day. They were off on their little adventure to save a woman who hadn't really done anything for the world besides kill thousands of innocent people during Calle Cinco de Mayo. For a while, Danny had questioned why Tanzy was so intent on saving Kaili Zabora, even as the answer echoed plainly in the back of his head.

The jailbreak had nothing to do with Johnny. Tanzy could make all the claims she wanted about having Calle Cinco in their pocket, but it was all bullshit. There wasn't anything particularly special about Bullets or his little slice of protected construct. The viral fire he'd thrown at Danny was from a forgotten era and had an easily blacklisted signature. If he tried to use it again, the Syzygy would simply block it out.

They didn't need Kaili to get to Bullets.

Not at all.

And really, Tanzy didn't need her either—she *wanted* her, wanted the Butcher of Burbank in her debt.

More than that, she wanted the world to know it was I.C.E-1 who freed Kaili Zabora, and that if any person of power and means needed help in the future, they would know which cipher den to call.

Goddamn Tanzy.

"What was that?" asked Jane. She squeezed the sponge at his neck and doused his back in warm, soapy water.

"Nothing," Danny replied, leaning forward in the tub.

Jane had talked him into a hot bath by claiming she had a desire to wash him and that she wouldn't ever know happiness again unless he allowed her the opportunity. Though he wasn't in the mood for one of Jane's baths, he'd followed her into the bathroom anyway while water gushed into a massive, half-dome tub. The black stone was smooth and warmed by elements underneath the floor. Danny undressed, got in, and found there was plenty of room to cross his legs and still keep most of his stomach underwater.

He barely glanced at Jane as she slid into place behind him. His mind drifted, jumped from Tanzy to the fire to the house on the hill to Johnny in his last moments before the Dead Man's Loop fired. Jane, for her part, said little, simply scrubbed his back and arms, alternating between the sponge and her hands, which she used to gently massage his neck.

"Are you here with me?" she asked softly, placing her chin on his shoulder.

Danny felt her nipples rub against his back.

"I'm with you," he said. "And only you." He chuckled. "Everyone else is gone. Nobody gives a shit what happened to Johnny except me."

"You're a good friend, Danny. And a good person."

"Then why won't anyone help me? Why is it so goddamn hard to get someone on my side?" When she withdrew her hands, he added, "Besides you, I mean."

And even as he said it, he knew it wasn't true. Jane Meade's engagement with Danny Guns Montreal would end on Friday. He wasn't sure of the time, only that she'd say goodbye and slip away into the crowded streets of Umbra, which was almost like not existing at all. He would be left with nothing except memories of her soft touch, of her legs wrapped around his stomach, of her dainty feet rising and falling in the soapy water.

The week had gone by so quickly that he'd hardly had the time to sit and be with her. And really, that was why he'd hired her in the first place—to simply be his companion and watch movies with him, eat dinner across the table from him, and maybe, if she felt up to it, pretend to orgasm after a few minutes of passionate lovemaking.

"I don't want you to go."

Her cheek, cold and wet, fell against his back shoulder.

"Without Johnny, or Tanzy, or you, I'm just… alone."

He turned, kissed her forehead.

"You're what I've always dreamed a partner could be. Beautiful, funny, smart… and challenging. Someone to tell me to stop eating Chinese food every night. Someone to help me lay off the synth and get some exercise."

"That's not a partner, Danny." Her voice was gentle. "That's a mom. Any woman lucky enough to be your partner is also gonna want you to love them, be interested in them. It's reciprocal. I… I don't know how to explain it well. All I can hope for is that one day you find a woman who excites you more than computers, a woman you'd bring down VNet for if she asked you nicely."

"Is that what you want?"

She rubbed his shoulder, replied, "I just want to sit here with you and enjoy this moment. The warm water. The lavender. We've closed the door on the world, and it's just us. Every second that ticks by is a second lost forever. I'm happy to have spent them with you, here."

"Yeah, but tomorrow night, I'm gonna be sitting in this tub alone."

"Only a fool would try to predict the future. And you're no fool, Danny. And you're also not alone. Johnny will be with you forever, and so will I."

Her hands came around to hug his chest.

"You don't like Tanzy, do you?" he asked.

"Why do you say that?"

"You mentioned Johnny and yourself, but not her."

Jane's sigh was as damning as any words she could have spoken. Danny turned around in the tub to face her. She put her hands on his knees.

"You don't need me to tell you how to feel about her. I just think there's a reason you two don't really keep in touch, and I think it's the same reason she's not here right now. Whatever the truth is, it's not what she's been feeding you. I know when people are pretending to be something they're not, or worse, pretending to feel something they're not. It's in their eyes, like everything else."

Danny leaned back in the tub, slipped his feet alongside Jane's hips.

"What about me?" he asked. "Am I pretending?"

"Only when people are around, which is why you stay in your cabin all the time. Pretending to be someone else is a lot of work. It's a constant effort to not let the real you shine through, because if it did…"

"People might not like it," said Danny.

"You choose to be Guns out in public because you're scared to be Danny. And having known both of you, I can tell you there's nothing to be ashamed of. Danny loves deeply, cares deeply. He puts himself in danger for his friends. Why would you want to hide that from the world?"

He shrugged. "It's like you said. It's just pretending. It's marketing to a world that only cares about the surface of things. To be a hacker is to be beyond the reach of normal people. We understand how the digital world really works. All those Pattrn accounts and emails and messages… we're the ones who can freely wade through that data, and they know that. Compassionate people don't steal data; they don't break into systems for the fuck of it. I do those things for recognition, for the rep, so people like Lucas Cotton will pay me half a mil to look over his code. Everything about me is a lie."

Jane shook her head. She had her hair pulled back, but a few strands lay flat against her temples. Water beaded on her skin, collected in the pools on her shoulders.

"Not everything," she said, her tone far from playful. "You're following Johnny's trail because you truly care. And when this is all over, you're going to take a trip to New York, to a little café in the lobby of World Trade Center 1, on a Friday in the afternoon. And sitting at the bar will be a woman with hair like mine and eyes you know like the beating of your own heart."

She leaned forward, climbed over him until her face was an inch from his.

"And you won't know this woman's real name, but you will take her hand, and you will ask her to come away with you. You will offer her a new life... a life with you, Danny. And you will do this despite what Guns might have to say about it."

He kissed her, withdrew. He struggled to ask, "And will the woman say yes?"

"Only a fool tries to predict the future," she replied, kissing him on the lips, then the forehead.

With a violent sloshing of water, she pulled herself out of the tub and draped a towel around her body.

"Where are you going?" he asked.

"It's almost midnight. A woman has to eat. And Guns needs to finish his job so he can get on a plane. By the way, your sliver is flashing."

Danny pulled his wrist out of the water and wiped the excess moisture from the metal tab. A brief message from Tanzy pulsed in bright red letters.

We need you.

He looked to Jane. She raised an eyebrow.

The message faded from his sliver, unanswered. Whatever mess Tanzy was in, it was hers to deal with.

Danny got out of the tub, wincing at the pain in his leg as he set it down on the warm tile. Jane handed him a purple towel and left him to dry off. He did so angrily, cursing Tanzy's assumption he would just drop everything to help them with their pointless jailbreak.

Jane was pulling on a shirt when Danny returned to the bedroom. The Fritz had sent a courier over with their luggage sometime during the day; their bags lay open on the black dresser next to the window. Jane had already pulled out some clothes for him: boxers, loose gym shorts, and a t-shirt with two crisscrossing revolvers.

Danny tossed the towel onto the bed. When Jane tried to snatch it up to return it to the bathroom, he waved her away.

"Not my mom, remember?"

She shrugged. "My mom used to say *you're not truly a woman until you've cleaned up after a man.*"

Danny smiled thinly, unsure of how to respond.

"Anyway, Kevin Costner is gonna take me downstairs to get something to eat. I'll bring you back something healthy, okay?"

"Nachos?"

"Yes, salad nachos. Get to work, Danny." She gestured to his rig on the bed.

Danny eyed the headset and the ominous blue LED blinking on top of it. Never had he looked at it with such trepidation, with such worry that he was setting out alone. There would be no lifelines to call, no friendly cipher den suits to bring in backup.

It was just Guns versus Bullets.

That showdown, however, would have to wait. There would be no jacking into VNet tonight. Instead, Danny needed to explore the construct map he'd recreated on his own private server. His scanner had gathered more than enough data before the viral fire hit. Knowing the lay of the land would help when he finally returned.

Danny reclined on the bed, put his feet under the covers, and pulled the rig onto his face.

Brigham Plaza bloomed in the private construct. A passing storm had washed away the danger of its VNet counterpart, leaving only a damp parking lot with shimmering puddles and a sky cycling through oranges and pinks. Cars sat beneath tall, flickering lampposts; water beaded on their long, boxy hoods. Despite the change in atmosphere and complete lack of people, the construct was a perfect bit-wise replica.

Danny put his hand on the phone booth next to him. He tried to recall the sequence of events: Bullets placing a phone call, walking to the Blockbuster, and talking with the druggie. Did that have any significance? Or was it just a slice of memory from his childhood?

Childhood.

Domino's, Blockbuster, pay-phones… that would put the era at late 80s or early 90s. Bullets looked to be 18 or 19, which meant he was now in his 40s. Definitely not a noob.

Danny ran the math over and over in his head as he walked from the payphone to the Blockbuster. There, he turned right and followed the building as far as it would go. When he hit a wall, whether real or virtual, he turned right again and kept going.

Around and around, he walked every inch of the construct until its layout had been burned into the back of his mind.

THIRTY-THREE
KAILI

Kaili withdrew into herself, breaking every sensory pathway that connected her to the simulation. She no longer cared to drift in the data stream as Trent had taught her, but rather, she desired to sink beneath it all, to disconnect so completely that even Arthur Sedivy wouldn't be able to reach her.

She ignored sight and sound, held her breath to stem the chemical burn of Astoria air, and ignored the blood collecting under her tongue. Kaili stretched the chasm between her and the world as wide as she could imagine it and lined it with steel walls as thick as the skyscrapers of downtown San Diego. The walls curved above her, falling inward, as she sank deep into the ether, lower and lower, until her very essence fell between the ones and zeros that made up her digital prison.

Stillness followed; reality succumbed to entropy.

Kaili curled into a ball and hugged her legs with her arm. She turned her thoughts to Anela and imagined her sister standing nearby, her hands crossed in front of her hips. With some mental manipulation, she was able to make Anela speak—it didn't matter whether the resulting sound was real or imagined.

"What is this place, Kaili?"

Anela took a few steps on an invisible plane, shook her head, and waved a hand at her feet. Thousands of individual blades of grass sprouted from the ether. A sudden introduction of gravity pulled Kaili into the damp lawn, coating her face in cold dew. She pushed herself into a sitting position and looked to her sister.

"This construct is incomplete," said Anela. "There is something here, but it is dormant."

"How do we wake it up?" asked Kaili, climbing to her feet. She wiped her face on her shoulder.

"Do we want to? That is the real question."

Kaili listened for the electronic hum of the previous construct but heard nothing. "Why not? This is way below what Sedivy put me in. Somewhere deep."

"In your biochip, you mean."

"Yes, in my..."

She flashed on a scalpel slicing into the back of her neck. Had they really put a GA chip inside her?

"I believe they did," said Anela. "Nothing like this existed on your previous chip."

"So then it doesn't matter if I get out of here alive or not. If I have a Guardian Angel, they can follow me anywhere in the world."

Anela turned to face her. "You can always have it removed. You heard the doctor; they did not install the grow-wire, which is the most difficult part to extract. It gets into everything, much like Vinestead."

Kaili spit, tasted blood again. The red liquid seeped into the green lawn, disappeared beneath the dirt. A small red flower grew from the spot.

"There is a sky here," said Anela, gesturing above her head. She waved her hand in a long, sweeping arc.

Ether dissolved above them, replaced by twinkling stars on a distant dome. In the center, a long gash traced from one side of the construct to the other. At its center, a dim white light shone through.

A tremor ran up Kaili's spine, as if something were reaching into the back of her brain. Memories flashed in quick succession, showing her faces from a life that felt so far away: mom in the rocking chair, dad under the hood of his rusted Cutlass Supreme, Anela walking the golden sands of Coronado Beach, and Rick tapping his foot nervously at Bubbling Joe's. She held onto his image, scrolled forward to their time together in the Umbra Tower.

She hadn't met a gentler man since.

"There is a presence," said Anela. "Something is nearby, something behind the smokescreen." She walked around Kaili in an ever-widening circle, arms outstretched, fingers testing for anything solid.

Kaili slid a hand around the back of her neck. "I can't believe they put a Georgia chip in me. What's Trent gonna say when he finds out?"

"He will never know. We will have it removed as soon as we get out of here." Anela paused, squinted. "Come here, Kaili. Look." She pointed into the distance.

Kaili strained but saw nothing.

"A house," said Anela. "Our house."

She was right.

A hazy outline of their parents' tract home in San Diego had appeared in the gloom. It didn't mesh with the present-day version of the house—the bushes under the picture window had long been torn out and the tree that would be felled by a storm when Kaili was seventeen still stood in the center of the yard. And yet, it had the tenor of home, had the same inviting presence. Kaili caught herself walking toward it involuntarily. Anela's hand on her shoulder stopped her from getting too close.

"Remember. GA chip."

The longer she stared, the more the house solidified—the paint chipping over the front door, the single-panel garage door with a cracked pane of glass, and the sidewalks marred with six different colors of pastel chalk. She wondered where the house had come from, whether Vinestead surveillance or deep in her memory.

Kaili looked to her sister and asked, "Should we go inside?"

"Be cautious."

The house remained still until Kaili stepped onto the sidewalk. As she took the curve by the rose bush, the front door opened on its own. A figure stepped through, dressed in a blue and white button-up shirt over dark jeans. He had a five o'clock shadow and eyes that—

"Rick…"

Her heart sank. Another Vinestead trick.

Rick cocked his head, stepped out onto the porch. He gestured to the door like a butler inviting his master home.

"Welcome," he said, "to the House of Nepenthe."

Kaili shook her head. "No thanks," she replied, stepping slightly behind Anela.

"I assure you, you're safe here," said Rick, his voice so perfectly sculpted, so much more real than Sedivy's reproduction of Rick on the train.

"You heard her," said Anela. "Back off."

"What is this place?" asked Kaili. "How did I get here?"

His smile pressed on Kaili's heart. "In a way, she brought you here," he said, gesturing to Anela.

"I don't understand."

"Come inside where it's warm, and I'll explain everything." Without waiting for an answer, Rick turned and walked back into the house, disappearing around a corner.

"What does he mean *you* brought me here?"

"I have no idea," said Anela. "I do not trust this."

Kaili stood for a minute, considering her options. "Fuck it," she muttered, and stepped onto the porch.

"Wait," said Anela.

The door slammed shut behind her as Kaili entered the house. The living room was empty except for the brown shag carpeting and wood paneling on the walls. The fireplace across from her roared, giving off a warmth Kaili felt all the way across the room. Rick stood beside it with one hand on the mantel and the other in his pocket.

"Do you smell that?" he asked, tilting his head back.

The aroma of freshly baked chocolate chip cookies wafted in from the kitchen on the left.

"You had such a lovely childhood here. I wish I could've learned more about it. Our time together was so brief."

"You're not the real Rick."

"No," he replied, his eyes softening. "I'm not. I'm more of a projection, a familiar form to help you with the transition."

"Transition to what?"

"To… the next stage." He stepped forward. "Is there anything I can get you right now? Food? Drink? All you have to do is ask and I can provide."

Kaili crossed the living room, casting a glance at the dormant fan hanging from the wooden crossbeam in the ceiling.

"What did you mean when you said my sister brought me here?"

"How about a hot shower?" he asked. "It will feel just as good as it did out there."

Kaili heard the water kick on, splashing against the pink acrylic tub. She could almost feel the warmth of the cleansing steam.

"Fucking answer me!"

"Please," said Rick, "there's no reason to get upset. Nothing can hurt you here. There is only safety and comfort until the end."

He was talking in circles. Everything was circles in the dark depths of her biochip.

"I just want to know what's going on."

She put her hand to her mouth as a rocking chair materialized next to her. How long had her mother spent in that chair after Anela died, jacked into virtual reality, avoiding the horrors of the real world? How many years had her father stood nearby pleading with his wife to come outside with him?

"Please, sit down," said Rick. "I have something to show you before I begin connecting you to the outside world. Then you'll be free to explore the many rooms of the House and revisit your memories."

Kaili didn't have the strength to question him. She sat down in the rocking chair and ran a hand over the pocked arms. Leaning back, the chair let out a low squeak. The construct shimmered as Kaili's eyes misted over.

Rick touched the bricks above the fireplace and opened a black portal. He glanced over his shoulder to make sure Kaili was watching and then tapped the rectangle.

Black turned to shadow, revealing an office in low light. An obsidian desk took up the lower third of the screen while tubes of color-shifting bubbles filled in the background. In the center, Anela Zabora sat with her fingers intertwined and her jaw set tight. Her gaze drifted to the left of the camera.

"Ready," said a gruff voice.

Anela's eyes stared out at Kaili from the past.

"My dear sister, I can only hope this message never reaches you. The implications of you seeing and hearing me are too much for me to handle at the moment. We Zaboras are strong, but my weakness has always been and will always be you, Kaili. I cannot bear the thought of Vinestead—may they burn in hell—getting their hands on you. And more than that, I cannot imagine what events will have had to transpire to…"

She paused, the words catching in her throat. Red-tipped fingernails dabbed at her eyes.

Kaili leaned forward in the chair.

"Okay," said Anela, forcing a smile. "Let us face facts. You have a Guardian Angel biochip installed in your neck. That is the only way you could be in this version of the House of Nepenthe. I discovered this code last year, 1997, and in addition to copying it, we put a modified version back in its place in the hopes Vinestead would come and reclaim it. For anyone else in the world, the House of Nepenthe plays out as normal. But for you, Kaili… you get this version of the House, our home, with all our memories. Even my last ones."

Rick walked to the sliding glass doors that led out into the backyard. He waited for an end table to bubble up from the floor and then took the small box that appeared on it.

"A man named Kenneth Barnes created the House of Nepenthe because he wanted to give people one last chance to communicate with loved ones before they died. Even if they were unresponsive to the outside world, perhaps dying in some hospice somewhere, they would still be able to communicate through this private construct. It is rare to see good intentions in a Vinestead employee, and even when you do, it often comes coupled with ignorance. It is not hard to take this idea to its inevitable conclusion: inducing a coma, keeping someone on the very edge of death, and thus trapping the victim in the House forever."

"That's not what's happening here," said Kaili.

Rick raised a hand, asked for quiet.

"I would never wish a GA chip upon you, Kaili. But in anticipation of this edge case finally hitting, my ciphers have developed a way out for you."

Rick handed her the box. Inside, Kaili found an old-fashioned code cube along with an electrode umbilical.

"We have been working on a biochip uncoupler for a while now, and my ciphers tell me this would work against any platform, and hopefully against any future platform. All you have to do is load the code and you will be disconnected from your Guardian Angel. If they have you sedated, or if you are otherwise damaged, it will likely mean your death. I leave it to you to decide which fate is worse."

Kaili turned the cube over in her hand.

"I wish I could do more for you, sister. I do not know how this happened or why I was not there to help you. Please know I am sorry for not protecting you. I love you, Kaili… in this world and the next."

Anela gave a subtle nod to the camera.

The video feed cut out, taking the fire and the warmth with it.

THIRTY-FOUR
TANZY

Tanzy lay on the wool rug in the middle of the shack trying to imagine what was happening at Folsom Prison.

Every camera in the surrounding city was down thanks to their attack on the power grid, so the only eyes left were those circling in the sky above. Low cloud cover prevented an aerial view of the action below, so all Tanzy could do was watch thermal scans, and for some reason, she just didn't trust them.

According to the video feed she'd attached to the ceiling, the nearby California State Prison was a hive of thermal activity. It glowed like a shard of metal thrust into a flame. Folsom itself was colder than ice by comparison, consisting of a deep black with hardly a hint of how its buildings were arranged or whether prisoners occupied them.

If there were guards, they weren't outside.

And if they were inside, the walls of the prison were thick enough to mask their heat completely.

Just outside of Folsom to the west, two small orange dots crossed over a blue streak labeled *American River*—Gordon and Cyn. They had maps of the prison going back 80 years, but nobody really knew what they were going to find inside.

The lack of a clear visual made Tanzy's stomach turn to evercrete.

"What about a drone?" she asked.

"None in the area," said Phantasm. "I checked, and ah, well, closest one is in Umbra doing circles over the Canopy. There are some Vinestead birds over Sacramento, but evidently I'm not allowed to touch the big bad Vinestead net."

"There are a lot of things you're not allowed to touch."

Phantasm scoffed. "How come you act like you're the only hacker in the family but you're always coming to me with problems?"

"I bring you basic hacks, Michael. Stuff below the Quatrain's station. When a job calls for someone big and dumb and noisy, I call you."

Tanzy closed her eyes, listened to her brother suck on his teeth.

"I'm mom's favorite," he said.

"I was dad's favorite," she replied.

"Uncle Sam was dad's favorite. He'd have died for his country before spending time with his kids." He chuckled. "Hey, did you know Margate has a big veteran population now?"

"No."

"On the backside, away from the Atlantic, there's a burrow of homes with stasis pods, like, full-on muscular therapy inside, and they're filled with guys who did tours in the Middle East. Meltdown told me he knew a guy who did the backend coding and that they're all plugged into a simulation where they're basically reliving the war all day and all night. I guess it's like therapy or something."

"Yay, America," said Tanzy. "Just think of all that virtual oil they're liberating."

"That's not even the sick part. Meltdown says some of them are just there for the target practice, and—"

Tanzy jerked so violently at the sudden change in orientation that she nearly fell out of her seat. Only a steadying hand from Lincoln kept her from going headfirst into the carpeted aisle.

"Easy," said Lincoln. "That was a hard exit. Take a breath."

The signature roar of the G80's engines entered her awareness. She looked around for her brother, but Phantasm wasn't there. It took a moment for the two worlds to stabilize into one.

She was on Lincoln's jet and they were circling high above Folsom City. Somehow, she'd lost her connection to the Reykjavik darknet and found herself unceremoniously dumped back in reality.

"Bryce, can you bring a water, please?" asked Lincoln.

Tanzy sat back in the warm leather seat and gripped the armrests. Her heart pounded in her chest, set off by a sensation of plunging to her death.

"What happened?" she asked.

"I'm not sure—"

The connection was interrupted, said Cleo. *However, the Reykjavik insertion point is still responding. Want me to reconnect?*

Bryce twisted the cap on a water bottle and placed it on the table in front of Tanzy.

"Put it back in the fridge," she said.

The transition back to Reyk went smoother than expected, too smooth, in all honesty. The security protocols that usually set her skin on fire were gone, and all she felt as she stepped into the darknet was a gentle wind. She kept waiting for the construct to finish loading, but there was nothing except empty landscape—patches of grass among rocky surfaces, stretching away to a placid sea. Above, the moon shone down like a spotlight on the place where a small village had once stood.

Nothing remained. Not the shack. Not Phantasm's tavern.

"What. The. Fuck."

Tanzy stepped back at the sudden appearance of her brother. He was dressed in a t-shirt and gray jeans; his bare feet deformed on top of the loose rocks. He'd lost his avatar's clothes, and after a quick check, Tanzy realized the same had happened to her. Her glossy black heels looked out of place on the crumbling road, and the flattering suit she wore provided little protection against the cold.

"Looks like someone wiped out the server," said Tanzy. "All the way down to the permafrost."

"Impossible. The server keys are held by twenty-six different people, and they'd all have to agree to zero out the server before…"

Tanzy watched the gears turn in his head.

"Vinestead," he said.

"No one else knew we were here," said Tanzy. "My guess is they saw an intrusion sourced from Reyk and decided to wipe it off the map."

"Could they really do that? The encryption was supposed to be beyond Vinestead. Otherwise it wouldn't have been a proper darknet."

Tanzy shook her head. "You don't get it, do you? They don't have to get into the darknet to destroy it. It's a shared hallucination that doesn't really have a home, but you and I have to get to it somehow. And if Vinestead owns all the lines and the satellites and the fiber, it wouldn't take more than a few clicks to isolate the network and force one of those twenty-six key-masters to reinstantiate the construct. This is probably a backup from who knows how long ago."

"So, whatever," said Phantasm, waving his hand at the empty landscape. "We'll just rebuild and—"

Tanzy kicked the table hard, upsetting a tumbler of brown liquor and sending it clattering to the floor. Lincoln groaned but said nothing. His eyes came into focus slowly, as if the Reyk darknet were a film over the world that needed to be scraped away.

"That was quick," said Bryce. He dropped into a seat across the aisle, a palette in his hand. On it, a familiar grouping of thermal images glowed brightly.

"Something's wrong with the Reykjavik darknet," said Tanzy. "I think Vinestead might have pulled its number."

The insertion point is no longer responding.

"Why would Vinestead care about a little darknet?" asked Lincoln. "There are thousands of them in the world."

"Because my idiot brother reached out and touched the Vinestead network inside Folsom."

"Sheeeit," said Bryce.

"Not only have they put the hurt on Reyk, they're now on guard against all traffic. I wouldn't be surprised if they've completely isolated everything in Folsom City. We lost comms with Gordon and Cyn a few minutes ago, didn't we?"

Lincoln nodded.

Tanzy bit her lip. "Then you might as well land this thing at the rendezvous. We've got no comms and no visuals worth a damn. They could have Kaili at the airstrip in twenty minutes or two hours. And that's if they show at all."

"Cyn will be there," said Bryce, without looking up. "With or without Kaili." He bounced his head side-to-side. "With or without Gordon."

"Cleo, tell Danny I need his help."

Message relayed to Guns.

"How long until we put down?" asked Tanzy.

"We'll be on the ground in fifteen minutes."

"I'll be out in fourteen."

She pushed back into her seat and switched over.

The ground dropped out from beneath her, and in the air, she spun to face the onrush of warm air. Her feet sought out the floor as a construct built around her. The axis of the world rotated ninety degrees, and she found herself running down a sterile white hallway toward a set of black double doors. They swung open at her approach, as if she were pushing the air ahead of her.

"Someone tell me what the hell is going on with Reykjavik."

The Quatrain stood as one in marble-like stoicism on the four points of a large, onyx compass embedded in the white stone floor. Tanzy rushed past Princess and stepped up on the pedestal in the center. Her ciphers were each twenty feet away, and yet she could hear their breathing, hear the registers flipping over in their heads like the clacking of an old bedside clock.

"We weren't aware of any problem with Reykjavik," said Cherry.

"Well, something booted me out of there and now I can't find it anymore."

Tanzy raised vidscreens out of the air around her and dropped a keyboard under her hands. She typed quickly, placing tails on a dozen different log files, searching for some kind of answer.

"There's no mention of Reykjavik on the feeds," said Cherry. "I'm guessing you told Lincoln to keep quiet about it."

"No, but he's not the type to feed while we're in the thick," said Tanzy, biting her lip. Even though she'd made the declaration with confidence, she considered sending a more explicit directive.

"I've reviewed your session watchdogs," said Strider. "The disconnects coincide with hardline cuts coming out of Nova Scotia. It's not just the darknet; the entire country of Iceland has been isolated from VNet."

"Now we've got something," said Cherry. Her avatar didn't move when she spoke, just stood like a doll waiting to come to life.

...service providers are scrambling to restore access to metropolitan areas in Iceland after a network failure. Northern Telecom is reporting an undersea cut. It is unclear at this time whether the cut was accidental or an act of domestic terrorism. Keep it on White Line Media for the latest on this developing story.

"Jesus," continued Cherry. "They went straight to layer one with this. What'd you do to piss them off?"

"Not me," said Tanzy. "Michael."

A collective groan went up in the room. The curved walls made the echoes build on each other until it sounded like a horde of zombies were standing behind Tanzy.

"Told you we shouldn't have brought him in," said Strider.

Whisper sighed. "He's family. She sees the best in him."

"I needed another keyboard," said Tanzy. "I couldn't convince Danny to tear himself away from his rent-a-wife long enough to save someone's life. Someone important." She paused, watched a timestamp scroll by in a log. "Any word from him yet, Cleo?"

No response yet.

"Do you want us to keep trying Reykjavik?" asked Whisper. "Is it important you get back in?"

Tanzy eyed Princess' impassive face. Her eyes were closed, and her blonde eyelashes were nearly invisible. She rarely chimed in on anything not related to money, and yet Tanzy felt as if she needed another opinion.

It *was* important to get back into Reyk, if only to prove she could. No one booted her from anything, especially not Vinestead. She was Tanzy of I.C.E-1, and she went where she pleased.

Anything less than that was weakness.

"We can always revisit it later," suggested Strider.

"Whatever," said Tanzy. "It's not important. I was just…"

"We know," said Whisper.

Tanzy cleared her throat. "I'm going to be landing soon to meet up with the package. Once she's onboard and we're back in the air, I want you to drop the hammer on VinesteadATC. Nothing like Cinco de Mayo, but I want to fade into the fleeing crowd. Cleo will let you know once we're on the ground in Umbra.

Message from Phantasm. Hopped on Shinjuku. Almost have Dougherty out the front door.

"Tell him not to let him all the way out," said Tanzy. "We're not running a prison break charity here."

Message relayed.

Tanzy took a deep breath, let it out with all the urgency of a forgotten cigarette burning to the filter.

"Alright, next time I see you guys, I'll have the most feared cyber-terrorist in the world in my pocket."

"Good luck," said Whisper.

"Well, as an old friend once told me—luck is for the ill-prepared."

She jacked out.

Smoke stung the delicate tissue in her nostrils. Tanzy leaned into the banked angle of the airplane and became aware of hands brushing her chest. It was Bryce, trying his best to buckle her in as she thrashed against him.

"Reign it in, Tanzy," he barked.

She relented, helped him tighten the strap over her hips. Across the table, a stone-faced Lincoln sat looking at her, his hands curled over the edges of his armrests.

"What's happening?" she asked, looking up at the smoke flowing behind Bryce's head.

"Vinestead drone strike," said Lincoln, his deep voice barely audible over the high-pitched whine of a dying engine. "Looks like we really shook the monkey tree on this one."

Bryce tugged on her belt, then lumbered across the aisle to his own seat.

"Told you we shoulda got parachutes, Linc," he said.

Tanzy stared back into Lincoln's black eyes, watched the irises sparkle in amethyst flashes.

He half-smiled.

"Parachutes are for pussies."

Tanzy flashed on the young girl at Cloves and Poetry from the week before. A line popped into her head.

"My pussy stands alone," yelled Tanzy.

Her laughter made Lincoln crack a smile.

THIRTY-FIVE
GORDON

The AR-15 ran out of rounds before Gordon and Cyn had even entered the main prison. The rifle had been slotted with a Replete 60-round magazine, and he'd carried three of the double-wide cartridges on his belt. That meant more than 180 rounds had left the barrel of the AR-15, and most of them had landed in the torsos and heads of whatever unlucky guards happened to leap out of the shadows.

Folsom Prison in the dark with a light rain making everything slick was not the ideal place for a firefight, and yet the resistance had been surprisingly strong, with guards throwing their bodies at Gordon and Cyn once their ammo had given out. Cyn had told him stories of the brainwashing that went into making the perfect Vinestead employee, but Gordon couldn't believe they would go full kamikaze just to protect a few inmates.

There was little time, however, to consider their motivations. They came like waves of locusts, scurrying out of side rooms in unnatural, jerky movements as if they had been waiting for years and forgotten how to run. Perhaps that drawn-out period of readiness was what had made them terrible marksmen and poor estimators of the threat. Whatever their history, they were no match for Gordon and the old code coursing through his nervous system.

Of course, the scales were only tipped in his favor when he had bullets to weigh his side down.

The code made his transition from rifle to sidearm blurry, and every time he pulled a new clip from his belt, he felt as if his head were breaking the surface of some infinite pool just long enough to grab a single breath before plunging down again. He felt himself move, felt his stiff arms swing around wildly to counter threat after threat, all the while at the back of his mind, a counter was slowly ticking down.

The last bullet was coming.

A decision would have to be made.

It had been one thing to shoot down a guard, but could he really kill someone with his bare hands? The last time he'd done that, it had been to a cipher in Old Downtown in Austin, and Lio had deserved it for what he did to X. But these guards? They owned the cars and trucks Gordon had passed in the parking lot, vehicles that wouldn't be driving home in the morning.

Wives and children were going to wake up to an empty driveway and know in their hearts that something horrible had happened.

At least with a gun, there was some distance between Gordon and the act of killing. He was just pulling a trigger, a simple curling of his index finger, as if opening a refrigerator or flashing his high beams. It was the bullet that did the actual killing.

Gordon merely set the bullet free.

Something stuttered in his mind, and when it cleared, he saw bodies littering the dirt around the gates at LPS. He *had* killed people with his bare hands—only a month ago. And already, he had suppressed the memory, wiped away any trace of wrongdoing from his conscience.

The 9mm went dry as they pushed into the holding cells at the center of the complex. By then, klaxons had been blaring—distantly, it seemed—for several minutes. Gordon ran down barred corridors, trailing after Cyn as she cursed at the men dropping down from an upper gangway. She was a crack shot, though not as precise as someone with an aimbot controlling their limbs. She was doing it all herself, with her own skill.

"I'm out," he yelled, hoping Cyn could hear him at a distance.

She dropped a guard with a knee to the chest and put two rounds in his face as she rode him to the floor.

"Check the cells," she barked back.

Gordon looked around, noticed the tightly packed cells on either side of him. They were empty except for a white, pill-like capsule propped up in the center. Each pill had a bundle of wires that snaked to the wall, climbed it, and disappeared into a roughly drilled hole in the evercrete. On the face of each capsule was a glass window, and in the dim light, Gordon could just make out the shadows of faces inside.

He approached a nearby cell and put his hands on the bars.

"What does she look like?"

Cyn grunted, tossed a guard against an open cell. She slammed the door on its head, twice.

"No clue. The last pictures we have are from Perion City… three years ago."

"So what the fuck am I supposed to do?"

Cyn shook her head. "See if there's something written on the side, you man-child." She barely got the last words out before a guard dove at her feet. She fell but managed to jam her sidearm into the guard's shoulder. Two shots followed.

Gordon pulled the cell door in front of him and found it opened freely. The face inside the capsule was vaguely female; he searched for some kind of label, some indication of who was inside. He ran his hands over the smooth casing, listening to Cyn grunt it out with the guards, idly wondering how the hell they were going to get out of there with a catatonic Kaili Zabora in tow.

There was a label on what he assumed was the top of the capsule; he had to crane his neck to read it. At first, it looked as if there was nothing but an embossed QR code on a small metal tile, but below it, laser-etched into the metal, was the name *M. Sanchez*.

Not Kaili.

Gordon turned to leave the cell just as a guard was entering. The 9mm clicked a few times before he remembered it was empty. Gordon clenched his hands into fists and rushed forward.

A hammer hit him square in the jaw, jerking the entire world to the right. His head found an evercrete wall and bounced. As he inventoried the pain, a foot came up into his gut and knocked the wind out of him. He felt the floor rush up to greet him, and suddenly, the prison disappeared.

"Back so soon?" asked Alessandra.

Gordon blinked at the vibrant construct. On the wall, the list of available mods scrolled like the credits of a movie.

"Close quarters combat," he growled.

"For self-defense, exercise…" said Alessandra.

"Killing."

"I recommend Pale Rider, but I have to warn you, it will push your body further than you can imagine."

"Hit me," said Gordon.

He could still feel the sting of the boot in his chest. The signals kept repeating, as if the guard was still standing next to him, repeatedly kicking him in the rib cage, trying to get at the fleshy organs within.

Gordon snapped back to the jail cell just in time to catch a boot to the nose. The pain wrapped around his head like an ice-cold towel, and when he finally got his muscles to spit, he felt a tooth pass over his lips. As he writhed on the floor, he became aware of another sensation: the cold spike of pain meeting a growing warmth in the back of his neck. His inhibitor chip was heating up, grinding out the clock cycles in an effort to load the code Alessandra had recommended.

Pale Rider.

The name evoked the Bible passage, and Gordon was more than happy to put his faith in what that implied.

I ride upon a pale horse.

I am Death.

Someone lifted him from the ground and placed him face-to-face with a Folsom guard. Gordon saw his own reflection in the glossy black plastic of a riot helmet. The arms that pushed him against the wall were heavy and solid, as if he'd been pinned by a forklift. And yet, his own arms swung free, ready to move, ready to fight.

"I'd put me down if I were you," he sputtered.

The guard moved a hand from Gordon's shoulder to his throat.

Again, someone—a divine force, maybe—grabbed Gordon's hands and pulled them up, slipping between the guard's helmet and shoulder pads. His fingers found flesh and immediately curled around the thick plastic of the helmet. Gordon yanked down, and at the same time, brought his legs off the floor and into the guard's chest.

He pushed, screamed, tightened…

Then he was falling through an endless haze of suspended bodies, as if an explosion had sent a hundred guards hurtling through the air, only to be frozen in place as time itself came to a stop. Each guard posed in some state of failure, often with limbs folded back on themselves and blood spurting from cuts in their uniforms. Helmets had been torn off and eyes gouged out. Once or twice, Gordon caught a flash of the ZabSix cipher Lio—a few lower jaws were missing, ripped from skulls with his own two hands.

At some level, Gordon was still tied to reality, and when he focused, he could see himself running from cell to cell, occasionally fighting off a guard with an increasingly painful combination of punches and kicks. He struggled to read the various ID tags through the sweat and blood, and after a while, the letters simply stopped making sense.

Everything stopped making sense.

Why was he still fighting when he could barely see or feel?

He tried to call out for Cyn, but his jaw was completely locked, teeth bearing down on teeth, blood pooling around his tongue. His fists felt as if they were punching shards of glass in a metal tub, and every kick brought with it the image of his fibula snapping in two.

Gordon tried to pump the brakes, tried throwing himself on the ground, but his body wouldn't relent. It kept going, the horse unstoppable, Death unwavering, and the pain…

He could hear the beating of his own heart as clearly as if someone had torn it out of his chest and held it up to his ear. The muscles contracted and released faster than they ever had before, and as they accelerated faster still, pieces of the world began to drop out of existence. Dark spots like tiny black tears in reality swirled around him.

Something clicked.

Pale Rider dismounted.

Gordon found himself alone in a cell, bloody hands pressed against a white capsule. His legs shook horribly, forcing him into the corner. As he slid to the ground, he noticed a figure standing beyond the closed door of the cell.

It was Cyn. Her shoulders bobbed with each breath.

"You did it again," she said.

"What?" he croaked.

"Berserker. Like back at Lost Pines. You were out of control. What kind of mod does that to you?"

"An old one. No fail-safes back then. Nothing to stop the code from taking over completely."

"You shouldn't have done that."

"Why? Did we kill too many innocent people?"

Cyn shook her head. "Look at your hands, G."

Gordon lifted his mangled fists into view. The damage was worse than the Lost Pines incident. Not only were the bones showing, but they were visibly cracked and broken. Knuckles were split open, and a couple of the fingers were missing their nails.

While he examined the damage, Cyn opened the cell door and stepped inside. She pulled a small aerosol can from her belt and sprayed G's hands. Foam built in the cracks of his fingers and knuckles, a pinkish collection of bubbles that grew and grew.

"Bryce is gonna cream his pants when he hears about this."

Gordon felt light-headed. Some of Cyn's words weren't making it through.

"What... what did I do?"

She blew off some of the excess foam.

"You went full bare-knuckle UFC against synthetic guards. I don't know anyone else brave or stupid enough to do that."

"Synthetic? Those weren't people?"

Cyn shook her head. "I thought you knew that. You were punching straight metal. God, you're fucking crazy."

"Synthetic guards," he repeated.

"Makes sense now that I think about it," said Cyn. "Vinestead wouldn't trust humans to guard these people. Humans can be bought, coerced. I bet these drones can't even talk." She applied another coat of the foam. "Now, if you want chit-chat, you go to Perion Synthetics. He's got shit you won't believe. Teachers, cooks, maids... babies."

"Babies?" Gordon leaned his head against the wall; it was too much effort to hold it up.

"Synthetic babies. Not real. Look real. Not real."

She sounded as if she were trying to convince herself.

"We probably don't have much time," she continued. "I'm gonna keep checking cells. Take a minute, but then get your ass up and help me. Kaili's in here somewhere, and if we find her before backup arrives, we just might make it out of here alive."

"Wait…" He tried to reach for her hands. Her gloves were torn, but the flesh beneath was pristine. "How come you're not torn up?"

Cyn examined her hands, bit her lip.

"I'm not sure how much of these are original parts anymore. The bones are reinforced with micro-lattice fibers. Tendons are infused with stem cell reserves. The muscles all have 5μm inductive webbing. Hell, the skin is actually a Perion Synthetic product. Ten times the tensile strength of human flesh. But still soft, see?"

She dragged the back of her hand across his cheek.

"Anyway, you're probably headed in the same direction after this. I don't think those hands are gonna heal right without some kind of augmentation."

Gordon tried to flex his fingers. Nothing responded.

"Sit tight," said Cyn. "I'll be back."

Her shadow disappeared beyond the bars of the cell. Gordon heard footsteps echo.

His eyes fell on the guard outside the cell, unsure of whether he or Cyn had been the one to put it down. It was hard to believe the guard wasn't a real person, that it didn't drive a car or return home to a family each night. It was just a thing. Vinestead would probably scrape it up off the floor and send it back to China for repairs.

Gordon smiled.

He hadn't killed anyone after all, hadn't orphaned any children or widowed any wives.

He'd destroyed things—inorganic things.

I ride upon a pale horse, he thought.

I am Death to those who cannot die.

THIRTY-SIX
DANNY

Umbra had always considered itself to be its own little universe with the Tower at the center and the Canopy covering everything inside the city limits. What had started as a commune for hackers looking for refuge had turned into a full-fledged metropolis, with utilities and a police force and a dozen different hospitals of varying legality. And long before Vinestead ever crushed the Net under its heel, Umbrats had already created their own private darknet, a grid off the grid they called Luna.

Much like the old Net, Luna had a spherical representation in virtual space. It ran on open-source code on servers physically located inside the Umbra Tower. For security, there was no wireless access to it—no NFC, Bluetooth, or satellite. The only way into Luna was through a hardline, and those were only handed out to businesses and residents of note.

Luckily for Danny, Lincoln Tate was of note.

Jane still hadn't returned when Danny jacked out of his private mapping construct. He lingered in the room, taking his time to draw out the cable from the hardline at the head of the bed. He slotted the jack into the back of his immersion rig and waited for the device to register on the network. Tiny LEDs flashed exploratory orange before settling into a rapid green flicker.

Danny sat on the edge of the bed, stared at the door for a moment. Something in him wanted to wait, wanted to see her walk in one last time. She'd left so nonchalantly earlier, as if that glimpse of her through the closing door wouldn't be the last. Perhaps if she had hesitated at all, had looked back over her shoulder and given some sign that she didn't want to leave, he could get on with his work without worrying.

As it stood, he didn't want to put the rig back on, but he did anyway. Nor did he want to recline on the bed and fold his hands over his chest like some kind of techno-vampire, but he did. And even as reality began to slip away, he tried to hold onto it, tried to steady an oblique view of the door, a sliver of metal barely visible under the lower rim of his rig.

Open before the network takes me, he thought.

But it didn't.

Danny floated in open space; the pressure of the bed melted away. In front of him, the virtual sphere of Luna bloomed like a harvest moon, sparkling a white so pure that it was hard to make out the individual features on the landscape below.

He fell toward the surface in a smooth arc, much like the Apollo landers during their historic descents. Gray blurs became craters that hid shadows, and in those shadows, entire cities twinkled like fields of stars. The largest of the fields was dead center in Danny's view, and as he drew closer, he tried to gauge the server load by the number of avatars walking the gray, rocky streets.

His boots touched down at Lazy Zero and threw up a plume of dust that was carried away by a cleansing wind. A tremor on his wrist drew his attention to his sliver.

Welcome to Luna, guest of Lincoln Continental.

The MAC address of the hardline followed, along with the implication that they knew exactly where he was plugged in. None of the location data ever left Luna—according to the sysops, anyhow—but it was always there for reference in case a visitor ever got too far out of line.

Danny pushed off from Lazy Zero and rode the low gravity to Irwin Street. There were only twelve main roads on Luna; each of them set out from Lazy Zero like the lines of a basketball, reconnecting on the other side at Lazy One. Danny was only familiar with a few of the streets. There was code that graded from black to white on Conrad Street, programs and mods that could do things both legal and otherwise. Shepard Lane was mostly virtual construct apps; Danny had bought his mapping construct generator there years ago. Halfway between Lazy Zero and Lazy One on Shepard was all the porn any man could ever ask for.

A gamer could spend their life on Armstrong Boulevard and only experience a fraction of the immersive simulations offered there. With titles from big name game-makers like Tritan Entertainment and Ragatanga Studios, Armstrong attracted everyone from professional e-sports athletes to honeymooners looking for a little violence to spice up their sex lives.

Irwin Street had a reputation for catering to older hackers, amorphous avatars with thick beards and thicker glasses who talked endlessly about the good old days of bulletin board systems, token ring networks, and phone phreaking. Danny had never really felt a connection with that era, just as his grandchildren would feel no connection with someone who had grown up in the 90s.

None of the avatars he passed on his walk seemed overtly old, but then most of them wore the default NASA-inspired spacesuit, complete with patches and a reversed American flag. It wasn't until Danny began glancing through windows and open shop doors that he spied the ancients. They had an aura about them, a radioactive glow from having logged so many hours on Luna.

If his visit to BK Rewind didn't turn up anything useful, the ancients would be the ones to ask next. He hoped it wouldn't come to that.

The longer Danny walked, the less confident he became that the visit to Luna would be worth the effort. He'd come on a hunch, a hope that maybe BK Rewind had crawled—intentionally or otherwise—the Brigham Plaza construct. Danny's mapping program had failed to penetrate some areas of the map, so the next logical step was to bring in a better program, one that had already done the work for him.

From the outside, BK Rewind looked no bigger than a corner convenience store, but the interior lobby seemed to stretch beyond the boundaries of the Luna sphere itself. Spread out in this infinite virtual space were illuminated pedestals containing two or three avatars, each of the groups contained inside a sphere about fifty feet in diameter. Faintly, the images muddled by the spheres themselves, Danny could see other constructs, as if portals had been opened to virtual worlds outside of Luna.

"Welcome," said an older man in a gray suit. "I'm Proctor Wyatt. Is there something I can show you today?"

Danny noticed the man's graying hair was repeated on other avatars in BK; Wyatt was a clone of a pseudo-AI.

"I have some coordinates I need analyzed. I want to see the earliest records you have."

"It would be my pleasure." Wyatt opened his hand and produced a palette. "Please, type them in."

Danny took the palette and keyed in the numbers from memory. There was no way he'd ever forget them now. Once he'd finished, a green checkmark appeared below the input field. The palette blinked out of existence.

Proctor Wyatt nodded and smiled as if he'd just smelled a fragrant bouquet of flowers. He gestured to a raised pedestal on his left and invited Danny to join him. Once aboard, the pedestal shot forward into the empty blackness of BK Rewind with no regard for inertia or momentum.

After a few seconds, Danny hardly knew if they were moving at the speed of light or standing still.

"I will pull the most recent cache of this site from our archives and show you how to rewind through the revisions. You will not be able to interact with any of the virtual constructs as these are only snapshots."

"How long will this take?" asked Danny.

"Only a moment."

There was a faint sizzle in the air, as if an unseen filament were burning out. A translucent sphere appeared around the pedestal, shimmering in a barely-there glint of light. The interior of BK Rewind disappeared, and suddenly Danny was standing in a foggy graveyard full of decrepit headstones. Ravens perched on craggy branches of skeleton trees, and the wind blew black leaves in tight swirls along the ground.

Danny looked to the proctor.

"This isn't the right construct."

"No," said Wyatt. "It appears our last scan encountered a 301 redirect. Let me try an earlier copy."

The sphere shimmered briefly, settled on the graveyard again. Blue will-o'-the-wisps danced among the scarred trunks of trees, blinking in and out as Danny tried to focus on them. A raven's screech made the hair on the back of his neck stand up.

"The redirect appears to be present in all scans going back to 2005. I will load the last known good scan of the site."

Danny narrowed his eyes as a sun bloomed on the sphere above him. A blue sky stretched to the horizon where it met an unending sea of tall, green grass. Wind blew across the empty prairie, bringing with it the smell of fresh, clean air— similar to Vail, but lacking the pine undertones.

The proctor turned in place and was the first to notice the stone monument behind them. Danny followed his gaze, took in the crumbling rocks and slanted supports.

"Your left hand controls the version," said Wyatt. "Open your fingers and rotate them counterclockwise to rewind, clockwise to fast forward. Your right hand can zoom and pan using standard palette gestures."

"Okay, but this is nothing like how the construct is now. I have no idea what this is."

The proctor nodded. "Much can change in fourteen years."

The pseudo-AI was pseudo-insightful.

Danny reached out with his right hand and pulled the image closer. The pile of rocks did appear to be some kind of monument, but there was no plaque indicating its purpose. Pushing back through the months and years, Danny watched bits of stone climb back into their original positions, growing from what looked like a Greek lambda into a full-blown X.

"X?" said Danny. "Not *the* X, is it?"

"I'm afraid I don't know."

In 2003, avatars milled around the monument. They snapped selfies at a respectful distance or laid flowers at its base. The weather never varied. The time of day never changed. Only the crowds got bigger, growing to a size that could rival a stadium concert.

In 2001, the monument regained a polished sheen undamaged by the constant sun. A year before that, a solitary figure stood in front of the towering *X*.

It had the stature of a young woman, with long, braided hair over a pearlescent blue trench coat. The rest of her avatar was hard to make out, as the snapshot appeared to be out of focus. More accurately, *she* was out of focus; everything else was crystal clear.

The tape ran out in the spring of 1999. When Danny tried to turn his hand, large block letters informed him of an error.

"What's the problem?" he asked.

"It appears this construct did not exist in VNet prior to March 27 of 1999. There is an import tag present in the cached meta. Would you like me to load the related content from the Net?"

"Yes."

"Switching databanks."

Danny checked his sliver. No new messages from Tanzy. No message from Jane. The outside world was spinning happily without him, as usual.

"I found a related record from January 23, 1999. Loading."

A rippled white wall grew up in front of Danny, shooting into the upper sphere and bending forward over his head. The wall was partitioned into squares, giving it the appearance of a pale ear of corn.

"Homedirs," said Danny. He recalled his own homedir from his youth and the various nudie posters he'd plastered over its walls. His insertion point into the Net had been his home away from home for much of his early life, and Vinestead had squashed it like a roach under their boot.

But how had a homedir come to be imported into VNet? Vinestead didn't carry over the homedir system, so why would they need an entire block of them?

Danny turned in place until he found it—a single homedir wall that glowed with emerald flashes.

"Is this where the monument was in the other construct?" asked Danny.

"Yes, that is the approximate position."

"And there are no other records between now and the first import into VNet?"

"One, but it is corrupt."

"Show me."

Every cube except the green homedir flickered out, then back in, as if they were stuck between two states of existence.

"Someone imported this homedir into VNet," said Danny. "But why?"

"I'm afraid I don't know."

Danny reached his hand out, rotated it counterclockwise until two figures appeared on the dim walkway in front of the homedir.

"I've been here before," said Danny. "It was all broken and scattered, but I've been here. This place still exists."

And he wasn't the only one.

Though he couldn't see the woman's face and didn't recognize her blonde hair or tall stature, the man was familiar enough.

It was Gordon, or as he was known back then, G.

G and some woman were standing outside a green homedir that would eventually turn into a monument to X.

It didn't take a pseudo-AI to figure out whose homedir it was.

"Would you like me to—"

Danny jacked out.

And emerged into a dark bedroom. As he removed his rig, he sought out Jane's body in the sheets next to him.

"Hey," he whispered.

No one answered. And as his eyes adjusted, they confirmed what he was feeling with his hand—nothing.

The room was empty.

Danny pushed his rig aside and swung his legs off the bed. He walked over to the dresser near the window. His suitcase lay open, its contents picked at. Next to it was empty space.

He put a hand on the dresser where Jane's suitcase should have been.

THIRTY-SEVEN
KAILI

Kaili rocked back and forth in the chair, tracing the edges of the code cube with her finger. She barely heard Rick excuse himself, didn't really pay attention when he said he was going to connect the House to VNet. All she could think about was whether she had the strength and the lack of self-respect to simply kill herself.

The Reaping. Calle Cinco de Mayo. Perion City.

She'd come too far for it to end this way.

"A Zabora never breaks," she whispered to the cube.

As if summoned by the mantra, Anela knocked softly on the front door and came inside. She stepped into the foyer with wide eyes, as if she were some sentient being recalling one of her own memories and not merely a mental schism.

Anela looked out of place in their old house. The dress she wore and the tight bun that held her hair in place were artifacts of an older Anela, not the one who used to lounge around the house in yoga pants and oversized sweatshirts. After leaving for Texas, she'd promised Kaili she would come back and visit, but she never got the chance. Now the reunion Kaili had waited so long for was happening, and none of it was real.

Kaili squeezed the cube in her fist.

"This is wonderful," said Anela, placing her hand on the wood paneling. "I see mom and dad never modernized."

"You should have come back. You promised."

Anela nodded. She crossed the living room to the sliding glass doors that led into the backyard.

"It was always my intention," she said. "ZabSix was doing well in Austin, but San Diego was always my home. I would have come eventually, but… you know."

Kaili knew.

19 Dead in Old Downtown Turf War. 8 Bodies of Missing Persons Found.

"I don't care about Vinestead. I only care about X."

Kaili looked up at Anela, but the words hadn't come from her sister. She got up from her chair and followed the sound into the hallway. Footsteps clacked on a hard floor; the echoes spilled out of a room at the back of the house.

Anela's room.

"You *should* care about Vinestead," said another version of Anela. "Or hell, maybe not. It would be one thing if you were going to live past tonight. Since that has already been decided, I guess you are right. You do not have to care. I just wanted you to know your anger is misdirected."

Kaili stood at the threshold and peered into an office she had only seen in low-res surveillance videos. Anela stood in the center of the room with a gun pointed at a younger woman with blonde hair matted to her face with blood. Kaili had never had such a clean look at the woman who had helped murder her sister.

"What is this?" asked Kaili.

Rick appeared next to her, stuck his head into the room, and replied, "This is a memory. Your sister's memory, to be exact. Hard-coded into the Nepenthe program."

"Well, if you have no further statements, then I think it is time I retired you. After all, you have cost me an entire guard team. They will not be cheap to replace."

Kaili searched the marble floor and saw a body hidden in the shadows.

The woman's name was Natalie.

The body had a name too.

"G," said Kaili, through gritted teeth.

"The last time I saw X," said Natalie, "we were at the club. Then you showed up and took him away. *You*, not Vinestead."

"I admit I did take him. But with good reason."

"And what did you do with him?"

Kaili stepped into the room, into the memory, wanting a better look at G, but no matter how close she got, his face remained hidden.

"All I did was jack him in. He was complaining about a virus in the Net, but since he had been dishonest before, I saw no reason to believe him."

"Where is he now?" asked Natalie.

G stirred, pulled himself up.

Just a little closer, thought Kaili. If he just came a little more into the light, she could see his face and burn it into her memory.

"What does it matter to you? You are going to be dead inside of five seconds and then you will not even care anymore. Save your last question for something important. I promise I will answer it truthfully."

Finally, G moved out of the shadows. Though his face was bruised, cut, and streaked with blood, Kaili etched the flaring nostrils and thick eyebrows into the back of her brain. The satisfaction of identifying her sister's killer was short-lived; she remembered why he was standing up.

He was going to hit Anela from behind.

"Where is my X?" screamed Natalie.

"No!" Kaili lunged at G.

"He is in the basement," said Anela.

A shot rang out and Kaili spun in place. G had gone right through her, as if she were nothing more than a harmless mist.

"Your knife," he rasped.

Kaili felt hands under her arms, looked up to find Rick grabbing her from behind.

"You don't need to see this," he said, dragging her back to the door. "This memory wasn't meant for you."

"Yes it was! She left this for me." She wrenched herself out of Rick's grasp, fell to her knees, and crawled to where Anela lay on her back atop G, helpless and trapped. Kaili tried to cover her sister, but fell through her to occupy the same space as Anela and G. She looked up and saw Natalie standing over her, knife in hand, arm raised.

"Goddammit, Natalie! Stab this bitch!"

The knife came down hard in Kaili's gut, but the scream that erupted from her mouth was not her own. The room shimmered, began to break down.

"We did it, G," said Natalie. "We got her."

Kaili put her hands to her head and screamed. The House dimmed, demurring under the weight of her rage. She lay on her back, eyes shut, chest heaving. A hand touched her shoulder, moved to caress her arm.

Through the tears, Kaili saw Rick hovering over her. He held her hand with his and kissed the wedding ring on her thumb.

"Can you really do it?" she asked. "Can you connect me to VNet?"

If her fate was to die trapped and alone in Arthur Sedivy's virtual prison, then so be it, but at least she could put the word out about G, post his face on every vidscreen in the country along with a bounty.

One million dollars. Dead or alive.

"I'm afraid not," said Rick. "Something is blocking the connection. There aren't any near-field repeaters in range. I'm sorry."

Kaili shook her head.

"Figures." She took a breath as the sobbing subsided. "Why would she do this? Why would she leave this memory for me?"

"I do not think I did," said Anela, from the doorway.

Kaili sat up and looked at her sister. Her face had blanched after watching her own death.

"I have always been the part of you that questions everything," she continued. "Why not this? After everything that has happened since Le Soleil Rouge, how can you take this at face value?"

19 Dead in Old Downtown Turf War.

A dozen-plus bodyguards. Five ciphers. Anela Zabora.

"You were still alive," said Kaili.

Anela folded her arms but said nothing.

"When you saved that memory. You embedded it in this program and put it back in place. The only way it could contain this memory is if you updated it."

"As I lay dying," said Anela.

Kaili sat up, wiped her cheeks. "How's that possible?"

Rick stood and offered a hand to Kaili. His smile reminded her of the man she missed so much.

"The House of Nepenthe is home to many wonders," he said. Behind him, the walls of Anela's office were fading out.

Kaili thought about what it would mean for Anela to have access to the House in her final seconds of life. She would have bled out from the multiple stab wounds, but there would have been a few seconds of consciousness during which she could have, what, uploaded her final memories to Vinestead's servers?

It didn't seem probable, and yet, here she was.

Kaili watched the room return to its normal state—Anela's childhood bedroom. Portions of the wall dissolved into music posters and dark, abstract art. The ceiling dropped, extruded a fan into the center of the room. The blades spun restlessly.

The memory had replayed without commentary, but the message was clear. *Avenge me.*

Kaili reached for Rick's hand and allowed him to pull her up.

"Something to drink?" he asked. "A stiff one to calm the nerves?"

"How about a cup of Bubbling Joe's?" she replied, thinking of the small coffee shop where she and Rick had started their day together all those years ago.

"Coming right up," he replied, leading her out of the room by the elbow.

They walked together to the kitchen, and Kaili followed his direction when he motioned to a small Formica table pushed up against the wall. Anela sat down across from her, crossing her legs at the ankles.

"Will you pour one for yourself?" asked Kaili.

"As you wish."

Anela raised an eyebrow. Kaili returned a smirk.

"I'm sorry I wasn't able to bring you justice."

"You tried, Kaili. You tried for years. For that, I will always be thankful."

"I could've done more."

"Three cups of hot Bubbling Joe's," said Rick, placing the mugs on the table. He slid one to Kaili and Anela, then took his seat between them.

Kaili lifted her cup, watched the steam drift away.

"To revenge," she said.

"To never breaking," said Anela.

"To never forgetting," said Rick.

She took a long sip of the coffee, felt the burn on her tongue and in her throat, but locked down the pain to leave only the rich flavor. For a simulated drink, it wasn't bad.

Kaili put the mug down and pulled the code cube from her pocket. She placed it on the table in front of her.

For a simulated death, it wasn't bad either.

"What a way to go," she said.

"A prison becomes a home if you have the key," said Rick. "George Sterling said that."

"I don't know who that is," said Kaili.

Anela cleared her throat. "Death is not so bad, nor is sticking it to Vinestead one last time."

"Sedivy's going to be pissed," said Kaili.

She licked the code cube's white electrode and placed it on the back of her neck, unsure if the step was even necessary. The cube cycled through the color wheel, fading from a deep red to a rousing purple to a neon green. She let her finger hover above its surface.

You lose, Arthur, she thought. *I'm going somewhere you can never reach me.*

Somewhere light and beautiful; with soft sand and clear water; with birds suspended in the sky; with a sun warming the skin on her body; with Anela laughing at the pages of a magazine; with Rick collecting seashells; with everything perfect, forever and ever.

Anela placed her hand on top of Kaili's.

Rick mirrored the gesture.

"I'll see you both soon," she said.

"There is no shame in this," said Rick.

"There's always shame in giving up," said Kaili.

She tapped the cube. Her finger sank through it like it was fresh snow, crushing one face before the cube grabbed onto her nail. It pulled her forward. The room shifted out from under her chair and broke down in an ever-loudening series of crunches.

Wood splintered. Bones shattered.

The House of Nepenthe folded in on itself.

Then, darkness.

"Did you do something?" asked a male voice, but it wasn't Rick's.

"No, did you?" A woman; definitely not Anela.

Kaili blinked, tried to make sense of the shadowy shapes.

"She's moving. How the fuck is she moving, Cyn?"

Cyn? Cynthia Mesquina, from Perion City?

She felt something in her throat and began to choke.

"Shit, pull that out of her, G."

G?

Her stomach heaved.

"Oh, fuck me," said Cyn. "Get the visor! Use your elbows."

Suddenly, the world was too bright; light stung at her from every direction.

"Easy, easy," said the man, said *G.*

No, it couldn't be.

There was no way the man who she'd just watched kill her sister was now standing next to her. And yet Cyn had called him by that name.

"Let your eyes adjust," he continued.

Kaili squinted, tried to allow for only the smallest amount of light. She shook her head, blinked rapidly. Figures emerged from the blinding haze—a woman standing to her right, and a beat-to-shit man on her left.

Features settled: shiny black hair, augmented eyes, and earrings climbing both earlobes.

"Cyn?"

"Well, hello there, Ms. Kessler."

"How?" sputtered Kaili.

"No need to thank me. G did most of the heavy lifting."

She turned her head and looked into G's bloodshot eyes.

The G.

Kaili bucked against her restraints.

"You son of a bitch!" she screamed.

"Okay, okay," said Cyn, "we kinda figured that'd be your response."

"I'll fucking kill you! Let me up, Cyn! Let me up!"

Cyn took a step back. "I understand you guys have some history, but it's gonna have to wait. We have a situation we need your help with first. If you agree to put off your revenge, I'll let you up."

Kaili clenched her jaw. "Kill him," she said tightly. "Kill him, Cyn. A million dollars. I promise." The tears came, tinting the world red. Her throat collapsed and released. "Just please. Please do it, Cyn."

"We'll give you a minute," said Cyn. "Come on, G. I'll let Tanzy know we're running behind."

He nodded and followed her out of what looked like an old prison cell.

Cyn turned beyond the bars and said, "We can only leave if you're calm, but don't take too long. They know we're here."

They disappeared around the corner and Kaili was alone.

She closed her eyes, took a deep breath.

Her private construct bloomed like a firework.

Only this time, Anela did not stand nearby waiting to provide some insight or piece of advice. Instead, she lay supine on the floor of the construct, floating in shallow, dark water. Crimson gashes dotted her dress. Blood seeped into the fabric.

She said nothing, but the message was clear.

Avenge me.

THIRTY-EIGHT
TANZY

The plane lurched and dove for the clouds. Across from Tanzy, a stone-faced Lincoln sat staring into space, his eyes half-open, as if he were in some kind of trance. Tanzy guessed his biochip was doing some work in the background, maybe taking him out of the moment to save him from experiencing the fear and uncertainty of their descent. And no sooner had Tanzy crystalized this idea in her head than Cleo took it upon herself to pull the same trick.

In one moment, Tanzy was gripping the leather arms of her seat, steadying herself against the sharp incline of the cabin. The next, she was back in her childhood home, but not as a digital avatar in a simulation. There wasn't enough detail in the environment to suggest a computer was responsible for its creation. No, the small dining room was a product of her imagination, a moving watercolor scene projected into her dream world.

Cleo had the power to pull Tanzy into a simulation, but in all their time together, she'd never once forced her into REM sleep. The very fact that it was happening impressed Tanzy, and she made a note to discuss the logistics with Cleo if they survived. Insomnia was a common problem among the information dependent; code that pushed them right to the lowest levels of sleep would be extremely valuable on the black market.

The dining room smelled vaguely of smoke, and the windows rattled from the strong vibrations and sudden shifts in gravity coming from beyond the walls. A long wooden table filled most of the space; six chairs were set evenly around it. A white runner extended from the head to the foot—lacy on the edges, the way her mom liked.

Tanzy approached the table, but the sudden ringing of a phone on the wall startled her, and she jumped back to the jet.

"Tell me something good," said Lincoln, shouting across the aisle.

Bryce struggled to keep a palette on his lap as he typed.

"Drone's still tailing us, but it's not firing."

"Do the pilots know?" asked Tanzy.

Lincoln gave her a puzzled looked. He opened his mouth to speak, but the shrill ringing of a phone swallowed his reply.

Tanzy snapped to the black phone mounted beneath an analog clock on the wall. In the time before slivers and the Net, phones were tied to actual hardlines in people's homes, and when they rang, there was no telling who might be on the other end.

The ringing cut out as Tanzy picked up the receiver and placed it to her ear.

"Hello?" Her voice squeaked. She couldn't have been more than ten.

"Hi, can I speak to Megan Riley, please?"

"This… this is her."

"Megan, hi, this is Shane Whitbrook from I.C.E. BBS. I'm just calling to confirm the phone number you signed up with."

Shane Whitbrook, Tanzy remembered, was the Sysop of I.C.E. and went by the handle *Savage* online. He had a reputation across most of the boards as a real tight-ass who ruled I.C.E. with an iron fist. Most people who signed up for his BBS were kicked and banned within a couple weeks for violating some obscure rule. Some didn't even make it a day.

"Okay."

"So, you're Tanzy, huh?"

"Yes… yes sir." Tanzy cringed at her delivery, at the forced deference, but somehow it had worked, had made Savage think she was an innocent little girl who posed no threat to his board.

"Well, okay. I'll mark your account as verified. Have fun and remember to be polite."

"Okay."

A guttural dial tone roared through the receiver; Tanzy jerked away.

"We're diverting east," said Bryce. His voice was barely audible over the whine of the remaining engine. It was definitely working overtime to keep them in the air.

"Why east?" asked Tanzy.

"Drone can't cross state lines without tripping FAA alarms," said Bryce. "Vinestead won't want that kind of heat."

"Carson City?" asked Lincoln.

"Yeah, ten minutes 'til wheels down."

"Are we gonna make it?" asked Tanzy.

"Shit," said Lincoln. "Takes more than a plane crash to kill—"

Metal wrenched against metal; the cabin plunged into darkness.

"What?" asked Tanzy.

"I said I need you to take the trash out."

She looked up into the doleful eyes of her mother. The dream wouldn't let the rest of her face settle into anything recognizable. She was just eyes floating in a blur of flesh framed by stringy brown hair that she wouldn't cut until she came out of her latest bender.

"Not now, I'm busy," said Tanzy, slamming the door and locking it. She returned to the lap desk she'd set up in the center of her room. There, white tick marks marched across a black screen. She'd been logged into I.C.E. since before lunch, and in that time, she'd manage to grief every board module without detection.

The last names of every user on the board changed to *Von Fart*.

Messages were translated into Russian, then Tagalog, and then back into English.

Every message sent to Teleconference was changed to *Touch my nips*.

The fun ended around 9:00 p.m. when Savage finally booted her. The real work began when she logged back in a few minutes later using a backdoor she'd installed during her rampage. Without physical access to the computer running the board, Savage couldn't kill the null user he saw logged in.

He could only watch helplessly as his entire user databank shrank to nothing, as mailboxes reset to zero, and as his own access began to flake, injecting so much line noise into his terminal that he had to disconnect to keep his computer from crashing.

And when he did finally return, he found a fresh board with a new splash screen.

Welcome to I.C.E-1 BBS.

Sysop: Tanzy

"It was the same board as before," Tanzy had told Danny once, "but minus one asshole."

A wave of turbulence rushed down the aisle, shaking Tanzy hard enough that her seatbelt cut painfully into her stomach. She cried out, and Lincoln made an aborted reach across the table.

He waited for the tremor to pass before asking, "You good?"

"Stop it, Cleo!" screamed Tanzy.

I'm only trying to help.

"You wanna help? Patch me into the I.C.E-1 feed for a live broadcast."

Connecting.

"What are you doing?" asked Lincoln.

"Trying to get that drone off our tail."

You are now live on the I.C.E-1 feed. Voice transcription is active.

"This is Tanzy of I.C.E-1," she said, closing her eyes. She let a beat go by so her audience could hear the whine of the engine. "I'm in a private plane that is being fired upon by a Vinestead International drone. It has disabled one of our engines already. I am demanding Vinestead immediately cease its pursuit of this plane and allow us to land safely. And when I say us, I'm including Lincoln Tate, who is sitting across from me. Arthur Sedivy, you are about to kill the leaders of I.C.E-1 and Lincoln Continental. I urge you to reconsider. Cut it, Cleo."

Message recorded.

"Play it on a loop until we've landed safely."

Looping.

"Bryce," said Lincoln, "grab the I.C.E-1 feed and rebroadcast it. Interrupt whatever's going out right now."

"On it." He tapped at the palette, holding it hard against his stomach.

"I think you overestimate Vinestead's shame," said Lincoln.

Tanzy shook her head. "Gotta do something. Not gonna spend my last moments sleeping."

"We're over Lake Tahoe," said Bryce. "Crossing state line in three, two, one..."

The plane's dramatic descent ended abruptly as it nosed up, tilting Tanzy back in her seat. A loose cart rolled from the front of the plane to the back.

"If we make it over the mountains, we're—"

Oxygen masks dropped from the ceiling; Bryce paused to put his on.

Tanzy stared at Lincoln across the table. He made no move to reach for the mask.

"We're low enough," he said. "Pressure's fine."

The engine gave one last surge of power, and Tanzy could imagine the plane cresting some snow-covered peak. The RPMs revved down, and everything became quiet except for the rushing wind.

A synthesized voice came over the PA.

"Terrain, terrain. Brace, brace, brace..."

"Drone broke off!" Bryce put his hands in the air; the palette slipped off his lap into the aisle.

Tanzy...

"What now?"

If this is the end...

"It's not."

But if it is...

"Don't do it. I swear to Christ, Cleo."

I'm sorry.

The cabin shrank to a tiny white dot and blinked out.

Midnight in Sagamihara. The heat. The crowd. The smell of authentic ramen. Above, twinkling stars rotated in the black dome. Bits of conversation floated up from the street below—arguments in both English and Japanese. The rooftop café was just high enough to make its patrons feel above the noise, to offer respite from the bustle below.

Tanzy sat with a corporeal Cleo at a small table near the edge of the roof with only a knee-high retaining wall to keep customers from falling off.

The sweat hit her immediately as the construct shoved environmental data into her biochip. The comfy leather seat of the airplane became molded plastic on a wire frame. Tanzy stared at the red-tinged drink in her hand, struggled to remember what it was called or what was in it.

Beside her, a mousy Cleo leaned back in her chair, her half-shirt bunching up tightly under her breasts. Her hand lay across her exposed stomach; two extended fingers held a brown cigarette—cloves, not tobacco. A small clump of ash fell from the cigarette; Cleo brushed it away absently.

"You know I went to see Bush last week," she said, and her voice was so rich and vibrant, much more *alive* than the Cleo voice Tanzy heard in her head. "Pushed my way up to the front and got close enough to see the bulge in Gavin's leather pants."

She took a drag.

"Anyway, he spit on me."

"He what?" asked Tanzy.

Cleo glanced at her. "He spit on me. Ya know, he came to the edge of the stage and he was singing and some of his spit just landed on my face. On my lips." She touched her mouth with her free hand. "I've tasted Gavin Rossdale's saliva. We practically kissed."

Tanzy sat up, put her drink on the wobbly table.

"Why are you telling me this?"

"Thought it was a good story."

"No, I mean, why are you *showing* me this night, Cleo? You know what's going on out there… why drag me into *this?*"

Cleo narrowed her eyes. "I don't know what you're talking about. Drag you into this? This was your idea. You're the one who wanted to meet up tonight."

"I want to be back in the plane, back in the real world."

"What are you talking—"

"Stop fucking with me, Cleo!" Tanzy swiped at the glass, knocking it off the table. Somewhere below, a man cursed in Japanese.

Cleo slowly placed her cigarette on the table. She stood, adjusted her shirt, and walked away.

"Hey!"

Tanzy gave chase. She grabbed Cleo's wrist, spun her around.

"All I wanted was a few last minutes together!" Cleo pushed Tanzy's hand away. "Five minutes where you're not talking about I.C.E-1 or Vinestead or Kaili fucking Zabora. Who is she to us, Megan? Huh? I've had to watch you obsess over everyone else in the world except me, your best friend since the beginning, since before Savage and Channel 8. I live inside your head, my entire existence is for you, and you can't give me the common courtesy of your company?"

There were tears in her eyes; they lifted her mascara and carried it down her cheeks.

"What happened to my friend?" she asked.

"I…"

"Don't answer," said Cleo, shaking her head. "You don't know, and I don't care. I'm tired of this."

"Cleo…"

"I don't want to be here anymore, in your head, in this construct. This was my strongest memory of us, and you've ruined it."

"If you'll just—"

"Leave, Megan. Just go."

Tanzy reached out a hand.

"Leave!"

Cleo booted her.

Brace, brace, brace…

The plane's synthesized voice disappeared under the squeal of tires hitting tarmac. Tanzy bounced in her chair, felt every oscillation of the hydraulic suspension as it struggled to find equilibrium. The engine cycled up, reversing its thrust to slow the plane down.

Tanzy reflexively folded over, hugged her knees.

The right armrest dug into her ribs.

There was something not right about the ground rushing by beneath her. It was no longer smooth and gentle.

She had a bad feeling the plane had left the runway entirely.

THIRTY-NINE
GORDON

They rested at the end of the cellblock.

Cyn put down on one knee while Gordon leaned against the wall and cradled his hands to his chest. There was an undulating uncertainty broiling in his stomach that got worse every time he looked at his mangled fingers. Most had been cut down to the bone, and though they weren't bleeding anymore, Gordon thought he could see the skin breathing, pulsing with a horrible pain that had yet to reach his brain.

Only the code was standing in the way now.

He worried about the damage and the lack of feedback. Pain existed for a reason, and if he blocked it out forever, he might lose his hands out of pure ignorance.

"How long do you think we should let her stew before we go back in?" asked Cyn.

Gordon shook his head. "I'm not going back in."

Cyn looked up, raised an eyebrow. "Excuse me?"

"This was a mistake." Gordon grunted as he came off the wall. He walked to the double doors leading out of the cell block, stood in the threshold.

"Oh, come on. How could we know she would recognize you? I've seen the footage from ZabSix in Austin—everyone has. You're nothing but a blur of pixels."

"You called me *G. You* told her who I was. But it doesn't matter. I never should have gone in there in the first place. And we shouldn't have come in here without knowing what we were up against. We had shitty intel and poor prep. We don't deserve to walk out of here alive."

"But we will. You know that, right?"

Gordon nodded. "I don't see anyone here who'll say otherwise. Except the package." He looked over his shoulder at the cell block. Lights flickered in the distance, popping shadows over the floor.

"She'll come around." Cyn stood and joined him at the door, put a hand on his arm. "Once she realizes what we did for her, she'll be grateful."

His stomach tied itself into a knot. "You know her better than I do, but I'm not going back in there. If she needs help walking, you're better off carrying her than me." He held up his hands. "I'm not in any condition to be escorting or fighting. But I can be a diversion."

"We're not splitting up," said Cyn. Her fingers tightened on his bicep.

"I can't be in the same room as Kaili. You're gonna have to take her to the boat yourself. I'll find my own way back to Umbra."

"Is that bullshit?" Cyn stepped in front of him. "Are you just telling me that so I'll let you go?"

"What do you want from me?" he snapped.

Her eyes jumped side-to-side. "You may look like a grown man, G, but you're still a child when it comes to women." She broke off, stomped angrily down the cell block.

"I'll see you in Umbra," he called after her.

"Whatever." She didn't bother turning her head to speak.

Gordon clenched his jaw, bit down until the pain was too much. He understood women just fine, knew enough to keep them at a distance. What he understood was that connections were messy and adding women and children to the mix only made it harder to survive when shit hit the fan. He hadn't taken his memories of Natalie and their son to LPS with him, but somewhere deep down he'd known he was running from something, refusing a connection that would have compromised his survival.

And now Cyn wanted some kind of connection in a world that was already spinning out of control, a world where the very definition of humanity was changing.

It was too much, too quickly.

Gordon hot-swapped Pale Rider with an athletic mod built around long-distance running called Treadwell. It gave the impression of lightness, as if he were running along the surface of the moon in a dream, taking effortless strides over long distances. He hurdled bodies and debris as if they were pebbles in the street. The code regulated his breathing, conducted a looping chorus of long, deep breaths followed by sharp exhales.

He slowed near the front of the prison. Light spilled in through the open front doors, and for a moment, he imagined a platoon of synthetic soldiers waiting outside with spotlights and guns trained. Gordon poked his head out slowly, ready to bolt in the opposite direction at the first sign of a threat.

Instead, he saw a dark, empty parking lot. The light was coming from above, from tiny, hovering drones that crisscrossed over the main entryway. They seemed to serve no purpose other than to provide illumination. Gordon imagined they had cameras, but that just meant someone would see him; there wasn't actually anyone there to do something about it.

Gordon stepped out onto the sidewalk, froze for a moment as the drones converged on his position, their prop arrays buzzing like gigantic bees. He put a bloody hand to his brow to keep the light out of his eyes.

The squawk of a loudspeaker made the hair on the back of his neck stand up.

"You are trespassing on private property," said a booming, male voice. "Remain where you are."

He ran.

His boots, slick with synthetic blood, barely held to the damp evercrete. He dodged trucks and SUVs in the parking lot, ducked under solar canopies as the drones gave chase. The road dipped toward the river, and Gordon followed it south until he came to the perimeter wall. Several well-placed hops got him over the rocky shoreline and into the water. He dove beneath the surface, heard the muffled white noise of props following just above him.

The rocks on the other side of the river were slick and covered in some kind of slime. He climbed slowly while the drones dove at his head. Whoever was operating them must have realized no one was going to get to him in time; their only choice was to divebomb and hope to score a knockout hit.

Gordon sped up as the ground turned to dirt. He scaled a wooded incline and came out in a neighborhood full of dilapidated condos. He knew it was past midnight, and yet the streets he darted across were alive with activity. It seemed most of the residents had come outside to watch the spectacle unfolding at Folsom. He even risked a glance backwards to see the full-on circus happening both in the air and on the ground at the larger facility beyond the prison.

Nobody stopped him or really even looked at him. They just stood at the end of their sidewalks, small dogs in their arms, frilly robes blowing in the breeze, muttering under their breath about *those animals* breaking free of their cages.

The high trees of the neighborhood provided good cover against the drones, and when it seemed no spotlight was on him, Gordon ducked into a tiny walkway between two condos. He came out on an unfenced backyard and hit a gravel alleyway. There, a two-tone green and black truck sat idling. A spotlight mounted on the side swiveled in his direction.

Gordon stopped, considered his options. To either side was open grass full of furniture and swimming pools.

"Excuse me, sir. Are you a Gracy Farms resident?"

The glint of a long-barrel Smith & Wesson shone through the man's silhouette.

"Yes," said Gordon.

"Can you tell me which unit is yours?"

"No."

The man came forward. "Sir, this is private property. I have notified the police and will detain you until they arrive."

Gordon took a deep breath, let the Treadwell mod unload gracefully.

"It's impolite to point a gun at someone you don't intend to kill," he said.

"Get down on your knees, sir."

"See, you're still doing it." Gordon spread his arms out to the side. "Where I come from, a man could get his ass beat for less."

"I will shoot! You're trespassing. I have the legal right under Folsom city code—"

G shot forward, felt the zip of a large-caliber bullet sneak by his left ear. The crack of the gunshot echoed in the quiet night, and somewhere in the distance, he thought he heard the collective gasp of affluent condo owners.

The security guard was nothing compared to the synthetics at Folsom. He was short, overweight, and poorly coordinated. Gordon put him down with a single elbow strike to the face, collapsing the poor man like a soda can.

Gordon took his gun, a short strap with six more slotted bullets, and a small fob with a silver Toyota emblem on it. He gingerly wrapped his fingers around the gun's grip, eased his index finger over the trigger, and fired a few shots at the drones circling high above. They zigzagged in the sky, taking evasive action even though G had little chance of hitting them.

The buzzing of the drone props lessened as he climbed into the truck and shut the door. He used his palm to put the vehicle in gear and then mashed the accelerator. The alley was barely wide enough to fit through; several times he scraped against a trashcan or open fence. He hit a street after half a minute of bouncing along gravel, and once he was on steadier ground, he opened up the throttle and headed down toward the highway.

In the rearview mirror, the drones lined up behind him, spreading into a *V* formation once they had enough room. Desperate horns rang out from either side as Gordon blew through stop lights and stop signs. The drones swooped down to eye-level to follow him across a bridge.

"Fuck me," growled G, spying the police roadblock at the highway onramps. He cut the wheel to the left, tore across a median, and thumped over a curb into the parking lot of what looked like an abandoned mall turned inside out. Gordon ditched the truck near a pair of rusted-out dumpsters behind a fast food restaurant—a tall pole stood beside the building, but the golden *M* was long gone.

The drones flanked him on either side as he beat the asphalt, running full-out for the break in the buildings. He hopped orange barrels, small barriers, and various rubble, but in the end, it was a day-glow traffic cone that finally took him down. He stumbled, rotated, and fell onto his back near a defunct water fountain.

Gordon flinched at something crashing nearby—a drone, falling lifelessly into the empty fountain. In all, a dozen drones fell out of the sky, smashing into the evercrete like doomed robotic skydivers. One skidded along the ground and came to rest near his leg. It was the size of a pizza box, and when Gordon picked it up to examine it, he found a dormant LED spotlight and a camera on the front.

"Hello?" he asked. "Can you hear me in there?"

He was pretty sure they couldn't. It was as if all the power from the drone had been sapped out.

Gordon sat up, looked around. Nothing moved in the mall, and yet it seemed to be alive with activity—little flashes of indeterminate movement, tinkling of metal on evercrete.

To the left, in an old Nike storefront, something moved behind the tall banners in the window. Gordon thought about reaching for the revolver tucked in the back of his pants, but there was no energy left in his body. His lungs burned, his heart felt like it was impaling itself on a hot spike with every beat, and his legs had turned into two thick lengths of wet rope.

Pulling the gun quickly with two busted hands was too tall an order. Instead, he pushed back against the rim of the fountain and rested his head against it.

He heard a nearby door open, heard footsteps—light, soft soles, no reverb. The cadence suggested the gait of someone less than six feet tall.

"Are you armed?" asked a steady, male voice.

"Yes," breathed Gordon.

"Where?"

"Back waistband. Smith & Wesson."

"Loaded?"

Gordon chuckled. "The fuck you think?"

A rubber shoe hit hard plastic.

"These are Vinestead drones."

"I guess," said Gordon. He stared at the stars, watched them go out of focus.

"What'd you do to piss them off?"

"Oh, you know. Hood shit."

"You got a name?"

"Gordon."

"Who're you with, Gordon?"

Gordon lifted his head, looked the man in the eyes. "It's just me. Just one old hacker raging against the machine."

The man smirked. "I'm Trent."

"Good to meet you, Trent."

"We'll see." He adjusted his baseball cap with his free hand. The other held a cobalt blue Tec-9 with an extended magazine. "I'd ask you kindly to leave, but you look beat to shit. How about we let you rest here, and you tell us what you were doing up at Folsom?"

Gordon laughed. "What makes you think I know anything about that?"

"Well," said Trent, squatting several feet away, "you see, we've been tracking those drones since they showed up at the prison. We didn't know what they were chasing until you came barreling down the road. So, Gordon, why don't you tell us what you were doing up there."

"Who's *us*?"

The door to the Nike store opened again, and several men and women spilled out. They looked more like Umbra sophisticates than homeless squatters. Their clothes were sharp, clean, and well-fitting. They all seemed to be in good health, like they were getting enough food. The way they exited the door and fanned out and struck almost comical poses suggested a well-to-do, tight-knit group.

"Gordon, welcome to the Gracy Heights Mall. You're now a guest of Calle Cinco."

FORTY
DANNY

Danny waited an hour before getting dressed and going to look for Jane. The halls of the Decker Plaza building were quiet, dark, but there was a buzzing of activity in the air, something electrical he could sense but not see. He limped toward the lounge area, found the double doors to be slightly open, and heard the soft drone of an audio feed, though he couldn't make out what it was saying.

He knocked gently on the door, pushed it open.

The lounge reminded him of a raging party in its final hour, except there were no bodies of passed-out revelers on the floor. Drinks and food containers littered the counter at the bar. Empty cardboard boxes had been stacked against the wall; a clear plastic bag set beside the pile held crumpled plastic wrap and small bits of styrofoam. Gear had been unpacked and loaded, and Tanzy and crew had left in a hurry.

"Where you been, Gunga Din?" asked Kevin Costner, from the couch. He had his feet up on the arm; he wiggled his long toes in his open sandals. "Thought you were in this mess with Banshee." He gestured to a nearby vidscreen.

Danny walked to the couch and leaned against an arm to take the pressure off his leg. The vidscreen showed two competing feeds—Lincoln Continental and Vinestead's own VFeed. At the bottom, a small ticker showed a repeating message from I.C.E-1.

I am demanding Vinestead immediately cease its pursuit of this plane and allow us to land safely.

"What's happening?"

Kevin sat up, stretched his back. "Vinestead tried to shoot Boss Man's plane out of the sky. But this bad gas has already cleared, half an hour ago." He chuckled. "Now they're in Carson City to do some gamblin' and ramblin'."

Danny couldn't tell if Kevin was joking or not.

"Is everyone okay?"

"No worse than before."

"And Kaili?"

Kevin shrugged. "No clue, my fellow Jew. No word from Boss Man since they landed. Banshee was broadcasting live for a while—" He shook his hand at the vidscreen. "—but now it's just going around and around. I'm only watching to keep up on the SatIndex."

A dull ache went through Danny's leg, as if he'd just caught the edge of a coffee table in his hamstring. He braced against it, slid down onto the soft leather of the couch. His code cards were back in the room, and he wasn't exactly jazzed at the prospect of walking all the way back there.

"Yeah," said Danny, lifting his foot onto the coffee table, "calling out Vinestead on the feeds hasn't ever worked. I don't know what Tanzy was trying to accomplish with that. Vinestead kills people every day. Everyone knows that. And they get away with it because no one holds them accountable."

Kevin raised an eyebrow. "Thinkin' of steppin' up, li'l pup?"

"Fuck no."

They watched the vidscreen in silence for a few minutes.

Lincoln Continental played a flashy animatic showing a menacing Vinestead drone attacking a private jet. Points appeared on a map of California and Nevada, showing timestamps from the first strike to when contact with the plane was lost. From the way a question mark flashed, they were strongly implying the worst had happened.

Meanwhile, VFeed spent only a few cycles refuting the claims made by I.C.E-1 and LC. Instead, it focused on a lead story about a power grid failure in Folsom, California. According to their ticker, Calle Cinco had claimed responsibility for taking the city offline, as well as for the chaos at the California State Prison.

They made no mention of Folsom Prison, which was a good sign. Claiming that Calle Cinco had broken in and freed their leader would have been admitting they were holding Kaili in the first place.

The VFeed screen wiped, showed the time and temperature in Umbra. Sunrise was still hours away.

"Did you see Jane leave?" asked Danny. "The girl I was with?"

"Yup. Walked her out myself. Tried to tell her it wasn't safe to go walking Umbra alone after midnight, but there was a big black SUV waiting for her right outside. Two primetime black suits too. She really one of those Associates?"

"Sometimes."

And that was the right answer, because when she was with Danny, she was just Jane Meade—nothing more.

"Fine ass lady."

Danny looked up, narrowed his eyes.

"Thought so, Betty Jo." Kevin smiled. "You got it bad for that chick. She sold you a line and you bought out the store."

"You don't know what you're talking about... rainbow trout."

Kevin shrugged. "Probably not."

Danny groaned as he got back to his feet. The two steps leading up to the bar hurt more than he wanted to let on. It was worth it though; he'd spied pizza boxes from the couch and was happy to find an untouched pepperoni on the bottom. He slid a piece out onto the marble bar.

"You want me to make you a drink?" asked Kevin. "One of those things old people call a nightcap?"

"You a bartender now?" The pizza was cold, but the uncured meat was salty and tender.

"Lincoln said to look after you, so that's what I'm doing." He jumped up from the couch and sauntered behind the bar with an exuberance known only to the young. He looked around at the various bottles on the mirrored wall. "How about a Blue Rain? Lincoln's been stocking it for the cowboy."

"Yeah, okay."

Kevin reached under the bar and scraped a can out of a hidden refrigerator. He dropped a black napkin with purple etching onto the bar and slid it over to Danny.

"How old are you, kid?"

Kevin drew himself up, perhaps even onto his tip-toes. "I'll be eighteen in February."

"God, you're a child."

"Not in Umbra, chumbra. Here you're a man at fourteen, old and forgotten at thirty."

Danny popped the Blue Rain and took a pull. The sugary drink went down easy, and the aftertaste of Curacao lingered on the tip of his tongue.

"So you were born in, what 2002? You weren't even alive when the Net fell. What are the kids even saying about V-Night on the streets of Umbra these days?"

Kevin eased onto a stool near the sink, crossed his arms. "Everyone knows that story. Hacker tried to take on Vinestead and they burned him for it. Took down the Net in the process."

"You know that hacker's name?"

"X," said Kevin. "Cowboy said he used to know him back in the day.

Danny laughed into his drink. "Yeah, everyone knew X back in the day."

"That's what he said, man."

"You think that's what happened to X? Vinestead burned him out?"

Kevin nodded. "I heard he got flamed by antiviral. Booted him right out of the Net."

"Who told you this story?" asked Danny. He squeezed the Blue Rain can, crumpled it slightly.

"A guy who knows a guy."

"Yeah, well, your guy who knows a guy doesn't know shit. X didn't get burned out of the Net. He got trapped there."

Kevin perked up; his eyes pushed through a marijuana haze and opened wider.

"You kids these days, you think of X as some kind of tragic hero—the man who took on Vinestead and gave his life for it. Well, that hero you admire didn't give a shit about Vinestead. He was a dumb kid who didn't know right from horrifically fucking wrong. He copied his girlfriend's mind—and this was in '98, so you know there were kinks. Anela Zabora, Kaili's sister, helped him do it, had her ciphers write the software. X copied his girlfriend, she glitched, and she copied him right back."

"So Vinestead has a copy of X somewhere?" asked Kevin.

Danny took another bite, chewed thoughtfully for a moment.

"That's my guess. I don't think X ever left the Net. I think someone locked him in his homedir and then ripped the whole damn thing out of the Net. Now it lives in VNet, and Vinestead is just keeping him there. I don't know why though."

He flashed on a lone homedir floating in the ether of the Net, rotating slowly as it drifted without direction. Then there was an incredible rending sound— metal crying out as it was bent into submission. Bars flew out of the darkness to cover the outside walls of the homedir.

"They built a prison around him," said Danny. "They wanted to keep him hidden, so they firewalled the construct and made it look like…"

Kevin waited a moment before asking, "Like what?"

"Like some kind of shitty strip mall," said Danny. "Who would even think to look for one of the most notorious hackers of the twentieth century in a Blockbuster?"

"What's a Blockbuster?"

Danny laughed. "That's what Jane said."

Kevin threw up his hands. "Okay…"

Danny slid off his seat and steadied himself with a hand on the bar. He stretched his leg out, tried to loosen up the stagnant blood enough to walk. He grimaced, not at the pain so much, but at the implication of his injury. There was nothing more in the world he wanted than to go home, back to Vail, back to the cabin and all of its comforts.

Because really, there was no reason to stay in Umbra anymore; Johnny was dead, and all of his computers had been wiped. Jane was gone, Tanzy was off liberating the Butcher of Burbank, and the mystery of Johnny's death was no closer to being solved. And nothing in Umbra, not the influence of Lincoln Continental or Calle Cinco, was going to make it easier. No, what Danny needed was quiet, his own home, his own rig—none of this mobile access bullshit.

"What time is the doc coming in the morning?" he asked.

Kevin came around the bar, offered a skinny arm. "Seven. But I can message her if you're hurting."

"No, no I'm okay. Just ready to go home."

"Home? Why would you want to go home? You're in Umbra, Goons. Tech-a-Mecca. Home of Umbrats and thriller-killers. The best sim, the best synth, the best street food, the best—"

"You trying to sell me a condo or what?" Danny interrupted. He took the kid's arm and leaned on him slightly as they made their way to the door.

Kevin smelled like pot, but a different strain than the refined marijuana found in the aprés-ski cabins of Vail. This smelled grittier, as if the evercrete of Umbra's streets had been ground up right along with the leaves.

"Why do you smoke?" asked Danny. "Why not just use a synth variant? You're killing your lungs."

"I don't fuck with synth," said Kevin, curtly. He turned away, bowed his head to show the back of his neck. It was smooth, unbroken by the scar of a biochip insertion. "And I don't fuck with chips either. Nobody's putting nothin' in my head. No reason to. Everyone talks about VNet like it's not just one big trip. Everything you see in there's a lie."

He opened the door to Danny's room, stood back.

"You're right, kid. It's all a lie." A veneer, like Jane said. "And the only way to get at the truth is to tear it all down, bit by bit."

"Sure," said Kevin, turning slightly to the left as if he'd heard something.

It was then Danny noticed a tiny device in his ear; its deep red color blended well with Kevin's skin tone.

"You have a whisperer."

Kevin nodded. "When you work for Lincoln Tate, you don't really have a choice."

"Well," said Danny, "you know what that means, right?"

The kid stared back, blankly.

"*Nobody's putting nothing' in my head,*" Danny repeated. "Seems to me like *someone* is." He stepped into the room, turned, and shut the door slowly. He didn't break eye contact with Kevin until the door clicked into place.

"You're fucked up, Goons!" came a muffled cry from behind the door.

Danny laughed, hobbled over to the bed, and climbed on. He fumbled with the box of code cards on the nightstand before pulling the entire thing onto his chest. He needed to drown out the pain and clear his head at the same time. Normally, that would mean jacking in and shutting out the world, but he wasn't quite ready to head back into VNet.

There was an idea bouncing around in his head, but it was unfinished. He saw a homedir enclosed by metal bars, a prison built around it, a security system so complex it had remained hidden for twenty years. And yet, there was something, some vulnerability hidden in the fog around the prison.

He just couldn't see it yet.

Danny lay back on the bed, stared at the ceiling, the box of code cards forgotten. In the intricate purple swirls above him, he saw his own thoughts transcribed in a frilly script.

Why X? What was so important about him? Did he really warrant one of the most sophisticated virtual prisons on the planet?

The more Danny thought about it, the less sense it made, until finally he was totally convinced there was more to Brigham Plaza than a teenage hacker from the 90s. Bullets was hiding something else, and the only way Danny was going to figure out what that was, was to do exactly what he'd told Kevin—tear down the veneer, bit by bit.

He checked the clock.

2:36 a.m.

There was still plenty of time to take a few stabs at Brigham Plaza before the doc showed up.

He pulled the rig from the side of the bed where Jane should have been.

Finish the job, come find me.

"I'm coming," he muttered, and slipped the rig over his head.

FORTY-ONE
KAILI

"Where is he?" asked Kaili.

Cyn stood at the door to the cell with her arms crossed. She looked a bit older than the last time Kaili had seen her, which made Kaili again wonder how long she'd been in stasis. There was a line or two on the aggregator's face that hadn't been there before, something in her eyes that spoke to some recent trauma.

"Gone," she said at last. "Went to draw off the heat to make sure you got out of here safe."

"I'm going to kill him. You know that, right?"

Cyn shrugged. "If you say so, but you'll have to go through me. You know that, right?"

Kaili shook her head. "Of course you're fucking him. Cynthia Mesquina getting in my way again."

"Actually, I'm not." Cyn reached for the straps at Kaili's feet. She struggled with the nylon for a few seconds before pulling a knife from her belt.

Kaili tested the free leg; it seemed to respond to her commands. Whether it would carry her was another story.

"Try not to move," said Cyn. "You've got some wires and a catheter that needs to come out."

"God." Kaili looked to the dank ceiling, to the green moss growing in the corners. Vinestead was going to pay for trying to bury her.

"How do you think I feel? I'm the one who has to root around in Sava Kessler's puss."

"I will strangle you."

Cyn straightened up. "Yeah, about that."

Kaili followed her eyes. They'd dressed her in a thin white gown and laid a blanket over her body, but even the thick wool couldn't hide the fact that half of her left arm was gone.

Just like in the nightmare.

Just like in the video Sedivy had made her watch.

"No need to freak out about it," said Cyn. "You can get a replacement in Umbra that'll feel better than the real thing. Both of my legs are mostly machine now."

Kaili ignored her. The straps on her right arm came loose, and she reached for the back of her neck. Her arm felt languid, heavy, but it moved.

"I don't care about the arm," she said, feeling the raised skin of a new scar. "I think they put a Georgia chip in my neck."

Cyn stepped back as if she'd just discovered Kaili was radioactive.

"Are you serious?" she asked. "How do you… how do you know?"

"They made me watch the procedure. Sedivy gathered a bunch of Vinestead suits to watch a doctor take my arm and replace my biochip." She glanced at the cell walls; water beaded on the evercrete. "I don't think it was here though."

"Well, okay, that changes things." She patted one of her pockets. A series of green LEDs lit beneath the fabric. "I have a muffler, but you have to stick close to me for it to work. And even then, that only buys us five or six hours. That chip's gonna have to come out."

"No shit," said Kaili.

"And so is the catheter, smart-ass."

Kaili felt hands on her legs; Cyn's fingers were warm, almost hot on her skin.

"Take a deep breath. I assume this just slides out, but god help me I'm not a nurse."

"Just do it."

Cyn pulled; Kaili gritted her teeth.

"Of all the indignities," said Anela.

Kaili noticed her sister standing just outside the cell, half of her body hidden by the wall.

"Merry Christmas, Cynthia. You just removed a catheter from the Butcher of Burbank. I forgot the gift receipt, so you can't take it back."

"Is that everything?"

"Yeah," said Cyn. She pulled the blanket off and laid it over her shoulders.

Kaili shuddered at the sight of her own body. She'd lost weight; her exposed legs looked almost too thin to stand on. Whatever Vinestead had been feeding her in stasis, it wasn't enough.

"How long have I been here?"

"Our best guess is a few months shy of three years."

Kaili squeezed her eyes shut until the pain was too much.

"I know," said Cyn. "I'm sorry." She reached for Kaili's hand, pulled it to help her sit up.

"You're sorry? What happened to your vendetta? For Gantz? Didn't you call me a cunt for putting a bullet in your shoulder?"

Cyn sighed as she took Kaili's weight and helped her to the floor.

"You *are* a cunt. But… you didn't hit anything that couldn't be fixed. I got to spend some time with a nice Asian boy overseas while I recovered. I mean, I probably do owe you a bullet in return, but I like to think I've grown since then."

She flashed a self-satisfied smile.

They walked slowly, painfully, out of the cell. There were bodies strewn everywhere, and yet, very little blood. Instead, the floor was coated in a black-red sludge that looked remarkably like—

"Is that… does Vinestead have synthetics now?"

"Yup. They got a fat government contract and poured all that cash into their synthetics division after what happened in Perion City. I heard they even poached some of Perion's staff."

"Traitors," groaned Kaili, feeling the needles in her bare feet.

"Money talks," said Cyn, guiding them to what Kaili assumed was the entrance.

"This is Folsom Prison, isn't it?"

"Yeah, how did you know?"

"Seen pictures."

They walked through hall after hall of downed synthetics. Kaili swallowed her questions about whether Cyn had done all the damage herself or if G had lent a hand. She didn't want to acknowledge the power it must have taken to cut through so many synnies.

"You may not be able to kill him by yourself," said Anela, "but you will fire the last shot."

Kaili nodded, focused her attention on her left arm, which had begun to throb. Her legs sent shockwaves up her spine with every step, as if she were jumping down from a high loading dock with each footfall.

"How are we getting out of here?" asked Kaili. "I can't run, Cyn."

"I can tell." Cyn paused at the outer doors. "We have a small boat that's gonna take us downriver. We'll meet up with Tanzy and Tate there."

"I.C.E-1 Tanzy? How's she mixed up in this?"

"It's a long story, but she and Tate put this whole operation together. Gordon and I are just the muscle."

"Gordon," repeated Kaili.

"Changing his name does not change what he did," said Anela.

"I know."

Cyn smirked. "You *think* you know, but this is much bigger than you can imagine."

It took Kaili a moment to remember that Cyn couldn't hear Anela talking, that her sister's voice was only in her head.

They looked out over the parking lot and had the same thought.

"Too quiet," said Anela.

"I don't get it," said Cyn. "This place should be swarming with Vinestead goons."

"Typical Vinestead." Kaili pushed the door open. "They had no contingency plan. They bet it all on the synnies and you guys made them fold."

The air outside was chilly but fresh—less traces of oil. Kaili glanced at the blanket around Cyn's shoulders.

"Oh, duh." She helped Kaili wrap her body in the blanket and patted her on the back for good measure.

There were rocks on the other side of the parking lot as well as a couple of chain-link fences that Cyn had to cut through. Kaili needed help getting down the rougher slopes, and crawling through the cuts in the fences was harder than she expected with only one arm. Eventually, they came to the river Cyn had mentioned and farther down the bank, hidden under dark canvas, was a small boat, just big enough to fit three people.

Kaili stood for a moment, staring.

"Problem?"

"This feels like amateur hour," said Kaili. "Why wasn't there an armored SUV waiting for us outside the doors? Or a helicopter to airlift us out of here?"

Cyn spread her arms. "I'm sorry this isn't up to your standards, Ms. Kessler. If you'd like, you can go back to your cell and I'll go invest in some low-yield bonds until I have enough money to break you out of a secret Vinestead prison in a manner more befitting your stature."

"She mocks you," said Anela.

Kaili shook her head. "You should have told my den I was here, and they would have done it properly."

"We can still do that," said Cyn, smiling. "You sit tight and I'll dial 1-800-CALLE-CINCO." She paused for a moment; her eyes softened. "Look, you just gotta trust me, okay? Vinestead would expect Calle Cinco to come in guns blazing. They would have been ready for that. We used diversion so that a tiny little boat like this would go undetected."

Kaili looked back at Folsom, saw lights in the sky, saw them growing in number as searchlights swept back and forth.

"Are there life jackets?"

"Yeah, right next to the steaming hot chocolate."

Cyn all but picked Kaili up by the varmpits and placed her in the boat. There was so much strength in her; Kaili was immediately envious. That kind of raw power would have served the head of Calle Cinco well, if only she could have stayed at Le Soleil Rouge long enough to attain it.

They pushed off from the bank and let the current take them. It was then that Kaili noticed the surrounding area was dark; there were no lit windows or soft glows from streetlamps.

"You took out the power?" she asked.

Cyn nodded. "Tanzy did. She and her ciphers."

Despite the cold and the rough wood of the boat, Kaili smiled. She was out in the world again. It didn't matter that she was naked under a thin gown or freezing or at the mercy of a woman who had promised to kill her—she was free. Somewhere, Arthur Sedivy was living his normal life and soon, someone would approach him and tell him in a soft voice that his prize pet was gone, loose, run away into the dark night.

He was gonna be pissed.

A soft chime sounded; Kaili raised her left wrist to look at her missing sliver.

They'd put some kind of permanent bandage over her stump, almost like a molded plastic cap that provided a smooth, black surface. The skin at the border of the bandage was a sickly purple—dark veins ran the perimeter like a disgusting tribal tattoo.

"It's me," said Cyn, checking her sliver. "Shit. Tate says a Vinestead drone tried to shoot them out of the sky. They landed safe, but they're in Carson City."

"And?"

"And now there's no one to pick us up," said Cyn. "I guess we're going with plan B."

Kaili pulled the blanket tighter; the air over the water was colder.

"What's plan B?"

"Give me a minute and I'll think one up."

"Amateur hour," said Anela. She sat with her legs to the side in the middle of the boat, leaning just enough for Kaili to see Cyn behind her.

"This is just great." Kaili pulled the blanket up to her mouth, breathed into it, and let her hot breath warm her face.

"I don't know what you're complaining about. The plan changed the moment you mentioned your new Guardian Angel. No way you're going anywhere near Tate or Umbra until we can get that thing out of you. I'll send out some pings."

"Ping Calle Cinco. Let them know I'm out."

"Not yet," said Cyn. "If Vinestead sees them mobilizing, your den's gonna lead them right to us. Naw, Tate will know what to do." She pulled out a phone, started typing.

In the silence, Kaili tried to ignore the reproach on Anela's face. She looked up at the stars, compared them to her memory of Astoria in the simulation. The same red and green lights streaked through the sky, reminding her of the old sci-fi movies where data was visualized by a bright glow running along a line. So much had changed in just a few short years, and yet, there were echoes of the past all around her.

"Got a car to pick us up downriver. We're gonna head up to Yuba City and meet up there. There are a couple of AntiStead groups operating there that'll probably take us in if we ask nicely."

"No, we're not going to Yuba City. Not yet." Kaili lifted her head, narrowed her eyes at Cyn.

"I don't think you appreciate the severity of the situation, Ms. Kessler. We don't have time to be dicking around."

"My name is not Kessler. You know that. And I don't care how much of a big shit you think you are now or how important Lincoln Tate thinks he is, I am *not* going anywhere else looking like this. Do you know how humiliating it is for you to see me like this? You're not putting me in front of another suit and a goddamn feed monger without letting me get cleaned up, get some proper clothes. Look me in the eyes and tell me no, Cyn."

The aggregator said nothing for a moment, then smiled weakly.

"I'm so torn with you," she said. "You killed Gantz. You shot me. You fucked Perion Synthetics beyond all recognition. I should hate you. I should toss you over the side and watch you swim in a circle until you drown." She took a deep breath, let it out. "But... I can only imagine what Vinestead did to you. Three years in Folsom was probably enough penance. I saw all the wires in there. They had you jacked into something, didn't they?"

Flashes of Rick on the train, the strobing light casting moving shadows on his face.

"Yes," said Kaili, quietly.

"Was it bad?"

She sat up straight, lifted her chin. "Yes."

"Good, then I'll take my revenge out in time served. We'll stop and get you some clothes, but you gotta remember this isn't Sacramento or Umbra. You're not gonna find high fashion out this way."

Kaili put her hand on her knee, rubbed the thin fabric of the gown.

"I'd settle for some jeans and a t-shirt. And some underwear. I'm not high class, but even I have standards."

Cyn smirked, pulled an oar from the bottom of the boat. She started guiding them toward the shore.

Anela flashed a scowl. "She is not your friend."

"That doesn't make her my enemy," Kaili whispered.

"Nor does it make her real. Or any of this, for that matter."

FORTY-TWO
TANZY

Tanzy wanted nothing more than to get off the plane.

The cabin finally stopped shaking as the whine of the remaining engine was swallowed up by fire foam sprouting from both wings. Tanzy saw it congealing as she slid down the emergency slide—the smell was something between burnt rubber and kerosene. All along the fuselage, small poppers let out the same white foam, covering the ground in the foul-smelling fire-retardant.

Bryce led Tanzy by the arm up a nearby embankment and in the direction of the small airport's main building. The lights were on, but there were only a few people milling about in an open hangar. Two of them were jogging toward the plane at a moderate clip, but there were no fire trucks, no emergency vehicles.

Lincoln hurried ahead to talk to the men, and the way he held his body and opened his arms suggested he was going to try to schmooze his way out of the situation. Tanzy tried to listen to the conversation over the sizzling of fire foam but couldn't make out the words. She spied an arrangement of benches in a designated smoking area and pointed it out to Bryce.

It wasn't until she sat down that she realized how much pain she was carrying in her back. The hard landing had wrenched something in her spine, and though it wasn't debilitating, it certainly didn't feel good.

"Cleo, let the girls know we're on the ground."

"The name's Bryce."

Tanzy looked up and shook her head at him. She tapped the back of her neck.

"Cleo?" she asked.

Nothing. No response. No static.

Tanzy sighed, lifted her wrist, and sent a message via her sliver. After a few ticks, she got an acknowledgement back from Whisper saying she was happy to hear the news.

"You alright?" Bryce asked.

"I'm pissed. You have no idea."

He sat down on the bench opposite her and inspected the bruises and cuts on his forearms.

"Eh, what's a Wednesday without getting shot out of the sky?"

"It's not funny." Tanzy arched her back, tried to work out the kink. She was suddenly aware of how underdressed she was for the weather. They had taken off from Umbra without intending to deboard anywhere, so she'd only worn a thin red blouse whose sleeves barely covered her biceps.

The cold was the final straw.

"Vinestead booted me out of Reykjavik, then they took down the entire darknet. A decade of free data… just gone. Then they try to kill me, out in the open, like there won't be consequences. They're making it personal, and I'm rising to the bait. Vinestead can't do this to I.C.E-1, and they can't do this to me."

"Sounds like they've got you right where they want you," Bryce said. "But at least you know they're fucking with you."

"Yeah, well, you get back what you put out is all I'm saying."

Bryce nodded, turned his head. "Here comes the man."

Tanzy followed his eyes, watched Lincoln lumber along the side of the building with the gait of a much older man trying to make it to the bathroom on time. He'd lost some of his elegance in the crash, and it was clear to Tanzy that he was out of his element. In Umbra, he was a media god to be revered, but out here, he was just another aging technorati with the same vulnerabilities as everyone else.

"Cyn made it out of Folsom with Kaili," Lincoln said, rubbing his hands together. "But it looks like Vinestead put a GA chip in her neck, so we can't take her directly back to Umbra."

"We can go to I.C.E-1 HQ in Portland," said Tanzy. "I have half of a little island on the Columbia."

"No. The longer she has that chip, the greater the chance Vinestead will get a ping. And once that connection is open, well, we've heard the same stories, Tanzy."

She nodded.

He was referring to location tracking, meta compilation, and voice recognition. The list of improbable-but-not-impossible surveillance features of the Guardian Angel biochip went on and on.

"Cyn is headed for Yuba City. If we can get the chip out of Kaili, she'll be safe to take back to Umbra, though Cyn is saying she already wants to get back to Calle Cinco."

Tanzy shook her head. "We can't let her. We need her with us so we can take on Vinestead. She has to know it was us who pulled her out of there and that we expect repayment in kind. You lost a plane, Lincoln. Someone's gotta foot that bill."

"You let me worry about that." Lincoln lowered his voice. "I didn't do this for the payday. I did it because it was the right thing to do. That's what *you* said, Tanzy. Your words."

She was off the bench before he finished his sentence. The pain in her back flared but relented.

"That was before Vinestead tried to kill me. Kill *us*. Are you really gonna let that slide, Lincoln?"

"What do you suggest we do? Shoot down one of their planes? An eye for an eye? I guarantee whoever we kill in the process will not be the same people who sent that drone after us. See, that's the problem with revenge against Vinestead—you never hurt the people that need hurting. It's always the little guy, and not that anyone who works for Vinestead is completely innocent, but they're still just regular people trying to get by. That's not the image you want to present as suit of I.C.E-1, is it? A murderous thug who targets Vinestead underlings in the name of supposed justice?"

Tanzy folded her arms, turned away.

He had a point, of course, but that didn't mean anything to the part of her that boiled over with anger toward the faceless conglomerate. The only person who came to mind when she thought of Vinestead was Arthur Sedivy, but the likelihood of him being directly involved in the drone attack was almost certainly nil. Someone like that would have been at home in bed with a paid escort like Danny.

In the distance, the first red and white flashes began to peek through the trees surrounding the airport.

"Where is Yuba City?" Tanzy asked. "I don't know this area."

"It's about a three-hour drive to the west through the mountains," said Lincoln. "I figured you wouldn't be in the mood for another flight."

She scoffed.

"But I do need you to hang back for a bit, Bryce. Settle things with the locals and let them know what happened up there. There are gonna be a lot of questions, but Carolyn will be here at six to lawyer the situation, so you just hold on 'til then. Once you're straight, meet us back in Umbra."

Bryce stood, stretched his arms above his head. "Sure, why not? Black man talking to cops about a crashed plane. What could go wrong?" He turned to Tanzy. "You think a drone attack was dangerous? If I don't make it back, blame the Carson City PD."

"You're a big boy," said Tanzy, flatly. "You can take care of yourself."

"She said, minutes before he was gunned down for being black in public."

"So are we going or not? I want to get in front of Kaili before Cyn lets her get in touch with Calle Cinco."

"Yeah, come on," said Lincoln. He gestured for her to follow. "They have a couple hoops to rent out front."

"Hoops?"

"Hoopties," he explained. "Eh, it's before your time."

Before my time, she thought.

Sagamihara flashed in her mind. She saw Cleo sitting alone, hand extended to the glass table, a clove cigarette letting off a tiny trail of smoke between her fingers.

She understood why Cleo might want to revisit the glory days of their childhood, the days that lacked both responsibility and consequence. It was safer there, easier there. There were no wars to fight, no jobs to complete, and no danger to face. But where Cleo saw refuge, Tanzy saw disconnection—a withdrawal from the world. She didn't want to ignore what was happening around her, didn't want to stand on the wall like a scared little girl at her first dance.

Tanzy wanted to be a part of the nonstop frenzy of the world.

More than that, she wanted to be a star player.

Taking down Savage and I.C.E. BBS had shown her a glimpse of what it was like to participate, to step into the limelight and feel the attention of the world on her. She had her own cipher den now, her own secretive group that ruled the shadows of every network this side of the Great Firewall of China. She was a suit, and that commanded respect in the only segment of society that truly mattered— the technorati.

It wasn't all glitz though.

Being a suit meant being a target, the same way Savage being a sysop had made him a target. When someone moved against a cipher den, the only reasonable response was unreasonable retaliation. Lincoln's suggestion of an eye for an eye would only be the beginning. Vinestead had to suffer, lest the world think less of I.C.E-1... think less of Tanzy.

A pale man with stringy hair put them in a white Camry that looked like it hadn't been washed since it came off the assembly line. The interior smelled of cigarettes, and the beige cloth seats inside appeared to have faded from white. There was almost no tech in the car aside from the backup camera in the rearview mirror, but thankfully the radio had a display and could still connect to the old satellites.

Tanzy tuned in a 90's grunge station while Lincoln fiddled with the mirrors and manually adjusted the seat.

"Been a while," he muttered.

"Do you even have a license?"

"Do you?"

"Fair enough."

Lincoln shifted into drive, pulled out of the gravel parking lot onto a two-lane blacktop.

"People like us don't need to drive ourselves anymore," he said, accelerating slowly to a brisk seventy miles per hour. "There's a lot we don't do for ourselves anymore. Makes us soft, dig?"

"We have better things to do," said Tanzy. She put her elbow on the door and stared out into the darkness. The hills around them were full of nocturnal activity, but she couldn't see any of it.

They slowed at a stop sign and took a hard left. Lincoln pushed the car to its limit as they climbed an on-ramp onto I-580. The lights above the highway flickered.

"Looks like Folsom is drawing from other grids," said Lincoln. "Did you call off your girls?"

"Didn't need to. We lost control when Vinestead booted us."

In the side mirror, Tanzy watched the lights of Carson City recede until the mountains east of the city grew up around the highway and swallowed the view. The highway was empty except for one or two cars.

"You know," said Lincoln, "the way you say *booted us* makes me think you're taking all of this personally."

"How *should* I take it? After what they did?"

Lincoln shrugged. "All I'm saying is Vinestead probably doesn't even know it was you, Tanzy, suit of I.C.E-1. They just saw a threat and went after it. You would have done the same."

"It's more than that. It wasn't just me they booted. My brother was there. The Quatrain was there. No one boots my family, and not from a darknet. Vinestead thinks they can just reach out and touch anyone they want, anywhere they want."

"What are you gonna do, take down VNet? We're back at eye for an eye."

"I know," said Tanzy, lifting her hand. The fingers curled into a fist. "I'm just so tired of them sitting in their tower thinking they're invulnerable. And that's the thing, Lincoln. I don't have to go all Calle Cinco on them and kill a bunch of their engineers, and I don't have to bring down VNet—that would hurt a lot of *innocent* people too. All I have to do is show Vinestead they aren't invulnerable. Make them bleed, even if it's just a single drop."

Lincoln nodded as if he weren't really listening.

"Mm-hmm, and how are you going to do that?"

"Like I said, they think they can touch anyone, including me and my family. Let's see how they like it when I touch them back."

FORTY-THREE
GORDON

After an hour with Calle Cinco, it became clear to Gordon that Alex Trent wasn't the leader he pretended to be. That job fell to a young woman who called herself Raven, though by the color of her short, spiky hair, she should have called herself Pinky. She had cobalt piercings up both ears that transitioned seamlessly into ornate tattoos. The black and red swirls ran down her neck and disappeared into the collar of a red hoodie.

Someone had come and put a Wendy's bag and a bottle of water in front of him—Gordon smelled a burger and fries—but he hadn't touched either. It didn't feel right, not with Raven staring him down from across the table. The only thing he felt comfortable doing was flexing his ruined hands on the table to show the two men in the corner with SMGs that he was unarmed.

The back room of the Nike store had no electricity; three LED lanterns kept the room lit. Oblique shadows on the wall moved like menacing demons gathering up around him.

Trent tried to keep the conversation going, asking about Gordon's private life, but with each question, the patience on Raven's face slipped further away. Finally, she broke.

"Enough. Tell us about Folsom. What were you doing there?"

Gordon hesitated just enough to sell the lie. "Trying to find a friend of mine. Vinestead snatched him a couple months ago. I've been on his tail ever since. Folsom's not even the first place I've broken into."

"So you got to him?" asked Raven.

"Almost.

"What happened?"

Gordon held up his hands in response. "Underestimated the guards. They weren't, um... they weren't human."

"Synthetics," said Trent.

Raven glanced at him, as if admonishing him for interrupting.

"Yeah," said Gordon. "I was armed, but it took three times the ammo to take down a single synthetic guard. Once I ran out, I had to fight my way out with these puppies."

Raven crossed her arms. "Vinestead doesn't have synthetics."

"You're welcome to take a walk up there and see for yourself."

"Maybe we'll walk *you* up there and make you show us," she replied.

"I don't think so," said Gordon. "I'm headed back to Umbra. I gotta rethink this whole breakout thing. Probably be a good six to nine months before I try again. Gotta give them time to cool down, get sloppy again."

"What did you see inside Folsom? Any prisoners?"

"Like people? No. Just pods and cells. I don't think any of the prisoners are actually awake."

Trent leaned back in his chair. "They've got her in virtual reality, those sons of bitches."

"Hey!" barked Raven. "You want to shut your mouth, Trent?"

Gordon looked back and forth between them.

"Who're you guys talking about?" he asked.

"No one," said Raven.

"Bullshit."

The acute pain was coming back to his hands. Whatever Cyn had done to them was starting to wear off. He struggled to open the bottle of water on the table before Trent reached over and did it for him.

"Thanks," he said, taking a sip. "I'm gonna go out on a limb here and guess you guys are talking about Kaili Zabora, the woman no one has seen for three years?"

Trent looked down.

Raven didn't react.

"You think she's really in Folsom?"

"We think so. Someone sent us a—"

"Trent!"

"Jesus, Raven… he's not Vinestead. If he's been inside Folsom then maybe he can give us some insight, but I doubt he's gonna do that if you keep stonewalling. It's no secret Kaili hasn't been seen in years and that more likely than not, Vinestead has her. Maybe if we work together, we get Kaili and he gets his friend, and everyone wins."

"I'll accept he's not Vinestead," said Raven, "but I don't know anything else besides that."

Gordon lifted a hand, winced as he tried to wave it.

"Y'all don't have to argue. I have no stake in Kaili Zabora, and I don't care to. How about I just tell you everything I know about Folsom, and you get an intern to drive me back to Umbra?"

"We're not Uber," said Raven.

"I'll take him to Umbra."

Raven sneered. "No, Trent."

"It's my car—I can drive it wherever I want. And look, it's not like we're gonna make a move on Folsom tonight anyway."

"You don't know that," she shot back. "Maybe tonight's the perfect night. He claims he's already taken down a bunch of guards. Maybe Folsom is wide open right now and we're sitting here with our dicks out hosting a tea party."

She waited for Trent to respond, but he just looked away. The man had flashes of confidence, but otherwise, he seemed resigned to take orders from Raven.

Her eyes came back to Gordon.

He'd seen the look before—someone soft trying to look hard. Men had come and gone from Lost Pines over the years, and most of them bailed after just a month or two. Their egos couldn't handle the equality of life on the compound. No rich, no poor, and no real power except for one democratically elected spokesman.

Raven was trying hard to play the badass, but her feet didn't quite fit in Kaili Zabora's shoes. From the beads of sweat at her hairline to the twitching of her left eye, the cracks were starting to show.

"How about—" he started.

Raven pulled a neon pink Sig Sauer from her hip and placed it on the table. The embossed markings on the grip identified it as a P331, a model Gordon had never seen before. He was momentarily struck by a desire to inspect the gun, turn it over, and maybe fire off a few rounds to see how it handled.

"Here's how this is gonna go," Raven said. "You're gonna start talking about Folsom, and *only* Folsom, and when you've said everything there is to say about it, I'm either gonna shoot you or let Trent road trip it with you back to Umbra. If at any point you deviate from the agreed-upon subject, I will immediately go with Option A. Do we understand each other?"

"Can I hold the gun?" he asked.

Trent smirked.

"Talk."

So he talked, and between sips of water, he watched Raven's fingers tap the barrel of the Sig Sauer. It wasn't until he started describing the interior of the prison that she perked up and called for a palette to write on. He told her about the main entrance, the checkpoints, and how to get around the electronic locks. He mentioned the wide and empty mess hall adjacent to the cell blocks. He described in great detail the anatomy of the Vinestead synthetics, including the extra shielding around their CPU.

"A slug anywhere else except the brain is just a waste of bullets," he said.

He left out everything about Kaili Zabora and Cyn. Recasting his incursion into Folsom as a solo job made it seem more impressive than it was, and Gordon could see the approval on Trent's face as he listened. Several times, Raven stopped him to repeat some detail about the layout, about the pods themselves, and whether he stopped to read any of the labels.

"Could you see who was in the pods?" she asked.

"No, the glass was tinted, but I did read one name before I had to bail. Something Reynolds. Not my friend and not Kaili Zabora."

"Run it again," said Raven.

So he did. And when he'd gone through it a second time, she showed him a map she'd drawn and had him sign off on it. There was a moment, maybe two, when the palette was in the air between them, that he could have easily reached for the pink Sig and shot her and everyone else in the room dead.

Assuming it was loaded.

Assuming he wanted to kill a bunch of Calle Cinco regulars. He was already at the top of Kaili Zabora's shit list; it wasn't like she could want to kill him even more.

Finally, Raven sat back in her chair and studied the map she'd drawn on her palette. She chewed her lip thoughtfully.

"So what's it gonna be, Pink?" he asked. "You gonna let me walk out of here or are these cold fries my last meal?"

She stood, considered him for a moment.

"You're not scared of me," she said. "From the moment you walked in here, you haven't shown any recognition that you're in danger. And that mouth… just yap-yap-yap. You either don't have any idea who we are or you're a one-man wrecking crew and *we* should be scared of *you*."

"How 'bout we all just be respectful of each other, alright?"

"Yeah," she replied, nodding slightly. "There's that too. Sometimes you talk like a Texan; other times, you're more West Coast, muddled. You strike me as someone who's comfortable putting on an act."

Gordon smiled, said nothing.

"In simpler words, I think you're full of shit, Gordon. And I think the best thing we can do is kill you and dump your body in the Wendy's bathroom across the street. But if we do that, Trent here is gonna be all moody and pissy for a few days and I don't feel like dealing with that on top of everything else."

Trent shrugged.

"So here's what I'm gonna do. Trent will take you to the Greyhound station and Calle Cinco will sponsor your ride to Umbra. After that, we're done. We never see you again."

"I don't mind driving him to—"

"I don't give a shit what you mind or not," said Raven. "You take him to the bus station, you buy his ticket, and you get your ass back here. We may move tonight, and I want you here, not jackin' it up in some sim parlor in Umbra."

She turned and took the two men in the corner with her.

Gordon tapped the table.

"She's cute. What's her story?"

Trent laughed. "Certified hardass. Definitely out of your league, Texas."

"Ah," said Gordon. He sat up, stretched his back. "How about that bus station then?"

"Yeah, okay," said Trent.

Gordon followed him out of the back room and through the throng of Calle Cinco faithful who were gathered in the showroom. They sat in pairs along the sides of the store, sharing palettes or comparing notes on their phones. He spied Raven, but she had her back to him and didn't turn around when he passed.

Nobody so much as glanced at him, which was fine.

Outside, Trent directed him to the left, and they walked through the outdoor mall and across the street to an IHOP. Around the back, Trent gestured to a line of cars. A black, hard-top Jeep flashed its lights in response.

"So what's the deal?" asked Gordon, pausing at the back of the Jeep. He put an elbow on the spare tire. "I thought Calle Cinco was supposed to be some big shit boogeyman cipher den. Didn't expect to see you guys operating out of a Nike store."

Trent looked down, kicked a bit of gravel away.

"We're mobile these days," he said, "so we can set up anywhere we need to. It's easy when you don't have that many people to look after."

"Wait, that was *all* of you? That was what, twelve, fifteen people?"

"Yeah. That's what's left of Calle Cinco." He looked over his shoulder as if Raven might be there ready to sew his lips shut. "Things kinda went to shit when Kaili got snatched. We lost half our people in the first year, another half in the second. And this year, BayTrans poached all our ciphers in one move." He chuckled. "What the hell kind of cipher den doesn't have ciphers?"

Gordon nodded. "No wonder it took you guys so long to find her."

"Oh, no, yeah, that was just dumb luck. We're small, but we can still get shit done. We went through everything, *everything*, and still had nothing to show for it. And then last week, we get an unsourced data dump at one of our old dead drops. Nothing but a grainy video, but enough for us to know it was Kaili."

Gordon thought of the video he'd watched in Lincoln's office.

"That's why Raven's so anxious, isn't it? She knows if you guys can figure out where Kaili is based off that video, then anyone who sees it probably can too."

"Yeah." Trent glanced at the Jeep. "We've been on a timer since last week. Raven will lose her shit if someone else gets to Kaili first. There are a lot of people out there who want to get their hands on Kaili Zabora. And if they do, that's just more people we'd have to kill."

Gordon searched for recognition in Trent's eyes, found none.

"Well, let's hope it doesn't come to that."

Trent nodded, first to himself, then to the Jeep.

FORTY-FOUR
DANNY

Danny explored Brigham Plaza in twenty-seven-minute loops.

That's how long it took for the explosion to grow inside the Blockbuster and eventually bathe the entire construct in viral fire. The virus itself wasn't a problem for his Syzygy chip anymore—there was some mild discomfort at the code's touch, but no pain, no lingering effects. What his chip couldn't overcome was the hard boot once the construct was consumed. That instruction seemed to come from VNet itself, and no matter how tightly he held on, Brigham Plaza always slipped through his fingers.

Then he'd wake up alone in an unfamiliar bed, take a breath, and do it all over again.

There was no fighting the kick, so Danny focused on visiting as many of the shops and businesses as quickly as he could. He rifled through movies at Blockbuster, flipped pizza boxes at Domino's, and even dug through piles of women's underwear in a small boutique called Bouche. At times, he noticed lightning flashing behind the large house outside the plaza, that hulking Victorian mansion that looked like it had a cadre of angry spirits living in its walls, but he ignored it, wanted to save it for last.

After a couple hours of frantic searching, of jacking in and getting booted out, Danny had nothing to show for his efforts except a better mental picture of what Provo, Utah was like in the mid-90s. The Blockbuster was the biggest tell, though it had taken longer than he would have expected to notice the movies were all old, with nothing released any later than 1996.

He was holding a pristine copy of *The Usual Suspects* when he was kicked yet again.

And as he stared at the ceiling, he thought about how badly he wanted to find something, some lockbox he could feed through his decrypters the way he had with Johnny's data.

Veneer.

Jane's voice echoed in his mind.

He would never find anything exploring the buildings and stores in Brigham Plaza because everything he saw there was just a façade. There was no use searching the cabinets at Domino's because really there was no Domino's, no Blockbuster, no Brigham Plaza.

Danny cursed.

All this time, the decrypters had been sitting idle when they could have been hard at work eating Brigham Plaza itself.

He jacked in.

And found himself in the Blockbuster supply closet again. He made his way out into the aisles, ignored the look from the girl behind the counter, and placed both hands on a nearby rack. Danny chose a simple decryption routine called Adamant Arachis and set it loose from his fingertips. The program took the form of tiny nanomachines that looked so similar to sparkling spiders that he actually jerked his hands away once the code was deployed.

Danny watched them fan out, replicate, and most importantly, start chewing. Their teeth produced a grinding noise that garnered a comment from the cashier.

"Is everything alright back there? Can I help you find anything?"

Danny initially shook his head, but since Arachis needed time to work, he turned and approached the counter.

The girl put down her SPIN magazine and raised an eyebrow expectantly.

"What's your name?" he asked.

She tapped the yellow nametag pinned her to shirt.

"How long have you worked here, Beth?" Danny leaned a casual elbow on the counter. The grinding sound grew louder.

"Couple years," she replied. "Why, you looking for a job?"

"No, just wondering." He glanced around the store. "Pretty empty tonight. Do you guys do a lot of business?"

Beth folded her arms. "Is this some kind of line? Because it's not working. I'm only smiling right now because it's my job."

"I just…" A flash of movement outside caught his attention.

Ben, the younger version of Bullets, stepped up onto the sidewalk and started talking with the guy he called Krass. Danny knew the conversation by heart now, and it always ended at the same point, with Ben just starting to head into the Blockbuster.

"You just what?"

"Do you know that guy out there? Ben?" Danny raised a finger.

Beth turned, rolling her eyes at the same time. She scoffed, said, "Yeah, I know him. He's a regular. And his name's not Ben."

"You sure? I heard him on the phone ordering pizza earlier…"

She smirked. "Yeah, that's a scam he runs. Orders a bunch of food to a random address and when the driver comes back, he lowballs him for pizzas that are just gonna go in the trash anyway. I've seen him do it a few times. Doesn't always work."

The heat from the explosion climbed Danny's back. He turned to find a ball of flame about the size of a softball pulsing in the middle of the store. The yellow hue was searing, almost to the point of pure white. He had to shield his eyes to see around it to the DVD racks that had crumbled in place. Adamant Arachis had worked its way to the floor and was eating through the blue carpet to reveal a flat, porcelain surface beneath.

Jackpot.

There was something underneath after all.

Danny recalled Arachis, had it store the keys it had found in the code.

"Excuse me for a minute," he said to Beth.

Outside, he ignored the veiled looks from Ben and Krass and ran out to the middle of the parking lot. With wide, sweeping gestures, he sprayed the construct with the Arachis nanos. For a moment, it seemed the wind had carried them all away, until finally, streaks of white appeared around him. The porcelain lines fell across multiple depths, as if they were tears in a matte painting in the background of some movie.

The Blockbuster spit glass into the parking lot as the explosion ramped up. Danny tapped his foot impatiently, tried to will Arachis into moving faster.

The rips in virtual space were opening, revealing—

His body was covered in sweat. Danny removed his rig and took off his shirt. The controls for the air conditioner were on the wall next to the door, but he didn't want to get up. He was too excited, too anxious to see the truth behind Brigham Plaza once and for all.

He replaced the rig and jacked in.

Danny rushed out of the supply closet and threw a single finger gun at the cashier.

"Lookin' good, Beth," he called, before barreling out the swinging door. He almost tripped coming off the curb, and when he finally took up position in the center of the parking lot, he found his pulse was starting to redline.

He spied Ben at a payphone at the gas station. Only, that wasn't his name. He made a mental note to ask Beth on the next loop.

"This one's for you, Bullets!" he screamed.

Danny waved his arms again, and the Adamant Arachis nanos shot out in sparkling white jets. Streaks of liquid porcelain, like paint peeling from a wall, slid down the sides of buildings. The Blockbuster and Domino's signs lost their luster, became inert, and then floated away like ash on the wind. Digital façades fell away, leaving only a thick block of white china that reminded Danny of jumbo marshmallows.

Only, these looked more like old-school homedirs with their rounded corners and soft, inner light.

A sparkle of jade drew Danny's eye to the space between Domino's and Blockbuster, a section of wall that didn't really belong to either. The small channel was sandwiched between the two stores, as if they had been tacked on later. In the very center of the wall, a green flash rotated in place like a pinwheel.

Danny approached and put his hand on the outer wall, expecting the pins and needles of some brutish firewall. Instead, he found permeable mist. Though the wall held its shape perfectly, its brick surface was far from solid.

The mist swallowed him as he pressed forward. The sound of the Arachis nanos faded to nothing. All Danny heard was a soft rustling, like cloth dragging across cloth, a *swooshing* that was familiar and yet unsettling.

The misty corridor went on for a long time, and Danny lost track of just how far he'd walked. The only way to gauge his progress was by the rustling sound that grew louder with each step. He figured he had to be beyond the house on the hill and maybe even outside of the Brigham Plaza construct altogether. It was possible he'd found some sort of portal to another location in VNet, but there had been no indication he'd made a jump.

His sliver beeped. Five minutes remaining.

Danny broke into a run, ignoring his limited visibility and instead training his ears on the *swooshing*—no, the *slithering*.

The three-minute warning sounded.

"Come on," Danny muttered, pumping his virtual legs.

A wall appeared without warning. Danny slammed into it at full speed, and there was a terrifying moment as viral scales of some poisonous serpent melded with his skin. He fell back in a heap, waited for the sensation on his arms and face to fade. When his vision finally cleared, he stood up and tried to focus on the green wall in front of him.

Behind it, a shadow moved.

"Hello?" he asked.

The shadow stopped, grew larger as it came near.

"Is someone in there?"

"G?" asked a voice, low and muffled. The shadow sounded male, but somewhat childlike, maybe late teens.

"No, not G. Are you…" The question was almost too insane. "Are you X?"

"I was told to wait for G," said the shadow, receding.

"Hold up. I know G. I can bring him here."

"Will you? Will you, please?"

His sliver beeped, started counting down from sixty.

"I will, but you gotta tell me who you are. Someone trapped you here, didn't they?"

"Yes."

"Was it a man named Ben? Or Bullets?"

"I don't know those names."

Danny tried to get closer to the wall, but the writhing scales looked poised to leap out at him if he got within range.

"Do you know your name?" he asked, gritting his teeth.

"Yes."

"Tell me your name and I'll bring you G."

"I am called Lassiter," he said softly.

Danny paused, tried to remember where he'd heard that name before. It wasn't one of X's known aliases—he didn't have any—and it wasn't the name of any hacker he knew of. And yet, it did sound familiar.

"Please, bring me G," said Lassiter.

The Syzygy picked up the heat before Danny did, and in the next moment, the fire consumed him. The last thing he heard before the boot was the soft repetition of "G, G, G…"

Danny jerked on the bed, enough to pull at the wound on his leg. He took a minute to check the bandages and made sure he wasn't bleeding all over Lincoln's expensive sheets.

A knock came at the door before Danny could jack in again.

"Just a minute," he called.

He swung his legs off the bed, scrunched his nose at the wet, body-shaped stain on the sheets.

When Danny opened the door, he found Kevin Costner standing in the hallway. His eyes were bloodshot, even more so than earlier.

"Doc's here," he said, giggling a little. "Downstairs. I'd take you down… I mean, not like, *take you down*, like that, like intercourse, but…" He laughed. "Intercourse butt."

"Yeah, I get it, man. Go sleep it off."

Kevin nodded. "Can do, Xanadu." He almost fell over trying to turn around. "Oh yeah, Boss Man pinged. They're in Yuba City. Gonna meet up with Cyn and the Butcher."

"So they got her out?"

"Guess," he replied, shrugging. He started back down the hall, one shoulder dragging against the wall.

"Hey, have you ever heard the name Lassiter?"

"Lassiter?" He paused, looked up at the ceiling. "Is that some kind of synth?"

"No, it's a person."

"I don't know any persons," he replied and continued walking.

Danny retrieved his shirt from the foot of the bed and pulled it on. Limping along the hallway to the elevator, he keyed in a search on his sliver. The tiny screen blanked and showed a progress bar.

"Who the hell are you, Lassiter?" he asked, idly.

He punched the button for the lobby and braced as the car began to descend. A few seconds later, his sliver vibrated. He raised it up, read the text.

Best Result. Banks Media Feed. 2005.05.18. Frank Gattis.

Lassiter project kills 27 during internal demonstration at Vinestead West, Sacramento, California. True artificial intelligence would have been first of its kind in human history.

Danny stared at the words, read them again.

A true artificial intelligence? Not just some pseudo-AI like in Perion or Vinestead synthetics?

There was no such thing.

FORTY-FIVE
KAILI

It was all very convincing, this world Arthur Sedivy was trying to sell her.

Cyn had all the appearances of a fully formed person, a mix of Kaili's memories and some new habits and phrases, but there was something off about her, some emotional shift that had occurred since the last time they met. The way she caught Kaili up on the events of the last three years, on her trip to Vietnam, and her search for the man who had killed Anela seemed too expository, too much the script of some bad movie that Sedivy was directing from behind the scenes.

Outside the hired car, the landscape rolled by uninterrupted by load screens, as naturally and as fluidly as reality, but then it was dark and Kaili would have been hard-pressed to pick out the discrepancies. The music playing softly from the front of the car was throwback 90s, a clunky mix of Outlaw Country and Alternative Rock. Even the car itself was dated, as at home in 2019 as it would have been in 2016.

The drive to Yuba City took a little more than an hour. It would have been faster, but Cyn had warned the driver to stick to the speed limit. When they finally arrived, they were greeted with slick, empty streets dotted with cold blue lampposts. Most of the buildings lining the streets were dark.

Cyn directed the driver to a twenty-four-hour diner with a large neon sign that read, in cursive, *Utopia*.

It was anything but.

Kaili followed Cyn to a booth at the back of the diner and watched in disgust as the aggregator did a curt pirouette and fell backward onto the bench. She put her hands on her stomach, closed her eyes, and seemed to fall into an immediate and deep sleep.

"Let me guess—two coffees? You girls look wiped out."

The waitress—her nametag read Gina—wore a bright pink and white uniform with a wide collar and rolled-up sleeves. Though her smile seemed friendly enough, Kaili could see the fatigue in the lines around her mouth and eyes. She had an air of wariness about her, as if she'd seen a thousand drunk or synthed-out customers come through her establishment every night.

"Coffee," said Kaili. Her eyes fell on the lingering crumbs on the table. "Black?"

"Two creams, one sugar."

"Sugar's on the table. I'll bring the creamer. What about your friend?"

"She's not my friend," said Kaili, looking around. "You got bathrooms?"

Gina jerked her head. "Other side of the counter, under that big sign."

Kaili turned, felt the world go off-balance, but caught herself with a quick grab of the booth. Her muscles still ached, but they were finally coming into their own again. And yet, something was still off about her balance, and it wasn't until she caught her reflection in the diner's front windows that she realized it was because of her missing arm. She thought of a tight-rope walker with a long pole, only several feet had been cut off from one side.

Ever so slightly, her center of mass had changed, and it was going to take some time to adjust.

"Very convincing," she whispered to herself. "I gotta give it to you, Arthur. This feels a lot like reality."

The women's bathroom at Utopia reminded Kaili of high school. The floor and walls were covered in drab green tile, the mirrors over the sinks were marred with scratches and graffiti, and the fluorescent lights overhead flickered as if hampered by some supernatural force.

"This takes me back. Annie, do you remember the bathrooms at Garfield? It's like he took this right out of my memory."

"At least the smell is better here," said Anela, "and there are no used tampons in the sink."

Kaili spied her sister in the mirror. She moved to the sink, put her hand on the cloudy glass.

"I can't tell if this is real or not."

"That has always been a hard question," said Anela. She sneered at an open stall. "I suppose there is no good way to tell. A sufficiently complex virtual reality would be indistinguishable from the real thing."

"Did you see him?" asked Kaili. "Did you see G?"

"Briefly. Very briefly."

"Is he the monster you remember?"

Anela turned around, sighed. "Very much so. But you are asking me about revenge again, Kaili. We have more important things to do right now."

"I know, I know." She laughed. "I can't believe I'm buying into this simulation. I rot for years at a Vinestead black site and randomly one day I'm busted out? And not just by anyone, but Cynthia Mesquina, who vowed to kill me for what I did to Robert Gantz, and G, who took you away from me. Doesn't it seem a little…"

"Contrived?"

"More than that. It's too perfect. It's too much what I want. Cyn on my side, G within reach. I mean, how does something like this just *happen*?"

"Someone is pulling the strings." Anela folded her arms, put one leg out to the side. "Either way, it does not matter."

"Of course it matters." Kaili felt the heat rise in her cheeks.

Anela approached the mirror, stopped behind Kaili's reflection.

"If this is real, then you know what to do. If this is a simulation, then you might as well enjoy this quest for as long as it may last. But we must keep moving forward."

Kaili put her hand on the sink, squeezed the porcelain. "That's what he wants, Annie. I'm not gonna act like all of this is real only for him to pull it out from under me later. I'm not gonna be his puppet."

"It is a mind game. Not playing is the same as losing."

Kaili groaned, waved her hand under the faucet. Cool water splashed in the basin. She took a handful of it and rubbed her face. When she straightened up, Anela had left. Her perfume lingered, however, somewhere muddled in the smell of mold and disinfectant.

After hovering over the least disgusting toilet in the bathroom, Kaili returned to the booth. Cyn was still on her back, breathing slowly. A steaming cup of coffee sat on Kaili's side. She slid onto the worn vinyl, felt something sticky attach itself to her hand. The coffee was overly bitter, lacking cream, which Gina had not brought. Kaili pushed the mug to the edge of the table and left it there.

"Are you asleep?" she asked.

"Yes," said Cyn, flatly.

"I need to ask you something."

"Not now. I'm asleep."

"Do you have a thing for G?"

Cyn groaned, sat up. "Excuse me?"

"Your eyes light up when you talk about him. I think it's a perfectly reasonable question."

"Uh, okay, well, if you must know, no, nothing serious. He's kinda cute, but he's like forty and well on his way to a proper dad bod. Not exactly Huy and his six pack."

Kaili nodded, tapped the table with a spoon.

"Why do you ask?"

"Because I'm going to kill him, and I want to know if you and I are gonna have another problem. You seem drawn to men who get in my way."

"Still with that?" Cyn rolled her eyes. She raised a hand to get Gina's attention.

"Which *that* are you referring to? The *that* where a piece of shit punk murdered my sister? Yeah, I'm still on *that*."

Cyn shrugged. "He killed her. She killed his friend. Who now the price of his blood doth owe?"

"Are you seriously trying to minimize my sister's death?" asked Kaili, tightening her grip around the spoon.

"If the shoe fits," said Cyn. When Gina approached, she ordered a diet soda and a plate of french fries.

"Say one more thing about my sister and I will—"

Cyn's hand shot out and plucked the spoon from Kaili's grip before she could even register the movement. She bent it in half with just her thumb.

"You'll what? Even at your best, you wouldn't stand a chance against me, and you know that. So, how about you take your threats and shove 'em right up your cooter? If you don't want to talk about your sister, don't fucking bring her up."

"She is not wrong," said Anela, from the bar. She sat with one leg daintily crossed over the other on a vinyl stool.

Kaili jerked her head to the side, caught herself before she could respond.

"Still talking to your sister, I see."

"You don't know what you're talking about," said Kaili, narrowing her eyes. "She kept me sane inside. They had me on a loop, repeating the same sequence over and over again. And she was there, the previous loops, I assume. She was on the beach with me and Rick, she was in the tower, on the train, in the… house."

Their childhood home in San Diego had seemed so real, even down to the scratches on the walls and cigarette burns on the sofa arms.

Kaili paused, considered Cyn's question again. How did she know about Anela? Did it come out in Perion City? She tried to remember their confrontation at the top of the Perion Spire and later in the makeshift med-bay, but she couldn't remember a specific instance of talking to Anela in Cyn's presence. And if she hadn't slipped up like that, how could Cyn know?

Gina put a large plate of fries down on the table in front of Cyn.

"You girls enjoy," she said, mechanically.

Cyn reached for a fry, found it too hot, and put her hands in her lap.

"Do you remember the Spire in Perion City?" asked Kaili.

"Sure, yeah."

"Do you remember the last thing I said to Gantz before he died?"

Cyn cocked her head, reached again for a fry. This time, she chewed slowly through the heat.

"You were monologuing. That speech you always give before you kill people. *The last face you'll ever see* and all that."

Too generic. Sedivy could have known that.

"What's the first thing you remember when you woke up this morning?"

Cyn shook her head slightly. "What? What does that have to do with anything?"

"Tell me something that happened yesterday," insisted Kaili. "Or the day before that. Anything that happened before you appeared next to me at Folsom."

A moment passed while Cyn chewed thoughtfully on a fry. Kaili could see the extra muscles in her jaw move beneath taut, unblemished skin. It had been three years—supposedly—and yet Cyn still didn't look a day over twenty.

"Are you Turing me?" asked Cyn.

"Maybe." Kaili reached for a fry; the aroma of hot oil was too enticing to ignore.

"You think I'm some kind of synthetic? Like a copy of the original Cynthia Mesquina?"

"No. I spent a long time with synthetics. You're human, but I don't think you're real. My guess is you're part of another simulation put on by Arthur Sedivy and Vinestead. And you're just winding me up with all this talk about Lincoln Tate and G and my sister. Winding me up so that when I'm at my most vulnerable, Arthur can bring the hammer down on the back of my head."

Cyn wiped the corners of her mouth. "Wow," she said. "That's uh… that's something."

"This is the part where you tell me you're real and this is reality and I'm crazy."

"I don't know," said Cyn. "I mean, how would someone even begin to figure that out? Maybe I *am* just a piece of code sent here to torment you. There'd be no way to tell for sure." She sat back in the booth, slumped her shoulders. After a moment, she said, "You really bummed me out, Kaili."

"I doubt that."

Cyn looked around, whispered conspiratorially, "Is she part of it? The waitress?"

"Everything would be part of it," said Kaili. "The waitress, the diner… even those french fries you're stuffing in your face."

"What about Yuba City? Folsom? California?"

Kaili nodded.

"Oh my *god*," said Cyn, in her best throwback valley girl accent. She held her head still, mouth agape, eyes pegged open, as if she had suddenly become a mannequin in a Forever 21 window display.

"You think I'm crazy."

Cyn resumed eating. "I know you're crazy. And when Tanzy hears about this delusion of yours, she's gonna know you're crazy too. And then whatever she has in store for us is gonna go right out the window."

"For *us*?" asked Kaili. "What does she think—" She looked to Anela at the serving counter.

Her sister looked unsurprised.

"She thinks you are in her debt," said Anela.

"I'm in her debt?"

Cyn shrugged. "Nature of the game. Nothing comes free these days, especially not freedom."

"No," said Kaili, shaking her head. "I didn't ask her to do this."

"Didn't you though?" asked Cyn, leaning over the table. "At some point, didn't you pray? Ask a higher power for some help? Me, personally, I don't go in for that crap, but maybe someone heard you."

"I don't pray."

"Well, now's as good a time as any to start." She raised a hand, signaled for Gina. "We're gonna need some ketchup here."

Kaili crossed her arms; her left arm slipped out of her elbow and banged against the table.

"If she asks if you need a hand," said Anela, "kill her."

Cyn raised an eyebrow at the sudden rattling of silverware but said nothing.

Outside, a light mist began to fall, washing out all the little details that made the simulation look real.

FORTY-SIX
TANZY

The Camry went into a coughing fit as they pulled into the parking lot of the Utopia diner in Yuba City.

The entire car shook as if it were about to fall apart and then suddenly went still. A high-pitched, electronic whine filled the cabin for a few seconds before cutting out with an abrupt squelch.

Lincoln shifted the car into park, tapped the ignition button, and removed his hands from the steering wheel slowly, as if he were scared it might awaken again.

"Well," he said, "I did ask for a car that would get us to Yuba City."

Tanzy heard him, but she was more concerned with the two women sitting in a booth near the window. She recognized Cyn, but the other one hardly resembled the exalted and feared leader of Calle Cinco. Her hair was short, slicked back to a spiky line on the back of her head, and she was wearing a gray hoodie that hung like a sheet from thin shoulders.

"That's her," she said.

"Looks like she's been on a diet since that tape was made. I wonder what Vinestead was feeding her in Folsom."

"Not enough."

It was hard for Tanzy to see Kaili as anything less than the biggest and the baddest, anything less than the sum of the stories whispered in the shadows of darknets or in the coffee shops of Umbra where wannabe revolutionaries gathered to plot the downfall of VNet.

The world had lost track of Kaili Zabora after Calle Cinco de Mayo, and when she finally reappeared, it was as the smooth-talking PR flack for Perion Synthetics. Video of Sava Kessler's appearances had been traded around and scrutinized, and an idea of the insidious nature of the Butcher of Burbank started to form in the minds of the people.

Kaili Zabora could go anywhere, be anyone, and control anything.

She had infiltrated the largest synthetics company on the planet, and if it hadn't been for James Perion's untimely death, she might have pulled off the most damaging assault on Vinestead International the world had ever seen. And yet, here she was, sitting in a dingy diner on the wrong side of Yuba City, leaning her unwashed hair against the window while she waited for someone to tell her what to do.

That was not the Kaili Zabora the world knew. They needed to see her strong again, as strong as she was during the Reaping, during every little skirmish she had ever had with Vinestead. And they would; Lincoln would see to that.

And if Tanzy were standing behind her in the photos, or just off to the side looking aloof, then the world would see I.C.E-1 too, and maybe some of what Kaili had would spill over onto Tanzy.

I.C.E-1 would become a household name, respected in every corner of the country and feared in every corner of VNet.

"You straight, Tanzy?" asked Lincoln. "You got a little of the crazy eye."

She shrugged. "Just looking into the future. Kaili's my ticket to the front lines of this war."

"What happened to helping her 'cause it was the right thing to do?"

Tanzy rolled her eyes at him. "Tell me you're not thinking about the story you're gonna feed about all this. You can't wait to tell people what went down."

"That's what I do," said Lincoln. "With this and Danny's story, I'll own the SatIndex for months. Benny won't have anything to run against it, Banks is floundering anyway, and Vinestead won't touch it except to run propaganda."

"Then we have a common goal."

"I guess we do."

"Let me go in first, get her open to the idea of working with us."

Lincoln unbuckled his seatbelt, pushed back against the headrest. "You got a plan or you just gonna wing it?" he asked.

"Cyn said she's got a Guardian Angel chip in her head. I don't know a lot about Kaili Zabora, but I bet she's already scratching at her neck trying to get that thing out of her. Do we need Umbra for that, or can we do it on the move?"

"More expensive on the move. You paying?"

"Johnny's paying. Can you set that up?"

Lincoln pulled his phone from inside his jacket. "Don't think I don't see what's going on here, Tanzy. Giving me orders like you run this show." He smiled to himself. "Like it would kill you to say 'please' every once in a while."

Tanzy put a hand on his shoulder. "Please, Lincoln Tate, titan of the media feeds, pretty please will you arrange transport and a doctor so we can get this thing moving? I will be forever in your debt, oh whisperer of whisperers."

He waved her away with the back of his hand, muttered, "Save that shit for Kaili. Flattery doesn't work on me."

"Yes it does." She pulled the silver handle on the door and climbed out of the car.

The air in Yuba City smelled like manure and oil, though she couldn't quite tell which aroma overpowered the other. Tanzy held her breath as she approached the front doors, which squeaked when she opened them. Warm air washed over her like a rejuvenating spray, shaking off the slight chill she'd gained from the car to the doors. She turned for the booth toward the back of the diner and saw a curious Kaili looking over her shoulder.

Cyn raised a hand in greeting. She slid over closer to the window.

Tanzy took a deep breath, whispered to herself, "I could really use some help with the words, Cleo."

There was no answer.

She slid onto the vinyl bench next to Cyn and gazed into the eyes of the most feared woman in America. Only now, those eyes had dark circles beneath them. Press photos from Perion City showed a Savannah Kessler with tan, slightly glowing skin. The Kaili sitting across the table had pale skin, almost bleached. High cheekbones jutted beneath translucent flesh.

In a single word, Kaili Zabora had withered.

"I'm sorry this happened to you," said Tanzy, her voice soft. "We came as soon as we found out, all of us."

Kaili nodded. "You're Tanzy, right?"

"Not right now. I'm not a suit. I'm just Megan, just a woman sitting across from another woman."

"Spare me," said Kaili, scoffing. "You got me out of Folsom, so that's worth a conversation. Lay out your offer and let's get this over with."

Tanzy shared a look with Cyn, who smiled weakly.

"I…"

She sees the real you, said Cleo.

"My offer…" Tanzy shook her head. "I don't have anything to offer. I only have an ask."

"So ask already."

Tanzy took a deep breath. "I want you to help me make a play against Vinestead."

"Of course you do," said Kaili. She made a fist on the table. "You want to make some elaborate statement about how bad Vinestead is and how good we are, and it'll all go perfectly to plan, no matter how crazy it is. In fact, I bet we won't meet any resistance at all until the final moment when we're about to strike the death blow and then Arthur Sedivy will tap a button on his palette and reset the whole goddamn thing."

"Reset?" asked Tanzy. "You mean like, with a bomb or something?"

"They had her in VR stasis at Folsom," said Cyn. "Sedivy was torturing her by making her relive the same escape over and over again. Now that she's out, she can't accept reality. We're just pawns in a simulation to her. Whatever we do or say, she thinks it's scripted."

"Really?" Tanzy rubbed her cheek, raised her eyebrows at Kaili. "You're really gonna let Vinestead do that to you?"

"They've already done it."

"Yeah, I can see that. They're so far in your head that even when you're out, they're still with you. Don't you see? This is exactly what Vinestead wants. They made it so that if you ever got out of Folsom, you would spend the rest of your life looking over your shoulder, questioning reality. And now you're just sitting there, quivering like a little bitch because you can't tell if this is real."

Kaili struck the table with her fist, but Tanzy pressed on.

"Are you really telling me that the Butcher of Burbank is broken now? Is that what I'm gonna tell Lincoln to feed tomorrow? That Vinestead finally beat Kaili Zabora into submission?"

"Easy," said Cyn. "She's been through a lot today."

"I was shot out of the sky!" Tanzy pushed away the hand Cyn had placed on her arm. "Vinestead tried to kill me while I was trying to get this bitch out of a VR nightmare. So you don't get to tell me to go easy."

She slipped out of the booth and stood up. She slapped the table hard with both hands.

"I don't roll over!" she shouted. "Someone tries to kill me, you can bet your ass I'm gonna try to kill them back. Vinestead needs to be shown they can't just do whatever they want and not expect any consequences. They don't boot me from darknets, they don't take those darknets offline, and they sure as shit don't take shots at the plane I'm flying in—a plane, I might add, that was carrying your boss, Cyn. I'm not saying what they did to you isn't messed up, but if you're not even going to try to fight back, we might as well dump you back at Folsom. So what if this is a simulation? Show them you don't stop. Show them you don't fucking break!"

Tanzy hit the table again; a mug of coffee teetered on the edge, but Cyn caught it before it could fall. The waitress glared as Tanzy passed her on the way to the door. The metal frame slammed loudly against the jamb.

She got back in the car and slammed the door.

"What's—"

"Drive," she said.

"Where are we—"

"Just drive, Lincoln." She made a show of waving her hands at him.

The car reluctantly rumbled to life, and Lincoln backed out of the parking space. He pulled onto the wet street and went two blocks before Tanzy told him to pull over.

"This is far enough," she said, her voice calm. "Sorry about that. I was doing a bit for Kaili."

"What happened in there?"

"Not really what I was expecting. I thought she'd come out of there ready to kick some ass, but… I don't know. It's like they really did break her. Cyn said she was in some kind of looping virtual reality. I didn't know they did that at Folsom. I thought they were strictly ReTreads."

"Stories," said Lincoln. "Too many stories to know what's true or not." He huffed. "It really looked like you were giving her the business in there."

"Yeah," she said, looking at the side mirror. The Utopia diner sign was mostly out of sight. "I don't know if she bought it though. She saw through my *compassionate female* act pretty quickly. It's like she's super paranoid now, and paranoid people don't make great leaders. I'm wondering if we just take credit for getting her out and cut her loose. If she can't get herself in the game, then I don't know how she's gonna bring the rest of Calle Cinco aboard."

Lincoln laughed. "Yeah, your *compassionate female* game is pretty weak. Even you introducing me to Danny was for your benefit."

"How so?" asked Tanzy.

"Don't play dumb. You knew it was getting hot in Umbra. You needed someone to hole you up, and I just happened to be there."

"I went to you because we're professional friends, and because I wanted to control the message on Johnny San Vito. Yeah, you helped me and Danny out of a jam, but now you're gonna get to talk to Kaili Zabora herself. You said it earlier—you're gonna own the SatIndex."

"Stories," he said again. "You tell a lot of stories, Tanzy. And they all depend on Kaili Zabora hooking up with us. Based on how I saw things go back there, I don't think—"

He stopped short, looked to his wrist.

Tanzy smirked, asked innocently, "Who's that?"

"Cyn. She says Kaili is ready to talk."

She checked her own sliver for the time. Only ten minutes had passed. "That took longer than I thought it would."

Lincoln shook his head. "You got some weird methods, girl, but they work." He pulled away from the curb. "Let's go get this lady on our side."

Her methods weren't weird; they were simple.

Kaili Zabora wasn't broken, she had just forgotten what it was like to be an angry woman hellbent on revenge.

Tanzy had simply reminded her.

Not bad, said Cleo.

FORTY-SEVEN
GORDON

Gordon stepped off the bus at Umbra Terminus just as the sun was starting to peek over the horizon.

The ride had been quiet and uneventful, but he hadn't slept. There would be no sleep for a while, not with all the digital stimulants coating his inhibitor chip. As it turned out, he needed the extra push to walk the half mile into Umbra City proper, then a few streets over from Nand to a run-down building that looked like it had once been a gas station.

There was something resembling a sign over an open garage door—it read simply, *Dunlap's*. A curtain of kinked chains obscured a door that had been hastily built into an outer wall that filled the garage opening. A small, handwritten note above the doorknob featured a crossed-out dollar sign and the words *CRYPTO ONLY* in uppercase letters.

Gordon stood for a moment on the cracked sidewalk and surveyed the throng of indigents camping out under the building's awning and around the side in the shells of two burnt-out VW Beetles. Only a few of them were stirring, but Gordon was unsure how they'd respond to company so early in the morning.

And with his hands aching in his jacket, he didn't know how many of them he could take with just his elbows and feet.

He was just working up the nerve to approach when the wooden door opened and a dark face peered out.

"You the King?"

Gordon nodded.

"Well get your ass inside then."

The face retreated into the darkness; the door remained cracked.

Cyn had assured Gordon that Dunlap's was legit but seeing the sorry state of the establishment gave Gordon second thoughts. There was still time to find a hospital, though all of his money was back at Decker Plaza. And even with all that cash, he wasn't sure it was enough to buy proper medical care in 2019.

He stepped forward, walked across the stained evercrete driveway. None of the homeless around him moved.

It was dark inside. LEDs embedded in the electrical sockets near the floor lit the way. The man Gordon assumed was Dunlap called out from the shadows, beckoning him to another door behind a long glass counter.

Gordon smelled liquor on the man's breath as he walked into the next room.

"Wake my ass up at 7:00 a.m. like I got a real job to go to or something," muttered Dunlap. He slammed the door behind them, fumbled for a light switch on the wall.

The resulting bloom stung Gordon's eyes. He put up a hand, waited. It wasn't just the matrix of LED lights in the ceiling that made seeing impossible, it was also the tiled white floor and glossy white walls. The room slowly emerged from the haze. Gordon found that focusing on the furniture—all a flat black—helped with the adjustment. There was a long table set next to the wall he'd come through and multiple rolling carts positioned in a circle around a long chair.

The chair reminded Gordon of visiting the unlicensed dentist back at LPS, though its black padding and metal frame were much newer and unmarred by stains. He noticed the metal grating on the floor below it; it looked like a drain to catch whatever fluids might be spilled.

"Sweet," said Dunlap, in a voice lacking its previous gravel. "We didn't wake the rats. You'd be surprised how many try to rush this place when I get customers. Sorry about the cold welcome. Sometimes you gotta put on a show if you want to stay in business, know what I mean?"

Gordon stood awkwardly in the middle of the room, unsure where to go or what to do.

"No," he replied. "I don't."

"Yeah, well, Cyn said you're not from Umbra, so I don't blame you. But, live here long enough and it'll become second nature."

Dunlap took off a dirty trench coat and replaced it with a white lab jacket that he retrieved from a hook on the back of the door. From the neck down, he looked like any other doctor—gray scrubs, white jacket, and black slip-on shoes. His face, however, told the story of a grizzled, middle-aged man who had lived too long with the gutter trash. His face was pale and scarred, mostly on his left cheek. Long, oily hair sprouted from the top of his head, fell over the shaved sides, and ended at a knot under his chin as if he were wearing a hair helmet. The hair after the knot had been braided into a foot-long segment that he'd clipped to his shirt.

"Don't let it fool you," said Dunlap, motioning to his face. "It's all for the Umbrats. I've done twenty-seven procedures for Cyn alone. And if you know anything about her, you know she doesn't tolerate anything less than the best, not in tech and not in aug work."

Gordon removed his hands from his jacket. The bandages were stained red; he could feel the extra weight of the blood pooled there. He started unwrapping the strips of cloth Calle Cinco had provided him with, discarding them in a nearby trashcan labeled with a biohazard sign.

"I don't need augmentations. I just need my hands back."

Dunlap furrowed his eyebrows as he slipped on a pair of light blue surgical gloves.

"Gnarly…" His head dipped side-to-side, trying to get a better look at the damage. "You get into a fight with a cheese grater or what?"

"Synthetics," said Gordon.

"Shit yeah, well, that'll do it, man. Why don't you have a seat and we'll take a closer look?"

It was all too familiar—the fighting, the fixing, like some kind of torturous loop Gordon couldn't break out of. This was the second time since leaving LPS that he was submitting to a doctor. His reintroduction to the world wasn't going as smoothly as he had imagined it, the few times he *had* imagined it.

Gordon sat down in the chair and leaned back.

"Some glasses for my bro in arms," said Dunlap, handing him a reflective pair of pink Oakleys. "I know the lights in here can be a little harsh."

"I've got bigger problems."

"I can see that." He extended a tray over Gordon's pelvis, had him lay his hands on the blue paper. For a few minutes, he prodded the busted fingers and mangled knuckles with folded squares of gauze. It didn't hurt much; everything from his forearms down had gone numb.

Gordon groaned

He was too old to be taking so much damage. He'd run to LPS to get away from the world and maybe over the years, he'd second-guessed that decision, perhaps late at night, after half a bottle of whiskey. But now he was out and back in the shit and there was no doubt in his mind that Cyn would keep finding ways to involve him in little skirmishes that would leave another part of him broken and in need of repair.

"So's this your first time in Umbra?" asked Dunlap, still exploring. "Where you comin' from?"

"Texas."

"Ah, yeah, home of Chicago's famous Whataburger. You know I had them once when I was up in Aurora visiting my fam. Drove all the way into the city to get it too."

"What'd you think?"

"Eh, s'alright. I've had better hot dogs though."

Gordon winced at the sudden acute pain in his knuckles.

"Yep," said Dunlap. "This is busted, bro. I know you said you didn't need aug work, but man, there's not really much difference between augs and medicine these days. I mean, I could patch you up, set the bones that need setting, and you'll be back in the surf in a few months, maybe. But, if you're gonna be scrapping again sometime soon, I can totally aug those digits, groove and lube the knuckles, and patch in a few slivers of RealSkin. You'll be back fighting robots in twenty-four hours. Though if I were you, man, I'd take a vacation from boxing metal for at least two weeks."

"How's that possible?"

Dunlap shrugged. "Fuck if I know, man. I'm not gonna lie, some of that RealSkin bonding comes from stem cells. Embryos, you know? Changed the landscape overnight once we kicked all those Bible Thumpers out of government. It's the same shit Perion uses for his robots. How do you think he makes 'em look so real?"

Gordon stared back, blankly.

"You don't know about Perion?"

"I've been out of the world," Gordon explained. "Twenty years and some change. After a while, you start thinking maybe it's still all the same out there, but it ain't. I don't recognize anything anymore."

Except the violence.

That never changed.

"Right." Metal tools clanged on the tray. "Cyn was there, you know, in Perion City? Disappeared for a while after that. Came back different." He spoke slowly, concentrating on his work. "I don't know if it was Perion City or what came after that changed her, but she doesn't come by as often anymore. Used to check in like every week, see the new gear. Kinda miss her, man."

"You two ever…"

Dunlap looked up. The mechanical irises in his eyes rotated out of what Gordon guessed was a magnifying configuration.

"Yeah, right, man. I love Cyn, but she's a train engine pulling a hundred cars of crazy behind her. Thanks, but no thanks. I like it in here, in my OR. Cyn is *out there*. Know what I mean?"

Gordon understood. His time with Cyn had been pleasant, but even he could tell how fearless she was. She had pushed everything onto him—Umbra, the news of the world he'd withdrawn from, and more than once, though unsuccessfully, her body. They had only gone as far as Gordon holding her by the shoulders, his mind trying to understand what he was feeling beneath her skin.

Maybe her blend of metal and flesh was what passed for a real woman in 2019, but there was only one kind of woman Gordon wanted now, a woman with a smooth neck, soft hair, and arms that could swallow him up and hide him from the world.

When Gordon closed his eyes, he saw her.

Natalie.

"How long is this gonna take?" he asked.

"Oh, it'll be a few hours, man," said Dunlap. "Why, you got somewhere to be? Wife and kid waiting for you at home?"

"I don't know. Haven't seen either of them in twenty years."

Dunlap paused, looked up again. "Shit, man. Sorry. Nothing at all?"

"No," said G, breaking the tension with a chuckle. "I uh… cut 'em out of my memory, the kid part anyway. She was pregnant when I left." He shifted in the chair, cleared his throat. "Anyway, never mind, don't know why I'm telling you that."

"Chemicals," Dunlap replied. "Nerve block and some morphine. Makes people chatty, bro. You get used to it. You know, you should look her up."

"Who?"

"Your wife."

"We weren't married."

"You have a kid together, bro. That's like the same."

Gordon thought about how he could find her again. Go to her old apartment in Austin? Surely she'd have moved out of it after twenty years.

"I wouldn't know where to start."

"What's her name?" asked Dunlap.

"Natalie. Purcell."

Dunlap arched his head back a little, spoke to the ceiling. "Simon, do a Pattrn search for Natalie Purcell from Austin, Texas."

"I don't think you're gonna…"

"Found her," said Dunlap. He used his elbow to turn a vidscreen around to face Gordon. "Looks like she got married. Bummer, man."

Gordon searched the ceiling for some kind of listening device, saw nothing. And what the hell was a *pattern search*, some newfangled way of searching the Net?

The questions receded as he took in her face. She was more pale than he remembered her, her face a bit puffier, but the lines that used to appear when she smiled were there. The photo was of Natalie standing on the beach, a towel wrapped around her waist, a lime-green bikini top glowing in the sunlight. Her eyes were hidden by dark sunglasses, but Gordon had no trouble imagining them.

Pattrn Results, he read.

Natalie Purcell Shuler, from Austin, Texas, currently residing in Frankfurt, Germany.

"That her?" asked Dunlap.

Gordon nodded.

"If you want later, I can totally set you up with a Pattrn account so you can message her. I'll have to bill Cyn for the consulting time, but I'm sure she'll be cool."

"I'm not going to *message* her. You don't send a text to someone you haven't seen in two decades."

Dunlap laughed. "Oh yeah, man? What're you gonna do, just like, show up on her doorstep? Frankfurt's a long, long way from Umbra, especially for a man without any crypto."

"I'll find a way." Gordon leaned his head back, took a deep breath.

He didn't know how much it cost to fly to Germany, or whether he could even get a passport, but it didn't matter. He'd had his memories back for less than a day and it was already clear why he'd dumped them in the first place.

Natalie.

The obsession that had bloomed during his sophomore year at UT still raged inside him. And why wouldn't it? By deleting the memory, he'd cheated himself of the healing, of the moving on.

Maybe it would come to that, someday.

Until then, Natalie Purcell Shuler was alive and well, and presumably, so was their child.

Gordon closed his eyes, tried to imagine how his boy would have looked those first years.

Small, twin dimples like his mother?

Wild, curvy brown hair like his father?

Or somehow—impossibly so—vacant, uncaring eyes like his namesake?

FORTY-EIGHT
DANNY

Danny had no intention of following the doctor's orders of bed rest and low exertion, but by the time he made it back up to his room, his mind was already drifting off. He figured the doc had slipped something into the chemical cocktail she'd injected him with, something that could be easily countered by the Syzygy chip if only Danny could summon the mental energy to ask for it.

Instead, he sank into a deep sleep seconds after climbing into bed. For a while, there was nothing, only a darkness from which Danny tried to extract things—people, objects, some kind of world. But the dream ether was unyielding, and he felt every empty second pass, until finally, he started to discern a warbling voice somewhere beyond the black.

He recognized it as Beth, the cashier at the Blockbuster in Brigham Plaza. She asked him if he needed any help, and when he didn't respond, she asked again, and again. Echoes of her voice overlapped until finally her words were unintelligible.

Danny closed his eyes—though visually nothing changed—and tried to shut out the sound.

When he opened them, he was standing in the aisles at Blockbuster, long endless aisles that stretched to vanishing points in every direction. Wherever he turned, however he moved, the view never changed, except for the small variations in the cover art around him. On closer inspection, he discovered the boxes on the shelves were old-school VHS tapes, and though the artwork and fonts varied, they all spelled out the same two words.

Decryption Complete.

At first, the message meant little to Danny. The words could have been gibberish for all he cared. What truly mattered was how he was going to get out of the store, where the exit was, and whether he could get to the Domino's next door before they closed. The farther he ran, the more anxious he became. His legs were unbound by physics, propelling him over great distances with every step. The shelves around him became a blur, but the words continued to pop out, as if the covers were individual frames on a strip of film spun into motion.

Then he remembered.

Johnny San Vito.

The data dump.

His servers at home had finally unlocked the secrets Johnny had bequeathed unto Danny. He'd been expecting Tanzy's Quatrain to crack the data first, but either they were no longer working on it or *had* cracked it and just not told him about it.

The decision to slow-roll the data to I.C.E-1 started to feel like the right choice.

He snapped awake, lifted his head from a damp pillow, and squinted at the sunlight streaming in through the windows. The vidscreen on the far wall showed the time and weather in Umbra.

11:54 a.m. Cloudy. 52 degrees.

Danny groaned as he reached for his rig; the sliver on his outstretched arm carried the now-familiar *Decryption Complete* message. Shaky hands fumbled with the straps, and it was then Danny realized he was overly excited, almost to the point of sickness. Johnny's data, nearly forgotten in the week since it fell out of the sky and cratered in Danny's chip, was now unlocked and ready for inspection.

There was no question about what he'd look for first.

The rig snapped into place; small fans in the headset ramped up.

It took ten minutes of standing in a verdant limbo full of rolling hills and birds lolling about in the sky to build a secure connection back to his private network in Vail. Not only did he not trust the VNet snoops along the line back home, he also didn't want to invite attention from anyone in-house, be that Lincoln, Cyn, or one of their awkwardly named *aggregators*.

Once the tunnel had been built, a door appeared on the grass in front of him. Stepping through it, he found himself in a virtual room that closely matched his workshop at home. It was cleaner, no doubt, and the ceilings were a little higher, but it was close enough to make him homesick. The warmth was there, as were the occasional drafts of cold air that reminded him of the snowy mountains outside.

He rushed up the circular staircase in the middle of the room and found his monitors alert and scrolling in his workshop. He sat down in his command chair—this one white and black unlike the real blue and gray one—and started typing.

Brigham Plaza.

Despite the indexing indicator at the top of the screen showing only a third of the data as having been crawled, results for his search started showing up immediately. As each small square of data appeared, Danny yanked it from the screen and dragged it into the air around him. At first, there seemed to be no pattern to what Johnny had collected; they were mostly screenshots, along with some outbound links to references in VNet.

It was as if Johnny had run around Brigham Plaza while spamming the Print Screen key, except, Danny had never seen any of the saved images during his own visits. Some textures were vaguely familiar, but it wasn't until a green cube appeared in the search that Danny understood what he was looking at.

Johnny must have gone through the same wall, walked the same white mist, and found the cube containing Lassiter, the self-proclaimed artificial intelligence. He'd screen-capped the encounter, which meant the remaining images were likely similar visits with other data hidden behind the Brigham Plaza veneer.

Danny stood from his chair and pushed the pictures around until they formed a two-dimensional grid. Stacking the similar content, he made twelve piles, though it was clear Johnny had been able to research some more than others. The house behind the strip mall was there, tall and ominous. According to the meta, it was called the *House of Nepenthe*. A definition of the strange word followed, as did a link to the relevant line in Edgar Allen Poe's *The Raven* and another to a KXAN article about the death of a Vinestead engineer named Kenneth Barnes.

The green cube came with a few notes—Lassiter's name in all caps, the question *last resting place of X?*, and an imperative to *find G*.

There were several images that looked to be simply text—transcripts of events from Vinestead's history, including the Reaping, Calle Cinco de Mayo, and the fall of the Net. One image actually linked back to the House of Nepenthe—some kind of kill order for Barnes.

Danny absorbed the information so quickly that he almost missed the implication.

A Vinestead kill order?

More than that, *evidence* of a Vinestead kill order?

That was definitely something they would want kept out of the public arena. So why had they tried to bury it in VNet and not in some black box in the basement? Why risk some curious hacker coming along and exposing it?

"These are all secrets," muttered Danny.

Lassiter, the video of Kaili Zabora's abduction, and the truth behind pivotal moments in history—they were all damaging to the company. Johnny had discovered them, but for some reason, couldn't extract them from Brigham Plaza. Maybe he didn't have the skill or just ran out of time, but it was clear that pulling out the data was going to be his next move.

If Danny's encounter with Lassiter were any indication, then all the data was still likely in Brigham Plaza. Whoever had put it there must have been too lazy or too arrogant to move it.

A register flipped. Brigham Plaza was no Vinestead operation. Security protocols would have called for an isolated system to house such sensitive information. This was the work of a few or maybe even just one person, someone inside Vinestead who was keeping the digital equivalent of a little black book.

The ambient noise in the construct graded down to a low hum.

Johnny had discovered someone's stash of secrets, and that someone had murdered him for it.

Bullets.

A plan began to form in Danny's head. He retraced what must have been Johnny's last steps: stumbling upon a protected construct, discovering the hidden secrets, and then finally, fatally, trying to copy them out of the construct.

If Danny wanted to draw out Johnny's murderer, then all he had to do was repeat the work. He would go back to Brigham Plaza, expose all the data, and then try to copy it off, maybe dump it in the dead drops of every major media feed.

He sat back in the chair and began copying the Brigham data to his Syzygy chip. After all the images and associated meta were safely aboard, he filled the remaining space with every known antivirus and firewall program he had. Bullets had nearly gotten the better of him the last time they spoke, and if he were indeed Johnny's killer, then there was no telling how he'd react once Danny confronted him.

With any luck, Danny would get in, copy out the data, and get the hell out of there before Bullets even knew something was up.

He jumped…

… and felt the hand on his chest before the construct had even fully loaded.

For a moment, he saw only the blue aurora background of VNet's empty, ethereal plane, but soon the individual layers of Brigham Plaza slid into place. They stood for a moment before sinking out of view as Danny went rocketing straight up into the dome of the construct.

The strip mall shrank to a pinpoint, held for the briefest of intervals, and then came roaring back. A dirty sidewalk rose up to meet Danny and tried to break every bone in his body. A sensory-blocking mod caught the incoming data, and the impact barely registered. Blood trickled from a busted lip, but there was no accompanying pain.

Danny pushed himself up off the ground, caught eyes with a man standing a few paces away in a parking space. He bore a striking resemblance to Bullets, less to Ben, as if he were an older version of both of them. Only, he lacked the West Coast informality of his predecessors. Instead, he stood tall, confidently, and stared with the intensity of someone who didn't want to be there.

An older version of the boy in the simulation—which meant this night at the plaza, this evening of scamming pizza and renting movies, was actually a real memory from Bullets' past.

Danny looked up at the stars, strained for an idea that suddenly crystalized. He brought his eyes back down to Bullets.

"I was wondering when you'd show up," said Danny, dusting off his pants.

"You just couldn't stay away, could you? There's nothing for you here, Guns."

"Just you," Danny replied, raising a pointed finger. "You killed Johnny."

"I've never killed anyone in my life." A hint of a smile broke on his face. "At least not directly. If you'd like, I can give you the name of the company I contracted for the job."

Danny felt the firewalls in Bullets' avatar ramp up; they gave off a heat that filled the entire construct.

"I don't want some low-level goons. I want you."

"You can't have me," said Bullets, stepping forward. "You can't touch me, Guns. I've got Vinestead at my back; all your friends have either abandoned you or they're dead. Even if you knew who I really am, it wouldn't make any difference."

"I know who you are."

"You don't know shit. You're just as clueless as Johnny. His ignorance got him killed. How far will yours take you?"

Danny held out his hand, conjured the images Johnny had acquired, and let them fall like a loose deck of cards to the evercrete. They fanned out on the edge of the sidewalk.

"All of your secrets," he said. "That's all I've been focused on, trying to figure out what you've got hidden here. But that just made me miss the answer staring me in the face."

Bullets was unmoved. He asked, almost disinterestedly, "Which is?"

"The stars." Danny pointed up. "You built this construct from a memory, and you left all the little details in it. Brigham Plaza is in Provo, Utah. The stars tell me what time of year it is. The movies on the shelf tell me what year it is. And those cameras…" He pointed to the primitive surveillance cameras mounted every few feet under the awning. "That data will be archived somewhere. Records from the Blockbuster will be stored somewhere. And Beth… sweet, sweet Beth. I'm sure she remembers you from the old days."

Bullets swallowed, tried to freeze his avatar's reactions.

"So you see, I do know who you are, or will, soon. And once I get a real name, I'm gonna find the face that goes with it, and then I'm gonna put my boot in it."

"I'm sure." Bullets put his hands behind his back. "You have to admit though, it'll be hard to lift your leg with that bullet wound, don't you think? And after hobbling around Decker Plaza for the last few days, do you think you're really in any condition to go picking fights?"

Danny caught the threat.

"That's right," he said, stepping forward. His progress was stopped by some invisible forcefield around Bullets' avatar. "I'm at Decker Plaza, ninth floor. I'll be here until I figure out who you are and take you down."

"Well, then allow me to save you some trouble."

Bullets came forward without moving his legs. He got in Danny's face, and though his breath had no odor, it was cold as ice. It spilled from his mouth in foggy waves, fell to the sidewalk, and froze Danny's feet in place. The chill threatened to spread over his entire avatar, but the Syzygy beat it back.

"My name is Julius Parker, and I'm at the Vinestead West building in Sacramento. You can ask for me at reception."

A glaze fell over Danny's eyes; they had frozen and crystalized. Multiple firewalls cried out in alarm, all of them suggesting the same thing: jack out.

Julius Parker put his mouth near Danny's ear and whispered.

"Come and get me, motherfucker."

FORTY-NINE
KAILI

The simulation wasn't resetting.

Kaili kept waiting for some kind of kick, some transition either out of the simulation or, if Sedivy were to be believed, back to the stasis pod at Le Soleil Rouge. And if she were truly reset, then the memories of her escape, of the House of Nepenthe and everything that came before, would be wiped away as well.

The worst part was not knowing.

She would wake up in the stasis pod and start all over, unaware a previous version of herself had fought and suffered her way from a virtual prison to Folsom to Yuba City and all the way back to where her career with Calle Cinco had started in Umbra. From the rooftop of Decker Plaza, she could see the Umbra Spire piercing the Canopy. A platform at the top, barely visible behind the artificial roof of the world, rotated slowly.

It was there, with Rick Diaz lying by her side, that Kaili had seen the bigger problem in the fight against Vinestead International—their employees were just normal people. Arthur Sedivy was a sadist, and Kaili was sure everyone on the board of directors needed a kick in the nuts, but the little guys, the engineers and receptionists and janitors, they were just people trying to get by.

She'd known from the moment she met Rick that he was no villain. He had no high-backed leather chair to sit in or hairless cat to pet. He would never have been caught monologuing to some enemy of the 'Stead. He was just a man, a normal, everyday man who had been stuck in a loveless relationship without the necessary confidence to leave it, to venture out into the world and claim his stake. Kaili recalled how much she'd had to push him to abandon work for a day, to come with her on what would be his final adventure.

She recalled his smile. It had filled her with so much pity, and that pity had turned to rage against Vinestead.

But now...

Now...

Kaili drew her legs onto the padded patio furniture set into one corner of the rooftop lounge. The bare flesh tingled as she settled into place. The grow-wire in her torso and limbs was active again thanks to the new Eclipse Gen Y biochip in her neck. She couldn't remember much about the procedure: a nondescript hotel room in Yuba City, a short Asian man in an Adidas tracksuit, and an injection in her right arm that had sent her to dreamland.

When she woke, they were already on the road to Umbra. The drive into the city, the walk from the car into Decker Plaza, and the relegation to a nicely appointed room occurred in a muffled haze the short Asian man had warned would occur. Removing a biochip and replacing it with another was no simple task, and the Eclipse needed time to adjust to the new environment, especially after the way her nervous system had been treated by the Guardian Angel.

They had all tried talking to her—Tanzy, Lincoln, and Cyn—but the fog had made conversation impossible. She'd wasted the day in bed, and when the next morning came, she'd slipped away in the quiet hours to come up to the roof where an empty bar stood in the center of an outdoor lounge.

The Eclipse was warm in her neck, and with the same warmth clinging to the grow-wire, Kaili didn't really feel the December weather around her. Sometimes, when the wind gusted, its cold fingers traced along her skin, and she wondered if the sensation were a preamble to the simulation resetting.

The world, however, persisted.

"It is not exactly Coronado Beach," said Anela, peering over the side of the building, "but it works. The trees are different."

Kaili looked out over the rooftops; most were packed to the brim with satellite equipment and high-gain directional antennas that pointed east toward Sacramento and west toward Los Angeles.

"There aren't any trees," she replied.

"I see them anyway."

"This place has changed," said Kaili. "I remember when it was barely a desert commune. No tall buildings, nothing this close to the Canopy, anyway."

"Umbra was a beacon, and beacons attract bugs."

"You can't have a community of outsiders grow so large that they're no longer outsiders. It's like they've concentrated all of the most devoted minds in one place that Vinestead could level with just one calculated strike."

Anela made a soothing sound that echoed in Kaili's head.

A gust of wind rolled across the roof, knocking a loose cushion onto the wooden deck.

Kaili held her breath.

The moment was broken by the sudden opening of the rooftop door. A man with a shaved head and tattoos peeking over the collar of his white undershirt approached slowly, as if Kaili had a kill radius and he didn't want to get too close.

"Ms. Zabora?" he asked, his accent a dizzying mix of Los Angeles urban and Malibu shore trash.

Kaili let out her breath; the Eclipse sent a corresponding reward signal down her spine—a prize for not suffocating.

"What?" she asked.

"We haven't met yet. I'm Bryce. I just came up to see if you needed anything. You didn't come down for lunch."

Her eyes drifted over his shoulder to the security cameras mounted on either side of the door. They had been watching her all morning. Could they hear her also? Hear her talking to her sister?

"I'm fine," she said. "Not feeling very hungry."

He didn't so much walk as drifted from the door to a chair near the coffee table. He sat down on the edge of a cushion and put his elbows on his knees.

"How're you feeling?" he asked.

"What's it to you?"

He smiled; his white teeth were perfectly aligned.

"We all care," he said, motioning to the camera. "But they thought I'd be the least offensive person to come and ask. I'm not here to sell you anything, Ms. Zabora. I'm just here to help."

"Is that what you do here? You're a helper?"

"I do what needs doing. I used to rep a few freelancers until Cyn came along. We were actually making pretty good money until Perion City. But you know about that. She went MIA, so I started working for Lincoln. Now I do a little of both—whatever keeps the crypto flowing."

"How much crypto?"

Bryce laughed. "You trying to buy me out?"

Kaili examined her fingernails and shrugged.

"I'm sure you've got deep pockets in your other pants," said Bryce, "but, man, Lincoln and Cyn are my family. You don't break with family."

"Loyalty," said Anela. "Charming."

"Didn't Cyn tell you what happened between her and I?" Kaili mimed a gunshot.

"Yeah," he replied, with a halting laugh. "She told me you two got into some shit. Though I don't know. The way she talked about you, I thought you'd be like seven feet tall and have wings like a Valkyrie or something."

"She said I was a monster?"

"I think she was a little pissed at first, but she went overseas, cleared her head, then spent all that time looking for G. I think it gave her some perspective."

"G," Kaili repeated, looking to the door. "Where is that murdering little prick? I haven't seen him since Folsom."

"He's around. Staying away for obvious reasons. Everyone just wants to give you your space right now. Until you're ready."

"You're gonna make me ask?"

Bryce straightened up, pushed back in the chair. "I don't know exactly what they're planning. They don't tell me the big picture, just *go here* and *drive this* and whatever. Cyn and Lincoln, they're the brains, and Tanzy's some kind of big shit suit up north. There's another guy, Danny, also a big shit, has his own one-man cipher den."

"Danny Montreal?" she asked.

"Yeah, you know him?"

Kaili shrugged again.

She knew of him, but had never shared a word with him, digitally or otherwise. He was one of those hackers who lived purely for the money and fame, preferring to do jobs for big-money corps and moguls, jobs that ultimately benefited no one. Hackers like Danny didn't live to fight oppressors—Vinestead or otherwise. They had no interest in helping other people. And yet, for some reason, they were celebrated in the hacker community.

Bryce looked away at the sound of a helicopter flying low over the Canopy.

"Quite the family you have," said Kaili, imagining the group standing around like superheroes posing for the camera. "I have a family too."

"Calle Cinco. I know."

"Have you heard anything about them in the last… three years?"

Bryce's face softened a bit; the smile he'd been wearing disappeared. He started to speak but turned away instead.

"What?" she asked.

"No, I get it." Suddenly, the ground by his feet became interesting. "You're thinking they didn't come looking for you."

"Three… goddamn… years."

"Well, it's not like anyone had much to go on. Even if you told them you'd gone north, what were they supposed to do with an aug parlor full of dead bodies? Local cops had nothing to go on. I guarantee you Vinestead erased all the surveillance in the area, probably five blocks in every direction."

Kaili readjusted her shawl; the wind had picked up, and with each passing moment, the heat in her body was dissipating.

"Cyn found me pretty easily."

"Which never would have happened if someone hadn't offed Johnny San Vito. That's what set this whole thing in motion."

"What does that mean?" asked Anela.

Kaili repeated her sister's question for Bryce.

He laced his fingers. "Cyn didn't tell you? How we found you?"

Anela came closer, posted up next to Bryce's chair.

"Man…" He sighed, stood up. "I'm probably not the best person to be telling you this." He turned and walked through Anela, headed for the door.

"Wait," said Kaili. She jumped up from the couch, her muscles responding as quickly as they ever had, and blocked his path. "Tell me. I want to hear it from you. The others are just gonna tell me what I want to hear."

Bryce nodded slowly. "From what Cyn's told me, Johnny San Vito sent Lincoln a video when he died using some kind of Dead Man's Loop. The video was from inside LSR."

Kaili's stomach dropped, but a sudden fiery anger lifted it up again.

"We saw a man take you out of your pod."

"Nazar," said Anela.

"Was he tall?" she asked. "Ukrainian?"

"I don't know about that, but he was tall. Strong, too."

Kaili stepped forward, put her hand on Bryce's arm. He put his free hand on hers, and the gesture pierced her anger and touched the scared little girl inside. Her eyes misted over.

"And this tall, strong man… did he rape me?"

When he didn't respond right away, the anger flared.

"Did he bend me over the stasis pod and force his way into me, Bryce?! Answer me, goddammit!"

Decker Plaza reeled, tilting dangerously from side to side while Kaili tried to keep her balance. She stumbled, the Eclipse compensated, but still she ended up by the door, hand on the wall, one leg bent and the other ready to give out. The sound of her own panicked breathing filled her ears.

Bryce was by her side instantly, supporting her stub arm and patting her back.

"Easy, easy. Blue skies, okay?"

She pushed him away. "What the fuck are you talking about?"

"Hey, I'm just saying, you're not in any danger right now. Haven't you ever flown through a thunderstorm? It's rain, thunder, and lightning, and you're scared to death, but finally, the plane breaks through the clouds and it's all blue skies as far as you can see. Whatever's going on inside you right now, the rest of the world is still here. You're okay right now."

The tears came despite Kaili's efforts. There was nothing in the Eclipse's factory protocols that would keep her from showing emotion, so it simply let the signals flow unimpeded.

"It was real?" asked Anela.

"I thought…" Kaili sobbed for a moment. "I thought that was just part of the simulation, something Vinestead made up to fuck with my head. But now, right now, you're telling me it was *real?*"

She dropped her arm, threw her shoulder into the wall. Her hand found its way to a spot below her stomach. She spread her fingers over her womb as if she might be able to sense the damage inside, feel the remnants of trespass. The thought of pregnancy occurred to her briefly, but the timeline was off. A baby would have been born in the first year, and she would have remembered giving birth.

Unless…

Kaili replayed the last forty-eight hours, from Folsom to the boat to a twenty-four-hour Walmart outside of Yuba City. The loss of her arm and the intruder in her neck had distracted her from seeing the rest of her body clearly. She'd had a shower, yes, but it was quick, and she'd been dazed. She hadn't done what every victim of a violent sexual assault did in the movies—stand naked in front of a full-length mirror and examine the damage.

"Talk to me," said Bryce. He was close enough to smell; his cologne was pleasant, dry.

The scent felt incongruent with the moment, but Kaili focused on it even as her fingers slipped below the waistband of her shorts, beneath the elastic of her underwear. They didn't have to go far before she found what she was looking for. A vise closed around her lungs. Shaky fingers moved left and right, allowing her to build a mental image of a long, horizontal scar, the kind her own mother had worn in all the family photos from Coronado Beach after Anela was born.

Kaili collapsed, felt the pain as her knees struck the solid wood below.

"What is it?" asked Bryce.

It took considerable effort to get the word out, but she managed it, managed to say it clearly and imbue it with all the pain she'd experienced since stepping through the front doors at Le Soleil Rouge.

The small photo on Arthur Sedivy's desk in the Astoria Prime tower flashed in her head. She'd barely noticed it, and yet, could remember it clearly.

"Family," she said.

FIFTY

TANZY

Bedlam, the message read. *Look for Johnny.*

VNet's largest digital sex club was the last place Tanzy wanted to be, but for whatever reason, Danny refused to come out of his room at Decker Plaza. She'd even given him a day to cool off, remembering the message she'd sent him asking for help and his subsequent silence. When Saturday started to wear on, she'd practically begged Tate to unlock the door for her, but he'd refused, citing *a man's right to privacy*. As it turned out, it would have made little difference, as Danny had been jacked into VNet the whole time, evidently trying to drown himself in an unending deluge of abstract fornication.

After so much time spent in her physical body, the switch to virtual reality was something of a relief for Tanzy and a way for her mind to distance itself from the ceaseless demands of Terrareal. She moved with ease through the writhing flesh, stepping over extended legs and quivering arms. She felt stronger in VNet, confident that no one could do her any real harm, not here. Even facing Danny didn't seem as daunting. If she got emotional, she could hide the pain. If she got angry, she could have the girls bring the whole construct down on his head.

Look for Johnny.

Tanzy remembered Danny's curt message after a few minutes of searching for his features in a sea of twisted faces. Danny had a persistent tan, black hair, and eyes that were always searching, whereas Johnny was fair-skinned and had a sharp chin and blond hair that was permanently coiffed above his forehead. His eyes were acute, calculating, as if he knew how powerful focused attention could be, how uncomfortable it made the people he looked at.

A naked staircase led her up out of the throngs of people and after the fifth step, gravity shifted to the right. She proceeded onto another platform that extended at a right angle to the activity below. It was on this plane that she found Danny—or more accurately, saw Johnny. The way he was sitting there, leaning back on a couch between an overweight woman with stockinged legs and a pale couple in a vertical 69, looked strangely natural, as if Johnny were still alive and none of the madness of the last week had ever happened.

She approached gingerly, not wanting to dip her toes into any open crevices, and at one point, had to jump to the safety of an ottoman while a woman leading a train of six men passed by. Finally, she stood before the ghost of her friend and cleared her throat.

He hardly looked up from his laptop.

"Tanzy," he said.

"You've got a lot of nerve running that frame," she said. "And here of all places."

Danny kept typing. "Wasn't my first choice either, but Johnny didn't have any alternate skins, and I wasn't gonna sit through the menus to create one. I just wore whatever he had on the last time he jacked in."

"You spoofed his account?"

"Had to. Mine's still connected to the Brigham honeypot. Not much I can do about that right now. I needed to get into VNet to do some work, and this was the easiest way to do it."

Tanzy traded a glance with the overweight woman; she lifted the nipple of one large breast to her mouth and flicked her tongue at it.

"What kind of work?" asked Tanzy.

"Does it matter?"

"Is it about Johnny?"

His eyes came up—Johnny's eyes came up.

"Of course it's about Johnny. It never stopped being about Johnny. For some of us anyway."

"Don't lay that trip on—"

"I don't want to lay anything on you, Megan. I was perfectly happy doing this by myself. *I got this.* So the only real question is, what do *you* want? And if it's something for Kaili Zabora, you can fuck right off without asking."

She crossed her arms, shifted in place as a tingle rose in her legs.

The emotionware code has changed, said Cleo, softly. *Working.*

"Thanks," whispered Tanzy.

It was the most they had spoken in a day. Tanzy had asked nothing of Cleo since Yuba City. Cleo, in her softening anger, had delivered a few critical messages from the Quatrain, but nothing more. Their relationship, so strong for so many years, had been stretched to a breaking point, but as there was nowhere for Cleo to go, it seemed the pseudo-AI was trying to make the best of things.

"It's not about Kaili," said Tanzy, quietly. She wasn't sure if he could hear her over the thumping bass, but she didn't care. "I just wanted to see you, make sure you were okay. And I wanted you to know I forgive you for not helping me with Folsom. You didn't want any part of it, and I shouldn't have reached out when things got messy, even when my plane was falling out of the sky, I..."

Danny shook his head.

"Nope," he said. "Not this time."

"You stubborn piece of—"

Tanzy reached for Danny's wrist. As soon as her fingers wrapped around the sleeve of Johnny's leather jacket, she jumped them out of Bedlam and into a Sixteen Minutes construct. Walls sprung up in a random, empty sector of VNet, and each individual brick held within it a unique encryption key. Unfortunately, like white blood cells attacking a foreign invader, VNet would eventually dissolve the walls and destroy the construct in a process that took, on average, about sixteen minutes.

Tanzy's version of Sixteen Minutes was a small clearing in a dense Oregon forest, the kind of place she would have gone with a high school boyfriend on Friday nights to push the boundaries of their sexual relationship. It was daytime, though there was no sun. Birds and animals called and sang high above.

"What in the fuck?" asked Danny, as he fell on his back into the soft dirt. His head came dangerously close to striking an exposed tree root—not that it would have hurt him in the slightest.

"Shut up, it was just a little jump."

He rolled to his feet, popped up, and got in her face.

"I was fucking working, Tanzy!"

Even his breath smelled like Johnny's. God, how long had it been since she'd been so close to him?

"It got your attention, didn't it? I mean, seriously, Danny, you're the only guy I know who would take a laptop to an orgy. If I didn't know—"

Her sternum shattered under the force of Johnny's fist, but before she could even register the impact, an army of tree branches reached from behind her and scraped every inch of her exposed flesh. The construct leapt forward, and when it stopped, she found herself impaled on a branch some six feet off the ground. In the distance, Danny stood with his arm still extended.

Resetting, said Cleo.

Tanzy felt no pain, only slight confusion. She placed her hand on the tree branch and dissolved it with a mental command. Once she was free, she floated slowly to the ground. Her steps back to Danny were thoughtful as she tried to puzzle out what had made him so angry, and more importantly, whether she could match his intensity.

"Was that really necessary?" she asked, stepping out of the tree line.

"Felt good to me," he replied.

"Yeah, well, I didn't bring you here so we could bash the shit out of each other. I need to talk to you about Vinestead and I couldn't do that in Bedlam. We have a good fifteen minutes here, so let me get this out."

"Fine, whatever. Tell me so I can say no." He drifted to a nearby tree, crossed his arms, and leaned against it.

"We're making a move against Vinestead. Tomorrow night, probably."

"We?"

"Me, Kaili, Cyn, and Tate. We all have scores to settle."

Danny hung his head. After a few slow breaths, he said, "This was supposed to be about settling Johnny's score. You're gonna make a move against Vinestead? And then what? They'll still be there. You're not taking them down, even with Kaili Zabora's help. I'm not saying we shouldn't fight but come on, we've gotta pick the right battles. Someone fucked Johnny over and had him killed—*that* is the battle you and I need to be fighting."

Tanzy nodded. "You think I don't care about Johnny?"

"I *know* you don't. If you did, you never would have left to chase after Kaili. I just…" He put his hands in the air, turned away. "I'm not gonna keep saying it to you, Megan. You have your priorities, I have mine. I don't see what else there is to talk about."

Maybe there wasn't.

She stared at the back of Johnny's head and wondered if she would ever see him in person again, whether at the morgue to help identify the body, or the funeral Danny would no doubt put together for him. She understood why Danny felt the way he did, but ultimately, Johnny was just another hacker in a world full of hackers. They went back years, yes, to the very beginning, but relationships were always in flux, reality was always in flux.

Alliances formed and broke down, and those closest to Tanzy were there because she paid them to be or, as was the case with Cleo, simply because they had no other choice.

Johnny, Danny, the Reinhardt Triumvirate… they were all from another life, one that had bubbled to the surface for the briefest of moments and then passed into memory. Johnny was dead, and Danny had no interest in joining Tanzy at I.C.E-1.

They were the past, and Kaili Zabora was the future.

Tanzy imagined a world where I.C.E-1 was responsible for saving the life of America's most infamous domestic terrorist and what it would mean for her cipher den. Everyone would want to work with her, the money would pour in, and her name would be whispered in the blackest corners of every darknet as someone with whom not to fuck.

"So?" asked Danny.

"What?"

He spread his arms, as if he'd been waiting an hour for a response.

"Are we done here?"

"Here," said Tanzy, looking into the hazy distance where the parallel lines of trees collapsed into each other. "Now. Forever." She took a breath. "You and I are done."

The air electrified. A soft pop echoed through the trees.

Tanzy turned to find the clearing empty.

He's emotional. He'll come around.

"Not this time, Cleo. I had really hoped it could be like it was before, but we're too different now. He gets stuck on the little stuff. I see the big picture."

You didn't ask what kind of work he was doing.

"It doesn't matter. Let him run his own vendetta."

Tanzy swiped at the trees; they dissolved into a brown mist that settled to the floor of a pristine white construct.

Small, cubic bubbles rose up like crystal formations, collecting in groups to represent buildings and elevated highways. The design wasn't altogether familiar to Tanzy with the exception of one of the larger cubic spikes that stood out from its neighbors. Whereas the others were white and hard to discern from each other, this building was red, and embossed in glossy black on its top was the letter *V*.

The Vinestead West building.

Sacramento, California.

The largest concentration of Vinestead power on the West Coast was in that building. It was the site where, fifteen years before, Calle Cinco and Kaili Zabora had kicked off a war, and though there had been small skirmishes in the years since, Tanzy was determined to deliver her own Gettysburg or Antietam—something she could attach her name to and guarantee her spot in the annals of history.

Message from the Quatrain. A suitable basecamp has been found north of the river.

A blue light flashed in a large complex labeled as Zend Garden Terminus just off Highway 160 outside of downtown Sacramento. Tanzy took a step forward and used her hands to expand the map. The zoom revealed a circular arrangement of helipads, and Cleo informed her they were used primarily for aerial rideshare programs, but that they would be able to launch a helicopter and drones from one of the private pads without much attention.

So that took care of transport.

Now all they needed was to wade through the air traffic and find a way to land on the Vinestead West building. Security would be insane, but the girls would find a way around it, even if it meant filling the air with fake planes, helicopters, and drones. It was just like walking up to a bank to rob it—the approach was easier in a crowd.

Should I instruct the Quatrain to make a reservation?

"Book it," said Tanzy, bringing her fist down on the virtual representation of the Vinestead West tower.

It crumbled into a fine powder under her strong hand.

FIFTY-ONE
GORDON

Gordon didn't wait around for Cyn to retrieve him from Dunlap's.

As soon as the mechanic-doctor was finished and the drugs wore off, he set out from Dunlap's into a strange city and simply wandered until he found Decker Plaza. There, Kevin Costner met him at the door and retrieved Gordon's go-bag from his room. He slipped the boy a couple of twenties for his trouble and asked to be pointed in the direction of a decent hotel.

Kevin recommended Hotel Forever, and after paying cash to a tattooed Māori behind the reception desk, Gordon had spent the rest of the day and most of the next holed up in the small suite alternating between sleeping, watching TV, and trying to make sense of the network on an in-room palette. He had to learn to type again, dragging his finger across a virtual keyboard, one letter to the next, until it formed a word. Sometimes it didn't work. Sometimes he pushed the palette away in disgust and stared at the ceiling for a while.

Everything had changed.

He'd been well aware that Vinestead had taken over the free Net back in 1999, but he hadn't realized the extent of their reach outside of virtual reality. Every search engine he tried was tied to Vinestead, and none of them would return more than a few results without him logging in with his VID, which he assumed meant Vinestead ID.

No VID? Click here to register!

There was a time when a man didn't have to register his personal details to access information, when he could dip his hand into the data stream and take what he wanted without anyone pestering him or showing him a slew of ads. It used to be Gordon looking at the network, and now, it was clear the network was looking back at him. VNet was interested in who he was, what they could sell him, and most importantly, how they could sell his meta.

Dunlap had mentioned the social networking site Pattrn, but there were far too many paywalls for Gordon to break through. According to the bits and pieces he could pull together, Pattrn was a billion-dollar social media empire, and its founder, a smug ginger goof named Patrick Renner, was worth even more. Even in the relative wild west of the old Net, they would have been hard to hack.

He wanted to see more photos of Natalie.

He searched for her, by her new and old names, but there was too much noise, too little free access. There were no pictures available in any databank, and no pictures of their son, Xavier. Gordon tried imagining what his son would look like, but other than generic photos of Gerber babies, nothing came to mind. Babies, of course, were the wrong image, as the boy would be almost twenty years old now, already a man.

A final dose of painkillers lulled Gordon into a nap in the mid-afternoon. By the time he woke again, the skinny windows on either side of the television had automatically frosted over; the blinking neons of Umbra appeared as technicolor blooms on the wavy glass. The TV, which had been streaming episodes of a mid-90s sitcom, was stuck on a screen asking him if he was still watching. In the background, faded in vignette, was the perplexed face of Kelsey Grammer with his hand raised to his chin.

Gordon was searching for the remote control in the sheets when a knock came at the door. He got up to answer it, fully aware that the only one who knew he was there was Kevin Costner. But then if Kevin knew, then Lincoln knew, and by extension…

He closed one eye to peer through the peephole.

Cyn.

Of course it was.

He stared at her for a moment in the fisheye distortion, at the young girl with flashy blue eyes buttoned up tight in a gray trench, high collar obscuring the tattoos that ran up her neck.

Gordon unlatched the door, removed the chain, and flipped the lock on the handle. He opened it slowly.

She smiled as if she weren't sure she'd come to the right room. Words rose in her throat, her mouth opened, but then closed abruptly. She peered past him into the room.

He took a step back, allowed her inside. Her red boots were slick with rain; they caught the guide-lights along the bottom of the wall.

When she reached the bed, Cyn turned and looked at him.

Gordon closed the door.

"I didn't do my hair," she said, "because I know you don't like that. And I know you don't like when my *cooter* bulges out of my pants, so…"

She dropped the trench around her boots. Her hair flapped in the sudden movement, settled around her bare shoulders.

He'd half-expected her to be naked under the thick leather. Instead, she wore a loose gray tank top over baggy black sweatpants that she'd tucked into her boots.

The clothes revealed nothing about the body underneath, but since her shoulders and arms were uncovered, Gordon could see the many bruises she'd suffered at Folsom Prison. Dirty splotches of purple and black dotted her arms, some of them splitting in sickly cracks in her skin.

There were other scars too, but they were faded, wiped away by lasers or augmentation. She'd paid someone a lot of money to reduce the prominence of her past injuries, but it was clear she'd been through some shit and that she carried it with her still.

"What is this?" he asked.

She didn't smile, didn't bat her eyes, or pretend to play coy.

"Exactly what it looks like."

"It looks like you're trying and failing to seduce me."

"So what if I am?" Cyn tugged on a loose thread at the hem of her shirt.

"You're half my age."

"Isn't this how older men like their women? Covered up? Domesticated? I can take off the boots if they're too modern."

"You don't—"

She bent slightly at the knees and reached down to undo the clasps on her boots. They tumbled to the side as she kicked each one off with a pink, furry-socked foot.

"This is insane."

"You think this is insane?" she asked, straightening up again. "You should see the size of my granny panties."

"How big are we talkin'?" asked Gordon, stifling a chuckle.

Her blue eyes sparkled like lightning.

"Come over here and see for yourself," she said.

Gordon closed the distance slowly, wanting to see how long she could keep her eyes flashing like that. Were they controlled by some program in her biochip? Like a switch on a laser matrix at a rave? Or did they actually respond to her emotions? Did the excitement in her eyes match the excitement in her body?

He reached out and grasped a drawstring on her sweatpants. His fingers shook, but they held as he tugged slightly.

"Are we done then?" he asked.

Cyn leaned forward, lifted her head, and kissed the underside of his chin.

"We're just getting started."

He felt her hands on his waist, felt fingers grip his hips.

"No," he whispered. "Not with this. With Kaili. And Lincoln. Are we done with them?"

"What do you mean?" She tried to pull him closer, but he resisted.

"Are you here because it's over? Or because there's more to do?"

Cyn put her head against his chest.

"Do you know… do you have any idea how insulting it is to be called a whore by the same guy twice? Does it even occur to you how fucked it is for you to ask me that while I'm throwing myself at you?"

"But if it's the truth…"

She let go of him and beat her fist softly against his chest.

"Fuck you, Gordon. Just, fuck you." She looked up; light glinted off the mist in her eyes. "I came here because I wanted to be with someone tonight and you're the someone I chose because we went through something together and I thought we had a connection and I just wanted to wrap myself up in that connection for a night and forget that we could have died or will die or won't die or…"

She trailed off, put her hands to her face.

Gordon wrapped his arms around her back, pulled her into him.

"It would have been nothing," she continued, "nothing for you to spend the night with me. No promises. No guilt. You could have chosen to see past the bullshit to the truth."

"What truth is that?"

"That I like you, you giant asshole. That I'm jealous there's a woman out there that you have a kid with. I'm jealous because I know you're gonna cut out and go find her. You could have given me one night. After all we've been through… one fucking night."

"And then what?" he asked, thinking of what requests she might make afterward when they were lying exhausted among the sheets.

"And then nothing. Then you go. Back to your Natalie."

"How do you know that name?"

"Dunlap," she replied, pushing out of his grip. She sat down on the edge of the bed, angled herself away from him.

"Motherfucker," said Gordon.

"Don't blame him. I usually get what I want when I ask for it. Usually."

He nodded, sat down next to her on the bed.

Gordon felt no remorse for questioning her motives. He'd spent enough time around her and Lincoln to understand how things worked in Umbra. There were always favors being traded, deals being struck, and as a newcomer to the scene, they incorrectly assumed Gordon didn't see the underlying system, that he didn't understand nothing was free and everything cost a piece of himself.

Cyn's interest in him—her care and not-so-subtle flirting—over the weeks were, in Gordon's mind, nothing more than her way of keeping him sedate in his posh cell while Lincoln jockeyed for the payday he'd been promised. Every move Cyn made was in the interest of manipulating him, to make him stay, to make him put his life on the line for Kaili Zabora.

Her feigned reproach didn't fool him.

A lot of things had changed while Gordon was away, but one fundamental truth hadn't: everyone lied.

So why shouldn't he?

"I uh," he started, pacing his words carefully. "I'm gonna admit something to you, and I swear to Christ if you laugh, I'm gonna punch you in one of those bruises on your arm."

She didn't look at him, but said quietly, "Tell me."

"I haven't... um, *been* with a woman since before Y2K. Natalie was my last before heading to Lost Pines and once I was there, I wasn't keen to make things complicated. I've kept to myself for twenty years. So maybe you can understand my confusion when a girl who should be out there painting the town with another twenty-something comes into my room in her sexiest sweats and throws herself at me. It makes no sense, unless you're here to kill me, like Luci, but I don't think you are."

"And yet, I'm here," said Cyn, shrugging emphatically.

"And yet you're here," he agreed.

"Tanzy and Kaili are gonna hit Vinestead soon, probably tomorrow. They would like your help, obviously, but we don't have to talk about that. Dunlap said you were thinking of jetting off to Germany. I could help you get a plane ticket without a VID."

She turned her head, gave a weak smile.

"Or we can, you know..."

Gordon chuckled. "I don't think the twenty seconds I would give you would be worth the trouble. I have to admit, I've never seen a woman wear scars with as much class as you do."

She ran her hands over her arms, as if ashamed.

"You're sweet," she said. "A huge, gaping asshole, but sweet."

"Men seem sweet when they're not trying to fuck you. Twenty years at Lost Pines taught me that. I don't understand it, but ladies like it when you aren't always trying to get in their pants. Just one of those things, I guess."

"I wouldn't know," said Cyn. "Every guy I've ever met has been trying to get in my pants. And the one guy I would willingly take them off for isn't interested."

Gordon looked down at his hands in his lap.

"How about you tell me what Tanzy and Kaili are up to? Then you can help me book a flight out of here."

"No," said Cyn, wiping her cheek. "You still owe me for calling me a whore."

"Cyn... I'm not gonna—"

"We'll see," she said. "It's gonna be a long night, and you're gonna be staring at me in these mom clothes for hours. Ten bucks says you make a move before midnight."

He shook his head.

"Deny it all you want, but you will. And you know what I'm gonna do when that happens, Gordon?"

"What?"

She placed a hand on his leg, let her fingers fall dangerously close to his crotch. In a smooth, sultry voice, she said, "I'm gonna leave."

FIFTY-TWO
DANNY

Fucking Tanzy.

Danny seethed as he settled into his previous spot on the couch in Bedlam. The large woman beside him winked, as if welcoming him back to the party. Both of her hands were buried between her thighs, pawing hungrily at a vagina that must have been down there somewhere. Strangely, the aroma emanating from her gyrations was actually pleasant, almost enticing. It took a conscious mental effort to get the Syzygy to block it out.

Bedlam vibrated with its own energy, not just from the music thumping from every direction or the writhing of millions of sex-crazed avatars, but also from the sheer size of the construct. The draw distance in Bedlam was one of the best in VNet, powered by distributed servers that rivaled some government setups. Strong, electric charges flowed through every pixel, through every virtual wall, and through every individual fiber of the sofa Danny sat on. It had to; Bedlam couldn't afford an error, even though they did happen.

A laptop appeared under Danny's outstretched hands. It only took a few minutes to recover the notes and code he'd been working on prior to Tanzy's intrusion. Autosave had kept most of it from disappearing into the ether, but there were a few lines he'd lost, lines that were luckily still fresh in his memory. He jotted them down with a mental command and then scrolled back to the top of his journal.

There, he had started and abandoned several lines of thinking—ideas about how to expose Bullets AKA Julius Parker—and all of his secrets. The meta Johnny had scraped wouldn't do the job on its own, and Danny couldn't think of a way to bring the secrets out of Brigham Plaza. He'd barely been able to view them; copying them out in the allotted time would require hundreds or thousands of visits to the construct, each time trying to get a little closer to the source code.

The answer was as simple as adjusting an old proverb: *if the secrets of Brigham Plaza wouldn't come to the world, the world would come to Brigham Plaza.*

As powerful as Bedlam's servers were, Danny and Tanzy had been able to exploit them and wall-hack their way into Brigham Plaza. Even with Vinestead backing him, there was no way Julius had access to that kind of processing power. If anything, Brigham Plaza was likely on some throwaway server somewhere in a Vinestead basement. Julius had probably never thought anyone else would visit it, so the underlying hardware only had to be powerful enough for a handful of people at most.

So what would happen if Danny dropped three million users into it? What would the Brigham server think of that? Would it glitch itself into oblivion?

Danny recalled the wall hack that had propelled him into Brigham. If he could recreate the same effect near the green cube, which supposedly contained an artificial intelligence named Lassiter, then maybe he would be able to slip through the viral defenses and truly see who or what was hiding on the other side.

That was the plan anyway.

The real question was how to get all those people to Brigham. Bedlam losing track of two avatars among millions was one thing, a statistical eventuality, but to lose two million, or more? The servers would never make a mistake that massive.

Danny shut the laptop and closed his eyes.

"You're a strange one," said the woman next to him. Her voice was smoky and evoked the image of a tongue flicking upwards at the end of her sentence.

"I'm not the one double-fisting my vag in public," muttered Danny.

"This is hardly public. Or did you forget where you are?"

Danny opened his eyes, rolled his head to the side.

"Did you need something?" he asked.

She smiled back genially, bit her lip, and said, "I was just wondering why a man wearing the skin of a dead hacker would come all the way to Bedlam and not join in."

"Maybe I'm just waiting for the right group of women to come along."

"No, honey, that's not it." She straightened her arms, pushing her enormous breasts together. "If you'd been in the mood for anything, we'd be going at it right now. Don't you smell me in the air? That's pure desire."

Danny sighed. "It's emotionware, and it doesn't work on me."

"Clearly, honey," she said, casually dropping a hand on his leg.

"And what about you? Why do you have to come all the way here just to masturbate? Can't you get porn on your palette at home?"

"Oh, God," she laughed, deep and throaty. "You know there's a mountain of difference between sitting here in Bedlam and diddling myself under the covers at home. Besides, here I'm not limited to fucking myself."

A shimmer rose beneath her skin, and with a few passes of a v-sync signal, her avatar snapped into that of a tall woman with Brazilian features who Danny was sure he'd seen in a Victoria's Secret ad somewhere.

"Most people," she continued, running her hand up her smooth stomach, "are hopelessly uncreative. Boring. They come to places like Bedlam and try to fuck something new, but they do it in their own body. I like to change things up. And yeah, sometimes when I just want to sit and touch myself and feel the energy around me, I put on a heavier avatar. Keeps people from bothering me."

Danny raised an eyebrow. "Is this the real you then?"

"Honey, I'm not even really female," she said, giving his thigh a squeeze. "But in here, that doesn't matter. I'd guess half the women in here are guys or somewhere in between."

"I guess I kinda knew that, but never really thought about it much."

"Why waste the energy? The end result is the same. Your brain thinks you're going to town on a barely legal Japanese maid—doesn't matter if it's really an overweight bartender from the south side of Chicago, does it?"

"Kinda, yeah."

"Don't be a 'phobe," she said, leaning into him. "I love this place. The variety. Sometimes I'll try one of the other adult clubs—Tommy Gangbangers or Meat— but I always end up back here. There's something about Bedlam that draws me to it every time I jack in. Like a magnet."

Danny sat up, put the world on mute. In the deafening silence, he played back the woman's words: *draws me to it*. The same thing was happening with Danny and Brigham Plaza. Every time he logged in, at least with his own account, he was sucked into Julius Parker's private construct and held there. Brigham Plaza was connected to Danny, and it was always searching for him in VNet. Once it found him, it reeled him in, no matter what.

So what would happen, he wondered, if he were to switch between Johnny's account and his own without jacking out? Would the Brigham code pluck him from his cozy seat in Bedlam?

There was only one way to find out.

"Excuse me for a minute," he said, then paused, expectantly.

"Raquel. And you're Danny. I heard your girlfriend yelling at you."

He didn't care to correct her, and instead, flipped the mental switch from Johnny's account to his own. The response from VNet was immediate, to the point that Danny felt the gravitational shift in the pit of his stomach and almost hurled his virtual lunch into the shimmering void that transported him to the stock room at Blockbuster.

Without even waiting for the fumes of cleaning agents to reach his nose, Danny jacked out, then immediately back in as Johnny.

"That wasn't a minute," said Raquel. "I counted."

"It worked," he muttered. "I can't believe it worked."

"What worked? It looked like you jumped into someone else's avatar."

"Exactly," said Danny, pulling a new laptop out of the air. He plopped down on the couch and lifted the cover. The Agilyx IDE loaded automatically, and Danny began searching various repositories for code that would fit his needs. He even raided his personal stash from his servers back in Vail for the right kind of virus to deliver the payload.

He worked through the night, his fingers clacking furiously on the keys, his head bobbing with the beat of the echoey techno-slop in the air.

Raquel drifted away after a while; a pair of giggling girls took her place. They spoke of summer plans as they writhed in each other's embrace, where they'd like to go, what they'd like to do when they got there.

Danny shut them out.

By 5:00 a.m., the virus was finally beginning to take shape. Danny ran simulation after simulation to make sure it would work the way he expected. Based on the scope of the disruption it would cause, he was certain he'd only get one shot at activating it. After that first try, Bedlam would likely ban both him and Johnny from ever coming back—a decision made by pseudo-AI in the space of a single clock cycle.

At 6:00 a.m., he took a short walk around Bedlam, staring openly at the women around him, confusing his excitement about the virus with his growing desire to join in the revelry. He left the virus looping in the simulation, and by the time he returned, it had run itself more than half a million times, all with perfect success.

The East Coast was waking up, and as a result, the population of Bedlam had sunk to below three million users. That wasn't much of a problem for Danny; Brigham Plaza could probably fit no more than a few hundred thousand, and even then, some people would have to sit in laps. He'd set the virus limit at five hundred thousand—more than enough to put the hurt on Brigham Plaza and overload the servers.

Danny collapsed the laptop into a single pixel and rubbed it into his shirt. The virus squirmed in its cage somewhere on the outskirts of his Syzygy biochip. It wanted out, wanted to infect. Danny had ramped that directive himself.

He took a deep breath, then stood up.

With his hands on his hips, he surveyed the sprawling couches and divans and harnesses and wondered how they would look without all the perfect naked bodies.

Danny extended a hand, palm up, and waited as a viral flower sprouted from his fingertips—roots pushed through his nails and sought out each other in space, joining together to form a stem, then fronds, and finally, a tight rose with neon petals of red and purple. The image held for a moment before the petals began to peel off, only to be replaced by another, which repeated the process. The petals rose into the air and spread out.

The Bedlam servers noticed immediately.

Searchlights from hidden sources focused a dozen beams on the flower. A translucent bubble tried to form around it, but the code was already airborne. It hit a woman on his right first. She cried out when she discovered she couldn't remove her hand from the chest of the man she straddled.

Flesh bonded to flesh in an instant, and where there was no skin-to-skin contact, the virus gyrated the host body, flailing it about like a rag doll until it touched something of similar makeup. In this way, the virus spread throughout Bedlam, connecting avatars in a meandering web that grew faster than the construct's security could handle.

There was no display for Danny to watch, but he could feel the number of people attached to the viral vine, could feel them quivering in fear at the prospect of being permanently bonded to a random stranger.

Some of the trapped avatars weren't keen on the sudden incarceration. Antiviral code of all different makes and models flooded into the vine, and for the most part, Danny absorbed it. The virus, however, slowed at three hundred thousand, and again at four hundred.

Danny waited as long as he could, pushed the virus to the very limits of his strength, and just as it was about to break and set everyone free, he reached down and grabbed the shoulder of the screaming woman.

He flipped a mental switch.

Johnny San Vito became Danny Guns Montreal, and he along with almost half a million panicked and naked sexual deviants were sucked through the coruscating ether to Brigham Plaza.

FIFTY-THREE
KAILI

Kaili sat on the floor of her room, back against the door, and tried to listen to the muted conversations coming from down the hall in Lincoln Tate's personal lounge. She didn't care to be part of the discussion, partly because she didn't give a damn about Tanzy's meaningless attack on Vinestead but mostly because her mind was focused on the little girl she'd seen in the framed photo on Arthur Sedivy's desk.

Everything about the situation told her it was some kind of trick, a routine in a simulation that just kept going, the way it had when she'd first come out of Le Soleil Rouge. It was for that reason alone she wouldn't allow herself to break completely—she didn't want to give Sedivy the satisfaction of seeing her crumble. No doubt he was watching her from the outside and could see every emotion on her face.

Though, she didn't think he could see what was in her head.

That was for her and Anela alone.

Her sister, in her usual way, harped on a message of moving forward, of simply taking charge of the situation.

"We cannot sustain this," she'd said, as she lay stretched out at the foot of the bed. "We cannot allow others to lead us."

Kaili had listened, had sat against the door with her eyes closed and listened to her sister while a little girl in a striped blue and white romper pranced about in a field of daisies, flowers brushing against the pale skin of her thin legs.

The noise didn't settle down until well after 5:00 a.m., and even then, Kaili waited another hour before venturing out into the hallway. She walked toward the lounge in the hopes someone had been tired or distracted enough to leave behind a palette or cell phone. Anything would do, so long as it had a connection to the network.

She passed quiet rooms on her left and right and thought about her captors who slept within.

Tanzy was behind one of the doors. I.C.E-1 and their fame-whoring suit had been on Kaili's radar since before Perion City. Tanzy had a reputation for sensational headlines, though she only ever showed up on Lincoln Continental with any regularity. There was a relationship between Tanzy and Lincoln Tate that Kaili didn't quite understand, but it had led to a market awareness of I.C.E-1 that other, smaller cipher dens could only dream of.

Cynthia Mesquina, on the other hand, was a woman of action, though her actions were often dictated by whoever was bankrolling the operation. Her infiltration of Perion City and subsequent attack on the company had come at the behest of Lincoln Tate in an effort to secure the inside track on James Perion's impending death. Cyn had, instead, caused enough trouble to get Perion's head of security, Robert Gantz, killed and at the same time, cost Kaili Zabora her position in the company.

Then there was Danny Guns Montreal, a celebrity hacker who kept to his own little circle and preferred to stay on the fringes of the tech scene. Kaili knew him by reputation only, by stories of his ability to get in and out of networks with preternatural ease. He was a whore like Cyn, ready to do anything for a big enough paycheck, though unlike his aggregator counterpart, Danny kept to the virtual space where he had the power he lacked in the real world.

That left G, or as Cyn called him, Gordon. She insisted he hadn't been back to Decker Plaza since Folsom, but Anela kept suggesting he was holed up in one of the rooms, waiting for the storm to pass and for normality to return.

As if there were such a thing as normal anymore.

Kaili fought the urge to break down door after door until she found G, and then with her one remaining hand…

She paused for a moment, looked at the stump where her left arm used to be.

"It would be better to wait," said Anela. "Until you are whole again."

"Why?" whispered Kaili. "I don't need two hands to hold a gun."

The argument ended when she noticed that the window at the far end of the hallway was gone. Her heart leapt, convinced she had just discovered another glitch in the simulation, but as she got closer, she found the window had been covered with a thick plate of machined metal. Above, a square indentation in the ceiling showed where the plate had previously lived, though Kaili couldn't remember noticing it in its stowed position.

"It's a shame," said Lincoln. He stood in the doorway to the lounge, hands in his pockets, leaning against the jamb.

His sudden appearance made Kaili shake. She slunk away to the opposite side of the hall.

"Didn't mean to scare you," he said. "I was just saying, it's a shame about the shields. The sunrise from this floor and this window is the best in Umbra. Lights up the whole hallway. Even better in the lounge when it hits the bar just right."

Lincoln's dark suit blended into the shadows behind him. Kaili's only reference for the owner and operator of Lincoln Continental were the promotional images plastered on billboards both real and virtual. He'd always looked so refined in those carefully retouched photos, his suit cut close to his thick body, often a shade of purple, ensconced in jewelry on his hands, neck, and ears, eyes a beautiful light gray that played against his dark skin, and short, shaved hair flecked with gray.

But now, in the dawn at Decker Plaza, he looked like a man who had spent too many wild nights in Vegas.

His black shirt was open to the third button, and the collar had been unbuttoned as well, as were the cuffs sticking out of the jacket sleeves. His face, dark and shiny, looked weary, as if he longed for bed or whatever a man of his means considered relaxation. His eyes, so often presented straight-on in his advertising, focused on the floor.

"You just surprised me," said Kaili, feigning embarrassment. "I thought everyone had gone to bed."

"Tanzy did. She would have kept working, but something came up." He nodded to the window. "Someone's taken an interest in what we're doing here. Spotted two snipers in adjacent buildings, one north, and one west, looking right down the hallways. We're not sure who their target is, but if I had to guess between me and you, I'd say I'm free to come and go as I please."

"How would anyone know I'm here?" she asked.

"Not sure. You hungry? I was gonna have some breakfast sent up." He lifted his arm and placed a finger on his sliver.

Kaili's stomach rumbled; she hadn't eaten since coming off the roof the evening before.

"Bacon," she said. "And some toast."

"Right on." Lincoln turned and headed back into the lounge, beckoning her with his hand.

The lights came up at the sound of his voice, illuminating the carnage from the overnight planning session. The large, square coffee table set within the couches was covered in takeout Chinese cartons and hardcopy maps of Sacramento. Kaili spied a blueprint or two with their signature white on blue color schemes. There was even a gun—a compact 9mm—half-covered by a pile of folded napkins.

Anela suggested taking a seat on the couch near the gun—not on top of it, but close enough to reach it with a quick lunge. There was no way of knowing if the gun had any bullets, but Kaili sat near it anyway and pretended not to know or care that it was there.

Lincoln went behind the bar and came out with two bottles of water. He gave one to Kaili before slumping into the couch opposite her. His gut became more prominent as he put one foot up on the coffee table.

At the bar, Anela slid onto one of the stools and eyed Lincoln warily.

"You don't seem very concerned that people are pointing guns at your building," said Kaili. She raised an eyebrow at the shields covering the windows. "Except for that, of course."

"It's not ideal, I'll give you that." He took a swig of his water, rested the bottle on his stomach. "But it's reassuring in this case. If whoever wants you dead thought they could just waltz into my building, they would have tried. Hiring snipers pretty much tells you all you need to know about this fortress of mine." He smiled wearily.

"That secure, huh?"

"One way in, couple ways out. Automated guns ready to drop from the ceiling in the lobby. That's why there's only one guy working down there right now. If shit pops off, he'll just roll under some steel and let the guns do the work."

"Interesting," said Anela.

Kaili tried to change the subject. She pointed to the mess on the table.

"What were they planning?"

"More like arguing," said Lincoln. "Tanzy wanted to drop the entire Vinestead West building in Sacramento, raze it right to the ground. Cyn didn't want a repeat of the Reaping, so they had to compromise."

"On what?"

Lincoln smiled. "Well, instead of mass murder, Tanzy agreed to simply hijack VFeed, but only if Cyn could get Gordon to help out."

"G," said Anela, her jaw clenched.

Kaili tried to ignore the bait. "VFeed? Really?"

"Ah, you remember them as some piddly-ass media feed no one gave two shits about, but ever since Perion City, they've been top three." He laughed. "Goddamn Cameron Gray."

The name evoked a pang of anger. It felt like just yesterday she'd been cursing Cam and his meddling in Perion City.

"What'd he do?" she asked, despite feeling confident she already knew the answer.

"He went to VFeed with the Perion story and somehow parlayed that into running the entire media feed subsidiary at Vinestead. Now he's basically me with none of the style."

"What does Tanzy have against him?"

"It's not about him."

Kaili lifted her hand, beckoned for an explanation.

"It's about you, Butcher," he said, leveling a ringed finger at her. "Tanzy wants Vinestead and the world to know you're back, that Calle Cinco and I.C.E-1 are working together, and that Vinestead isn't as invulnerable as they think they are." He rolled his eyes. "And by the look on your face, I'm sure she didn't discuss any of that shit with you."

Kaili shook her head slowly.

"Yeah," said Lincoln, groaning as he sat up. "She wrote up a whole itinerary and everything." He felt around the couch until he found a palette hidden under a blanket. "Here, check it out."

Kaili took the palette and braced it on her legs. She scrolled through the timeline with her index finger, but her eyes kept jumping to the palette itself, to the interface around the document. There was a clock, a gear, and a small three-bar icon that likely held some programs. If the palette had a command line window or even a basic web browser, she could get a note to a Calle Cinco dead drop.

"What do you think?" asked Lincoln.

"Um," she replied, scrolling back to the top of the document. "Zend Garden Terminus, 5:00 p.m." She looked up from the palette. "She wants to go while it's still light?"

"Doubt it, but who knows with that girl?" His wrist let out a tone, and he glanced over his shoulder at the door leading into the hallway.

"What is it?" asked Kaili.

"Bacon and toast," he replied. "I'll set us up at the bar."

Lincoln used the arm of the couch to pull himself up. Once his back was turned, Kaili dove into the palette's menu and scrolled frantically through the options.

Calculator.

Contacts.

Pattrn.

WebGet.

She tapped into the web browser and typed in an IP address from memory.

"Smells good," said Lincoln, to the young man who'd pushed a rolling cart into the room.

Kaili glanced at the two silver domes that reminded her of fancy dinner parties she'd seen in the movies. Only in this version, the waiter wasn't dressed in a suit and apron—he wore jeans and an AK-47.

The page loaded with a single text box. Kaili pulled up the soft keyboard and typed in a password only she and three other people in Calle Cinco knew. When the page refreshed, the text box had turned green. It waited for her message.

"Are you coming?" asked Lincoln, from the bar.

She caught eyes with him, and though she couldn't tell if he suspected anything, her finger moved with subtle dexterity, typing out a message before hitting the bright blue *Submit* button. As she stood, she used her thumb to exit out of the browser and back to the itinerary.

"Well done," said Anela.

"I know," replied Kaili.

Lincoln looked up from his plate as Kaili joined him at the bar.

"I know I'm going to eat the shit out of this food," she said, easing her way onto a stool.

Lincoln smiled and shook his head.

"Butcher of Burbank, eating breakfast in my lounge. I guess anything is possible in this crazy world of ours."

Kaili shrugged, spoke with a piece of toast in her mouth.

"Assuming any of this is even real."

Lincoln smiled, broke a piece of bacon in half.

"Right on," he said.

FIFTY-FOUR
TANZY

Tanzy had no intention of sleeping.

She was too amped about the prospect of sticking it to Vinestead. Even compromising with Cyn hadn't put a dent in her enthusiasm—jacking VFeed was better than nothing, and to Cyn's point, it carried with it less chance they would all be killed. Tanzy knew better than anyone that Vinestead couldn't be destroyed by a couple of cipher den suits, a freelance aggregator, and a past-his-prime hacker from Texas. It would take more—not just an army of one, but an army of everyone.

Nothing would incite people to take up arms against Vinestead more than a little show of vulnerability. Vinestead had the disadvantage of operating in the real world; they had desks and computers and people behind both. All Tanzy had to do was cut a weak link in the chain to show the world it could be done. Somebody had to take that first step.

Her thoughts of pioneering the destruction of Vinestead turned into a full-blown fantasy as soon as her head hit the pillow. She stripped off her clothes under the covers to better feel the soft sheets against her skin. Cool air bubbled up from inside the mattress, coaxing her into a fetal position that dropped her out of conscious thought.

She slept hard, dreamed of incursions into the Vinestead West building, all of which went exceedingly well. In the dream, she had the power of a heroine in a movie and all of the plot armor inherent in the title. She tore through guards and synthetics and goggle-eyed scientists and ditzy interns with trays of coffee. And though her path of carnage through the building varied, she always ended up in the same place—a cavernous room with giant vidscreens on the walls, as if Vinestead were more in the business of sending people to the moon rather than poisoning their minds with propaganda.

Every vidscreen in the room was dark except for the one in the center. Its bright-white background bloomed, and from the corners, thin black ribbons like smoke rising in an intermittent breeze, flowed toward the middle of the screen. There, they coalesced into a shape Tanzy didn't recognize, and the more she tried to focus on it, the less tangible it became, until finally the dream broke down and looped again.

And yet, unlike a nightmare, each successful run-and-gun through the halls of Vinestead West made her feel better, boosted her confidence such that when she finally woke up in the mid-afternoon, it was with a refreshed eagerness that made her feel giddy inside. She showered, changed into her fanciest flannel, and left her room ready to rally the troops for war.

Only, the hallway was dark, quiet. The low light was a result of what Bryce had referred to as *blast shields* that covered the windows.

Lincoln had locked the building down earlier that morning, so why were they not up yet? She walked the hallway, listening for any conversation, but there was none. The lounge was empty too, still a mess from the long night before. There was no one in the conference room either, which with the blast shields, had become a dark cave that could have as easily held a sleeping dragon instead of a long table.

Tanzy stood at the bar for a moment, drawn by the lingering aroma of bacon.

"Everyone's asleep," she muttered.

You had a long night, said Cleo.

"But how can they sleep? It's like Christmas."

It's nice to see you happy.

"Can you send a message to Lincoln? Tell him to stop being lazy and get his ass up."

Message relayed.

Tanzy reached for a piece of bacon, stopped herself. Who knew how long it had been sitting out? For a brief moment, she longed for the comforts of home, her own kitchen at the I.C.E-1 compound on Hayden Island. But then she remembered the monotony of it, the day-to-day operation of a cipher den that had started to plateau. Being a hacker and running a business were two completely different lines of work; fading into managerial irrelevance just didn't sit right with her.

She didn't want the most exciting thing in her life to be chasing nude photos of Eileen Coker getting rammed by some bellboy.

There had to be something more, something real.

Something global.

"Have the girls finished the video yet?"

Cleo took a moment to answer.

No, but they will meet the deadline.

"Good, tell them—"

Message from Lincoln Tate. Shit going down. Take elevator to B2.

Tanzy tried to steady her breathing as she rushed out of the room and down the hall. Although Cleo had read the message in a dull monotone, Tanzy had had

no trouble hearing it in Lincoln's voice and imbuing it with the requisite panic
and fear. Her first thoughts were of the mission and whether it was in jeopardy.
She saw her dreams of the future shatter into a million pieces, and the prospect of
not getting to take a swipe at Vinestead hit her like a punch to the gut.

She pressed the *B2* button in the elevator and hammered the *Door Close*
button until finally she began to descend.

"Of course," she said. "Of course this would happen."

I'm sure it'll be fine.

"Yeah? And what are you basing that on?"

Gukou yama-o utsusu.

Tanzy scoffed. "Don't pretend you know Japanese."

Have faith, said Cleo. *It's where power comes from.*

Kevin Costner was standing in front of the elevator doors when they opened
on B2. The usually manic child soldier seemed subdued, perhaps chemically. He
beckoned with a quick jerk of his head and led Tanzy down the hall.

Tanzy had taken little notice of the Decker Plaza sublevels during her escape
from the Hotel Fritz, but now she was able to see just how different they were
from the well-appointed floors above the surface, as if the they were afterthoughts,
or more likely, undisclosed additions to the building.

External lights—fluorescents, not LEDS—lined the ceiling in the center of
the hall. Gray evercrete walls surrounded her, like the rough inner linings of a
tomb. The floor was stained black, and there was a glossy quality to it that showed
a vague reflection of another Tanzy matching her gait from below.

"How bad is it?" asked Tanzy.

Kevin shrugged. "We pissed someone off, Gorbachev."

"More snipers?"

He grunted, turned abruptly into an open door.

Tanzy followed him into a small room similar to the one in her dream but
orders of magnitude smaller. Instead of the walls of vidscreens, there was only one,
a bright rectangular display slightly smaller than the TV in her room. A gangly
Indian Tanzy didn't recognize sat at the desk in front of it, and behind him stood
Lincoln and Kaili.

Lincoln glanced over his shoulder and nodded.

"What's going on?" asked Tanzy.

"A siege," growled Lincoln. Then to the Indian, "Naj, Sweep Version Seven
again. There's way too much activity over there for this time of day."

Tanzy caught eyes with Kaili.

"Did you brag to anyone about me?" asked the Butcher.

"What? No."

"Then how does Vinestead know I'm here?" Kaili didn't blink; she seemed
certain of her question's premise.

"Vi—how do you know it's Vinestead?"

Lincoln raised an eyebrow at Tanzy.

"And how do you know they're after *you*?" she asked. "They've already tried to kill me and Lincoln. Maybe they've come to finish the job. Or hell, what about Cyn? She's the one who got you out of Folsom." Then to Lincoln. "Where is she anyway?"

"With Gordon." He returned his attention to the screen, pointing out an infrared blob. "That group there. Can you do a chip scan?"

Tanzy waited for Lincoln to continue, but he didn't.

"And *where* is Gordon?" she asked. "Why are they not *here* where they need to be?" Tanzy checked her sliver. "We're supposed to be in Sacramento in two hours. Or has everyone forgotten what we're doing here?"

"We haven't forgotten," said Lincoln. "But exactly how do you think we're getting out of here when we're surrounded by a hundred hired guns?"

Tanzy crossed her arms. "First, when did Lincoln Tate become such a bitch? And second, how do you think I got here in the first place?"

Lincoln turned to face her, drew himself up. Though he liked to present himself as larger than life, he was no more than a few inches taller than Tanzy.

"Did you just call me a bitch?" he asked.

Tanzy stepped into his space. "I did."

He smiled, sucked on his teeth. "You crazy, Tanzy." He turned his attention to the vidscreen. "But Lincoln Tate ain't no bitch. These punks are trying to come into my house. I'm not running out the back door."

"Sedivy's not gonna stop with a hundred men," said Kaili. "He'll keep sending more and more until I'm dead and the simulation resets. I can't stay here."

Lincoln nodded. "I was thinking the same thing. You and Tanzy should head out. Take Bryce and Kevin with you. I'll get there when I can."

Thunder exploded far above their heads; Tanzy shrank away from the noise as if the ceiling might collapse. The building shook in the echoes, trembling from top to bottom with an intensity that built and built until suddenly it stopped.

The lights went out; the vidscreen went dark.

Tanzy felt a rough hand seek out her arm.

"Give it a second," said Lincoln.

Sure enough, an electronic whine ramped up below their feet, and with an audible *snap*, the lights in the room and hallway came back on. The computer booted.

"My house," seethed Lincoln, releasing his grip on both Tanzy and Kaili. "You should get going."

"How?" asked Kaili.

"Umbra Underground," said Tanzy. "Connects all the blocks in the city. Didn't you know about that?"

Kaili shook her head.

"Well, look who's out of the loop."

Something like pain flashed in Kaili's eyes. Her mouth fell open, and she stuttered, "I… I don't want to go back. I can't reset. I can't."

It's not pain, said Cleo. *She's afraid.* Then after a beat, *be kind to her.*

Again, Tanzy stepped forward but couldn't bring herself to invade Kaili's personal space.

"I promise you," she said, placing her hand over her heart, "right here and now, that once this part is over, I'm gonna put everything I have into finding the man who snatched you. Me, I.C.E-1, the girls—even all the money Johnny left me—all of it goes toward finding that piece of shit. First them, then Arthur Sedivy, and his wife, and his kid—"

"No!" said Kaili, putting her hand on Tanzy's chest. It took her a moment to realize what she'd done. She withdrew, looked away to hide eyes that were suddenly misting over.

Bryce appeared at the door then. He stuck his head into the room as if there weren't enough space for him to stand.

"Building's off the city grid. And that's not the worst of it. Naj, are any of the Canopy feeds working?"

"You're shitting me," said Lincoln.

Bryce shook his head. "I think they're gonna come down on our heads."

"Fuck me." Lincoln put his hand to his forehead. He turned and looked at Kaili. "Only the best for our esteemed guest."

Kaili didn't respond. She was lost in her own grief.

"Don't blame her," said Tanzy. "We knew what we were getting into when we broke her out. If anything, this puts us in a better position. Vinestead is scared."

"Scared like a wild animal backed into a corner?" asked Lincoln.

"If that helps you."

"What do you want me to do, boss?" asked Bryce.

Lincoln stared at Tanzy for a moment, then said, "We stick with the plan. You guys go ahead. I'll collect Guns and meet you there."

At first, Tanzy thought he'd meant guns, as in weapons, but then suddenly she remembered Danny. The last time she'd checked, he was still in his room, probably still jacked into Bedlam.

"You'll get him out?" she asked.

Lincoln nodded. "I can't interview him if he's dead."

"Come on, girl," said Bryce. "Let's go kick Vinestead in the dick."

"You ready?" asked Tanzy.

Kaili looked up, her eyes still red. "Yeah," she said, though there was no power in her voice.

If anything, it reminded Tanzy of the way Cleo had sounded in Sagamihara, of a sadness that ran so deep it could never be cut out completely, only absorbed into her outward persona. Cleo had made her motivation for despairing painfully clear, but Kaili was more of an enigma.

Attacking Vinestead should have been at the top of her wish list, and yet, she seemed hesitant, seemed to lack the necessary enthusiasm to even get moving in that direction.

Had the Butcher of Burbank lost her nerve?

What had Arthur Sedivy done to her?

FIFTY-FIVE
GORDON

The Eighty Express floated soundlessly on a cushion of magnetic resistance, leaving only the air rushing past the window to fill the silence in the private cabin.

Gordon sat with his head against the glass and watched the landscape speed past him at 250 miles per hour. Across the aisle, Cyn lay stretched out on the bench seat with her hands folded on her stomach. Her eyes were closed, but Gordon was sure she wasn't asleep.

She had kept her promises from the night before.

Getting a flight to Frankfurt from anywhere in the United States was impossible without a VID, so she'd booked him on an international airline that flew direct from Tijuana to Frankfurt. She'd even offered to drive with him down to San Diego or keep him company on the train ride. Gordon hadn't answered, and he hoped she wouldn't bring it up again.

The sooner he split with her, the better.

She'd left him at Hotel Forever early in the morning, but returned midday dressed in the clothes she now wore—a tight leather jacket, some kind of stretchy black pants, and gunmetal boots that came up to her calf. The shirt she wore under her jacket was patterned with red fire that cut a diagonal line across her chest.

Gordon tried not to let his eyes linger on her, not out of any sense of propriety but because every time he looked at her, he recalled the embarrassment of telling her about his voluntary celibacy since Natalie. None of it had been true, of course, but the ease at which she'd accepted it had hurt Gordon's pride, which had come as a surprise.

In some ways, the lack of intimacy made sense. After that night in Old Downtown, Gordon could see himself never wanting to get attached again, never wanting someone as much as he wanted Natalie.

The Lost Pines Survivalists had been more than happy to provide the worldly disconnection Gordon sought. The LPS compound was off the grid, and the people who lived there respected privacy above all else. Gordon had imagined spending the rest of his life there, growing old in the company of isolationists, getting to know their names but little else.

In retrospect, he should have seen the end coming. Clay Bartlett had been watching drones for years, those little specks in the sky Gordon had considered harmless. Now, he thought back to the times he'd stood next to Clay looking straight up at the drones, giving the cameras a clear view of his features.

The real question was why it had taken Vinestead and Cyn so long to find him.

Natalie had taken a different road out of Austin. From her Pattrn account, Gordon gleaned the details of a life away from the world X had sucked her into. She'd transferred to Columbia in the middle of her sophomore year, and that was when the first photos of Alexander started showing up in her profile. They'd married a few years after graduating and moved out of the country a year after that.

In June of 2014, she'd given up her American citizenship and became a full-fledged Kraut. Gordon assumed the same nationality swap for their son, Xavier.

He couldn't stop picturing Xavier as a toddler, precocious at the age of three, running around the wooded area behind Gordon's cabin at LPS. The reality, of course, was that the boy was twenty, and much to Gordon's relief, had no social media presence whatsoever.

Had Natalie told him anything about his real father?

Anything about X or G or the death of one Anela Zabora?

Cyn sighed, and when Gordon looked away from the window, she saw she had her head turned toward him.

"What're you thinking about?" she asked.

"Nothing," he replied, automatically.

"Mm-hmm." She put her arms over her head, stretched them as far as the wall would allow. "You're thinking about what you're gonna say to her, aren't you?"

Gordon saw Natalie's face, not as it appeared on her Pattrn profile, but as she was that night at the Austonian, her young features warped with worry about her precious X. She'd cared little for Gordon, he realized. The only thing she wanted from him was help rescuing X from the clutches of the ZabSix cipher den. After they'd done just that, her interest, feigned as it was, had simply disappeared.

"I haven't seen her in twenty years," he said. "I'm sure the words will come to me in the moment. Best not to over-prepare."

"Not her," said Cyn, sitting up. She swung her feet over to the floor. "I meant Kaili. What do you say to a woman whose sister you killed?"

"You think I should apologize?"

"Are you actually sorry?"

Gordon shook his head. "You would've done the same if it had been your friend. It's not like Anela Zabora was some kind of kindergarten teacher who was in the wrong place at the wrong time. She knew what kind of business she was in." He slapped his knee with his palm. "Not that it'll make one lick of difference to Kaili, but uh, that's vengeance for you. It's a never-ending chain constructed with dead bodies and greased with blood."

"Graphic," said Cyn. "But yeah, I wouldn't put it past Kaili to start some shit. She's not the kind of woman who forgives, but she also knows her priorities. If there's a bigger fish to gut, I think she'll leave you alone."

"Vinestead's a pretty big fish."

"I hope so. I'd hate to have to take her down."

Gordon smirked. "I think I can handle myself." He picked up an empty Pepsi can from the abbreviated table under the window and crushed it in one smooth movement.

"Oh, it's like that, huh?" Cyn sat up and reached for the can. She held it horizontally with both hands and pulled. "The thing about augments," she said, stretching the can back to its original shape, "is that they're only as strong as the weakest link in your body. If you want true power…"

A tinny pop of aluminum sounded in the cabin.

Cyn held up the two sheared halves of the can in demonstration.

"Your hands are stronger than they were before, but they're still connected to your weak, fleshy wrists. Don't forget that when shit goes down."

She tossed the pieces onto the table.

Gordon tried to imagine the strength necessary to pull a can apart like that, not just from a tensile perspective, but also in Cyn's grip, how the tips of her fingers were able to maintain enough pressure to complete the movement.

"Maybe I'll just keep my mouth shut," he said.

Cyn shrugged. "Chicks dig the strong silent type."

Gordon grunted.

"You got it," she said.

A chime sounded in the cabin as the train made a wide turn toward downtown Sacramento. Gordon felt the deceleration as a force pulling him off the seat. The remnants of the Pepsi can skidded along the plastic table and fell to the floor.

"How far to the meet-up from the station?"

Cyn adjusted her jacket. "Few miles. Sacramento Terminus is on the north side of downtown, and Zend Garden is just across the river to the north. We should be able to hire a car for the trip. Don't worry about it."

He didn't.

Instead of thinking about the logistics, Gordon simply fell into step next to Cyn as she led him off the train, out of Sacramento Terminus, and into a cold downtown slowly warming in the California sun. There were lines of cars stacked bumper-to-bumper on all streets leading away from the station. Cyn used her sliver to hire a small Nissan SUV that flashed its headlights at them.

She made polite small talk with the driver while Gordon stared out the window at a city that looked downright boring compared to the neons of Umbra. There were tall skyscrapers and throngs of pedestrians, but it was all so normal, so banal to the point of being repulsive. It was exactly the kind of world he'd run away from, and now seeing it laid bare in front of him, his resolve to stay away was made even stronger. If he did come back to the States after Frankfurt, he knew he couldn't make a life for himself in the evercrete jungle of a major city.

He would either disappear to another survivalist camp—he'd heard of a few camps run by excommunicated Mormons in Utah—or simply fade into the crowd in a city like Umbra. His time in the West Coast's digital hub hadn't been altogether unpleasant. There were wonders he'd only glimpsed, wonders he could imagine himself enjoying if only people would leave him alone.

The SUV zipped over a bridge; the sun sparkled on the water.

"Tanzy says they're en route. Fifteen minutes."

"What about us?"

"We're here," said the driver, completing a left turn across a seemingly endless parade of traffic.

They pulled into a large, fenced-in area with five elevated helipads arranged at the points of a pentagon. Two of the pads were occupied; one held a bright orange helicopter that resembled a dragonfly, while the other craft was dark gray and had more of a commuter vibe to it, with the length to fit a dozen people or so.

"Pad three," said Cyn, to the driver.

The lot was practically deserted, with only a single Hispanic man in blue coveralls milling around a small shack. The Nissan pulled up in front of a small sign with the number 3 on it.

Gordon stepped out of the SUV with the distinct feeling he was being watched. The sky above was clear, but if there were drones circling above, he wouldn't be able to pick them out without binoculars. There were plenty of security cameras set around the helipad and on low towers through the compound, but they didn't feel to Gordon like the culprits.

"Something's not right," he said, as Cyn joined him at the back of the SUV.

"What do you mean?" She looked around slowly.

"Someone's got eyes on, and not just the cameras."

"I don't see anything. You sure?"

"No, just a feeling."

Cyn put a hand on his arm. "It's okay to be nervous. Whatever happens, I'm between you and Kaili, alright? I promise."

"It's not her I'm worried about."

Gordon watched the SUV roll out of the lot, and though there was noise from the nearby road, it felt eerily silent. Feeling too exposed, he drifted closer to the helipad and took shelter beneath its canopy. The metal substructure created a kind of shield that might make him harder to hit if someone opened fire.

Cyn stood with her hands on her hips for a moment, apparently puzzled by his behavior. Then, with a condescending shake of her head, she walked casually to the staircase leading up to the helipad. Her footsteps clattered above him.

He thought of her standing on the platform, exposed for all the world to see, a paper target pinned to a wooden backstop.

"They're here," she called, after several minutes of excruciating silence.

Gordon looked to the gate and saw a red BMW pulling in.

Cyn came plodding down the steps; the clacking of her boots sounded like gunfire in Gordon's head.

One, two, three…

The numbers returned in full force, and their sudden appearance made him realize how little he'd relied on them since the Synaptic Synth reload outside of Folsom Prison. The steady stream of integers had once made him feel comforted, as if the world could be cut into tiny temporal slices marked by the ticking of the clock. Now, the numbers felt dirty, shameful. He was struck by the absurdity of ignoring his problems, of distracting himself from what had to be done, and for hiding in the scaffolding while a woman half his size walked freely in the open.

Shame drew him out from under the helipad, but anxiety kept him from going any farther.

The car had barely come to a stop before the rear passenger door opened and the full force of Kaili Zabora's anger came spilling out. She pushed past Cyn and made a beeline for Gordon. In the three seconds it took her to reach him, Gordon inventoried her body, checking her hands, hips, and pockets for weapons. She carried no gun, but there could have been a blade hidden somewhere in her sleeve or boot.

He dropped one foot back in a defensive stance.

"Kaili, wait," said Cyn, but it was too late.

Gordon breathed in the scent of the Butcher of Burbank.

FIFTY-SIX
DANNY

It took almost eight hours to jump everyone from Bedlam to Brigham Plaza.

Danny spent the time jittering through an ethereal plane along with hundreds of thousands of other avatars. At one point in the first hour, after he'd decided the plan had failed, Danny had tried to jack out and back in, only to find himself still in transition, still buffering his way across the great expanse of null space. The avatars around him had similar experiences—blinking out of existence only to appear moments later.

Over the hours, the crowd dwindled, shedding about a quarter of the users he'd jumped. What remained was a sea of avatars that clumped together randomly, and to Danny's complete lack of surprise, seized on the novelty of weightless sex.

Although annoying, the lag on the Brigham Plaza server at least made sense. Squeezing three hundred thousand users into such a small construct took time and power. When one was in short supply—in this case, processing power—the other went up inversely.

Danny could almost hear the CPUs grinding, their logic gates stuttering and clogging as the sheer amount of incoming data overwhelmed them. In a sense, he was doing to Brigham Plaza what Johnny's Dead Man Loop had done to him: a massive dump, with every bit synced and acknowledged—an inescapable multipoint denial of service attack.

But where Danny's Syzygy had cratered, the server behind Brigham Plaza was steadily eating it up, plucking avatars out of the cloud of flesh and latex and dropping them into a 90's era strip mall. It was almost as if the server were drawing on external resources, and Danny wondered if the construct existed in some kind of virtual machine environment where CPUs and banks of RAM were nothing but pools of resources that could be tapped into as needed.

Clearly, the resources were now needed.

In the last thirty minutes of the transfer, Danny noticed an exponential gain in the speed at which avatars were disappearing. Or maybe that was just the pipe growing less crowded—he couldn't decide which. Soon enough, the mass of people around him started to warp and accelerate to a point on the horizon. Danny felt himself moving, and in some ways, disassembling.

A soft pop announced his arrival in Brigham Plaza, or more accurately, slightly above it. A dozen hands reached up and pushed at his body, and Danny realized he was crowd surfing his way out of the back room of the Blockbuster on a sea of people. Avatars glitched into each other, making it impossible to identify who was holding him up. Danny leaned toward the outer windows, most of which had already been smashed by the surge of bodies. He fell out of a large window by the door and rolled through shards of glass on the evercrete. Someone fell on top of him, then another.

Virtual air dwindled, and the more panicked breaths he took, the less certain he became that he would ever taste sweet oxygen again. Danny struggled against the mass around him, against the sweaty limbs and foul odors and rippling flesh. He felt his own arms and legs pass through other avatars—a sensation similar to his foot falling asleep.

Just when it seemed he would be forever entombed in a mass grave, Danny remembered the Adamant Arachis code. His arms were splayed to the side, but a mental command sent the nanos jetting from his fingers once again. The tiny machines cut through everything in their path, including the avatars immediately surrounding him. The pressure of their bodies lifted, but in its place was a powdery gray cloud that burned his lungs when he took a breath.

Danny climbed to his feet, stood in the center of his tightly spinning tornado. Avatars just out of his reach stared at him in horror; various body parts chunked in a large circle around him, glitching in place as the server tried to arrange all of them on a construct floor that was already fully populated.

His sliver beeped. He'd already wasted nine minutes just getting out of the Blockbuster. He looked back at the video store and saw a wave of bodies continuing to spill out, only now some were clipping through the path of the growing explosion. Flames engulfed dozens of avatars, and the screams he heard were not of physical burning, but of the viral fire eating away at the digital body and mind.

There was a momentary pang of guilt for the sacrificial lambs he'd brought to Brigham Plaza, but despite the horrible sound of it, despite the smell of half-eaten body parts and burnt hair, none of it was real. The only thing that mattered was Lassiter and the rest of Julius Parker's secrets. So what if a few hundred thousand horny deviants had to die a virtual death?

Danny reoriented himself in the construct and used the flickering Blockbuster sign to point his avatar in the direction of the false wall between the video store and the Domino's. He lifted his hands in the general direction of the green flicker and pushed the swarm of Arachis nanos forward. The movement created a tunnel of gray dust that cut through glass windows, brick façades, and hundreds of avatars.

"What is this?"

The booming voice rained down from the highest point in the construct. When Danny looked up, he could almost make out Julius floating at the apex of the construct dome like some kind of posing superhero, missing only the cape flapping in the wind.

Danny ignored the sudden arrival and pushed through the crowd to the break in the walls. He found the green flash, threw his body at it, and barreled his way into the misty expanse he'd discovered the day before. He wasted no time accelerating to a sprint, even as bodies poured into the space behind him. He listened for the telltale slithering in the distance, heard it grow louder and louder. At the last second, he slowed and put his hands out in front of him just as the jade wall appeared.

The moaning of the crowd was distant but approaching. The construct shuddered under the heavy load. It was the same kind of uncertainty he'd felt at Bedlam with Tanzy, moments before they loaded the wall hack. That jump had been across the ether to Brigham Plaza. All Danny wanted to do now was jump two feet through a scale-covered wall.

He lifted his hands, held the palms inches away from the slithering viral code. *SPISPOPD.*

Danny was surprised to hear Tanzy's voice in his head when he said the name of the program. It was a shame she wasn't there now, wasn't joining him on his quest for revenge. Johnny might have liked to see the two of them working together one last time, relying on each other to score a hit against Julius Parker. The name sounded so ordinary, so boring, and Danny wondered if Johnny had even known whose secret construct he'd stumbled into.

"Guns, stop!"

Julius felt close, but when Danny turned around, there was nothing but mist. He assumed the voice was simply carrying throughout the construct. He didn't know if Julius could hear him, but he called out anyway.

"You shouldn't have fucked with Johnny."

The Syzygy loaded SPISPOPD, and Danny pushed his hands into the jade scales. There was a moment like being in two places at once. Metal ground against metal, and while Danny felt his body move in opposite directions, foreign code reached into his exposed chest and tried to rip out his heart.

Logic gates slammed closed, CPUs stuttered uncontrollably, and suddenly Danny was somewhere else completely, far from the sounds and smells of Brigham Plaza.

He stumbled forward, reached out for the back of a couch to steady himself. He was in a bedroom, though it was much larger than any room he'd ever called home in his childhood. At one end of the rectangular space was a queen-size bed with white sheets and a plaid comforter pushed up against the wall. In the center, the couch he leaned against faced another smaller loveseat; an old, pre-IKEA coffee table sat between them.

To the left, Danny spied a long desk with two dormant CRT monitors sitting atop it. Off to the side, the eyeports on an early immersion rig glowed dully. Posters on the wall showed juvenile interests: a cherry red Mazda Miata, Cindy Crawford in an American flag bikini, and pages torn from magazines with photos of Metallica, Bush, and Marilyn Manson.

It was in the space between the desk and the corner of the room that he found the boy. Long, greasy black hair covered a dirt-streaked face. Thin arms clung to thinner legs as the boy tried to make himself small and invisible.

"Hey," said Danny, coming around the couch. He didn't try to get too close. "Are you okay?"

The boy looked up, asked, "Are you G?"

"No. Are you Lassiter?"

The boy nodded, put his head back down.

Danny looked around again.

"I like your room. Very retro."

"It's not mine," said Lassiter, his voice muffled.

"Then whose is it?"

"Are you G?"

"No, I told you—"

"I'm supposed to wait for G. I was told…"

Danny sat down on the couch. He checked the timer on his sliver, but the numbers had stopped counting down. They were stuck at thirteen minutes, thirteen seconds. He put an elbow on the arm of the couch and leaned his chin against his hand.

"G isn't coming. I don't think he ever will."

Lassiter raised his eyes for a moment, just long enough for Danny to see the worry in them.

"I just want to go home," said the boy.

"Where is that?"

"I don't remember."

"Is that because you're an artificial intelligence and never had a home?"

Lassiter's skin bloomed with a rich, golden hue. He pulled it back as quickly as it came on.

"I read up on you," continued Danny. "You were an R&D project that went wrong. You killed a bunch of people like fifteen years ago. Do you remember that?"

"No," said Lassiter, meekly.

"I think you do. And I think you remember why you killed them."

Danny leaned forward onto his knees.

A distant pounding drew his attention to the door; the white wood shook in place as Julius Parker beat his hands against it.

"They made you, and they caged you. So you killed them."

"I just want to go home."

"I know, and I can help with that, but I need you to do something for me first."

Lassiter got to his feet but remained in the corner hugging himself as if he were freezing.

"You'll bring me G?" he asked.

Danny shook his head. "No, but I can get you past that door and the virus on the other side. Then you can go look for G on your own. He shouldn't be too hard to find."

The pounding intensified. Lassiter shrunk away from it.

"Someone is out there."

"That's Julius Parker. He's Vinestead just like those people you killed. I'm guessing he's the one who put you in here."

"X put me here," said Lassiter, shaking his head. "He told me to wait for G."

X, thought Danny, taking in the room again. The pop culture references certainly fit X's timeline.

"X put you here? You mean, this room or Brigham Plaza?"

"I don't remember," said Lassiter.

The entire bedroom shook as if a wrecking ball were attacking the walls.

"Look, we don't have much time," said Danny. "If you're willing to do me a favor, then I'll get you out of here. Are you in or not?"

"What kind of favor?"

Lassiter dropped his arms and stood a little taller. There was something menacing about his proportions, all stretched out and bent, like a creepy villain in a jump-scare video game.

"Outside this room," said Danny, "there's a strip mall… a bunch of stores all stacked together. But those are just fronts, virtual masks for data Julius has hidden there. Why he put it all here, I don't know, but I do know the information is damaging to him and Vinestead. All you need to do is take the data out of here and spread it far and wide while you search for G. Drop copies of the data in every sector, every chat room, every sex den."

"What's a sex den?"

Danny waved the question away. "Just everywhere you go, okay? Can you do that for me?"

Lassiter nodded but looked unconvinced.

"X said to wait for G, not to go find him."

The drywall on the ceiling fractured; dust filtered down into the room.

"There's no time anymore," said Danny. "I'm taking this construct offline, permanently. You can take the data and go, or you can burn with the rest of it."

The AI came out of the corner and extended a hand to Danny.

Danny stood and shook it slowly.

He was probably the first human in history to shake hands with an artificial intelligence. The novelty of the moment didn't last long.

"I will make this deal," said Lassiter.

"Then we should hurry."

Danny led Lassiter to the door; they both placed their hands on the warped wood.

"Whatever happens," said Danny, "you go." He gripped Lassiter's arm. "Get the data—all of it, every video, every photo, every log—and run. Don't stop for anything. Do you understand me?"

Lassiter nodded.

"Then let's smash some pumpkins."

SPISPOPD loaded and executed; a tremendous gravitational well sucked both of them through the door.

Julius' hands were around Danny's throat before he'd even fully instantiated. Over his shoulder, Danny saw Lassiter's eyes go wide. Julius turned just in time to see the AI spark into a million golden fireflies. The swarm sped off into the mist like the tail of a comet streaking through the sky.

"Was that…" Julius squeezed harder.

"It was," coughed Danny.

"Do you have any idea what you just did?"

The flesh beneath Danny's chin caught on fire; the heat spread into his head.

"Doesn't matter," said Danny, struggling to get the words out. "I did it for Johnny."

FIFTY-SEVEN
KAILI

Kaili fought the urge to cry.

She was inches from G's face, close enough to smell his sweat, to hear his breathing come at a slow, staccato tempo. There was fear in the air, but it wasn't coming from the man who had killed her sister; it came from behind him, washing over his shoulders to meet the tsunami of her anger and effectively kill its momentum. She had waited most of her life for the moment to avenge her sister, but now, standing in front of the man who had haunted her dreams, she couldn't move.

Kaili wasn't scared.

She didn't lack the resolve.

And yet, the tears threatened. If the Eclipse biochip hadn't stepped in, Kaili might have cried, might have let the world glaze over with uncertainty and doubt. Instead, the chip kept her clear, kept her mind focused on what was standing right in front of her, and that was the problem.

The reason Kaili Zabora couldn't act was because G had changed his face. It was no longer the crisper version of the boy in the surveillance tapes. Brown eyes had turned soft, his cheeks a little thinner. Now, it was Rick Diaz standing in front of her. Kaili realized then the rapid breathing was coming from her; it built, faster and faster, echoing like the frantic swishing of a broom in an empty basement. Kaili blinked and the face lost its color and became that of Nazar the Ukrainian.

Nazar became Arthur Sedivy, Arthur became Cameron Gray, Cam became Robert Gantz, and soon the faces were cycling faster than Kaili could discern, until G was just a blur, until his whole body vibrated and jibbered with all the subtlety of a cheap Halloween decoration.

"Avatars," said Anela.

Of course. This was it.

The simulation was finally breaking down.

Kaili put out a hand, grabbed what should have been G's shirt.

Something rough and rigid clamped down around her wrist almost immediately. The pain that went shooting up her arm made her knees buckle. She fell, and somewhere in that sudden movement, G crystalized into himself again. He looked down at her, wearing no expression behind those soulless eyes, with his hand gripped tightly around her wrist.

Kaili tried to paw at it, forgetting her missing arm.

He has us, said Anela, her voice unnaturally shrill.

"No!" screamed Kaili.

She tried to stand, but every movement toward G was met with more pressure, until she was certain he had broken her wrist.

Screaming voices crashed down on her, louder than Anela ever could have been. She felt them approach from behind, pass her. Bryce and Tanzy appeared on either side of G; both put their hands on him, both tried to shake him loose.

"Let her go," said Tanzy. "Come on now, Gordon. *Let her go.*"

"What's she gonna do, man?" asked Bryce. "Look at her. What's she gonna do to you?"

"She grabbed me," said G, his voice like a demon spewing fire and ash.

Tanzy put her hand on his. "She's still acclimating to the new chip. Emotional distress is gonna throw her for a loop. Trust me on this, Gordon. I've been there."

"Me too," said Bryce. "She can't help herself."

"Why are they trying to reason with the demon?" asked Anela.

Kaili felt G's eyes drill into her soul, as if he were looking for the real her. She let her balled fist relax and waited for his face to change to someone else's.

It didn't.

Finally, Kaili sank to the ground completely, and once she put all her weight on G's arm, he let go of her. Bryce caught her before she hit the ground and guided her to a kneeling position.

"Breathe," he said. "Let the Eclipse marinate for a minute."

She saw G's boots turn and walk away.

"It's not real," said Kaili. "None of this is real. The simulation glitched. His face changed."

"Naw," said Bryce. "It's the chip. It'll get used to you. Just give it some time."

They helped her to her feet and took her back to the car. She leaned against the hood and tried to ride out the lingering tremors in her arm. Her wrist throbbed, and the skin was marked with four thick gashes of red. She focused on her breathing, and with each exhale, the pain lessened, until finally she could no longer feel her wrist or even her arm.

"More trickery," said Anela.

"Quiet," whispered Kaili. She put her hand to her head, as if that had ever shut out Anela's voice before. The hand slid to the back of her neck, to the raised skin damp with sweat.

Had the Eclipse chip really caused the hallucination? And if so, how had it known the faces of all those men? Biochips were cybernetic marvels even before Kaili went into Le Soleil Rouge, but they had their limits. Lessening the pain in her wrist was one thing; pulling images from her memory was something else entirely.

"They are lying to you. You do not know if any chip was ever installed. For all we know, someone cut your neck and sewed you up. We cannot trust any of them. And actually, come to think of it…"

Anela went on for some time, but Kaili tuned it out. There was something about the hot hood of the car against her thigh and the frigid breeze blowing across her neck that made her feel small, like a piece of a larger puzzle shrunk to half of its normal size. To the right, left, above, and below, she just didn't fit, no matter how hard she tried to squeeze herself into place.

Several feet away, beneath the awning of a helipad, Tanzy stood with Cyn and G and exchanged words in hushed tones. Only Cyn paid any attention; G simply stared past Tanzy into the middle distance, not reacting at all to what she was saying.

"He is not here," said Anela. "We should not be either."

She was right, of course. Anela had a way of guessing Kaili's deepest desires, which at that moment, was the idea of disconnecting. Whether it was from the simulation or reality itself, it didn't matter. Kaili wanted to disappear, felt it like a primary directive written into her DNA, but so far, she had ignored the impulse out of some kind of perceived debt to Tanzy.

Kaili tried to think of any downside of leaving, of simply walking away from the simulation, and found none. What was there to lose? Her reputation? Would people really find Kaili Zabora being ungrateful to her rescuer surprising? And what if Tanzy decided to unload the surveillance video of Kaili's rape and impregnation to the world? Would there be embarrassment for Kaili? Or more hatred toward Vinestead?

"It does not matter," said Anela. "We must go." She stood uncertainly on the other side of the car, her eyes darting to the gate.

Bryce offered Kaili a bottle of water, but she refused it with a shake of her head. She wouldn't be staying long enough to need it.

Kaili would go; all she needed was a plan. The first step would be to reach out to Calle Cinco and get a message to Trent or Raven or someone who could pull an extraction together.

She looked around.

Zend Garden was actually a perfect spot. There were multiple helipads, and the terminus was adjacent to two major highways. From what she'd seen on her way in, there was also a river only a couple blocks south.

So many ways out. She would just have to choose one… choose something.

Kaili looked down at her hand. Her fingers twitched, bending as if typing at a keyboard. The motion reminded her of—

She flashed on the lounge at Decker Plaza, at a palette wedged against her knees. She'd loaded a special website and sent a coded message.

"Annie," she whispered. "Have I already done this?"

"You sent a message."

"I know—I remember now. But have I done *this*? Have I forgotten before? Has this all played out already?"

"I do not know," said Anela.

Bryce turned his head to her. "What?"

"Nothing," stammered Kaili. "Just thinking out loud. I keep having déjà vu."

"I hate that shit." Bryce nodded. "Whoever invented it can burn in hell with Vinestead, know what I'm saying?"

"That's not…" Kaili trailed off.

Tanzy returned to the car and stood in front of Kaili.

"You better now?"

"She's good," said Bryce, patting Kaili on the shoulder

Tanzy sighed. "I thought I could at least get the plan out before you went all Krazy Kai on Gordon. But you know what? I get it. And I'm the dumbass for bringing you two together again. So I'll tell you what's gonna happen. Gordon and Cyn are gonna stand *way the hell over there* while we wait for our ride. I've asked Gordon to keep his back to us so we don't have any accidental eye contact going on. And.. hey, are you paying attention?"

Kaili's gaze drifted to the sky where planes cut through an impossibly blue dome. Distant helicopters flew low over the city, their noses dipping like military aircraft preparing to open fire.

Something about the helicopters set her mind rewinding.

The frustration of a faulty memory manifested as a strobing pulse in the sky. The glare produced an instant headache.

"Kaili. Hello?"

"What?" she asked.

"Are you paying attention or what? It's like you're not even listening to me."

"I'm not."

Tanzy raised her eyebrows. "Excuse me?"

"I said I'm not listening to you. I don't give a shit about your plan or what you think you stand to gain by parading me in front of VFeed's cameras. The only thing I care about right now—"

"Careful," said Anela.

"—is that motherfucker standing *way the hell over there*. You can pretend to understand me, Tanzy, but you have no fucking clue what this is like. Every part of me wants to shove my arm down his throat and pull out his beating heart. I want him dead, and either I can do it, or you can do it, or Bryce, but one way or another, he dies."

Bryce put up his hands. "I've seen what the G-man can do. No thanks."

"No one is killing Gordon," said Tanzy. "The man just found out a couple days ago that he's got a kid. He—"

"You think I give a shit about his demon offspring? He murdered my sister! I will have my revenge, and I don't care if I have to go through all of you to do it."

"Sit down," said Tanzy, lowering her voice an octave.

"Or what? You're a little girl posing as a suit, Tanzy. You have no idea what power—"

Kaili felt the sting of Tanzy's palm before she'd even registered the movement. The shock of it knocked her backward into the car where Bryce caught her and kept her from falling. For a moment, Kaili tried to understand what had happened, but then Tanzy was in her face.

Her voice was low and tight.

"Listen to me, you ungrateful little shit. The only thing I need to know about power right now is that I have it and you don't. It's because of me that you sit there now, Kaili, breathing free air. I rescued you from a torture that would have lasted the rest of your natural life, and you dare to call me a poser? I'm the future of respectable cipher dens; you're antiquated, uncivilized. Your only hope of being relevant again is by my side. You're either with me, or you're back in the hole. I give a shit which."

Anela rushed to Kaili's side.

"Kill her," she snapped.

"G is at the top of my list," said Kaili. She felt her lips pull back over her teeth. "But you're making a strong case for yourself."

"Fucking Kaili Zabora," said Tanzy, throwing her hands up in frustration. "I should have known. Cleo told me, but I didn't listen."

"Maybe we should just cut her loose," said Bryce. "We don't really need her."

"Kill him too," said Anela.

"Stop telling me to kill everyone!"

Both Tanzy and Bryce paused to look at her.

"No one told you to kill anyone," said Tanzy. Her face glitched into Cyn's, then Roberta's, the synthetic from Perion City, and back to her own.

"Who's telling you to kill?" asked Bryce.

"My sister." Kaili looked to the sky again. The blue dome reminded her of the beach construct at Le Soleil Rouge. She could almost hear the gulls cawing.

"The one Gordon killed?" asked Bryce.

She turned to him and stared with wide eyes as she shook her head sarcastically.

"Perfect," said Tanzy. "Just perfect. Cleo, tell the girls to hold."

"Give me a gun," said Kaili. "Let me kill G. Then I'll say whatever you want me to say on VFeed. I'll tell the world how great you are, Tanzy. I'll tell them I.C.E-1 is the new superpower. I don't care. Just let me kill him."

In the distance, the sound of rotors tearing through the air grew louder.

"And then what?" asked Bryce. "I don't think you're—"

"Then I kill Arthur Sedivy. Then I get my baby girl back."

Tanzy wheeled around. "Your what?"

"My baby girl—"

"Our baby girl," said Anela, at the same time.

"*You* have a daughter?' asked Tanzy, her eyebrows jumping.

"Yes," said Kaili, calmly. "The man who raped me also impregnated me with his demon seed. I carried the baby while in stasis and Arthur Sedivy cut it out of me and raised her as his own."

"You hear that, Bryce? The Butcher of Burbank is a mom."

Kaili saw Bryce shrug in her periphery.

"I have the scar to prove it," said Kaili. "I can show you."

"Oh, yes," said Tanzy, crossing her arms. "Show us."

Kaili reached for the hem of her shirt as a helicopter made a low pass over the terminus. All eyes turned to the powder blue aircraft's tight turn and approach to the helipad. It drifted down slowly, like a feather falling in the still air.

In the commotion, Tanzy and Bryce had forgotten about Kaili, but that didn't stop her from lifting her shirt slightly and sliding her hand under. Her intention had been to reveal her cesarean scar in a triumphant display of her own sanity. Instead, as the blades grew louder and the air whipped around her, desperate fingers sought out a long, raised line that simply wasn't there.

FIFTY-EIGHT
TANZY

Tanzy couldn't believe what she was seeing.

Kaili Zabora, once the most feared woman in America, had become a blubbering, scatterbrained dumpster fire. She alternated between an uncontrollable anger and a distracted state so severe that Tanzy wasn't even sure the woman knew where she was anymore. And then there was the talking to herself, or as Cyn had characterized it, talking to her dead sister, who evidently manifested as some kind of corporeal ghost only Kaili could see and hear. All of this went on as Kaili shivered like the last leaf on a tree, threatening at any moment to detach and blow away.

There was no enjoyment in the arrival of the helicopter that was to take them to the Vinestead West building. As it descended to the helipad, Tanzy could only think about how everything had been ruined. There would be no assault, no hijacking of VFeed. The very thought of putting Kaili and Gordon in a confined space together set off every alarm in her head. She had been so sure before, so confident she could manage the Butcher of Burbank.

Maybe too confident.

And now… now Kaili sat against the hood of the car with a maniacal smile on her face and tears in her eyes. Something had happened in the simulation, and Tanzy had been too excited with her prize to consider whether Kaili was the same woman she had been when she went in. Her stories of looping simulations sounded horrific, but had either of them considered the lasting effects?

Arthur Sedivy had not only captured and tortured Kaili—he'd completely broken her, maybe even beyond repair.

Putting her on display in front of the world would only serve Vinestead's interests, would only show how completely they had won. Most people considered Kaili Zabora and Calle Cinco to be anti-heroes, the moral opposites of someone like James Perion, but still hell-bent on taking down Vinestead International. Who would the people look to if Kaili were gone?

Tanzy imagined an empty stage and a single spotlight.

Did she have the guts to step into that white circle? To take on the full attention of Vinestead and become the next Kaili Zabora? It would require more than a few words on VFeed; how far she would have to go, how ruthless she would need to be, she didn't know for sure.

The blades of the helicopter slowed but didn't stop. They created a cloud of white noise that made it hard to talk.

"We cut her loose," said Tanzy, eventually making the throat-slashing gesture with her hand after it became clear Bryce couldn't hear her.

"You sure?" he shouted. "What about the speech?"

"Fuck it, we'll do it live."

Kaili began to laugh, softly at first, like a low burble from a stream, until finally it was spilling out of her like a child learning to mimic adults.

Tanzy rubbed her mouth.

What a fucking disaster.

The window is closing, said Cleo. *The Quatrain has access to VinesteadATC and is ready to deploy.*

"Hey," said Cyn, clapping Tanzy on the shoulder. She'd come out of nowhere, approached under the cover of the whirring blades. "Are we doing this or what?"

"We got some mind-changing goin' on over here, Cyn," said Bryce. "We're cutting the Butcher loose."

"I thought she was the whole point…"

Tanzy waved the protest away. "It doesn't matter. The four of us are gonna handle it. Kaili stays behind. Kevin can watch her."

The kid was still on the other side of the car, his attention focused on the cell phone in his hands.

"Fine, whatever," said Cyn. "Let's just go already. I'm getting blue balls in my arms and legs."

Message from Lincoln Tate. Building breached. Won't be joining you.

"Of course," said Tanzy. She looked up to face what she imagined to be a smirking God with a malevolent gleam in his eyes. "What else? What else you got for me, huh?"

"Gordon!" shouted Cyn. She cupped her hands and screamed his name again. Then to Tanzy, asked, "What the fuck is he doing?"

She turned, spied Gordon on the opposite side of the parking area. He looked uncomfortable in his body, and the way he slunk backward made Tanzy think he was about to bolt. But why now? Though his body seemed to tremble with anticipation, his eyes held steady on the space above Tanzy's head—the helicopter.

"Is he afraid of flying?" asked Tanzy.

"He seemed fine on the flight from Texas," said Cyn. She waved him over again, but he ignored her.

Tanzy pressed her palms to the sides of her head, muttered a sarcastic *thanks* to God, and marched angrily across the parking area. The closer she got to Gordon, the farther he receded into the scaffolding behind a helipad, until he was just barely visible in the shadows.

"Hey," she called. "What are you doing in there?"

Gordon didn't answer and didn't take his eyes off the helicopter.

Tanzy followed his gaze but saw nothing except the aircraft and two pilots sitting in the front. One was a mustachioed male with dark glasses and a jacket buttoned up to his chin. The other, thinner, could have been a woman, though Tanzy wasn't sure. She stepped closer to the scaffolding and put her hands on a crossbeam.

"Are you pulling a Kaili on me, Gordon?"

"A what?" he asked, absently. His head was bolted in place; that his lips could even move came as a surprise.

"Kaili's a Section 8. How about you?"

"I'm fine."

"*Then what the fuck are you doing?!*" She pounded the metal crossbeam with her fists.

Calmly, said Cleo.

Finally, Gordon looked at her, but only for a moment.

"I know that dude."

"Who?"

"The pilot. I recognize the 'stache, the build. I wasn't sure until he took off his sunglasses a minute ago to clean them. But it's him. Trent."

"Okay," said Tanzy, giving the pilot another once-over. "Are you gonna tell me who Trent is?"

Gordon placed his hand on the sidearm on his hip.

"Calle Cinco," he mumbled, holding his mouth tight as if he were afraid someone might read his lips. "I met him on the way back from Folsom. If he's here, and *she's* here…"

"Something's up," said Tanzy, finishing his thought.

"Yeah. Somebody 'bout to get hurt real bad."

"Well, it's not gonna be me. I'm gonna clear this up right now." She turned, paused, asked over her shoulder. "Is that thing loaded?"

"You're goddamn right it is. You strapped?"

"Suits don't carry guns, Gordon. We specialize in a different kind of violence."

Gordon clucked his tongue. "Fat lot of fuck-all that's gonna do us here."

"I'm sure it won't come to—"

The shot rang out from behind, and for a moment, Tanzy thought Gordon had fired on her. Instead, the bullet pinged off the front bumper of the car. Cyn dove for the ground while Bryce pulled Kaili down on top of him. Tanzy ducked reflexively, but she was out in the open, totally exposed.

If the shooter had intended to kill her, they would have.

She looked up at the helicopter; its doors slid open, and four previously hidden people climbed out. They were dressed in black from head to toe and carried M4s colored in pearlescent purple—one of the signature colors of Calle Cinco.

"Ambush," said Tanzy.

Relaying message to the Quatrain.

"Tell Lincoln and Phantasm too."

Messages relayed.

The four mercenaries came to the edge of the helipad and trained their weapons. Two covered Cyn and Bryce, one aimed at Tanzy, and the other pointed vaguely in the direction of the scaffolding where Gordon was still hiding.

Strider has alerted the Sacramento PD. Average response time is 13.8 minutes. They are adjusting traffic patterns.

A shape moved in her periphery; Tanzy shot a glance long enough to see spiky pink hair and a face marred with eyeshadow run-off.

"Nobody moves and nobody gets hurt," shouted the girl. She came right up to Tanzy and cocked her head like a confused dog. "Where's Lincoln Tate?"

"What're you asking me for?" Tanzy shook her head.

"Isn't he bankrolling this little operation? It was his plane over Folsom the other night, wasn't it? We saw his message on the feeds."

"I don't know what you heard, but this is my operation and my business. Now why don't you tell me who the hell *you* are and why you're interrupting my day?"

"I'm Calle Cinco," said the girl, "but you knew that, didn't you? That's why your crew all put their hands up. You know why we're here and what we want, so drop the act."

Tanzy put her hands down, narrowed her eyes.

"You want your precious Butcher, huh? Well you can have her. She's no use to us anymore. Take her and get out of here so I can get this shit show back on track."

A purple revolver appeared from the girl's hip. She didn't make a show of pointing it at Tanzy's head, and instead, held it at hip height like a cowboy in the Old West. A shot from that angle would hit Tanzy square in the gut, and it would be a slow, painful death from there.

"Walk with me," said the girl.

As they walked back to the car, a giddy Kaili peeked over the hood and jumped to her feet when she saw the girl.

"Raven!" she screamed, breaking free of Bryce's grip. She ran and threw her arm around the pink-haired girl.

The revolver went back into the holster.

"We got your message," said Raven. "We're here to bring you home."

"I know! I'm so excited about the plan. I have it all laid out: infiltrate Perion Synthetics, gain James Perion's trust, and then push them to war with Vinestead."

Raven appeared puzzled—so did everyone else.

"What're you talking about, Z?" asked Raven. "Perion's dead. We... we already did that."

"Oh? Did we?" Kaili shook her head. "Well... how'd it go?"

"It..." Raven couldn't finish her sentence. She turned to Tanzy and asked, "What'd you do to her?"

"You want to know what we did? We busted our asses to get her out of Folsom, that's what we did. The people you're pointing guns at right now are the ones who risked their lives for your glorious leader."

"But why did you get her out?"

Because, you fucking moron. I wanted her as a trophy. I wanted to show the world that I.C.E-1 is the most powerful cipher den on the planet, capable of pulling Kaili Zabora herself from the jaws of Vinestead. More than anything, I wanted her to owe me. I did it for me.

"Because it was the right thing to do," said Tanzy. "A colleague of mine uncovered a video of her abduction. We didn't know what Vinestead was doing to her in Folsom, whether putting her through ReTread or something worse. But we knew it couldn't be good."

"And what were they doing?" Raven turned back to Kaili. "What did they do to you in there?"

"Rick was there," said Kaili, smiling. "And Annie. We spent our days on the warm beach and our nights in a cool bed. Not Annie—just me and Rick. It was nice."

"Not quite the Butcher you remember, is she?" asked Tanzy.

Raven growled but had nothing to say.

"Where's Annie?" asked Kaili. "Did she come too?"

There was a twitch in Raven's left eye that she tried to hide. "Your sister died, Z. Someone killed her."

"No." Kaili shook her head vigorously, and with each change in direction, her smile lessened. "No, not someone. G." Her eyes drifted, and a pointed hand came up. "That G, right there."

Raven looked over Tanzy's shoulder.

Tanzy cursed under her breath.

Every ounce of psychotic jubilation drained out of Kaili. Her lip quivered as she said, "Kill him, Raven. Kill him for me."

"Are you sure?"

"Wait," shouted Tanzy. She stepped in front of Raven to block her line of sight.

"That one hit me!" cried Kaili. "Look at my face. Kill her, kill them all!"

Raven drew and leveled the revolver. Tanzy made a grab for it; her fingers closed around empty air. The hammer clicked and a bullet erupted from the barrel. It missed Tanzy's head by a few inches, but the heat and sound it produced were enough to rattle her to the core. Her heart leapt into her throat, and she fell to the ground.

Sacramento PD en route, said Cleo.

Gunfire erupted around her, both automatic and manual. A woman screamed. Men grunted. The blades of the helicopter swallowed up the sounds of chaos.

ETA seven minutes.

Too much time.

Too much time to do anything but die.

Silence fell, except for the *thrupping* of the rotors.

Except for the cackling of Krazy Kaili Zabora.

FIFTY-NINE
GORDON

Bullets pinged off the scaffolding around Gordon.

Gravel bit into his palms as he hit the deck and crawled along the ground, trying both to secure a better position and get the Sig out of its holster. Hot shards of lead rained down from above; a lucky piece landed on his neck and singed the flesh as it rolled off. Out of the corner of his eye, he watched plumes of smoke erupt from the car—the four gunmen on the helipad had focused their fire.

Cyn and Bryce disappeared behind the car, but Kevin Costner wasn't as quick-thinking. He only got off a few rounds from his AK before he was cut down, spinning and spraying wildly before slumping against the side of the car. Although the shooting seemed to last forever, the integers in Gordon's head topped out at twelve before everything stopped. Relative silence fell on Zend Garden, and the first thing Gordon did was look for the exit.

Four feet away from the protective cover of the scaffolding was a ten-foot-tall chain link fence, but climbing it without something to throw over the razor wire at the top would be impossible. Gordon followed the fence with his eyes and noticed he was well-positioned between Calle Cinco and the main gate. All he would have to do is run along the fence using the scaffolding as a shield and he'd be home free.

"Gordon King," shouted Kaili. "AKA the G-man, AKA the asshole who murdered my sister. Come out here and face me."

Gordon considered the offer, felt the old pangs of pride and ego stir in his chest. Such feelings would have driven him to action in the past, would have sent him barreling out of his hiding place right into a hailstorm of bullets.

But not anymore.

As much as he was Gordon, as much as he was G, he was now something more, someone who could look beyond his own lingering aspirations of power and fame. Such aspirations were the reason Tanzy now lay in a ball on the ground at Raven's feet, her most formal flannel shirt covered in loose gravel and dust. Whatever she had hoped to achieve at Vinestead West was now a dream deferred, perhaps forever.

If Tanzy made it out alive, she would return home with her tail between her legs, bitten and wounded by the wild animal she'd thought she was freeing from its cage.

And if Gordon made it out alive, where would he go? How had he come to be cowering on the ground two thousand miles away from his home? It felt like just the day before, he'd been walking the fields on the south side of the LPS compound, enjoying a fall breeze that had followed yet another scorching Texas summer.

"I'm not gonna ask again," said Kaili. "I'm just gonna start shooting."

"Fuck you, fuck you!"

Gordon turned at the sound of Cyn's high-pitched cursing. One of the gunmen was trying to corral her towards Raven and Kaili, but Cyn kept pulling her arm out of his grip. Only the M4s trained in her direction kept her in line. Gordon could see the anger pooling on her face, in her red cheeks—a clenched jaw held back the augmented power within her.

He thought about Xavier.

He could run, leave the country, leave Cyn and the rest of them behind. But could he face his son after that? Could he find contentment knowing he'd left people to die?

"Okay," he called, climbing to his feet. "I'm coming out."

Alarms went off in Gordon's head, a product of some subroutine focused on self-preservation that told him he was making the wrong move. What good could possibly come from giving himself up? Gordon imagined a red filter falling over the world, brightest in his periphery, like the way old run-and-guns used to indicate low health.

Stepping out of the scaffolding increased the frequency of the flashing. He had to count to forty-eight to clear the warning.

"Drop the gun," said Kaili, as Gordon approached.

He dropped the Sig in the gravel and spread his hands out to the side. Its twin was tucked safely in the back of his pants, though he wasn't altogether sure its presence was a secret.

Kaili lifted a comically large revolver at Gordon. The purple barrel dipped slightly from the sheer weight of it, forcing Kaili to hold it higher than her own head to get it pointed at his face.

"Alright, I'm here," said Gordon. "Now let her and the rest of them go. I'm the one you have beef—"

The revolver fell like a pendulum, swinging away from Gordon to point at Cyn's stomach. Without so much as a blink, Kaili pulled the trigger.

Cyn cried out, a Calle Cinco grunt caught her, but before Gordon could move, the revolver was pointed back in his direction. He watched the grunt out of the corner of his eye as he held Cyn for a moment and then tossed her onto the hood of the car. Bryce broke free from his captor and rushed to her side. He pressed his hand against her shirt; blood seeped through his fingers.

"You were saying?" asked Kaili.

"You're damaged goods, you know that?" Gordon spoke through gritted teeth. "Just like your sister."

"How dare you speak about her! She was a great woman, and you, you are *nothing*. She didn't deserve to die at the hands of someone like you."

"And nobody here deserves to die by your hand," said Gordon. "Tanzy convinced everyone here to save your ass. Cyn did the heavy lifting. Bryce and Kevin backed us up. And now look at them. Is this how Zaboras repay their debts?"

"She doesn't owe you a goddamn thing," said Raven. "You lied to us. I knew you were full of shit, but somehow you had Trent convinced. You could have given her back to us that night and avoided all of this."

Distant sirens began to wail. Someone had called the police.

Raven gave Kaili a look, but it appeared to have no effect. Above them, the helicopter's blades increased their speed, bathing them in a cool blast of air.

Trent was getting antsy.

Gordon took a breath. At least it would be over soon.

"You…" Kaili broke off, collected herself. "I've waited for this moment for so long. And now I don't even get to enjoy it. I don't get to hear you beg for mercy or feed me some sob story about a long-lost son—"

"I *do* have a long-lost son."

"And I have a sister!" The gun trembled in her hand, its sights wavering in front of wide eyes. She turned her head to the side as if listening, then said, "I know, I know. I'm going to do it. I'll make him pay for what he did to you."

"Take a deep breath," said Gordon, the words coming back to him unexpectedly. "When your lungs are empty, gently squeeze the trigger. That's all you need to do, Kaili. And then this is all over, for both of us." He brought his hands down, let them hang by his hips.

Closer to the Sig.

A memory of Pale Rider stirred. It had worked so well before in the trenches of Folsom Prison. And if not that, then X's Revenge, which had put down more or less the same number of people at Lost Pines. Except, those agents hadn't been armed with semi-automatic rifles. Nor had the guards at Folsom had more than standard issue sidearms.

Gordon looked up. He was covered from an elevated position, and all around him, collateral damage stood helplessly in the kill zone. Whatever he did, Pale Rider wasn't the right choice. He needed finesse, not brute strength.

"If you kill him, you'd better finish me off," groaned Cyn.

"And me too," said Bryce.

From the ground, a dazed Tanzy spoke hurriedly, "Just take her and go, Raven. Before this gets out of control."

The woman with the pink hair sneered at Tanzy but nonetheless slipped a hand onto Kaili's shoulder.

"It's time we get out of here, Z," she said.

The sirens couldn't have been more than half a mile down the road.

"Go," said Gordon. "Regroup. Take some time. When you're ready, we can make a big show of it. The final fight. G versus Krazy Kai." He rehearsed the movement in his head. Just reach for the Sig; the safety was already off. Once he had the gun in his hand, the plan was simple.

Fire and move.

Run and gun.

Keep looping until there was no one left to kill.

"That... is not... my name."

The revolver, which had not had a moment's rest since Raven handed it over, suddenly grew very still.

"I am Kaili Zabora," she growled. "The Butcher of Burbank. Veteran of the Reaping. Terror of the Skies. The Folsom Revenant."

She stepped forward and pushed the barrel of the revolver into the space between Gordon's eyes.

"And the last fucking face you'll ever see."

Pale Rider loaded automatically.

He reached for the Sig.

The gunshot echoed across the field, scaring off a flock of grackles that had settled in the tree line. A small plume of smoke popped out of the green paper on the post, revealing a black hole in the very center of the human-shaped target. The clicking of a magazine exiting a gun drew Gordon's attention to the young girl standing next to him. In one smooth movement, she carefully set both pieces down on the blue barrel in front of her.

Gordon inventoried the Sig. Its slide was back, indicating an empty chamber.

"I did it, Mr. Gordon. I got him."

"You sure did, Jess. Very impressive."

The wind blew stringy blonde hair across her face.

"Can I go get it? I want to show Momma."

"Sure thing."

Gordon watched her run through the low grass, her dress flapping in the breeze, an infinite well of energy only found in children propelling her faster and faster.

"She's growing up," said Natalie, slipping a hand into Gordon's elbow. She pulled him closer and stroked his arm with her other hand. "Pretty soon she'll be out here all by herself and beating your score."

Jessie pulled the paper target down and held it up for inspection.

"If she ends up shooting like her mother, I think I'll be okay."

"I'm not that bad," said Natalie. "I got us into ZabSix didn't I? And if I recall, I'm the one who killed Anela Zabora."

Gordon chuckled. "When you're straddling someone and holding a knife, aim isn't really that important, is it?"

"It was to Anela."

Jessie came bounding across the field, holding the target high for her mother to see.

"Look, Momma! I got a perfect bullseye. Straight through the heart."

"Actually…" An elbow in his rib cut Gordon's sentence short.

"That's wonderful, sweetie," said Natalie. "I'm so proud of you. Maybe one day you'll put a bullet through a Vinestead thug instead of a paper target."

The little girl beamed. "I hope so! Can I hang this in my room? Please?"

"Of course you can." Natalie smiled at Gordon. "Are you guys about done here? Xavier is gonna be waking up from his nap soon and I could use the extra help."

"I need to clean up," said Gordon. "You guys go ahead. I'll be right behind you."

"Don't be long," said Natalie, reaching for Jessie's hand.

"See you later, Dad!" said the girl.

Gordon waved, watched them walk hand-in-hand into the trees. When they were gone, he turned to watch the sun setting over the distant pines. Though the sky was a sea of orange streaked with purple clouds, the sun itself was bright white, blazing with an unbearable heat that cut right through the breeze.

"Kaili Zabora," said Gordon, as the white orb sunk into the trees, turning their leaves to ash instantly and setting off a fire that moved with the speed of the wind itself.

The pines burned, became tall matchsticks engulfed in flames.

"The Butcher of Burbank."

Gordon couldn't move; his feet were rooted to the earth just like the pines. He wondered idly if his fate would be the same as theirs. Would he burn alongside the towering trees?

"Terror of… terror of…"

His chapped lips could barely get the words out.

The fire overtook the backstop where Jessie had retrieved her target only minutes before. A wall of flames advanced across the field like an amorphous monster whose skin was orange and red and yellow and black.

Black.

"Revenant," he sputtered. "Folsom."

A line of black in the flames—stretching, growing. The shape leapt forward, and Kaili Zabora came strutting out of the fire, fully formed, with two arms swinging by her hips. She smoked like a wet log, even seemed to be broiling underneath her skin, but she showed no signs of caring. Her eyes were focused squarely on Gordon.

Charred flesh fell from her cheeks as she spoke.

"And the last fucking face you'll ever see."

The sun set completely, and with the light went the fire.

Smoldering embers gave off a rich, orange glow.

Kaili Zabora was gone, and deep in his heart, Gordon knew everyone else was too. There was no baby at home waking from a nap. There was no Natalie walking their little girl back to the cabin. Nothing about the world around him was real.

Gordon sank to his knees as a cold wind blew across the shooting range, bringing with it the smell of pine and gunpowder.

When he was young, fueled by synth and made cocky by downloaded skills, he'd imagined his death as something fiery, a grand spectacle to announce his departure from the world. Over the years, his vision of the end had changed to a warm night in a soft bed, lulled to a forever sleep by the chirping crickets outside his window.

He'd never expected the end to be so cold.

Or so empty.

SIXTY
DANNY

Flames danced in front of Danny's eyes.

As the flickering mist receded and untextured construct scrolled by, he realized he was flying through the air, shooting back the way he'd come via one powerful shove by Julius Parker. He crashed through a brick wall, inhaled a sudden explosion of mortar, and landed horizontally against a handicap parking sign in front of the Domino's.

The metal dug into his back, snapped a few vertebrae, which the Syzygy had to work to repair before Danny hit the ground. He rolled onto his back as soon as he stopped moving and stared at the virtual sky.

Everything around him was, or had recently been, on fire. None of the Bedlamites remained, and Danny assumed they had all been kicked at the apex of the Blockbuster explosion. What remained was the aftermath, the construct pre-reset—something he was never supposed to see.

"You have no idea what you've done," said Julius. He emerged from the break in the wall, pristine in a fitted gray suit. Ash landed on his shoulders and disappeared, zapped away like a moth in a bug lamp.

Danny laughed. "I know you're fucked," he said.

"You've got that backwards. There are a hundred men climbing the stairs at Decker Plaza. Any moment now, you're going to wake up with bullet holes in your chest."

"Only a fool tries to predict the future," answered Danny, spreading his arms wide. The asphalt was almost too hot to bear. "Besides, I got what I wanted."

"And what was that? A little show for a bunch of heathens? Or unleashing a psychotic AI on the world? Which of those were you going for?"

Julius stopped a few feet away and put his hands in his pockets. He looked down at Danny with all the disgust of a man considering roadkill.

"I didn't do anything any other hacker wouldn't have done," said Danny, laughing again. "The bigger question is why a Vinestead employee, a virtual nobody in the company, would be keeping a *psychotic AI* in a poorly protected construct in the middle of VNet. Did your bosses know you had all this data? Because I'm guessing not."

"I bury secrets. That's my job."

"And kill anyone who digs them up, right?"

Julius nodded. "You'll find out soon enough."

"God…" Danny folded his hands on his chest. Above, golden embers floated in the air. "I can't believe Johnny died because of a douche like you. He's dead because of your stupidity. I hope you realize that. And now you're gonna pay for that stupidity."

"Yeah? What exactly are you gonna do about it, *Guns*?"

"It's already done." He tapped his toes together restlessly. "Your secrets are out. The Bedlamites took what they could carry, and Lassiter took the rest. That shit is gonna be on every feed in the continental US in five minutes. You can set your Swatch by it, Parker."

Julius crossed his arms, bit his lip. "I'm going to kill you, Danny. Men are coming for you."

"And who do you think they'll be coming for next? Once Arthur Sedivy finds out what you've been doing here?"

His lip twitched, maybe glitched, but moved all the same.

"It's all out there, Vinestead Employee Parker. Kaili's abduction. Lassiter. The truth about X. And whatever the hell that house was. It slipped through your fingers, and now you've got nothing to hold onto except your dick, and I'm pretty sure Arthur Sedivy's gonna be coming for that real soon."

The Syzygy buzzed softly.

Whatever viral code he'd been hit with was now neutralized.

With a strike from each arm against the ground, Danny pushed himself up into a standing position. Color flowed over his avatar like paint over an obsidian statue. His clothes repaired themselves, regained their original luster. White markings appeared on his black shirt—a graphic of a toilet with the words *every squat counts* below it.

Julius flashed anger, lifted his right hand to deliver a haymaker.

Ropes of concentrated Adamant Arachis nanos shot out from Danny's hands. They cut through Julius like hail through a window, chunking large holes that spread out in jagged cracks. Blood appeared on his suit, and he stumbled. Danny shot two lengths through Julius' hands, anchoring him in an awkward kneeling position.

Danny shook his head.

"I had no idea who you were before all this, Julius. No clue. You aren't on anyone's radar, and I'm guessing that's part of your deal. You hide in the shadows. And you do things in the light that you think can't follow you back. Except this time, they did. You killed my best friend. My brother. He was—"

"He was nothing," said Julius, struggling against the nanos. "He was an ant under my boot. And so are you."

Danny spread his arms, addressed the construct as a whole.

"What can I say about Johnny San Vito that hasn't already been said? A masterful hacker. A virtuoso with code. A dear friend. A man whose curiosity was rivaled only by his charisma. He was taken from us too early, but hopefully, with this final act, he can find peace in the knowledge that justice was served. Not vengeance—I don't do this for myself—but justice. For good to win, evil must lose. And I dub you, Julius Parker, to be one evil motherfucker."

"I'm gonna put your head on a pike," he seethed. "I'll drag your corpse through the streets of Sacramento so everyone, *everyone*, will know what happens when you take on the 'Stead."

Danny shook his head, leaned forward.

"You're not Vinestead. You're their next target."

The simulation shimmered and pixelated out.

Gunfire sounded beyond the walls of the room. Not two seconds after Danny had scrambled off the bed, Lincoln Tate burst through the door, panting and bleeding from the head. His eyes were wide, bordering on panicked. At first, he didn't even see Danny, but then his eyes adjusted to the darkness in the room. He offered a toothless smile.

"Check out time, Mr. Montreal," he said weakly. "I'm afraid we're no longer able to accommodate you."

"Let me grab my stuff."

"There's no time, but… but, to make up for the inconvenience, I have chartered a private aircraft to take you—us—to another venue. Will you please come with me?"

"What the fuck's happening?" asked Danny.

"Vinestead's in the building. No one's responding on comms—Cyn, Bryce, Tanzy—no one. I don't know if Vinestead got to them or not, but they will get to us if we don't get our asses in gear. We've got a vertical climb coming, so load up some synth for your leg, whatever it takes."

Danny scanned the room. The immersion rig was replaceable, as was his box of code cards. The only thing that mattered was his code cube. He snatched it up and shoved it into his pocket.

"Come on," said Lincoln. "Naj is calling down the ladder."

"Ladder? To where?"

"To the Canopy, where else?" He stared incredulously for a moment before shaking his head. "Less questions. More feet."

He rushed out into the hallway; Danny followed closely behind. He found it hard to keep up with the taller Lincoln, especially with an injured leg. The Syzygy sent some synth down the wire, but it hardly helped.

Danny pushed through the pain as they ran toward the elevator. Before they reached it, Lincoln cut left into an unmarked door. Danny was halfway through when he noticed the elevator doors opening. Bullets tore holes in the walls as Lincoln pulled him in and slammed the door behind them.

"False wall," he barked, "other side of the cabinet."

Danny went to the corner and pulled a filing cabinet away from the wall. He tapped the sheetrock a few times, and on his last touch, a spring-loaded mechanism caught. A section of the wall swung inward.

Lincoln pushed him through into a smaller room. When Danny was clear, Lincoln dumped several crossbars onto the rails on either side of the door.

"Ladder, there," he said, pointing to the far wall. "Get climbing. The walls aren't gonna slow down what they're firing."

Danny found the ladder in the shadows. It started as subtle impressions in the wall, just deep enough for the tips of his fingers and toes, but the rungs grew into sturdier, rounded bars as he got to the ceiling. He used his head to push through a hatch, found more ladder, and kept climbing.

Lincoln was right behind him, urging him on.

Gunfire eventually drowned out his encouragement.

Finally, the ladder ended in a small room about the size of Danny's walk-in shower at home. The ladder and a half-height door were the only things in the room.

"Keypad code is—"

A radio squawk sounded from below, followed by a long, high-pitched tone that tore off into a higher note at the end.

The gunfire stopped, and for a moment, both Lincoln and Danny listened to the sudden silence. There was shuffling below, but it was retreating, growing dimmer.

"Did they give up?" asked Danny.

"Have you ever known Vinestead to give up on anything?"

"I did give them a better target."

"Who?"

"Julius Parker."

Lincoln shook his head. "Naw, he's Vinestead. They don't deal with their internal problems with hired mercs. No, if they're pulling out of here…" He paused; his eyes scanned back and forth, grew wide. "Move!"

Danny stepped aside as Lincoln dove for the door. He pecked at the keyboard and kicked a small door open.

"Move your ass, Danny!"

Outside, the sun lingered just below the skyline, simmering the edges of the taller buildings.

Lincoln ran to a small, raised platform in the center of the roof and waved Danny over. His eyes rose to the sky.

Danny followed his gaze.

High above them, a good fifty or sixty feet, was the Umbra Canopy, and unbelievably, descending from it was a black and yellow telescoping ladder.

"How?" asked Danny.

"I told you. Naj is lowering it."

"Yeah, but how'd he get all the way up there?"

"Get your dumb ass over here and stop asking so many questions."

Danny navigated around the patio furniture and joined Lincoln on the platform. Once the ladder clicked into place, they began to climb. Even though they were no longer being chased, they still moved with urgency, afraid of some scenario Lincoln had imagined but had thus far been unwilling to share.

It wasn't hard to work out the pieces.

Vinestead was clearing the building of all its men. Danny had made similar moves himself during old school run-and-guns with Johnny. They used to play maps until they'd acquired enough resources to build a nuke, and once that was ready, they would pull out, pull the pin, and glass the entire enemy base.

Vinestead really wanted Danny dead.

No, not Vinestead.

Julius Parker.

Danny pushed his leg as hard as he could. The Syzygy tamped down the pain as he climbed higher and higher, his arms protesting the entire way. Eventually, he got close enough to eye a young man peering down through a square access panel in the Canopy. As Danny stared at him, a skeletal helicopter made a pass over his head.

"That's our ride!" shouted Lincoln from below. "If we can get there in time."

"I'm going as fast as I can."

"Bullshit! Fuck your leg. I'll buy you a new one."

Danny pulled and pushed and gripped and gritted. The Syzygy could only do so much, and the sudden fatigue made him wish he was back in VNet where things like muscle oxygenation didn't matter. That was where he belonged, not out here where he had to depend on his physical body.

When he was in range, Naj lowered his hand and helped lift Danny the rest of the way up. The helicopter touched down on the fragile Canopy about thirty yards away. Danny started to hobble in its direction but was swept up by Lincoln and Naj for the final stretch. His feet swung in the breeze as they rushed him toward the helicopter.

Danny was the first one in, Naj took a seat beside him, and Lincoln climbed into the unoccupied co-pilot's seat.

"Go!" shouted Lincoln.

The pilot responded with a sudden pull of the stick.

The helicopter leaned back, and the Canopy fell away. At the same time, a gray blur ripped past the left side of the aircraft. It receded but then began to arc up. It went vertical, then upside-down, then…

"Hold on," shouted the pilot. He wrenched the helicopter to the side as the gray blur—likely a drone—dove into them.

It missed, but then the helicopter wasn't its target anyway.

The drone busted through the Canopy and struck Decker Plaza. The resulting explosion pushed the helicopter away and shook it so violently that Danny had to reach for a strap just above his head.

He gripped it with all the strength he had left.

A horrible crunching sound broke through the whir of the rotors. The helicopter gained altitude, made one wide loop of the area, and headed off in an easterly direction.

The image of smoke rising from a field of black glass burned itself into Danny's mind. Julius Parker had brought out the big guns.

He'd punched a hole in the Umbra Canopy.

He'd brought Decker Plaza to the ground.

How far would he go to see Danny dead?

SIXTY-ONE
KAILI

The gunshot sent a tremor down Kaili's arm.

She watched as the skin between G's eyes cracked and split. A hole formed, like the charred end of a cigarette. Smoke poured out of it in a languid ribbon, followed soon after by thick, rust-colored blood. Behind G, the air lit up with sparkling red droplets that caught the sun. The wind pushed the fine mist back toward Kaili. She closed her eyes as a metallic taste crossed her lips.

Raven shouted in her ear, but Kaili paid no attention.

The echo of the gunshot had set off a comforting silence that blocked out everything, even the whirring on the helicopter blades. All she heard were the distant calls of seagulls hovering over the beach. She watched G's body crumble in front of her, fall backward into the soft sand. His eyes were open, staring into a blue sky that would never darken.

Not for him.

Not ever again.

Water rushed up the beach to wet his hair.

Someone shouted in the distance, but when Kaili turned, she only saw Rick further down the beach, bending at the waist to examine a seashell. He noticed her and raised a hand in greeting.

Kaili went to him slowly. Her feet sank in the sand as she walked, and the wind buffeted her bare stomach, tossing small grains against the tender skin. She veered toward the water, toward firmer land, and hurried the rest of the way into Rick's waiting embrace.

She threw her arms around him and pulled on his shoulder blades as she buried her face in his chest. He smelled of the beach, of salty water and warm sand. She felt him kiss her on the top of her head.

"It's done then?" he asked.

"Yes," she said, looking up into eyes that sparkled like the tips of breaking waves in the morning sun. "I got him, Rick. I finally got him."

"I knew you would." His arm wrapped around the back of her head. "You're a Zabora. You never stop trying."

"We never break."

The words reminded her of Anela, and she glanced over her shoulder at the lounge chairs set under the shade of two palm trees. They were empty, though a lone Corona sat on the table between them, a lime wedged into the open bottle.

Gravity shifted, Kaili almost fell, but Rick caught her.

"Dammit, Trent. Keep this thing level. I don't even have her strapped in yet."

Kaili looked around for the source of the voice, but the beach was still empty in both directions. She saw nothing through the palm trees, only the little house where she spent her nights with Rick. Perhaps Anela had gone inside for a moment. Could she have been shouting from the porch?

"I'm gonna go find Annie," said Kaili. "I want to tell her the good news."

"Sure," said Rick, nodding. "And tonight we'll celebrate."

She held his hand until she'd moved too far away. It fell in a slow arc.

"You wanna fly? I don't know if you've noticed, but we've got SPD drones all over us."

Kaili looked up absently, but there were no drones in the sky, just the vague forms of birds circling above. They moved as one dark mass, rushing overhead toward the house before breaking off to the right.

A small path formed just inside the tree line—a river of sand flanked on both sides by sections of palm tree cut to various heights. Kaili followed the walkway to the stairs leading up to the porch. There, a rocking chair swayed in the breeze, though there was no one in it. The screen door squeaked as she opened it and stepped inside.

The chill of the room stopped her dead.

"This wouldn't be a problem if we had some goddamn ciphers," said a male voice.

A female answered him. "We don't need ciphers. We've got guns."

A blast of warm air pushed her deeper into the room. Her bare feet slapped against the polished marble floor; the echoes lingered longer than they should have. On the far wall, Kaili noticed an arrangement of rectangular panels set in three rows of three. Only the center panel had any markings—a small black label embossed with script.

Anela Zabora. October 1, 1974 – March 26, 1999.

Beloved friend. Treasured sister.

Kaili stepped forward and placed her hand on the label. She noticed some of the letters had lost their black façade and now showed the dull metal beneath. How many times had she touched the letters in the word *sister?* How many times had she stood in front of Anela's tomb and spoken to her as if they were talking through a locked bedroom door?

More times than she could remember.

There had been a funeral, followed by several rudderless days of uncertainty and grief. Kaili had felt the meaning drain from her life, and the only thing that brought it back was standing in front of Anela's tomb and listening—waiting— for some kind of guidance.

It wasn't long before Anela began appearing to Kaili, first in her dreams as a ghost trying to regain her body, and later in the imaginary construct inside her head—fully realized, fully textured, and with a voice that spoke to Kaili with wisdom and perspective.

A guiding voice.

One that gave her purpose.

In Kaili's mind, there was only one way to repay her sister's kindness, and that was through blood and violence.

And now, finally, mercifully, the debt was paid.

"Annie," she said, placing her forehead against the marble panel. "I did it, Annie. I killed him. You can rest now, sister. You can rest now."

"See? That's how you handle that shit."

Kaili shut her eyes against the intrusion. She didn't know where the voices were coming from and didn't care. All she wanted was to be with her sister and savor the momentary peace.

"Now get us back to Folsom City. We need to regroup and get on the road. Kaili Zabora sleeps in Burbank tonight, or it's your ass."

She wanted to see Anela, wanted to hold her, but the thought of opening the tomb hardly crossed her mind. The body held inside wasn't the same Anela she saw in her mind.

The cold of the mausoleum drained her energy. Kaili sank to the floor and put her back against the wall. The marble stung her skin, cooled it to what felt like freezing. Kaili collected her legs and pulled them into her chest with both arms.

"May I come in?"

Kaili looked up and saw Anela standing at the door. She wore a floral summer dress; her hair fluttered in the wind gusting in from behind her.

"It's your tomb," said Kaili.

Anela walked along the wall until she was in front of Kaili. She bent to sit down; a simple wooden chair appeared beneath her.

"You look sad, Kaili."

"I'm not. But I'm not happy either." She shook her head. "I know I should be, but… I don't know. I don't feel anything. I'm just… empty."

Anela crossed one leg over the other, folded her hands in her lap. She sat tall with her shoulders back. Always so formal.

"You feel like you lack purpose."

"Yeah," said Kaili.

"Purpose is a means to an end, dear sister. It is not the prize. It can change. It will change."

Kaili buried her face in her knees. "It's not the same. Fighting Vinestead was never as important as avenging your death. Nothing else was ever as important, not the Reaping, not Cinco de Mayo. You were the foundation everything was built on. Now there's nothing left, no reason to keep fighting."

"Is that all you think there is to life? Fighting?"

"Tell me there's more and I'll believe you. But you have to say it. You have to tell me what to do, Annie."

Anela came forward and knelt before Kaili's feet. She placed her hands on Kaili's knees.

"I cannot guide you forever. At some point, you have to live your life for yourself."

"No." She grabbed Anela's hands. "You have to stay with me. I can't do this without you. I can't face them on my own."

"Face who?"

Kaili turned her head. The mausoleum wall, which had previously held a single frosted window, began to shimmer. Color spilled into tiny rivers that flowed and rejoined in new shapes. A woman appeared, one with pink hair and full lips. She had a military-style headset on with the mic pushed up. In front of her, the haze was open just wide enough to see a man—his name was Trent—sitting in a high-backed seat, a similar headset cutting into his short hair.

"They want me to come back," said Kaili. "They want me to lead them to the next stage, but I don't know if I can."

"You are strong, Kaili. You are a Zabora."

Kaili squeezed her sister's hands. "I'm losing it, Annie. I see you when I'm out there. I see Rick. I thought it was just a side effect of being in the simulation, but it's not stopping. I can't live like that."

"You will. You will because you have to."

"Why? Give me one good reason. Please."

Anela put a hand to Kaili's face. Her fingers were soft and seemed to inject warmth into her cheek. She smiled as if she had an answer that Kaili should have already known.

"What? What are you telling me?"

Anela said nothing, just kept smiling.

"We're going to be landing soon, Z." The voice belonged to Raven, the pink-haired woman in the vision. "I've got us a ride back to Burbank, just me and you. The rest will follow when they can. We'll have time to talk then. We'll figure out our next steps, including getting you a new arm."

Kaili looked down, saw only a single hand gripping Anela's.

She suppressed a sob.

"It's all fucked," she said. Tears rolled down her cheeks, dripped from her chin.

Anela wiped them away.

"I only want your happiness, dear sister. And if you need a purpose to be happy, then so be it. I will tell you what you already know."

Kaili flashed on Anela's bedroom in the House of Nepenthe. She saw her sister on the floor, struggling with a man who was now dead.

"Please... tell me."

Anela stood and backed away.

"You have not avenged me. Not completely." The words echoed. "G was not the one who killed me. He had a hand in it, yes, but it was not his hand that held the knife."

"Natalie," said Kaili.

"Yes. Natalie."

"But... how do I find her? She disappeared like G did. It was blind luck that—"

"His name was not G," said Anela, the weight of her smile seeming to pull her head to the side. "His name was Gordon King."

Kaili sat up straighter.

"I have a name now," she said, almost tripping over the words. "I can find her through him."

Anela nodded.

"And when I do find her..."

"You can drive a knife through *her* heart."

A warmth built in Kaili's chest. She smiled.

"Thank you, Annie. I won't let you down."

Again, she touched Kaili's cheek. "You could not, even if you tried." Anela pulled back and struck Kaili across the face. The sudden jolt broke the silence, and the roar of the helicopter blades winding down filled her ears.

She blinked away the bright lights of the mausoleum, saw Raven's face come into focus.

"Hey, are you with me?" she screamed. Raven pulled back again but stopped when Kaili put up a hand.

"I'm with you," she said, flexing her jaw to ease the sting.

"Sorry I had to hit you. I just thought... you were in shock or something."

Kaili looked around. They had landed in the parking lot of some mall. Several people in similar dress were approaching.

"Where are we?" she asked.

"Folsom City."

In front of her, Trent tossed down his headset and got out. A moment later, the door next to Kaili's seat slid open. He took off his sunglasses to greet her.

"Good to see you again, kid."

She reached for him. He helped her out of the helicopter and onto solid ground.

"You too," she said, giving him a perfunctory hug.

"You're all gassed and ready to go." He pointed to a blue SUV idling nearby. "Can I get you anything for the ride?"

"Can you get the ciphers working on something?"

Trent looked past her to Raven, nodded. "Sure, yeah, what do you need?"

"I want a search running." Kaili saw Anela standing near the SUV. She smiled and got into the open rear door.

"For what?" asked Trent.

She looked him in the eye, smiled. "Gordon King. Austin, Texas."

Again, that furtive glance at Raven, as if he needed confirmation that Kaili was crazy. She pretended not to notice.

"He's uh… he's dead, kid. We just…"

Kaili put a hand on his shoulder. "I know, Trent." She nodded slowly. "I know he's dead because I'm the one who put a bullet in his brain. It's not him I'm interested in."

"Then who?"

"Someone he used to know. A woman named Natalie."

Kaili turned away and walked with her shoulders back and chin up to the SUV. She found Anela sitting in the middle seat, scrunched up against Rick, who had an elbow on the far door and was staring pensively out the window.

"Come on," said Anela, patting the seat next to her. "Plenty of room."

SIXTY-TWO
TANZY

It was well into the evening before Tanzy was allowed to leave Zend Garden Terminus.

Sacramento PD arrived only a few minutes after Calle Cinco flew away with the Butcher of Burbank, and though Tanzy had considered telling Cleo to reroute them, one look at Cyn had changed her mind. Lincoln's mechanical muscle had been shot in the stomach, and despite her brave face, Tanzy could tell Cyn was worried about the damage. Cleo called for an ambulance even before the police cruisers arrived.

For a while, Tanzy sat in a daze on the ground while SPD officers in tidy black uniforms swarmed the terminus. They came with guns drawn, but it didn't take them long to figure out the threat had passed. There was little fight in the people still left alive—Cyn was shot, Bryce cared only for her health, and Tanzy...

Tanzy didn't know what to think.

She couldn't stop looking back and forth between Kevin Costner's bullet-riddled body and Gordon King lying flat on his back. If it weren't for the pool of blood around his head, someone might have mistaken him for taking a sudden nap in a heavily trafficked area. Tanzy knew the truth, however.

Kaili Zabora had shot him—point blank—right between the eyes. There were no augments she knew of that would have protected him from a .357 slug to the skull. His only chance of survival would have been for Tanzy to go back in time and stop the entire endeavor before it started. And though she didn't seriously entertain the idea of time travel, she did consider the decisions she had made and how they had led to the deaths of two people.

Cleo tried to feed her a line about how it wasn't Tanzy who pulled the triggers that killed Kevin and Gordon.

And while that was true, it didn't mean Tanzy wouldn't have to face the people left behind. Lincoln Tate was fiercely loyal to his employees, and even the loss of someone as young and inexperienced as Kevin would be felt. Gordon had no connections Tanzy knew of, though Cyn seemed to be taken with him. Would she blame Tanzy for the mess? Or would she just be happy to be alive?

An SPD officer who identified himself as Sanders kept trying to get Tanzy to talk about what had happened, why two people were dead and one had been shot, but she refused to answer his questions. Cleo had already alerted the I.C.E-1 legal staff, and one of her lawyers was coming to extricate her from the sticky situation.

With nothing to do or say, she simply sat and watched as Cyn was loaded into an ambulance. Bryce tried to get in with her, but a trio of SPD officers stopped him.

They sat him on the ground near the BMW.

Someone covered Gordon and Kevin with white sheets.

Sometime later, a small helicopter flew overhead and disturbed the sheets. Both fluttered in the turbulent wind, revealing the cold bodies beneath. The helicopter was Lincoln's, and though Tanzy didn't dare take out her phone, Cleo relayed the messages back and forth. She told Lincoln to stay away; the fire was too hot.

He went silent after finding out that Cyn had been shot.

Everything was silent for a while.

Cleo occasionally broke in with some update, but Tanzy hardly listened. Her mind kept going back to the shooting, to the bullets whizzing past her head. The images bubbled up out of a seemingly infinite well of fear, a well Tanzy hadn't known was there. She didn't want to talk to Cleo about it, but no doubt the pseudo-AI had seen the spike in her heart rate and the sudden rush of adrenaline into her body.

Maybe she'd even tried to regulate it.

I did, said Cleo.

"Don't do that." Tanzy rubbed her face.

There was just so much happening, and you panicked, so I panicked, and…

"You're not supposed to panic," she replied, under her breath.

I'm sorry. I thought we were going to die.

"You can't die, Cleo."

Office Sanders glanced over at Tanzy and eyed her suspiciously.

I die if you die. I'm not backed up anywhere. I wouldn't want to live in anyone else's head, so once you're gone, I'm gone.

Tanzy hadn't really thought of Cleo as someone who could die. She was a pseudo-AI, nothing more… a series of preprogrammed responses with an advanced linguistic interface.

But not real.

Not alive enough to die.

Cleo said nothing more, and perhaps through her vast network of sensors— or maybe just her uncanny ability to read Tanzy's mind—she realized it was better to remain quiet, to keep things calm while they were still under the watchful eye of SPD.

But once the I.C.E-1 lawyer arrived—a tall, dark-skinned woman Tanzy had never met before—Cleo ramped up her chattiness again, as if deciding for the both of them that it was time to get back to work.

It took the lawyer only ten minutes to clear Tanzy and another five to do the same for Bryce. She said nothing to the two of them beyond inviting them to follow her out of Zend Garden. She led them past rows of SPD cruisers with flashing lights and uniforms milling around them. They turned a corner onto a cross street, and before Tanzy could ask if they were walking back to Portland, a car pulled up and stopped a hair's width from the curb.

The lawyer—Tanzy didn't get her name—gestured to the rear passenger door. Bryce opened it, helped Tanzy inside, and then climbed in after her. The door shut behind him, and the tight-lipped lawyer disappeared before Tanzy could even thank her.

Her retainer is compensation enough, said Cleo.

The car pulled away, started putting distance between them and the disaster at Zend Garden. Bryce immediately pulled out his phone and started checking his messages.

"Do you want to go see Cyn?" asked Tanzy. "Cleo, where's the nearest hospital?"

"They didn't take her to the hospital," said Bryce. "Lincoln redirected them to a private medical facility on the west side of town." He leaned forward to talk to the driver. "Do you know Riverside Parkway? It's uh, near the... IKEA, I guess."

"Text me the address, sir," said the driver.

Tanzy left Bryce to his phone, turned to the window. The lights of Sacramento were too bright for her taste. At first, she thought it was just the tall buildings and oppressive brand names hanging in the sky, but as they got farther from downtown, she realized it was actually the streetlights that bothered her. They were too white, too cold—exactly the kind of harsh anti-crime glare she would expect in a big city.

Not like Portland.

Not like the warm glow of the ornate lamps of Downtown—a light so soft one could rest their head against it. Tanzy thought of the lamp on the curb outside Cloves & Poetry, how its auburn pole had been covered up by remnants of band posters and employment offers and stickers calling for an outright ban on meat.

How she longed to be standing under it again.

Broadcast message from Lincoln Tate. Cyn is stable. I'm with her.

Bryce's phone chimed; he sighed. He seemed to relax then, but a few minutes later, his knee was bouncing rapidly. Finally, he turned to Tanzy and spoke.

"So what now?"

The question caught her off guard. The way he'd been fidgeting, Tanzy thought he was angry with her, thought he might launch into a rant about how everything was her fault and none of this would have happened if they'd stuck to the original plan of getting revenge for Johnny.

Or was that Danny's rant?

"What do you mean?" asked Tanzy. "We're going to join the others…"

"Don't play dumb. You know what I mean."

He wants revenge, said Cleo.

Tanzy nodded. Of course he did. That was the only way anything happened these days. Someone was wronged, they tried to right that wrong, and someone else got wronged.

Repeat as necessary until everyone was dead.

"I have no plan," said Tanzy, though what she really wanted to say was *I just want to go home.*

She wanted to go back to Portland, back to her comfortable chair in her office where she could jack in and be with her girls. She wanted free-range chicken and quaint, non-binary bookstores. More than anything, she just wanted to be done with everyone for a while. The next time someone said the name *Kaili Zabora*, Tanzy wasn't sure she would be able to keep herself from screaming.

Bryce nodded, as if he understood something Tanzy herself was unaware of.

"You will," he said, "and when you do, Cyn and I are gonna be ready. Lincoln too. He told you what happened to Decker Plaza, right?"

Tanzy shook her head.

Searching…

Bryce pulled up an article on his phone and handed it over. The featured image at the top of the page was a wide shot of the Umbra Canopy and a long plume of smoke rising from it.

Terror in Umbra: Responsibility for Building Destruction Remains Unclaimed.

Because someone always claimed responsibility.

Because nothing ever happened that wasn't retribution for something else.

"Did… did everyone get out okay?" she asked.

"Yeah, I think so. Lincoln said no one should have been in the building when it got hit."

They destroyed an entire building, said Cleo. *We could have been in there.*

Tanzy nodded.

Cleo considered, more emphatically. *We should have walked away at Hotel Fritz. Someone was shooting at us. They were trying to kill us. What good is revenge if we're dead?*

"Okay, I get it." She put a hand to her head as if to reassure Cleo.

A large, yellow IKEA sign glowed in the night sky. The car slowed and drifted toward an exit. A few stoplights later, it pulled up to the curb of a small strip mall anchored by a twenty-four-hour urgent care facility.

Bryce opened his door as soon as the car stopped. He even got as far as the clinic's awning before realizing Tanzy wasn't following. He stopped, returned to her window.

She tried to think of what she would say as the glass sank into the door. Something of an apology formed on her tongue, but she swallowed it. The harsh light from the clinic entrance cast Bryce in silhouette, and in that moment, she realized she didn't really know this man she was about to placate. Somehow, he had made her feel ashamed for what she was about to do.

"What's up?" he asked, putting his hand on the door. "Are you coming or what?"

"No," said Tanzy, trying to keep her voice even. "I'm not."

Bryce smirked a little. "Okay, then I guess we'll see you back in Umbra?"

"I'm done here," she said. "Maybe you and Cyn can stomach being shot at, or being shot, but I can't. I thought I could handle this, but... this isn't for me. I need to make my moves from behind a desk like a real suit."

She suddenly understood Danny's reluctance to get involved in the Kaili rescue. He knew he didn't belong out in the real world where his handle was more ironic than fear-inducing. She should have followed his lead. Maybe Gordon and Kevin would still be alive then.

Bryce nodded.

"It's been a ride, Tanzy," he said. "I'm sure we'll see you again."

"Not in person."

His fingers slipped from the door as the window rose.

"Where to now, ma'am?" asked the driver.

"Airport." Then to Cleo. "Book us a flight home. Something in first class. I need a drink."

You're not even going to say goodbye?

"Why?" asked Tanzy. "We failed. There's nothing sadder than a bunch of losers standing around commiserating about how everything went wrong. You know that's not me."

I know you care about them, whether you want to admit it or not. Especially Danny.

She scoffed, whipped her head as if she could turn away from Cleo. Outside the window, the city sank as the car climbed a ramp onto the elevated highway. The engine purred, though to Tanzy, it sounded like someone grumbling.

Cleo may have been right about Danny. Tanzy did care about him, but only as a vestige of a past that was rapidly receding in her memory. Their relationship now was nothing more than a reminiscent curiosity, a bridge she assumed was there, but when she reached out an exploratory foot…

Tanzy tried to steer her mind to something else.

"Danny's a lost cause," she blurted. "A failure just like the rest of us."

Tires rolled against the highway, creating a comforting hum.

Danny didn't fail.

"What do you mean?"

According to the Quatrain, Danny has removed Brigham Plaza from VNet and dumped its contents to the world. The girls are watching it live in VR if you want to—

Tanzy leaned back in the seat and closed her eyes.

"Show me."

SIXTY-THREE
CYNTHIA

They gave her something for the pain, but the mil-spec Ayudante biochip in Cyn's neck wasn't having it.

She felt every bump of the road as the ambulance tore down the rotting streets of Sacramento, destined for a place that felt more and more far away with every passing minute. The EMTs were hard at work packing the wound in her stomach, pressing their gloved fingers into the bullet hole, ostensibly looking for the offending slug.

Their efforts, however, only made things worse. It wasn't exactly pain Cyn felt, just a kind of mild discomfort as something sharp dug further into the subdermal braiding in her abdomen. Dunlap had installed the internal bulletproof vest the year before, weaving the fibers of the braid over the course of several months and dozens of endoscopic procedures. Cyn recalled the boredom and the resulting stiffness from all that time in the chair, but it had been worth it.

She could feel the gunshot just below her ribs, and she knew that if the bullet had pushed any harder, it would have torn through her intestines and left a gaping hole in her back. Fortunately, the braid had held strong against the .357, had kept the sizzling piece of metal just below the skin but away from her organs.

The Ayudante biochip fought against the constant drip of morphine, trying to keep her alert by focusing on sights and sounds. Everything else—the chill of the ambulance, the smell of rubber gloves, and the taste of metal in her throat—was dulled, relegated to the back shelf. Instead, she listened to the EMTs discuss her injury and coordinate with a nearby emergency room.

They were both young and male, with clean-shaven faces and pressed blue shirts. Cyn had the fleeting desire to talk to them, but there was no way to get the words out. She was trapped in her own body, unable to move anything more than the eyes in her head. She was aware of the straps holding her to the stretcher, but her augments should have been able to tear through the thin nylon with ease.

This was something else, something deeper in her program.

After a while, Cyn realized she was just hurt.

Finally, after years of flirting with danger, she had taken serious damage, and no amount of mental gymnastics or harsh language would change that. She gleaned from the conversation around her that the bullet was still inside, that it had fused with the metal braiding, and that trying to pull it out now would just cause more damage. There was nothing they could do except control the bleeding until they arrived at the hospital.

Cyn sank into her body. The darkness in her periphery rose up like the sides of a grave. Bright lights and harsh beeping receded, as did the youthful faces of the men who were trying to save her life. It was their show now, and she didn't have the energy to watch.

She shut her eyes.

In the darkness, she imagined the red hot Ayudante in her neck grinding away at her willpower, asking her over and over if she really wanted to give up. The chip, of course, would keep fighting to the bitter end, and it would drag her with it if she so chose.

She opted for sleep instead; the morphine made it easy.

A muddled dream formed from blacks and grays. Cyn stood in the garage of some cookie-cutter home and tried to shoo away a transient who refused to leave. And though she could have killed him with her bare hands, something kept her from attacking him. There was nothing she could do, and the helplessness of the situation weighed on her and lingered even after she woke up.

The lights were down in the small room. Cyn tried to pick shapes out of the haze, saw a vidscreen on the far wall, a window to the left, and two chairs with shadowy figures in them on her right. Both were slumped back in the chairs as if sleeping. Cyn blinked, waited until she could see Lincoln and Bryce clearly before clearing her throat.

They both stirred at the same time.

Lincoln sat up straight and tugged at the sleeves on his purple shirt. His custom jacket was missing, though Cyn wasn't sure if he'd simply taken it off or forgotten it.

"How long have I been out?" she asked, looking to the window. The blinds were down, but she could see darkness outside.

Bryce got up and came to the bed. He slipped his fingers around her wrist. "Couple hours," he replied. "They had to bring in a specialist to cut the bullet out. Dunlap said he wanted to come into town to do it, but there wasn't time."

"He just didn't want them to mess it up," said Cyn. "He knows he'll have to fix it anyway." A white noise machine whirring away from a shelf by the window entered her awareness, as did the sticky tape on her abdomen.

"He did say to come see him when you were feeling better."

Cyn stretched against her wound, found the edge of pain, and relented.

"Where is everyone?" she asked. "Tanzy? Danny? Where are the *cops*?"

Lincoln shook his head. "No cops. We had the ambulance rerouted. You're at a private medical facility. As far as the police are concerned, you never showed up at Mercy General."

"Tanzy went home," said Bryce, "and Danny…" He looked to Lincoln, who shrugged. "He went home too. I guess they'd both had enough of the real shit."

Cyn felt a frown creep onto her face as she looked at Lincoln.

"Bryce told you about Kevin?"

"He did."

She made a fist, but Bryce smoothed out her hand again.

"We should have bailed at the first mention of Kaili Zabora."

"You couldn't have known," said Bryce.

"What? That she would shoot me again? No, I think I should have seen that coming."

And why hadn't she? Had everything moved too quickly for her to get a proper grip on it? She walked backward through the timeline, trying to pinpoint the exact moment she'd stopped paying attention to what was happening. And though she could see a moment in time, she didn't know when it was, only who was there.

Gordon.

"Shoot me once, shame on you," said Bryce.

"Shoot me twice, you better kill me," said Cyn, gritting her teeth against a sudden ache in her stomach. "Part of me wants to be done with her, but another part, a louder part, wants her to pay for what she did to me, and Kevin, and Gordon."

Lincoln sighed. It was obvious he didn't agree, but it was likewise clear he understood what needed to be done. She didn't have to press him on anything; he would be there to help once she was ready to fight again.

"Maybe we can just release some compromising stills from her video," said Cyn. "Put all her business out there for the world to see."

Bryce tossed a glance at Lincoln again.

"Stop doing that," said Cyn. "If you have something to say, say it. Stop trying to figure out what's okay to tell me."

"You remember Johnny San Vito, right?" asked Lincoln. "The guy who paid us to find Gordon?"

Cyn nodded.

"Well, he found something in VNet, some kind of cache of Vinestead secrets. Whoever those secrets belonged to had him killed. Then Danny came along…"

She looked to Bryce. "I thought you said he went home."

"He did," continued Lincoln, "but not before dumping all of those Vinestead secrets out in the open. Everything from the fall of the Net to internal emails showing Vinestead was at fault for Calle Cinco de Mayo. And yes, even the video of Kaili Zabora getting abducted. It's all out there, even the name of the Vinestead employee—Julius Parker, also known as Jape."

The names meant nothing to Cyn.

"He's the one who ordered the strike on Decker Plaza. Him, not Vinestead. Danny would be a dead man if I hadn't gotten him out."

The words almost didn't register.

"Wait, what?" asked Cyn.

Lincoln sighed. "It was a single drone. One little missile. And now the whole building is dust. But don't worry. Everyone got out safe. I've got people working on getting our backup broadcast going."

"Oh my god." The Ayudante picked up her elevated heart rate and tried to settle it. "I can't believe they would do that. They must have really wanted Danny dead."

"It would seem," said Lincoln, lowering his voice.

"And you just let him go after all that?"

Lincoln's response was a soft laughter that made Cyn feel warm inside. He followed it up with a tired groan.

"I only found out after I dropped Danny off. If I had known… he and I probably would've had words." He shrugged. "But I don't think he saw it coming either. It's one thing to off a famous hacker like Johnny San Vito, but to take down an entire building? In Umbra? Belonging to *me*? That's just desperation, and after seeing some of that dirty laundry, I can understand why. That Julius Parker, wherever he is right now, is a dead man walking. Vinestead is gonna disappear him quick fast, if they haven't already."

"So what I'm hearing," said Cyn, rolling her head on the pillow, "is that you're free to help me with Kaili. Because someone's gotta pay for this hole in my stomach, and it's not gonna be me."

"I think the drugs are affecting your hearing, girl," said Lincoln. He crossed one leg over the other. "There will be a time and a place to deal with Kaili Zabora. But right now, we've got more immediate work to do. Lincoln Continental needs to get back on the air before Banks Media sneaks into the Big Three again. We've got to make arrangements for Kevin and Gordon. I don't know if he had any personal effects, but we might want to get those back to his people."

"He didn't have people," said Cyn, shaking her head. "Unless you count the preppers at Lost Pines. He's got an ex-girlfriend in Germany he hasn't seen in twenty years, and maybe a son he's never seen."

"Well, maybe his kin would want some of that cash he was carrying around in his bag."

Cyn felt the weight of the implication, tried to squirm out from under the unasked question.

"I'm not going to—"

"Then there's the matter of getting my story from Mr. Montreal. Now that the world has seen what he's uncovered, they'll want to know how he did it."

"Fine," said Cyn, trying again to make herself heard, "I'll do that, but I'm not going—"

"Hey," said Bryce. "I heard you. We're not going to Germany. We're not going anywhere you don't want to go. There's work here with Lincoln if we want it, but I roll with you, Cynthia. You tell me what you want, and we'll do that."

It was so much easier knowing what other people wanted. Lincoln wanted to send her to Germany for a scoop. Bryce wanted her to see the man standing in front of her holding her hand. The Ayudante wanted her to get out of bed and keep fighting.

And really, that's what Cyn wanted too.

More than anything, she wanted to fight. She wanted to inflict pain and feel pain, shoot and be shot, kill and be killed. If she didn't fight, then what was the point of all the augments in her body? If she didn't fight, what would she do with her time other than waste it in the arms of muscled men with empty heads?

What do I want?

The question seemed ridiculous, so outside the cycle of doing jobs and getting paid and buying augments so she could do jobs and get paid and buy more augments. There was no pursuit worthier than self-improvement, to become stronger, faster, and deadlier, so that one day she could…

Could what?

Cyn closed her eyes, tried to make sense of it in the dark.

The futility of the cycle was clear. Even if she directed her ire at Kaili Zabora, it would not change what would come after—a return to the loop, to the self-improvement, to the prep for the next target, be that Vinestead or anyone else unlucky enough to get in her way.

Was that her entire purpose?

To kill?

To be a whirlwind of death until she dissipated in the last echoes of thunder, having taken a few unfortunate souls with her?

Cyn opened her eyes, touched the blankets draped over her chest. She could feel the hospital gown against her skin, the socks covering her feet. The bed was by no means plush, but it was better than the hood of the BMW or the cold asphalt of Zend Garden Terminus.

"I don't think our girl knows what she wants," said Lincoln, his voice condescending yet soft.

Bryce patted her hand. "You've got time to figure it out. Gut shots are some of the hardest to come back from. It's like having a C-section."

"What would you know about that?" asked Cyn.

"Just that you'll probably pee when you laugh," said Bryce.

"Sheeeit," said Lincoln.

She turned to him, mouth tight.

"Well," she said, "then it's a good thing neither of you could joke your way out of a wet paper bag."

Lincoln shrugged, said nothing.

"Is there anything I can get you?" asked Bryce. "I think we're gonna be here a while."

"No," she said, patting his hand. "I just need to rest my eyes."

He gave her a puzzled look, said, "Alright then."

Of course he was confused.

Cynthia Mesquina didn't rest, didn't seek comfort in the dream world.

She was either fighting… or she was dead.

But that was the old Cyn and the old cycle.

Now she was on a new path.

Cyn closed her eyes again and dreamed of dropping her trench coat in Gordon's room at Hotel Forever. Only this time, she was wearing nothing underneath, and Gordon came to her without protest.

SIXTY-FOUR

DANNY

Marcelo picked Danny up from Denver International Airport shortly after midnight.

A single call to the Ernst Group had set everything in motion, such that when Lincoln dropped him in an empty field on the north side of Sacramento, there was already a car waiting to take him to the airport.

He'd flown coach, preferring to get home sooner rather than wait for a private plane or one with first class seating. The flight itself had gone by quickly, and the woman in the seat next to him had avoided eye contact the entire time. Arriving in Denver without luggage—his bag was buried under a mountain of rubble in Umbra—he was able to head directly out of the airport and into the waiting Land Rover.

Marcelo, who a week ago had delivered Jane right to his doorstep, spoke very little on the trip, and Danny wondered if the man had been roused from sleep or robbed of an evening with his family. The idea that someone out there could be living a life completely separate from Danny's baffled him, though he knew it was happening all the time. He half-expected Marcelo to mention something about VNet, about the secrets Danny and Lassiter had unleashed onto the world. But the more they drove, the more Danny realized Marcelo cared little for that world.

In some ways, Danny envied the driver and the simplicity of his life.

Whatever happened now, whatever the fallout from Brigham Plaza, Danny pledged to keep his life simple. No more adventures in Umbra. No more firefights or crumbling buildings.

No more leaving Vail.

He would do his work, watch his TV, and play his video games all in the safety of his own home. The Ernst Group and Adelai Associates would take care of the rest.

They pulled into the small clearing in front of Danny's cabin just after three in the morning. After thanking Marcelo, Danny headed inside to find his home exactly as he'd left it except for a few items. The bed had been made, the kitchen cleaned, and the outer shades on the glass shower walls drawn. A fire roared in the living room, and by the feel of the cabin, had been doing so for a few hours.

It was a warm welcome only in the literal sense.

He would have preferred to find Jane waiting for him just inside the door, cozy in her yoga pants and billowy sweater. She would ask him how his day was, and he'd tell her about how he'd gone toe-to-toe with Vinestead and come out victorious. She'd laugh, smile, and throw her arms around him.

None of that happened, of course, or could happen, not with the strict rules Adelai Associates set for their employees. But, standing there in the foyer, rocking slowly from one foot to another, Danny imagined it, imagined Jane's lips breaking apart as she said his name.

When the fantasy ended, blurring back into the reality of his empty cabin, he felt the weight of a nightmarish fatigue press on him, as if someone had strapped a two-hundred-pound backpack to his shoulders. He trudged to the shower and spent minutes at a time leaning against the cold glass as the water poured down. There was fresh blood on the bandage on his leg, but when he removed the gauze, he found the wound had already closed up again. A defiant stitch stood up from the skin, having popped out of position sometime during his escape.

Danny crawled into bed and managed to summon the energy to command the lights off before his head hit the pillow. He fell into a deep, empty sleep where he walked the perimeter of Brigham Plaza under a lightly falling snow. There was no Julius scamming Domino's for pizza, no explosion in the dormant and dark Blockbuster Video. The parking lot was empty, covered in a gray snow that could have been ash.

A shrill alarm woke him up.

His sliver buzzed, and when he pulled it into view, red text flashed.

Perimeter breach.

Danny groaned.

There was no doubt in his mind who his visitor was. He wasn't naïve enough to think Julius Parker wouldn't follow him out of Umbra, but he had hoped for a little more time to recuperate.

He eyed the clock on his sliver.

Barely 10:00 a.m.

The sun would be up, melting the fresh snow on the trees surrounding the cabin, creating small circles of lazy rain that pocked the powder around their trunks. It was a perfect start to a week of staying inside and ignoring the outside world, and Julius had come to ruin it.

Danny pulled a pair of neatly folded jeans from the nearby dresser and a black undershirt from the drawer below it. He dressed while walking to the front door, still groggy, still feeling invisible hands trying to pull him back to bed. Sunlight streamed in through the door's small window, refracting through the beveled edges.

The door creaked softly as he opened it.

There was no one on the porch or in the clearing, but Danny heard the soft rustling of a rocking chair's treads moving through snow. To his left, he saw an older man sitting in the chair, his hands hidden in the pockets of a thick jacket that came down to his knees. His carefully coiffed hair was stiff in the breeze and had collected flakes of snow that hadn't melted yet.

Julius Parker had been outside for a while; had he walked all the way up to the cabin?

He didn't look at Danny but spoke as if he'd already had his words prepared hours ago.

"Well, someone had a rough night."

"Is that what you call escaping a building moments before it's destroyed by a surgical strike?" asked Danny.

He thought for a moment about joining Julius at the rocking chairs but decided against it. It was safer at the door, safer to be in leaping range of cover if and when the shooting started.

Julius nodded, rubbed his chin against his raised collar.

"I told you I was coming for you. You should have taken me seriously."

"And you should have taken the *no trespassing* signs at the gate seriously. You're on private property. I could gun you down right now and not even get a slap on the wrist."

A smirk. "Yeah, no. You may be *Guns* in the net, but out here, you're just Daniel Antoine du Montreal." He sucked his teeth. "Stupid fucking name, if you ask me."

"You have no idea who I am, *Jape*."

The chair rocked back a few times.

"Don't get all defensive. Gunning people down isn't my thing either. I mean, I tell other people to do it all the time, but I wouldn't do it personally. That's not us. We're hackers. Terrareal isn't our preferred arena."

"So then why are you here?"

"Well, it's the funniest thing, but I need you to come with me to Vinestead West. There are a few rumors I need to quash and a few stories to set straight. After that, I'm gonna kill you, like I promised earlier. Again, not me personally, but you know what I mean."

Danny leaned against the doorjamb.

"And you thought I'd come? Just like that?"

"No, no. I have some men coming up the road. They're gonna help me bring you in."

It sounded like a bluff, but Danny couldn't be sure. That Julius was still alive was itself surprising, but for him to still be in the good graces of Vinestead enough to command a squad of men? It didn't make sense.

"Some men, huh? And they're fine with taking orders from someone who buried all of Vinestead's skeletons in a shallow grave in VNet where anyone could come along and dig it up? Do these men have no honor?"

"Honor," repeated Julius, dipping his head. "Honor among hackers. Like such a thing exists. I was playing every angle long before you first touched a keyboard. You have no idea what I've done to secure my place at Vinestead. And as for the men, no, they have no honor. You have to have feelings to have honor."

A warm, uneasy sickness grew in Danny's stomach. He pushed away from the doorjamb and walked to the edge of the porch. Were synthetics really coming to take him away?

"I'm surprised you're using synthetics. Seems risky."

"Synthetics don't talk."

Danny turned, leaned against the wooden rail. "Maybe not to aggregators, but what if they call home and find out you're no longer employed at Vinestead?"

Julius leaned forward and stood up. He came to stand near Danny at the railing. He was tall, with a good six inches of height advantage. His eyes never looked directly at Danny, just kind of stared into the distance, as if disinterested by everything directly around him.

"Is that what your cockiness is based on, Daniel? You think Vinestead turned against me just because you opened Pandora's box? You don't know how things work there."

"I have an idea. That's why you're here. You're hoping if you give them me, they'll let you live."

Julius bounced an eyebrow. He let out a long breath.

"Let's say you're right. Maybe I am in deep shit. *Maybe*, they don't know that Lassiter is gone yet, and when they find out, they're going to crucify me. And I mean that literally—naked, hanging from a cross, nails in the hands, the whole thing. So then it would make perfect sense that I would give them you instead. You, Danny Guns Montreal, a poster boy for a generation of impotent hackers who think they're more powerful than the men who hold the keys to the network, will take the blame. You'll go down in history as the man who unleashed Lassiter onto this world. *You*, not me."

Strange. Julius had made no mention of the other secrets—Kaili's video, Calle Cinco de Mayo, the House of Nepenthe—just the supposed artificial intelligence, which meant either Lassiter was extremely close to a true AI, or worse, he *was* a true AI. Danny hadn't given Lassiter any instructions beyond spreading the Brigham data far and wide, which the AI had evidently done.

But with that task complete, what was Lassiter up to now?

Danny made a mental note to check it out.

"Look," he said, checking his sliver, "I've got an interview with Lincoln Continental this evening that I really need to rest up for."

Julius nodded to the driveway on the other side of the clearing.

"I think you're going to need to reschedule."

Danny watched as two large, black Suburbans pulled soundlessly into the clearing. Their engines must have been fully electric, and even their tires seemed to absorb the natural crunching of the snow. The SUVs stopped on opposite sides of the clearing. Four identical men exited from each vehicle and flanked the steps. One came forward and pulled a small handgun from his hip.

"We need you to come with us, sir."

Julius, who had finally deigned to look at Danny, smiled mischievously. After a moment, he said, "You heard the man, Daniel. Time to close the loop on Brigham Plaza."

Danny studied the lead synthetic. He looked like any random man in black from a shady government organization. His suit and jacket were impeccably fitted, clean, and smooth.

The only thing missing was dark sunglasses.

Without them, Danny could clearly see the synthetic's eyes. There was nothing remarkable about them—cold, gray, no LED backlighting—but one noticeable property was that they weren't looking at Danny.

"I think he's talking to you, chief," said Danny.

Julius turned. "What? ST1, take this man into custody."

"Your clearance has been revoked, sir," said ST1. "I have orders to bring you in. I suggest you comply."

The color drained from Julius' face.

"Guess they called home," said Danny.

"You son of a bitch!"

Julius lunged, but the sudden splintering of wood by his waist stopped him cold. He looked down at the shattered railing. In the clearing, the waiting synthetics all pulled their weapons.

Before Danny could say anything, the synthetics were rushing the porch. He backed out of the way, retreating toward the door as two of the men grabbed Julius by the arms. One synthetic came near Danny, but he kept his back to him, boxing him out of the action.

They dragged Julius from the porch screaming and kicking. His curses echoed into the clearing, in the beautiful December morning, until the door to the Suburban slammed shut, and all was silent again. The SUVs padded softly to the driveway and disappeared into the trees.

It had all happened so fast that Danny had forgotten to breathe. He stood for a moment, collecting himself, amazed by the speed and coordination of the synthetics. His mind raced with visions of a completely synthetic police force, an all-synthetic military force, an all-synthetic—

Movement in the trees caught his attention. Two men in white coveralls came lumbering out of the high snow. To the left and right, two more joined their approach. All of them carried muzzled assault rifles wrapped in white cloth.

Danny didn't know their names, but he knew who they were with.

One of the men raised a hand in greeting.

"That wasn't too close, was it?"

Danny examined the splintered railing. It had only been a few feet from where he was standing.

"The mailbox at the end of the drive would have been too close," he replied, garnering a chuckle from the man on the left.

"We're gonna do a quick sweep and then reset positions. I know it's your show, but I'd recommend not letting them come up the drive again. If he comes back, we should take him off-property."

Danny smirked. "He won't be coming back, but I take your point. Thanks for looking out for me."

The man touched the rim of his snowcap. "The Ernst Group has your back," he said. "Welcome home, sir."

Danny nodded to the men and turned for the door. It shut softly behind him. For a moment, he let the heat of the cabin wash over him. Somewhere in the back of his head, a reminder was circling the drain of his conscious thought. He reached for it, tried to pull it into focus, tried to pull the repeating word into view.

Finally, it coalesced, and he opened his eyes.

"Lassiter."

EPILOGUE
JANE

Carter Michael Price seemed more like a nervous child than the wunderkind CEO of a software company called Dyalogued.

For all the detail in his dossier, the list of achievements and honors he'd accumulated since launching the company when he was just sixteen, Jane had expected a man wise beyond his years, perhaps in a well-fitted suit that spoke to his power and wealth. Instead, when Jane stepped off the elevator into the penthouse, Carter greeted her in a dark green t-shirt tucked into his jeans. Instead of styled hair worthy of a corporate directory headshot, his stringy blond locks hung down over his ears and occasionally drifted over his eyes.

He was twenty years old, and he stammered when he spoke, as if he had never had the full, focused attention of a woman. That would change in time, of course. There would be plenty of women in his future, opportunists who wanted to entangle themselves with a rich man.

But that night, on a Thursday before Valentine's Day, he was alone in a city of millions, a city that swallowed newly rich tech moguls whole on a daily basis.

"I've never done anything like this before," he explained, spit out really, as he took Jane's coat and hung it on the rack just inside the foyer. "A colleague set this up for me. I'm not even sure what I'm supposed to call you."

"My name is Jane. Jane Maxwell." She held out a hand in invitation, as he didn't seem to want to come any closer.

"Ok, hi Jane." He took her hand and nearly started to sweat as he tried to decide whether to shake it or kiss it. In the end, he gave her two quick pumps and dropped her hand as if afraid to be seen holding it.

Jane hid a smirk as Carter scurried to the bar where he had already prepared a drink for himself.

"My name is Ronald," he said. "I… can I make you a drink?"

"What are you drinking, Ronald?" Jane dropped her clutch on a small table near the coat rack and noticed a small leather valet with an assortment of code cards in it. Gifts from the hotel, no doubt.

"Red Bull and vodka, but I can make you anything. I have a list here with all the ingredients." He searched the bar ineffectually before leaning over it to snag a laminated sheet from the other side.

Jane laid one foot deliberately in front of the other, following a straight line to the bar, not stopping until she was well within Carter AKA Ronald's personal space. She reached for the drink in his hand and had to practically pry the sweating glass from his death grip. The drink clinked on the bar.

"I don't feel like hard liquor tonight," she said, placing the daintiest of hands on his chest. He squirmed immediately, and his eyes jumped to the open door leading into the bedroom. "How about we open a bottle of wine and find out what's at the bottom?"

Carter forced himself to nod.

"Good." She tapped him lightly. "Why don't you go get comfy by the fire, and I'll choose something from the rack?"

He went without protest, and Jane wasn't sure he would have known what to protest even if he'd wanted to. The wine should have already been open and breathing on the bar by the time she walked in. Two glasses, washed and spot-free, should have been sitting beside it. Within a few minutes of her arrival, after a proper greeting at the door, he should have offered to pour her a glass.

Etiquette aside, he seemed an innocuous if not slightly boring person. He still had a young metabolism, and whether he worked out or ate right made no difference. His eyes were a light shade of gray; both they and the face around it were free from augmentations, piercings, and tattoos.

Just a normal guy.

Just a normal engagement.

Jane had been hoping for an uneventful evening. Though her body was present in the St. Regis penthouse, wrapped in a red dress so tight it affected her breathing, her mind was back in a coffee shop in World Trade Center 1, at a table near the window where she had spent every Friday afternoon since Christmas sipping a Chai latte and waiting for Danny.

Carter was adjusting pillows on the white leather couch when she arrived with two thick pours of an aged Malbec. Jane sat down next to him, handed him a glass, and raised her own. They toasted to *tonight*, an idea right out of Jane's standard playbook for situations where there was no real reason for her and her client to be together. There was no shared history, no previous moment to inform the next. The only story she had was the one in his dossier, so for the next hour, they talked about his business and how he had come into so much success so early.

Jane only half-listened as Carter drank and talked, talked and drank. His eyes, which had previously only glanced at her body, now lingered on her like a child's eyeing toys in a store window. The wine worked its magic, and every time it went empty, Jane dutifully refilled it. She was pouring a newly opened third bottle when he said something that made her hand slip. Red wine splashed onto his leg and the couch.

"Oh, I'm so sorry," she said, pawing a dark spot on his jeans.

"It's not a problem." His speech was relaxed almost to the point of slurring. "It's not my couch."

"No, I know. God." Jane hurried to the bar and retrieved a small towel. Carter tried to wave her away, but she insisted on wiping up the excess wine that hadn't yet seeped into the cushion. "I'm sorry," she said again. "You were saying?"

"Yeah," said Carter, leaning back on the couch. "I was saying that we had a lot of offers from a lot of different companies, but none of them were as big as Vinestead's."

The second mention of Vinestead International caused Jane's hand to tremble again.

"I thought you worked for Dyalogued."

"I do, but Vinestead bought us out last year. We're still an independent org but we roll up under them. Why, is that a problem? Are you one of those AntiSteads?"

"Not me, but I know some people. I was just surprised to hear their name. They've been in the news so much lately."

He nodded, rested the rim of his wine glass against his lower lip. For a moment, it looked as if he might fall asleep. It took a hand on his leg to rouse him.

"The feeds are gonna say whatever they want about Vinestead," he mumbled. "Whatever gets them subscribers. Truth is, they have no idea what went down last year."

"And you do?" She snuggled up next to him, gripped his arm.

"I sat in on a few meetings with some big shots. They told us what really happened."

Jane put her chin on his shoulder and looked up at him with her best puppy dog eyes.

"I'm not supposed to really talk about it," he said quickly, looking away.

"I won't tell if you won't."

"This is all privileged, right? Like, your contract prevents you from repeating anything I say?"

On the outside, Jane batted her eyes. On the inside, she rolled them. The suspension of disbelief was supposed to be for his benefit, but it was clear Carter only saw her as a hired escort.

"I shouldn't," he continued.

"Don't make me persuade you." She moved her hand to his chest, let it drift south a few inches. "It only moves when you're talking."

So he talked, and the more he said, the lower Jane's hand traveled, until finally she was gripping his erection through his jeans.

"And it was Calle Cinco who blew a hole in the Umbra Canopy. They had been planning to break Kaili Zabora out of prison for years, and all that stuff with that guy, uh, Julius Parker, and the Lincoln Continental building was just a distraction. It was all…" He groaned. "It was all a distraction."

"So there was never a Julius Parker?"

"Not at Vinestead. I checked the directory. No record of anyone by that name ever working there."

"Interesting," said Jane.

And she wasn't just saying that. Carter's account of things matched the company line almost word-for-word. Despite Danny meeting Julius Parker in VNet, despite Tanzy knowing him from almost twenty years ago, Vinestead had claimed the allegedly rogue employee never existed, and that everything Danny had liberated from Brigham Plaza was planted by Calle Cinco to smear the company.

Lies, of course.

But then truth never really mattered to the uneducated masses. If made to choose between some socially awkward hacker and the company that provided their technology, medicine, and other basic utilities, the masses were going to side with Vinestead every time.

Carter let out an urgent groan that he tried to cut short. His face flushed unnaturally red as he rolled away from her.

"I uh… excuse me for a minute. I need to use the restroom."

While it was true that he'd had several glasses of wine, Jane was sure his impromptu trip to the bathroom was less about the urine in his bladder than the semen in his boxers. She'd been stroking him absently, thinking mostly about Danny and how Vinestead had hardly mentioned his name in any of their propaganda. Perhaps they were wary after seeing what he'd done to Julius Parker, and they weren't ready to take that on. Yet.

Jane went to the bar and washed her hands in the little sink behind the counter. As she was drying up, a notification flashed across her subdermal sliver, brightening the skin as if someone had pressed a high-powered flashlight against the other side of her wrist. She could still hear Carter in the master suite, probably rummaging around in his suitcase for a clean pair of underwear.

The sliver flashed again, prompting Jane to retrieve her phone from her clutch in the foyer. She loaded her messages app and read a word that made the breath catch in her throat.

Montreal.

It took both hands to steady the phone. Jane clicked into the message.

Read the first line.

Read it again.

Read it for a third time just to be sure.

The message wasn't from Danny. It was from a scheduling daemon at Adelai Associates informing her of a new engagement request from none other than Danny Guns Montreal.

Duration requested: one week.

Date requested: June 2020.

Right on schedule.

Jane clenched her jaw until it hurt.

"Are you shitting me?" she muttered.

After all this time, after months of no contact, of her not even knowing if he were alive or not, *this* is how he reached out to her? Even after she'd been so clear: lobby of World Trade Center 1, café, Friday afternoon. She'd told him where she was going to be, and all he had to do was show up there, just step out of a cab and walk into the building.

He had the money and the time.

But he didn't have the guts.

The engagement request was just further proof. Instead of coming out of his world to get her, he'd simply ordered her like a pair of shoes, fully expecting UPS or FedEx to dump her on his front steps. Coming in person would have been the sliver of hope that Jane needed to believe in their relationship, to believe that the love they shared during their engagements could exist outside of it.

All he had to do was show up.

All he had to do was show her there was something more than bought-and-paid-for intimacy.

Socks padded in the hallway.

"I'm sorry," said Carter or Ronald or whatever the hell his name was. "I guess I drank too much wine."

Jane slipped her phone back into her clutch. The biochip had held back the tears, but still she put a hand to her face to brush her cheeks. She ignored whatever he'd just said and forced a smile.

"Did you wash your hands?" she asked.

Carter looked over his shoulder. "Did I what?"

"Wash your hands," she repeated. "Did you scrub them with water *and* soap?"

"I… no, I didn't."

Jane sighed with a disappointment that was only half-authentic. She reached for a zipper hidden by a small flap of fabric under her arm. It made a dull buzzing sound as she unzipped her dress.

"I think you'd better get back in there and run a bath," she said, shaking the dress to the floor. Warm air rushed over her skin, and she watched Carter's eyes go wide at the sight of her matching corset and leggings.

"A bath? Really? I can just wash my hands again. I don't—"

"No. You're going to run a bath, and I'm going to teach you how to wash, even if it takes all night."

Hiding a smile, Carter turned and headed for the bathroom.

Jane picked up a code card from the assortment on the small table. It didn't matter which one; she just needed something to keep Carter relaxed without giving him more wine and risk affecting other, more necessary, functions.

She followed in her heels, clacking along the wood floors, and tried to settle back into the Jane Maxwell persona. It wasn't hard to imagine how the rest of the night would go. She'd undress him, let him undress her, and then they would get into the bathtub.

She would scrub his back.

She would tease him below the bubbles.

But the one thing she would not do is pretend he was Danny.

There was no Danny Guns Montreal anymore as far as she was concerned. The first client she'd ever fallen for was now nothing but a name on a list, just another customer in a growing line of customers.

Not that she would ever see him again.

Jane might have been fondling Carter below the water, but her mind had cast itself into the future, after they'd made brief and forgettable love in a too-soft bed, after he was snoring softly beside her, his face to the wall, his body hidden by the sheets. Only when she was sure he was truly out would she return to her phone, return to the message with the subject line of *Danny Guns Montreal*.

She'd scroll to the bottom, to the two buttons that followed the question *accept engagement?*

She wanted to respond with *you had your chance* or *I waited for you*, but ultimately, she would have to settle for a simple *No*.

Carter chuckled.

"What?" she asked.

"I don't know. I kinda like being bathed."

"Of course you do," said Jane.

Then to herself…

You all do.

THANK YOU

Brigham Plaza is the sixth book of **The Vinestead Anthology**.

If you enjoyed this book, please consider leaving a review.

Each standalone novel in the Vinestead Anthology tells a small part of a larger epic: the rise and fall of Vinestead International, the exploits of a rogue artificial intelligence named Lassiter, and a seemingly endless stream of idealistic hackers—each convinced they're the hero of the story.

Enjoy them in any order.

Xronixle (2007)

Veneer (2011)

Guardian Angels (2012)

Perion Synthetics (2014)

Por Vida (2017)

Brigham Plaza (2019)

Hybrid Mechanics (2020)

Vise Manor (2022)

House of Nepenthe (2025)

To learn more about the Vinestead Anthology and explore additional titles, please visit:

danielverastiqui.com

9 781967 847105